PRAISE FOR
Red Dirt Country

'Fleur McDonald has created once again a gripping, powerful story . . . one of the best.' *Blue Wolf Reviews*

'When Fleur McDonald publishes a book, readers can be confident that it will be worth reading . . . equally at home in the red soil and harsh terrain of the north, the softer landscapes of Queensland and the streets, malls and suburbia of the major cities.'

Queensland Reviewers Collective

'With its engaging mystery and authentic rural setting, I enjoyed *Red Dirt Country* . . . anticipating the next instalment.' *Book'd Out*

Fleur McDonald has lived and worked on farms for much of her life. After growing up in the small town of Orroroo in South Australia, she went jillarooing, eventually co-owning an 8000-acre property in regional Western Australia.

Fleur likes to write about strong women overcoming adversity, drawing inspiration from her own experiences in rural Australia. She has two children, an energetic kelpie and a Jack Russell terrier.

Website: www.fleurmcdonald.com
Facebook: FleurMcDonaldAuthor
Instagram: fleurmcdonald

FLEUR McDONALD

Red Dirt Country

ALLEN&UNWIN

SYDNEY · MELBOURNE · AUCKLAND · LONDON

This edition published in 2021
First published in 2020

Allen & Unwin
83 Alexander Street
Crows Nest NSW 2065
Australia
Phone: (61 2) 8425 0100
Email: info@allenandunwin.com
Web: www.allenandunwin.com

A catalogue record for this
book is available from the
National Library of Australia

ISBN 978 1 76087 897 9

Set in Sabon LT Pro by Bookhouse, Sydney
Printed in Australia by McPherson's Printing Group

10 9 8 7 6 5 4

MIX
Paper from
responsible sources
FSC® C001695

The paper in this book is FSC® certified.
FSC® promotes environmentally responsible,
socially beneficial and economically viable
management of the world's forests.

They say that a feather is a symbol of those who have passed, sending love and support from realms beyond. Every time I see a feather, I think of you.

◦⁓

In memory of the beautiful Amy Milne, publicist wonder, dear friend and Pooh-bear lover, who died far too young and left such a gaping hole in many lives.

And to those who are precious.

Chapter 1

2000

Deep ragged breaths tore from Dave as his heart hammered against his chest wall. Heat pulsed through him and sweat trickled down his brow, onto his cheek. Impatiently, he tried to flick the beads away. He wanted to cry out. To fill his lungs ... They were burning with the effort of dragging air into them.

Heavy footsteps pounded behind him on the pavement. Were they closer? He had to resist turning around to check, so he put his head down and concentrated on running. Running away. One foot in front of the other.

His muscles ached with the exertion, and fear swirled around his body.

'No,' he muttered as he felt a hand on his shoulder. Dave twisted his body one way, then the other, feeling freedom again, before he stumbled.

Head down, he faltered again, regained his footing and kept his pace consistent. Fast enough to just be out of reach. Away, away, away.

Crack! The sound of a shotgun.

Dave's instinct was to yell out. He opened his mouth, but something else, something more deep-seated—terror, maybe—made him close it before he could utter a sound. They'd hear him if he cried out and then they would know where he was.

Three more steps, then he lurched as if he'd been pushed forwards.

Heat seared through him; he wasn't sure where it was coming from. Only heat, not pain.

His chest was burning too; he couldn't catch his breath and his whole body was on fire. He had to stop. No choice.

Don't stop, don't stop, don't stop, he thought, reaching up to touch his shoulder. Now he could smell blood. He knew without looking that his hand would be red.

The river, he had to get to the river . . .

But he was too late. His slowing had meant Bulldust was on top of him, pulling him to the ground, shaking him by the shoulders.

'You're dead!' Bulldust's breath was acrid in his face.

'Get off me,' roared Dave, trying to throw his arm back, but his arm was too heavy. As much as he tried, he couldn't raise it to fend off Bulldust. Instead he twisted and tried to roll away, kicking out as he moved.

'Thought you were cleverer than me, didn't you?'

'Get off . . .' He tried again to fling Bulldust from his body. 'Dave!'

'No,' he grunted as he felt Bulldust shake him even harder.

'Dave, wake up. You're having another dream!'

Not Bulldust. Melinda.

His eyes flicked open and he saw the pale glow of the bedside light and Melinda above him, frowning. Her hands were on his arm. 'What?'

'You were having another nightmare,' she said.

Dave licked his lips as he tried to get his bearings. His heart felt like it was pounding in his temples, and when he reached up to touch his forehead, his fingers came away damp with sweat. He automatically touched his shoulder. No blood. No open wound. Only the ever-present ache from where the bullet had entered his flesh a few months before.

'Sorry,' he muttered, sitting up and reaching for the glass of water on the bedside table. 'Didn't mean to wake you.'

Melinda was upright now, her arms crossed over her pregnant stomach. 'It's the third time this week. I think you're going to have to do something about the nightmares, Dave. You can't go on like this. I can't keep waking up every night. God knows it's going to be bad enough when the baby comes.'

Dave threw back the covers and swung his legs out of bed, his feet checking the floor to make sure it was solid, not like the shifting ground of his dream. He stood up and rubbed at his face. 'Sorry,' he said again. 'Go back to sleep.'

'Fat chance of that now,' she huffed, starting to pull the covers up and roll over. 'Between the baby kicking and you moaning, there's not a lot of rest to be had.'

Dave switched off the bedside lamp and ran his hand over Melinda's hair. 'Try to go back to sleep,' he said, before shutting the door quietly.

He walked out into the kitchen and stood by the sink. The nightmare had seemed so real—he had smelled Bulldust's sweat and breath. Heard his heavy breathing as he chased him. Felt his hand on his shoulder. Listened as Bulldust threatened him. So real.

Swallowing hard, he poured himself a glass of water and drank it, staring at his reflection in the window. Bulldust had changed his life. Changed the way he looked at the job; made Dave want to get back out onto the streets, to chase down those bastards who thought they were above the law.

The ache of his shoulder reminded him of the vow he'd made as he'd walked out of the Brisbane hospital: he would track down Bulldust and his brother Scotty, and he would make sure they went to jail.

Dave knew he wouldn't go back to sleep now. The gnawing pain had seen to that, but so had his thoughts. Glancing at the clock, he saw it was 3.09 a.m.

That was the time he'd been waking up at, most nights, since he returned to Perth from Queensland. Not always to a bad dream. Not always to Bulldust chasing him. Sometimes he just woke up. He would go from being in a deep sleep to staring at the ceiling, wondering what had woken him.

He usually had the unsettling feeling that Bulldust was watching him.

Of course, it wasn't the case.

Or was it?

How could they really be sure that the brothers hadn't tracked down Dave and his family to where they lived and were just biding their time?

Dave grabbed two painkillers from the packet on the bench and refilled his glass. Swallowing them, he hoped that the pills would stop the pain and make him sleepy enough to stop thinking. He walked through the house until he reached the lounge. Here, he pulled back the curtain and stood in front of the window, almost daring Bulldust to come and find him.

Looking into the darkness, he tried to see if there was any movement in the bushes that hid his house from the road. There was no moon tonight, so it was hard to tell. Perhaps the bushes were shifting in the gentle breeze. Maybe he should go out and look. Just to be sure.

A dog barked in the distance and Dave froze. Spencer, his previous partner at Barrabine, the one who had suggested Dave go undercover, had said he was suffering from the effects of being shot.

'Mate, it's a traumatic thing to have to go through,' he'd said when they'd talked on the phone yesterday.

'I should be tougher than that,' Dave had answered. 'I'm a copper.'

'Don't see how that makes you exempt. Plenty of other fellas out there who have been through the same, more or less, and feel the way you do. No shame in it. How many times have I told you that?'

Dave had harrumphed, still feeling that he shouldn't be reacting this way. The doctors were hoping he would be able to get back to work in another week, but he wasn't sure he could wait that long. He needed to keep himself busy. Get his mind occupied again.

Of course, it hadn't helped that Mel's father had visited yesterday and made some pointed remarks about him being off work.

'Planning on going back to work any time soon? I shouldn't have thought a gunshot would stop you for too long. Seemed like you love your work more than your family.'

The remarks had made Dave want to punch Mark again; he'd done it once before and had never felt the need to apologise. Oh, he'd thought about saying sorry since he'd returned home after being undercover in Nundrew, but every time he came close, Mark made a snide remark and Dave only wanted to hit him all over again.

Even though being around the house all day was hard, he had to admit that part of him loved it. He got to play with Bec and be involved with her daily life. Things he'd missed out on for a while. Yesterday, he'd taken her to playgroup while Melinda had had a pre-natal appointment. He'd wanted to go to that too, but Melinda had said it would be too hard with Bec there.

Sometimes Melinda made him feel like a hired babysitter rather than Bec's father. And when she was having her afternoon sleeps, the house was so quiet. Silent enough to hear the clock tick. This was when he most craved the noise and adrenalin-filled rush of detective work. The phone calls and call-outs. Being on a high-pressure job.

Spencer had reminded Dave that it wasn't like that all the time, only when they were nearing the end of a case. Most times, the detectives would be labouring over photographs, witness statements and answering phone calls from victims who wanted answers. That was easy to forget when he longed for the stimulation of a case.

I know, I know, he thought to himself as he continued to stare out the window. *But I miss it.* He shut his eyes and leaned his head against the cold pane. *And maybe it would help my head.*

❧

Melinda handed a wriggling Bec to Dave. 'Can you give her breakfast? I've got to get ready for my doctor's appointment.'

Bec gurgled with laughter as Dave held her under his arm and tickled her tummy. 'We can do that, can't we, princess?' He looked over at Mel who had picked up the sponge and was wiping the bench down. Her stomach was pressing against the bench, her hair swept up into a loose bun. From where Dave was standing, she looked beautiful.

'Hey.' He reached out and touched her cheek. 'I'm sorry about last night. You look gorgeous today. Having my baby suits you.' He didn't mention the black rings under her eyes, or that she looked exhausted. He was sure he looked the same. The only one who was sleeping just fine was Bec, and her energy showed that.

A flicker of a frown crossed Melinda's face before she smiled. 'I wish you'd talk to someone about how you're feeling, Dave. Maybe you should see a different counsellor or something.' She covered his hand with hers for a moment, then dropped it again as Bec began to wriggle in protest. 'This one doesn't seem to be making progress with you.'

It was on the tip of his tongue to remind her that the police were paying for his sessions and he had to be cleared by *this* lady before he could return to work. The police force couldn't have a person back at work who was unfit, physically or mentally. Dave decided against saying so. Considering how little sleep they had both had, it would start an argument. Instead, he nodded as if he agreed.

He didn't, of course. The counsellor was fine, and the appointments were just something he needed to do so he could get back to work. He knew he'd be better off at the pub with some of his colleagues; men and women who understood what it was like to be shot for the greater good. To be shot taking down some hardened criminal.

To fear. Fear never seeing his family again. Fear that he'd lose his life in the process. Fear that he wouldn't catch the criminals he was chasing.

A counsellor could only provide coping strategies, not the real understanding of someone who had been in the situation Dave had. With someone bearing down on him, wanting him dead.

'Daddy!' Bec slapped her chubby hand against his shoulder to get his attention.

'Sorry, princess.' He set her down on the floor and opened a kitchen cabinet. 'There's a bowl in here,' he sang to the tune of the *Play School* jingle. 'And a spoon as well. We're looking for the Weet-Bix ... and the milk ...' He broke off as Mel grabbed her handbag.

'I'll be back late morning,' she said. 'Hopefully the doctor will be on time and I won't get held up there.'

'Do you have to have any blood tests or anything today?' Dave asked, as he helped Bec get out one Weet-Bix. 'You can crush it up,' he said to his daughter.

'Not today. Just the normal urine tests. I'll let you know if there's anything amiss.' She walked around to Bec and gave her a kiss. 'Be good for Daddy,' she said.

'Bye, Mummy,' Bec answered, looking up from the bowl of breakfast cereal.

'Little Miss Princess and I will be just fine here, won't we?' He leaned over to give Mel a kiss goodbye, but she'd already turned away and was heading out the door. 'See you then,' he said to her disappearing back.

Dave watched her raise her hand and give a little wave without turning around. Life with Mel hadn't got any easier since he'd come back from undercover. He'd thought it would be perfect. They'd both agreed they wanted to be with each other. To try. His near-death experience had reminded them both what they felt for each other and what life would be like without the other. With this in mind, he'd thought their relationship would be fail-safe.

Dave had agreed to move to Perth, but not Bunbury, where her parents were. Perth was closer to them than where he'd been stationed, at Barrabine, and he'd felt it was a good compromise. But then her parents had moved to Perth instead. Only two suburbs over from where he, Melinda and Bec lived.

Dave had tried his hardest to fit in with this new life in the six months he'd been back. He'd been promoted to Detective Senior Constable in the stock squad—where he'd always wanted to work—but he hadn't yet started. Maybe the counsellor would sign off on his mental fitness after his next appointment. Until then, he was in limbo.

As he listened to the car start and his wife drive away, he thought, *The sooner I get back to work, the better.*

Chapter 2

Kevin swung the Toyota Land Cruiser across the red ground and headed towards the windmill. The cattle pads were deep in the earth and made the ute shake and clatter as the vehicle ran over them. He inspected the feed, bushes and trees as he drove. Some rain wouldn't go astray. The seasons had started to change, and it wasn't long before the Wet was supposed to start. The temperature had risen in the last couple of weeks from the balmy high twenties to the more intense high thirties and, over the weekend, the first lot of thunderclouds had turned up, but dissipated as quickly as they'd arrived.

His father, Jackie, had been sitting next to the fire back at the homestead, talking to other Elders from the community, and Kevin had joined them to ask if they thought the Wet might come early this year.

'Nup. Not this year, boy. Still too cold.'

Kevin had frowned as he'd looked out across the bush-land. Last year had been dry too. If it didn't rain, he'd have to bring in hay from down south and that was a costly exercise. Not something he wanted to do if he could avoid it.

As he rattled across the bush, the steering wheel vibrating under his hand, he realised that the grasses were more than dry—they'd started to break down. The bushes and trees had the telltale signs of broken branches and leaves stripped off. The cattle were eating them now. Kevin knew that when the cattle started to eat the bloodbush and leaves, most of the more palatable feed had been eaten.

Off to the side, the flick of a tail caught his attention. A mob of about twenty red Brahman cattle were camped in a grove of shrubs, their heads down, eyes closed, with their ears and tail continuing to twitch, keeping the flies at bay.

He turned the wheel to drive up for a closer look.

That's contentment, he thought, smiling as a cow opened her eyes to look at him, assessing the danger, then shut them again.

They were holding their condition well, considering the lack of decent feed, he decided, before driving on.

A few kilometres of rough track and creek crossings further on, he pulled up at one of the troughs in the large paddock. He could see that the water was lapping about an inch below the rim. Full.

Kevin swung the door open and jumped out with the energy of youth and stretched as he looked around the land. There was fresh cattle shit near the trough and tracks that the wind hadn't yet covered. The cattle were happy coming in here to drink. And he could see the dirty rub marks and hair on the posts of the fence that surrounded the tank, which trickled water into the trough. Cattle loved to scratch.

Smiling, he felt the same kind of satisfaction that he imagined the cattle would be feeling. He'd made a difference to this land, this station, since he'd come back here. The Elders had put a lot of faith in him when he'd won the scholarship to study agriculture down south. The decision had been controversial with some of the community. But the ones who hadn't been in favour were beginning to come around now, seeing the improvements Kevin had made. There was, however, still a long way to go.

Deciding he should check the levels in the tank, he jumped the fence and walked over, feeling the warmth of the sun on his skin. He adjusted his hat and sunglasses before climbing the ladder to check inside. The steel was hot to the touch and he glanced up at the sky, wondering what the time was. About two-thirty in the afternoon, he guessed. Just time to check here, then the solar pump about another forty-odd ks down the track and get home again.

Peering inside, he saw the tank was full.

The windmill was in good working order too; even so, he walked around it just to make sure it was pumping smoothly and everything was okay. He didn't want to leave anything to chance with the weather warming up and the cattle needing to drink.

Back in the ute, he felt another surge of fulfilment. Who would've thought that when he'd left his homeland to go to that fancy school in Perth, he would've ended up back on Spinifex Downs as the manager? Of course, that had always been the plan, but he'd been unsure it would eventuate exactly as the Elders had hoped.

Kevin had copped a bit of flak from the fellas he'd grown up with when he'd got back home. 'Don't go bringing all your fine words and education back here, brother. You're no different to the rest of us, no matter what they say.' That had come from Morgan, his best mate when he'd been a kid.

Sure, it had hurt him, but he'd been prepared for a backlash. His father had warned him it would happen. 'You won't be seen as one of us anymore. You'll be an outsider now.'

Kevin had ignored the comments. He knew he was doing the right thing by his people. Improving the herd, the station, their land. They would all see it in time, but it would take just that. Time. Once he'd united them all again, given them a purpose and dignity, then he'd be accepted.

And time had begun to work its magic in the last couple of months. Kevin could feel and see the difference in the community. Just little steps, but that was all he was asking for. The kids were happy, and Morgan had started to talk to him on the same level again. His jackaroos Cyril, Charlie, Jimbo, Harry and Nicky were happily working the cattle and maintaining Spinifex Downs the way Kevin had hoped they would.

Spinifex Downs was an Aboriginal lease linked to a community. There were fifty women and children who lived just back from the creek in small houses that had been built by the government. There were about the same number of men, along with one young white woman, Paula, who taught the kids.

Kevin lived in the homestead, about half a kilometre from the community, with white lime-washed walls and high ceilings, and fans that gently swung while the generator was on. The homestead also housed his office. He would never admit it but he missed living among his people, down along the creek banks. He missed being involved with his family and the friendships; the kids, laughing and barefoot, kicking the footy on the dry, dusty ground; the smell of wood-fire smoke and the chatter of the women while they cooked the meals.

Kevin knew, though, his purpose was more important than everything he missed. He was going to take his people forwards. Help keep their culture, beliefs and land strong. Give them pride. He knew he was making progress.

He dusted his hands on his already dirty denim jeans and adjusted his hat again, before getting back into the ute. Another forty ks and he'd be on the boundary of Spinifex Downs and Deep-Water Station, where there was the last lot of water he had to check today. Cotton Bush Bore.

Looking at his diary, he saw that Jimbo and Harry had checked it last about a week ago. They were good lads, and they were getting better under his guidance, so he hoped he wouldn't find any problems when he got there.

As Kevin drove, he hung his arm out of the window, enjoying the feeling of the warm breeze on his skin. The ranges rose in front of him, catching the afternoon sun, glowing ochre red, and he could see the black dot of a wedgetail eagle riding the thermals. The bush and spindly white-trunked trees grew to just before the summit, where the barren rocky outcrop took over, reaching towards the sky, turning the ranges the colour of maple.

Kevin couldn't imagine living anywhere else. During the eight years he'd spent in Perth, he'd felt like he'd been ripped away from all he loved. When he'd first arrived in the city, the noise had almost driven him to distraction. There wasn't quiet or stillness anywhere—no silent corner for him to escape to and think. No place to hear the birds and feel the wind. He'd missed his family and the space. Holidays were the highlight of the terms, and the homesickness had never really left him until he returned to Spinifex Downs.

The two-wheel track, which Kevin was following, ran along the fence line, ducking and weaving through the scrub that lead to Cotton Bush Bore. As he drove, he thought about the next few weeks. The muster was finished and all the cattle intended for market had been sold. They were now in maintenance mode; making sure that all the waters and fences were in tiptop shape before the Wet came. He didn't want any of his cattle straying onto his neighbours' properties during the big rains.

He knew there were a couple of internal fences that needed tightening and floodgates to be erected in at least one of the deeper river systems. He'd made a note that he wanted the boundary fences ridden by men on horses to make sure they were as tight and in good condition as they could be.

When the top of the windmill, gently circling, came into view, it took him a moment to realise what he was looking at, he'd been so lost in his thoughts.

He ran through the facts about Cotton Bush Bore and the part of the paddock it watered. There should be five hundred cattle in this twenty-thousand-hectare paddock. It had eight watering points, five of them were new ring dams and the rest were still the old version of troughs and windmills or pumps.

When he'd returned home three years earlier, building more dams had been the first priority. The men hadn't been maintaining the mills and often the cattle were left without water for days. During the Dry, that was unacceptable.

He scanned the landscape but didn't see any of the herd of red cattle he'd painstakingly started to build back up again. They'd be around somewhere, he knew. Sometimes they were like dingos—they blended in with the landscape and were hard to see. Laughable really, with how large cattle were.

As he drove closer to the trough, he noticed there weren't any cattle prints or fresh shits around. The dirt wasn't disturbed as it would have been if the cattle had been coming in daily for a drink, and there were a couple of dead birds near the tank. Even without getting out of the vehicle, Kevin knew there was something wrong with this bore.

'Musta got a bit hot for you,' he muttered to the birds as he drove past. 'At least, that's what I'm hoping.'

He pulled up next to the trough. The cement was dry and the mud in the bottom was crumbly and cracked. Didn't appear as if there had been water in it for a few days. He looked around quickly, scanning the landscape. The trees and bushes hadn't been eaten, the way they had back at the previous watering point. The only good news at this point was that he couldn't see any dead cattle. That would mean they'd worked out there was another watering point and gone there.

Jumping out of the ute, he ran to the tank and tapped the side. It echoed hollowly and Kevin swore.

Empty.

The creaking and groaning from the old mill caught his attention. All old mills made noise, talking to the empty landscape. With this one, there was movement and noise, but the water wasn't being pumped. A quick glance at the column showed Kevin the pump rods were undone.

'Bastards!' he spat and jogged over to the fence to look around. With his boots jarring on the dry land, he walked the fence line, occasionally stopping to tug on the wire. It felt tight for the first one hundred and eighty odd metres, then he saw it.

The dirt was scuffed up and Kevin could see cattle tracks on either side of the boundary fence. He pulled at the bottom wire and it came away easily in his hand.

'Damn it to hell!' he yelled, and his words bounced off the ranges and echoed around him. 'You bastards!' He knew his cattle were now on the neighbour's place and he was sure they weren't there by accident.

Back at the ute, Kevin rummaged around for the video camera he kept with him at all times in case he found things he wanted to show the community. He jogged to the sabotaged areas and recorded footage of the tracks and fence. Not that he would be able to do anything with it. His father's words were already sounding in his head: 'They won't take any notice of what's going on out here, boy. The law won't help us, so don't involve the coppers.'

The burn of anger made him try to get over the fence more forcefully than he normally would and he tripped on the top wire, tumbling face first into the red soil. 'Bastards,' he muttered again, getting to his feet and wiping his hands on his jeans.

Kevin followed the cattle tracks for the first kilometre then realised the sun had started to sink behind the range. It would be dark very soon and he shouldn't be out here alone.

❧

Kevin pulled up at the homestead and looked at his father, who was still sitting outside by the fire. Charlie, another one of the ringers, was sitting next to him and they were both working on leather whips.

'Workin' on some new ones,' Jackie said as Kevin walked over to them and sat down in the dirt. Kevin was holding a brand-new football and was tossing it up and down.

'Need some for next muster, for sure,' Kevin said. The frustration was burning in his chest, but he had to keep it in until Charlie had gone. He sat down next to them, putting the ball in his lap, and reached out to look at the leatherwork.

'Pretty good there, Charlie. You making it for yourself?'

'Yeah. Broke mine when we were mustering out in Lemongrass paddock. Got caught around a bull's horns and he ripped it from my hands. Bloody thing.'

'You should have it finished well enough in time then. Where's your boy, Charlie?' Kevin asked, letting the leather fall from his hands and taking the piece his father handed to him, twisting it around his fingers.

'Probably playing footy down at the creek. Footy mad. And that Miss Paula, she gets right in there with them. All the kids love it!' He grinned, his white teeth flashing.

Kevin grinned and held up the football. 'I've got this for him and the rest of the kids. Signed by David Wirrpanda.'

Charlie's grin got wider. 'Good on you, Kev. They'll like that.'

'You can take it to him now if you like.' He handballed the footy over to Charlie, who caught it and turned it around to see the signature. He ran his weathered fingers over the black texta marks, then handballed it up in the air a couple of times, catching it nimbly.

'Cheers, boss.' Charlie got to his feet. 'See ya, old man,' he said to Jackie, who just nodded and kept working.

The ringer sauntered away, whistling and twirling the ball in his hands.

Jackie looked up at Kevin, a question on his face.

'They're at it again.' Kevin spat the words out.

Jackie didn't say anything, but looked down and continued to weave the leather quietly.

'We've got to put a stop to this, Dad!' Kevin threw the leather onto the ground and ran his fingers through his hair.

What he really wanted to do was get up and pace—that's how he thought things through, by walking. It wasn't done like that out here though. He knew he had to stay sitting down. And try to be calm.

Jackie shook his head. 'Let's not cause any trouble.'

'Dad, are you going to let them win all the time?'

'There's to be no trouble, boy.' Jackie put down his leatherwork.

Kevin noticed how intense his father's eyes were as they looked at him steadily. 'It'll be the third time they've stolen cattle from us,' he said.

'Just so long as they leave us some.'

'If they keep doing this, there won't be enough cattle to make money! We have to stand up to them. Go to the police.'

'No! I've told you. This has happened before. You don't know what it was like back then, Kevvy. Don't stir up trouble. That's all there is to it.' As if that put a stop to any further conversation, he returned to his leatherwork, refusing to look at Kevin anymore.

Kevin reached over and grabbed a log from next to the fire and threw it onto the coals. Sparks shot into the copper-coloured sky, just as a mob of screeching corellas came in to land on the gum trees nearby.

Kevin lowered his voice and chose his words carefully. 'Dad, the coppers, they're here to help us. They—'

'The coppers aren't interested. Look, we just want to live the quiet life out here. Raise a few cattle and live on our land. You want to go stirring things up? We can't do that.

Let it go. It's the way it's been for generations, no point in trying to buck the system.'

Kevin looked around, clenching his fists. 'I didn't come back here to let this go on. I came back to recreate the pride our people once knew. Letting these bastards get away with taking our cattle isn't helping the pride. We need to do something.'

The fire crackled and sent cheery flames licking either side of the wood. The laughter of the kids drifted over from the makeshift dirt oval near the creek. Jackie looked straight at Kevin again, but this time he brought his hand up and pointed his finger at his son.

'I'm telling you again. Don't go to the police. Don't cause trouble.' He looked back down at his leatherwork and didn't say another word.

Chapter 3

The phone rang and Dave snatched it up, hoping it was the call he'd been waiting for. 'Burrows.'

'Dave, it's Kelly Dalton. I've just reviewed your notes after our last appointment. I think you're right to go back to work.'

Dave shut his eyes and clenched his fist. Thank god! If his counsellor had been in front of him rather than on the other end of the phone, he would've hugged her. Instead he cleared his throat and said, 'Great. Thanks.'

'I know you're still getting the nightmares, but they have decreased, so I'm happy. I think another strategy would be to do some meditation before you go to bed, or some yoga perhaps. It may help clear your mind of some of the bad things you've been dreaming about.'

Dave rolled his eyes. *You've got to be kidding me,* he thought, but found himself agreeing anyway.

In the other room, Dave could hear Bec singing to herself. 'Twinkle, twinkle . . .' He refocused on the conversation.

'Again, you'll need to keep up with the exercises the physio has given you—not only for your arm, but because exercise is great for mental health. I spoke with Rachael just before I rang you. She's happy with your progress as well, but stressed not to forget that the strengthening exercises are as important as the mobility ones. And to keep up the low-impact gym work you've been doing.

'If the nightmares increase, or change, or if you find you're not sleeping, you'll need to come in and see me. Otherwise, let's make your appointments fortnightly now.'

'No problems.' Kelly's words were like balm. He was going back to work.

'Right-oh. I'll get my receptionist to send you through an appointment schedule. Feel free to change any if they interfere with work.'

Dave hung up and stood for a moment, thinking about the phone call and feeling his shoulder. For once there wasn't an ache, as if the news about going back to work had taken the pain away. It had been six months since he'd been shot.

Six months. How his life had changed in that time.

'Daddy?'

A warm glow began in his stomach, coupled with a bubble of excitement. He was going back to work! He swung around and saw Bec standing behind him. Swooping down, he picked her up and tossed her in the air.

'Daddy's going back to work, princess! Isn't that good news?'

Bec screamed with laughter as Dave caught her and put her back on the ground.

'I think we should go to the café down the road and have a hot chocolate to celebrate, don't you?'

Bec nodded. 'And a piece of cake.'

'I think we can stretch to one of those too. I just need to make a phone call and then we'll go, okay? Can you get your shoes?'

Nodding again, Bec ran out of the room and Dave picked up the phone. He dialled Spencer's number and waited as it rang.

'Spencer Brown.'

'I'm good to go,' he said.

There was a silence and Dave knew Spencer would be checking off all the return-to-work criteria in his head. Yes, he'd seen the counsellor. Yes, he'd been to the physio. Yes, yes, yes. As far as Dave knew, every box had been ticked.

'Great news,' Spencer said after a second. 'I'll get it organised. When do you want to start?'

'About three weeks ago!'

Spencer laughed. 'Patience, grasshopper. I'll have to get in contact with Bob Holden and let him know you're coming. Give me two days to get it organised. Shouldn't take much longer.'

'Okay. I can live with that.' Dave couldn't keep the grin from his face. 'Tell me about the fellas there.'

'Bob's a great bloke. Been through some pretty tough shit in his career, but he's an excellent detective. Not sure who else is in the squad these days. You'll find out soon enough. What are you going to do to celebrate? Going to have a beer with the boys?'

Bec came back into the room with her shoes on but the laces untied. In a second glance, Dave saw she had them on the wrong feet. He smiled. 'I'm taking a certain very pretty little lady out for a hot chocolate. That's our celebration.'

'Sounds great.' Spencer hesitated before saying, 'How is everything going at home?'

Dave squatted down, the phone tucked between his ear and shoulder as he took one shoe from Bec's foot then the other. 'Same as it was last time we talked.' He was careful about what he said in front of Bec. Only yesterday, she'd repeated a swearword he'd muttered as he did his exercises, when the pain had hit him.

Bec's parroting had earned him another scowl from Mel. 'Right.'

Dave heard Spencer let out a sigh and gathered that his friend wasn't sure where to go with this line of conversation.

He was about to ask about Kathy and what was happening at the Barrabine station, when he heard a key in the lock. It was his turn to frown; he hadn't heard the car pull up. Dave changed Bec's shoes over and started to tie her laces. 'I'd better head off. Sounds like Mel's home. Talk to you soon.'

'No worries, I'll get everything organised. Cheers, buddy.'

'Cheers.'

'Hello? I'm home.' Mel called from the front door.

'Mummy!' Bec tried to get off the floor but Dave hadn't finished tying her laces and she flopped back down again. 'Daddy's putting my shoes on.'

'We're in the lounge room,' Dave said as he heard the clatter of keys on the kitchen bench.

'Where are you off to?' Mel asked, appearing in the doorway. 'Hello, you,' she said smiling down at Bec. 'You're all dressed up!'

'We're getting hot chocolate,' Bec said, getting to her feet as Dave finished tying the lace.

'That sounds exciting.' Mel glanced at Dave curiously. 'It's nearly four o'clock and time for Bec's tea.'

'I've finally got the call that I can go back to work,' Dave said, getting to his feet and walking towards her, his arms outstretched. 'We're celebrating. Why don't you come too?'

Mel stared at him before burying her face in his chest. 'You're going back to work? What about the nightmares? Are you sure you can cope?'

Dave could hear the anxiety in her voice.

'What's the saying about getting back on the horse?' he said as he dropped a kiss on her head.

'Yay! Daddy's going back to work,' Bec said, jumping up and down. 'Come on.' She tugged at Mel's hand. 'Come on, Mummy. Let's go!'

Mel pulled away from Dave. He watched as she rearranged her face from troubled to smiling.

'We'd better go and celebrate then, hadn't we?'

Dave held out both his hands to the two most important people in his life and pulled them towards him. 'Hot chocolates all round,' he said, trying to jolly Mel along. He wasn't sure why she was troubled. Maybe she was frightened he'd get shot again, but that wasn't going to happen. He wouldn't let it. The pull to go back to work was too strong to give much thought to Mel's feelings.

❧

Out on the street, Bec wobbled on her three-wheeled scooter a couple of metres in front of them. Dave took Mel's hand and was relieved when she didn't pull away. Instead she put her other hand to her chest and looked at the ground as they walked, tapping her fingers over her heart.

'Don't go near the road,' Mel called to Bec.

Dave asked, 'What do you think about me going back to work?' He knew his tone sounded hesitant, but he also understood that his wife wasn't happy. He couldn't remember the last time she had been and he wasn't sure if it was the thought of his work or something else. Their marriage had been wobbly for a while. In fact, it had been the reason he'd gone undercover in the first place. Then there had been the revelation that Mel was pregnant again. He'd sometimes thought that if there hadn't been a new baby on the way they wouldn't have reconciled when he returned from undercover work.

When they'd been reunited, she'd run towards him as he'd come through the Qantas gates. Her smile had been wide and there had been a look of adoration and relief.

Those emotions had been short-lived, though, and lately her face had only shown tiredness and strain.

'It had to happen,' she answered.

Dave glanced over at her; she was watching Bec.

'But . . .' He left the sentence hanging, knowing there was much more to come.

'The nightmares, Dave.'

'They're just part of it. I've spent a while talking to the counsellor about them. They're not worsening so she says they'll go over time.' That was a white lie. She hadn't said they would go, just that he should go back and see her if they got worse.

'Yeah, they said that when you first came home. They haven't stopped yet.'

'Rome wasn't built in a day, love. And it's really not been that long. Guess we've just got to give me time.' Dave's eyes scanned the area as they walked—looking for potential hazards was second nature to him now. As he checked where Bec was, and then for cars, he turned his eyes back to Mel and saw her mouth open. She looked as if she was going to say something, but then she seemed to change her mind.

'What's wrong?' Dave asked as they walked in step with one another. He watched their feet as they walked and couldn't help but think maybe this was the only time they were in step with each other in any way.

'No, nothing,' she answered shortly.

Dave paused, knowing he had another subject to broach with her. He'd received an email earlier in the day, and he'd need to choose his words carefully in telling Mel about it.

Justin Parker was the Senior Sergeant in Nundrew and had been his contact when Dave had been undercover. When Dave had been shot, he'd been trying to escape not only Bulldust and Scotty—the two cattle duffers—but also a dirty cop named Joe. He'd been informing for Bulldust and checking on the people Bulldust employed in his mustering business.

'I received an email from Justin today,' Dave said, tightening his grip on Mel's hand. 'The court case is coming up in about six weeks. I'm going to need to go back to Brisbane to give evidence at Joe's trial.'

Mel shook her head and was silent.

'I'll only be over there for the time I need to give my testimony,' he continued, trying to downplay the fact he would have to leave close to the birth of their baby. 'A couple of days at most.'

'Well, I guess you've got to do what you've got to do,' Mel said, extracting her hand and picking up her pace. 'Bec, you need to stop now,' she called out. 'We're nearly at the café.'

'Mel . . .' Dave tried to catch up with her but Mel stopped suddenly and turned to him, putting her hand on his cheek.

'I mean it. You do what you have to. I mean that. Bec and I, and bub, when it turns up, we'll be just fine.'

Somehow, Dave didn't feel comforted by her words.

The phone rang early the next morning, before Mel had got up. Dave slipped out of bed quietly to answer it. Last night had been the first in many that he hadn't had a nightmare and they had all slept peacefully. Maybe it was knowing he was going back to work that had kept his mind calm, or perhaps it had been the two-kilometre run he'd gone on after they'd all got back from the café.

Whatever it was, he decided he needed more of it in his life.

'Burrows,' he answered, his voice low, glancing at his watch. Six-thirty.

The trouble with their house was, even though it was brick, voices seemed to travel easily through the walls, and he didn't want to wake up either Mel or Bec.

'Spencer, here.'

'What's going on?'

'You're good to go. Spoke with Bob yesterday. He's keen to have you and he's found you a desk. Start on Monday at 0700. You'll be at the bottom of the ladder for a while, but don't forget that Bob's coming up for retirement in a few years. If you work hard, you'll be able to apply for his job.'

'How many are on the team?'

'Another four, as far as I know. You'll meet them all on Monday. I don't know any of them, so you'll have to form your own opinions. But Bob? Like I said last time, he's a nice fella. I worked out of the same station as him a shit-load of years ago. He's a fair bit younger than me, so he was just getting started. It was before I moved to Barrabine.'

'Sounds great.' He paused. 'Anyone else there who might want to go for his job when Bob retires?'

Spencer gave a laugh. 'How about you get your foot in the door and see if you actually like it before you start writing your resume?'

It was Dave's turn to laugh. Spencer always had some one-liner that made him crack up.

'When was the last time you rode a horse?' Spencer asked.

'What? Never!'

'You might have to brush up on that skill if you get sent north. Most of the stock squad ride horses over in Queensland and, if you head north, I guess there'll be spots that are only accessible with a horse and a chopper.'

Dave frowned at the thought. Not that he was frightened of horses, they'd just never really been an animal he'd had a lot to do with.

'Bikes can go most places,' he said knowing that wasn't strictly true. He turned towards the passageway as he heard movement from Bec's bedroom. Dave hoped his daughter wouldn't wake up just yet. Mel didn't like it when Bec appeared before 7.30 a.m.

Spencer laughed. 'Can't really imagine you on a horse. Those long gangly legs of yours would get tangled up in the stirrups.'

'I should learn just to prove you wrong,' Dave retorted good-naturedly.

Spencer's voice sobered. 'I was talking to Justin yesterday.'

Dave felt himself nodding, then realised that Spencer couldn't see him. 'Yeah, I got an email.'

'How do you feel about that?'

'Well, shit, Spencer, it's about the time the baby's due.'

'Crap. I bet that news didn't go down well.'

Dave deflected the comment. 'Just have to hope like hell it doesn't come while I'm away. I don't want to miss the birth.'

'Nah, course not. No one does. Well, not that the mum has a choice.' He was silent again. 'I guess you might be able to video your testimony.'

'The case is still a little way away. We've got time to put something in place if we need to. Mel was two weeks over with Bec and there's every chance that'll happen again, I guess, but let's keep that up our sleeves.'

'Do you reckon even thinking about going to Brisbane is a good idea with all the angst around your place at the moment.'

Dave rubbed his scalp. 'Probably not but, hell, this is what I do. Just so long as I don't miss the birth.'

'Maybe I'll see if Kathy can come up and visit Mel while you're gone.'

Dave thought about Spencer's wife and how kind she'd been to them both when they had shifted to Barrabine. 'I think Mel would like that.' He didn't mention that Mel might be too busy with her parents to fit Kathy in. The daily visits to her parents' house were peppered by them coming to his. Usually he disappeared to the back shed until they'd left. Another good reason to go back to work; his shed was the cleanest it had ever been.

'I'd better get on, mate,' Spencer said. 'Got a heap to do today. So many B and Es and mind-numbing stuff. Need to get you back here to make something exciting happen. Good cases seem to follow you.'

'I'd rather they didn't,' Dave said, a smile in his voice. 'Thanks for the info and chat.'

'Good luck. Let me know how you go.'

Dave put down the phone and listened again. There was silence. Bec must have gone back to sleep.

He let himself quietly out the sliding door in the lounge and stepped onto the lawn. The leaves were wet with dew and the magpies were singing from the top of the tall gum tree in the backyard. In the pre-dawn light, Dave smiled. He was going back to work.

Chapter 4

Kit Redman parked his white Toyota Land Cruiser ute in front of the post office in Boogarin, a small town in the north of Western Australia.

His window was down, so he felt the heat before he got out of the vehicle. The warmth always seemed more intense in town than out on the station. He supposed it was from the bitumen that sealed the main road.

On the footpath he looked around to see if he recognised any of the cars parked along the street. The late morning sun was catching the tall antennas on the edge of town—they helped everyone stay in contact—and the white dishes alongside the tall steel structures provided satellite internet. The technology was new and many in town thought they weren't necessary. They were the backward thinkers, Kit knew, because this was going to be the way of the future, even though the towers were an eyesore.

Ghost gums lined the roads, and at the end of the main street a large hill rose into the endless sky. Against the vividness of the blue, the rich colour of the ochre soil clashed and made Kit want to put on a darker pair of sunglasses.

This had been his town for a long time—he'd guided the shire council to make good decisions for the people who lived here and in the surrounding areas. He'd acted as a mediator between the mining companies, Aboriginal Australians and station owners.

A dirt-covered white Toyota wagon with a caravan hitched behind was pulled up near the steel cut-outs of a kangaroo, lizard and eagle. An older couple were out, taking photos, posing against each structure. He hoped they'd spend a bit of money in Boogarin later. Maybe buy a coffee at the café or a burger at the pub. If they went into the craft shop right at the top of the main street and bought some tourist paraphernalia they'd make Jay-Jay very happy.

Another vehicle pulled up next to his and a woman got out. Kit touched his Akubra to Jenn Davies.

'Nice to see you, Kit,' she said, stopping in front of him. 'Haven't run into you in town for ages. Are you here for the shire council meeting?'

'Not this time, Jenn,' Kit answered, pushing his hat back on his head. 'Few other things going on.'

'Geez, Kit, we could do with you back in the president's chair, I reckon. The fool that's there now just isn't doing the right thing by the people.'

'Now, don't you think fifteen years as the shire president is enough? I'd be old and stale if I went back in. New blood is always good. How's Charlotte?' He pushed his hat back as he talked and scratched his forehead.

His daughter, Kia, and Jenn's daughter, Charlotte, had gone through School of the Air together and then on to boarding school, where they were both now in Year Eleven. They sat next to each other on the plane to and from school and had shared a room in the boarding house since Year Ten.

'She's fine, thanks. Studying hard. ATAR is such a hard slog for kids that aren't book smart. Poor Charlotte just has to keep working at it. Not like your Kia. Brain on legs, she is!'

Kit smiled. 'She got her mother's intelligence, for sure.'

Jenn laughed. 'And speaking of the brains, how is Tara?'

'She's fine. But not at home at the moment. I'm baching. She's visiting her dad. Old Jim had a fall a couple of weeks ago. He's okay, but needing a bit of support,' he said as Jenn's hand flew to her mouth.

'Oh no!' She sighed reflectively. 'Isn't it hard when the parents start to get old and we're so far away?' Jenn batted some flies away from her face. 'You blokes, all of your families are still up here. It's the ring-ins—the ones who came in to marry you all—who find it hard.'

'I guess that's true. Hadn't thought about it like that.' He nodded. 'Anyway, Jenn, I'd better keep moving. Got a few things to pick up and jobs to do.'

'Hopefully you've got the storeroom packed to the brim. The Wet shouldn't be too far off now.'

They both glanced at the bright blue sky, which didn't hold a cloud anywhere.

'Love your optimism,' Kit said, and again touched his finger to his hat. 'See you round.' He walked off down the street with the swagger of a man who had spent most of his fifty-five years on a horse.

'Morning, Kit!' a male voice called from a ute as he drove past, and Kit threw his hand up in acknowledgement.

Pushing open the door to the newsagency, Kit was greeted by a blast of cool air and two kids with balloons and tiger face-paint.

'Roooaarrr!' growled one of them, her fingers curled over as if she had claws. The other opened his mouth but no sound came out.

'Ah, hell!' Kit gave a start and pretended to stumble backwards. 'Help! Someone help! There's a tiger in the newsagency.'

A high-pitched giggle came from behind the paint. 'It's only me, Mr Redman. Cally. And Evan.'

'Good lord, have you eaten Cally, Mr Tiger?' Kit asked, looking closely at the little girl. 'I can hear her voice, but you don't look like her.'

'Mr Redman,' Cally said in a kind tone, 'it's me. I've just got my face painted.'

Kit looked up and saw Cally's father, Jamie Crowden. He winked at Jamie and turned back to the kids. 'Well, I'll be,' Kit said, scratching his head. 'I don't think I've ever seen you look so scary, Cally. You too, Evan. Where'd you get your faces looking like that?'

'Miss Mitchell painted them at daycare this morning. Dad didn't think it was us when he came to pick us up either.'

'Miss Mitchell has some hidden talents. We'll have to get her painting faces at the next show,' Kit said. He turned his attention to Jamie. 'How's it going, Crow?' he asked using Jamie's nickname.

'Good, mate. Just on the way home. Picked up a heap of cattle lick blocks and some poly pipe. Got some new land we need to get water to.'

'Got some good help out there?' Kit asked as he straightened up.

'Yeah. Couple of young blokes who seem pretty switched on. Need another one for the next muster, but we'll have to get through the Wet first. Not that there's any sign of it.'

'Still real early, Crow. Don't panic yet.'

'I know. But last year was drier than normal. Feed's getting a bit scarce. Bought a few truckloads of hay from down south and it cost me about half a year's profit!'

'Yeah. I know things are a bit short. But it's not real bad yet.'

'That's true.'

'Now, mate, while I've got you here,' he glanced around to see where the kids were, but they were in the kids' corner playing with toys and the young girl behind the counter seemed to be more engrossed in flicking through a glossy magazine than listening to what Kit was about to say. 'Don't suppose you've noticed any unusual tracks on your place? Or anything out of the ordinary at all?'

'As in vehicle tracks? Get 'em all the time. Tourists looking for a place to camp. Drives me spare.'

'I'd say more single vehicle tracks—you know, like a ute. In strange places, around bores and troughs and the like.'

Jamie squinted as he thought. 'Can't say I have. What sort of trouble are you having?'

Kit shoved his hands in his pockets and rocked back and forth on his heels. 'Not trouble as such. Just some unexplained happenings, I guess. Found the carcass of a freshly killed beast on the side of the road a couple of weeks ago. Looked like a bush butcher's job.'

'That happens from time to time.'

'Yeah, it does.' He paused as the door opened and another man walked in. Boyd Shepard. A bloke who used to be a local but had shifted further south. Seemed he couldn't stay away from the place. He nodded to him before turning back to Jamie. 'Not missing any cattle?'

'Haven't seen any signs of that.'

'Well, that's good.' Kit nodded. 'I'd best get on. Only came in to grab the *Farm Weekly*.'

The girl behind the counter looked up. 'I've still got 'em out the back. Haven't put 'em out on the shelf yet. Been run off my feet.' She closed the magazine and walked towards the office at the back of the shop. 'I'll just grab you one.'

Kit and Boyd exchanged glances. Perhaps if she hadn't been reading the gossip pages . . .

'Better make that two, love,' Jamie called after her.

Walking over to the other side of the shop, Kit stood next to Boyd Shepard. 'What's going on, Shep?' he asked quietly, his hands in his pockets.

'Not much,' he answered, not looking at Kit.

'Up here for a reason?'

'Nah, mate. Just the usual.'

Kit nodded. 'Guess I'll see you a bit later then.'

Boyd nodded and Kit walked back to the counter and waited for the *Farm Weekly*.

Ten minutes later and he was back outside in the glare of the sunlight. He adjusted his sunglasses and hat and this time walked towards the farm merchandise store.

Two small Aboriginal boys ran along the street in bare feet, a can of Coke their hands, and an old-timer sat under the shade of a tree, a cigarette hanging from his mouth. The sun was warm enough to raise a sweat and bring the bush flies out. They clustered around Kit's forehead.

Inside the store, he was greeted warmly again. Without too much chat, Kit left his order and then wandered down to the police station. He knew that his old mate, Glenn King, would be shutting the police station for an hour while he went to lunch. Kit intended to buy him lunch today.

His high-top boots clicked on the cement as he walked up the steps to the station, and just as he reached the top, Glenn came out, a large bunch of keys in his hand.

The grey-haired man dressed in uniform stopped when he saw Kit and a smile spread across his face. 'Well, well,

well, if it isn't the king of Boogarin Shire! How are you, old mate?' Glenn held out his hand and they both shook hard.

'Been a while, Kingy. Want a feed?'

Kit watched as Glenn's eyes narrowed just slightly. He knew Kit wasn't here on a social visit.

'Sure. I'll lock up and then how about we ask Mae over at the pub if she can find us a place where we can talk privately?'

'Sounds like a plan.'

❧

They sat at the back of the dining room. Being a Monday, there weren't any other people looking for lunch, so they had the place to themselves.

Kit ordered his usual steak with chips, and Glenn ordered a beef parmi.

'Thanks, fellas,' Mae said as she jotted the orders down. 'Any drinks?'

'Not for me,' Kit said. 'I've still got business to get on to after I've finished here.'

'And you'd better not have one, Senior Sergeant Boss Man,' Mae said with a wink as Glenn shook his head too. She pushed her pen behind her ear and smiled at the men. 'Won't be long.'

Mae walked away, pushing open the kitchen door and disappearing into the smell of deep-fried food and steak.

Kit noticed Glenn watching her with raw appreciation and raised his eyebrows.

'What's going on there?' he asked, picking up his fork and turning it around in his large fingers.

'What do you mean?'

'Looks like you're salivating.'

Glenn looked sheepish. 'That obvious?'

'Only to me.' He paused. 'Guess it's pretty lonely for you now?'

Glenn's wife had died two years earlier and Kit knew her ashes still sat next to Glenn's bed, along with a photo of them both on their thirtieth wedding anniversary.

'I hate it. Hate going home to an empty house. Cooking my own dinner and having to sit there without anyone to talk to.' He put his elbows on the table. 'Anyway, you didn't come into town to talk to me about that. What's up?'

Kit wanted to comment on what Glenn had said, offer some kind of support, but he knew that his friend didn't want him to. Glenn had told him as a fact and that was all. Instead he nodded and tapped his fingers on the table before saying in a quiet voice: 'There's some strange happenings beginning to get about. I reckon we're losing some cattle.'

Glenn sat back, rubbing his chin. 'Losing as in lost or stolen?'

Kit thought Glenn sounded hopeful at the 'losing' part. 'I wouldn't like to assume, but probably more the latter.'

'Damn! Been a while since that happened around here. What makes you think that?'

'Well, there're a few tracks that I can't account for on fence lines and boundaries. Looks like the fence has been dropped and cattle run over the top of it. Wondering if someone has been mustering wide.' As he said it, he imagined a chopper taking a wide arc out around his land

and seeing what cattle were close by that they could run over the fence. Calves that didn't have a brand on them were prime targets. Usually he didn't run cleanskin cattle close to the boundary's fences for that very reason. Neighbours and musterers couldn't always be trusted.

He knew of mustering contractors who had taken a cut of the sales when the cleanskins had been sold by the owners, so they were encouraged to muster wide. Not all mustering companies were like that, but in recent times, when diesel prices and wages were high and so were cattle prices, it added a bit of extra incentive to be dishonest.

And once cattle were marked with someone else's brand, it was difficult to prove they belonged to you.

'I see.' Glenn frowned. 'Should I ask what side of the property you're talking about?'

Kit raised his eyebrows. 'Do you even have to ask? And there was a beast used as a ration on the side of the road. Professional bush butchering job.'

'I had hoped that had all stopped for good.' Glenn folded his arms across his chest.

'A leopard can't change its spots.'

Chapter 5

As Dave pulled up in front of the stock squad office in a suburb on the outskirts of Perth, a buzz of excitement ran through him. He was here.

Finally, here.

He had achieved what he had set out to do all those years ago, after he'd been kicked off the farm. Getting his head around the fact he wasn't going to be able to farm had taken some time. He'd tried working for someone else, but it had been a bust; the job as a farmhand hadn't suited him. Often he'd had better ideas than the owner—or at least so he thought—and he'd found it impossible not to tell them what to do, especially when he could see a better way of doing things. Mostly, his employers hadn't liked his forthrightness. He'd decided he needed to find a job that let him work with animals and be interactive with farmers and graziers, but in some other capacity.

A newspaper article had caught his eye just after he'd left his last seeding job; twenty-five sheep had been stolen from a property out of Albany and the blokes had been caught red-handed at the saleyards after transporting them in a decked-out horse float. Somehow, they'd turned the float into a two-deck sheep crate, and they'd been discovered when detectives had noticed urine and sheep shit coming out of the holes along the bottom of the floor. Now, it wasn't unusual for hobby farmers to cart their stock in unconventional ways, but not having the right paperwork was more than a bit of a problem. Dave had followed the case all the way through until the men had been charged and sentenced.

The case had piqued Dave's interest and he had made some enquiries about how to become a detective . . . Now here he was, standing out the front of a nondescript white house which was headquarters for the Stock Squad WA.

To this day, he still bought the *Farm Weekly* and kept current with what was going on in farming—he knew what lambs were worth and whether grain prices were good. He had stayed up to date with some of the stock agents' names across the state—they didn't know him, but he knew who they were.

He was informed.

Taking a deep breath, Dave opened his car door and walked up the path, his palms sweating. He pushed open the door and went inside.

His first impression was the office was busy. There was a bit of noise—typing and phones ringing—and two detectives were talking to each other in front of a white-board. There were another two people at desks, looking at paperwork, and one on the phone. Dave assumed the one on the phone was Bob, because he was older than the others and his desk, at the front of the room, was the largest.

Bob turned at the sound of the door and smiled, waving Dave in.

'Gotta go, mate,' he said to the person on the other end of the line. 'Our new celebrity detective has turned up.' He slammed the phone down and called out, 'G'day, Dave. At least, I guess you're Dave and not some random who's walked in off the street! We're pleased to have you.' He got up and came towards him, holding out his hand.

The others turned around and looked at Dave; he felt like a deer in the spotlight. Holding up his hand he gave a bit of wave and then grasped the man's hand.

'Bob Holden,' the man confirmed. Bob turned to the rest of the investigators. 'This bloke,' Bob said in a reverent tone, 'is Dave Burrows. He single-handedly took down a mustering company who were stealing cattle in Queensland. And he took a bullet for his effort.' He pumped Dave's hand up and down again, ignoring Dave's grimace as his shoulder got a workout. 'So you fellas be respectful and nice.'

The other detectives thumped the table and whooped, before getting up to make themselves known to Dave.

A whirl of names: 'Perry Randall, great to know ya.'

'Toby Parke, but everyone calls me Parksey.'

'Blake Murray.'

The last one to introduce herself was Lorri Prior. 'I've heard a lot about you,' she said. 'Looking forward to working with you.'

Dave was impressed by the strength of her handshake. 'I'm really glad to be here,' he said to them all.

Bob took charge. 'This will be your desk, right alongside me, Dave,' he said, indicating a desk in the corner. It faced out towards the other detectives and Dave realised he'd be able to see the whole room, which suited him well. There was a computer and phone on the top and what looked like a case file. It had a couple of handwritten notes scrawled on the outside, but he couldn't read them from where he was. His fingers itched to pick the folder up and flick through it, as well as read what was on the whiteboard. He just wanted to get started!

'We're not that busy at the moment. You and I'll take a run to the saleyards tomorrow. Got the sheep sales on in the morning. Check a few weigh bills and chat to a few of the farmers and truckies. You'll need to meet the stock agents and auctioneers—get some relationships going with those blokes. They're easier to get to know than the farmers, you'll find.' Bob indicated for Dave to walk with him. 'Come on, I'll show you over the place.'

He took another breath then continued as they walked outside. 'Farmers are a funny breed of cattle, you see. Hard to get to know. Play their cards pretty close to their chest. You'll have to bring them flowers and buy 'em a beer to get 'em to open up most of the time. Treat 'em nice and all.'

Dave nodded. 'Yeah, I've known a few of them. More often than not they don't like to report stolen things.'

'Dead right there, mate.' Bob pointed at a large iron shed that took up most of the back area. 'Now this is the storage shed. Need it big so we can fit in all the equipment. You'll see we've got our motorbikes and other paraphernalia in here. We're each responsible for maintaining our own machinery. We'll supply you with your own ute; it'll be kitted out with everything you need: two-way radio, scanner, kangaroo jack, water tanks, siren and lights, all that sort of thing. You shouldn't want for anything really. Guessing you've got your own swag?' Bob pulled on the large sliding door and it rolled open with ease.

Dave nodded and peered inside. Six motorbikes were lined up on one side of the shed. There was a set of transportable sheep and cattle yards and two trailers. On the wall were bridles, and saddles were hung over rails that lined the walls. He could smell oil and leather and was transported back to his grandfather's farm and the tack he used with his Clydesdales, oiled to keep it supple.

'We've got a tractor out at the farm . . .'

'You've got a farm?'

Bob nodded. 'Yeah. About nine hundred hectares out of Wagin. It's where we take stock we know has been stolen, be it horses, cattle, sheep. Just so long as there's not too many of them. Gives us a place to keep them until we've finished the investigation. See, the stock is classed as evidence, so even if we find the owners, we can't give it back until the investigation is finished, charges have been laid and the person of interest has been found guilty. Need to show that the POI has altered the earmark or changed the brand, and if they're in our care, then we can do it straight away.' Bob pulled the roller door shut. 'Anyway, enough about all of this. Tell me about your undercover work. Far more interesting than this mundane stuff.'

Dave gave a laugh. 'I disagree! I reckon this is more interesting. Plus, there's not that much to tell. We got the employees but not the employers. We know who's behind the rustling, but they're still in the wind.'

Bob looked at him. 'They got a price on your head?' he asked seriously.

Dave had a flashback to his dream, where Bulldust was chasing him. He tried to put it out of his mind and instead shook his head. 'They wouldn't know who I was, looking like this. I was pretty different when I was undercover, so I doubt it. Haven't heard anything and if there was a whisper, I'm sure I would've. We've got ears everywhere.'

Leaning in close, even though there wasn't anyone around, Bob said, 'And I heard one of us was dirty. Bad, bad thing that.'

'I've got the court case coming up in about six weeks. I'll have to go back over to give evidence.' Dave wasn't entering into any conversation about the cop he'd found to be giving information to Bulldust and Scotty.

Bob let out a belly laugh. 'That'll keep you busy, mate! Let's hope we don't tie you up on a big case while all that's going on.' He glanced at the large silver watch on his wrist.

'Gawd, look at the time. Close enough to lunch already. Let's round up the rest of the crew and get a counter meal at the Berkley. It's just around the corner from here.'

Surprised, Dave said, 'What, all of us? Shouldn't there be someone in the office? And we can't drink while we're on duty!'

'Mate, one isn't going to hurt you. This is how we woo our farmers. Just breaking you in gently, so I am.' He clapped Dave on the shoulder. 'Come on.'

Dave had wanted to fire up his computer and look at the software they used. The file on his desk was calling him too—what was in it?

Guess I can do that afterwards, he thought and followed Bob back into the office.

～

Laughter rose up from the table as Bob raised his glass to Dave. His cheeks were glowing from the alcohol and Dave was sure he hadn't just had one, but there was only one half-empty glass in front of him.

No one else was drinking but they all seemed quite relaxed about Bob having a beer. Maybe the culture was different in the stock squad, he thought.

But even so . . . *We're supposed to uphold the law and how can we do that if we're three-parts pissed?* he wondered.

'Right-oh, you riff-raff, quieten down. I'm going to make a toast.' Bob pushed his plate aside, not before wiping his finger around the edge to get the last of the gravy that had covered his schnitzel. 'We're damn excited to have you, Dave. Here's to many a long year with the stock squad. Just hope you don't have to take a bullet for us here.'

Parksey let out a long whistle while the rest of team banged on the table and made some noise.

Dave was embarrassed and held up his hands. 'Enough already! I'm glad to be here and thanks for being so welcoming.' He paused and looked at each one of them. 'I'm *really* glad to be in the team with you all.'

Parksey leaned forwards. 'Tell us about it. You know, the case and being undercover and all.'

Dave shrugged. 'Not much to tell. I went over there and did my job.' He wasn't sure he could articulate how thrilling it had been; how frightening and exciting at the same time. Until it came to that final chase and he had felt the bullet enter his shoulder.

It didn't seem so exhilarating in the middle of the night when the nightmares were taking hold of him. As he listened to the dog's bark as they hunted through the bush that night. The shock of the cold water as he'd submerged himself in the river and the tightness in his chest as he'd held his breath for so long he thought he might not surface again.

'You've gotta have a couple of war stories you can tell us about,' Perry encouraged, also leaning forwards in anticipation.

Taking a sip of his lemon squash, Dave debated what he could tell them. Finally, he leaned back in his chair and looked at them all. 'Well,' he said, 'when I first arrived in Nundrew, on an old motorbike, I had to speed down the main street to get the coppers' attention. It was the ploy, you know? Make a loud entrance, the cops start to watch you and the crims decide you're okay, because the cops are out to arrest your arse. It worked too, because when I parked the bike on the verandah of the pub and left it there, it caused a bit of a stir. That got me an introduction to the local police.' He paused and watched their faces. His colleagues were enthralled.

Spencer had told him not many cops ever went undercover, and most were fascinated by the experience. And scared at the same time. He'd warned him that he'd be treated like a celebrity and Dave hated this part. But he was a good storyteller, so he went with it.

Only for today, he thought.

He shrugged. 'Here's the most glamorous part. First night? I slept on the floor of the public toilets. Cement floor. No lights. All that sort of stuff.' Taking a breath, he remembered the coldness of the cement, even through the swag mattress.

'Why did you stay there?' Lorri wanted to know.

'I had to play the part of a drifter,' he said. 'Drifters don't have money, so no hotel.'

'Geez,' Blake looked repulsed. 'Hope it wasn't on the nose.'

'Wouldn't have mattered if it was. It was the spot to camp the night. Was pretty lucky after that. Hooked up with the POI and I camped with them until the job was finished.'

Bob waded into the conversation. 'See you all gotta remember, boys and girl, it's about acting. You're playing a role. So you can't be who you are normally, isn't that right?'

'You're on the money. It's the little details; I put a stone in my shoe so I walked differently, had contact lenses to change the colour of my eyes. I was someone my own mother wouldn't have recognised, and the personality had to be the same. You been under, Bob?'

'Nah. The undercover gig isn't for me, but I've been a handler a couple of times. That's as close to the action as I want to get. More drinks anyone?' Bob asked as he started to get up.

Everyone shook their heads.

'Actually, we should get back to the office,' Perry said. 'I've got a couple of phone calls to make.'

Chairs scraped backwards and everyone got up, while Bob headed back to the bar.

'What are you working on?' Dave asked, falling into step alongside Perry, hungry for information.

'I've got a case of trespassing on a property down south. The victims farm marron and they've had people going on their place and fishing their dams.'

'Got any leads?'

'Not yet. It's frustrating because it's happened twice, but the MO isn't the same. I think they've been hit by two different POIs. Between the two hits, they've lost half their marron supply and all of their markets, because they can't supply what they were contracted to.'

Dave grimaced. 'The hidden side of rural crime. People losing their livelihoods.'

'Yeah. Heartbreaking when you see the families—sometimes they've got little kids and other times it's the old farmer who has had the farm in the family for generations and they can't keep it anymore. Crime doesn't discriminate.' He raised his voice as a car rushed past on the busy road.

'Any type of crime,' Dave agreed. 'Anyone else got something in the wings?'

'There're always a few reports of the greener crops being grown on Crown land or even on some of the farming land that doesn't have people living on it full time. I think Lorri has one of them going right now.'

'Using my name in vain?' Lorri asked as she came alongside.

'Dave just asked what was going on in the office and I was telling him about your greenery case.'

'Oh yeah. Growing them along the Avon River.' She shook her head. 'They're so stupid. These types are the easiest to solve. We just set up some cameras and silent alarms and catch them checking the crop, then turn up when they are there next and arrest their sorry arse!'

Perry and Dave laughed.

'Good job, Lorri,' Perry said.

Bob, having drained his second beer quickly, fell into step with them. 'I gotta go out,' he said. 'Be back in a couple of hours. Dave, if you've gone by the time I turn back up again, it's sale day tomorrow. We'll hit the yards at oh-six-hundred, okay?'

'Sure thing, boss.'

Chapter 6

Kevin saw the dust before he saw the car.

The cloud of red swirled high into the bright blue sky and a little later on the growl of the engine reached him too. From the shed, where he had been helping Jackie change the oil in one of the utes, he walked towards the dirt track that ran past the shed, then stopped, his hands on his hips. They weren't expecting anyone.

'Looks like we've got company,' he said. It was unusual to have people come out here without calling first, and an unexpected visitor meant one of two things: tourists on the wrong track, or trouble.

'Who's comin'?' Jackie asked, walking up to stand alongside Kevin, wiping his hands on a rag.

'Can't tell from here,' Kevin answered.

'Hmm. Whoever it is, I don't think they'll be bringing any good,' Jackie said, turning away. 'I can feel it.'

'Might be lost.'

'Nah, no good will come of this. You'll see. No one turns up unannounced out here and brings good news.' A burst of children's laughter from the edge of the creek rose into the still air and intermingled with engine noise growing louder. A round of barking from the dogs and then the *thwump* of bare feet on leather. The kids were playing their afternoon game of footy.

'No good,' Jackie repeated from a distance this time.

Kevin turned around in time to see his father disappear into the murky darkness of the shed. He frowned as he swung back to look for the dust again. Instead, he saw a white four-wheel-drive troopy with police stripes down the side. He narrowed his eyes and didn't change his stance.

Maybe his father was right.

The vehicle pulled up to a stop and the policeman waved through the window. 'G'day there, Kevin,' Glenn said, getting out of the vehicle and putting his Akubra on his head with large meaty hands. 'How're you going, mate?' He adjusted his heavy belt, which had a gun and handcuffs hanging from it, before reaching into the back of the vehicle and bringing out three litres of fresh milk and three loaves of bread.

Rule number one of the bush: never arrive at a station empty-handed.

'G'day,' Kevin answered.

Glenn walked over, his hand outstretched, and Kevin didn't see that he had any option other than to shake it.

'Things looking a bit dry out this way,' Glenn said.

'You're a bit off the beaten track. What brings you out here, Senior Sergeant King?' Kevin asked as he took the bread and milk. 'Cheers for these.' He didn't move or offer him a cuppa.

'Just thought I'd come for a little chat. Find out how things have been going since you've come back up. Been a while since I've seen you in town.'

Kevin watched the man closely. His eyes were flicking everywhere as if he were searching for something. Finally they settled on Kevin's face. Glenn looked him straight in the eye, his face solemn as he patted the small black bush flies away.

'Got no reason to be in town unless I need supplies or stuff for the station. Only go in once every couple of months. We're pretty self-sufficient out here. What did you want to chat about?' Kevin asked. He kept eye contact as a single white corella flew overhead. The swish of its wings was the only noise in the silence stretching between the two men.

A sense of foreboding trickled through Kevin's stomach, but he didn't let it show.

'How about we go and sit down?' Glenn asked.

'I'm happy here. What's this all about? I think we both know you don't make courtesy calls, Sergeant.'

Glenn pushed his hat back on his head and scratched at his hairline before pulling it back down. 'Right. Well, then. How are you getting on? No trouble since you've got back?'

Kevin thought of the cattle that had been pushed over the fence and his damaged windmill.

'Everything is fine,' he answered. 'Nothing that a bit of rain wouldn't fix.'

Glenn seemed to grasp at that line of conversation. 'Yeah, she's been dry for a while. Got enough feed for all your cattle or are you needing to shift some?'

'We're good for the moment.'

'The Wet can't be too far away.' He looked up. 'Although no build-up yet.'

'It'll come.'

'Yeah, Kit Redman said the same thing. Guess you're right.'

Kevin stiffened at the name. Kit was his neighbour and the owner of Deep-Water Station. Kevin didn't want to enter into any discussion about him.

'I've got to get on,' Kevin said, starting to move towards his ute in the shed, still holding the bread and milk. 'Pretty busy, you know. Was just about to head out on a bore run. Anything else I can help you with?' He hoped that would dissuade Glenn from asking any more questions.

'Well, actually, mate, there is.' Glenn took off his hat and wiped his brow.

In the open, it was blazing hot; it would be much cooler in the shade or the shed, but Kevin wasn't letting the police officer in there until he knew what this was all about—he didn't want the man getting comfortable.

Glenn started to follow Kevin, who stopped and turned around to face him.

'What's that?' Kevin said.

'Well, speaking of Kit, he came to see me the other day. On business, you know?'

Kevin stood and listened.

'He reckons he's seeing a few strange things around his place.' Glenn scratched his arm then put his hand in his pocket. When Kevin didn't say anything, he continued. 'He's seen cattle tracks on his place, and it looks like someone has laid a fence down. Could be heading in this direction.'

Kevin felt the burn of fury in his throat, in his stomach. 'What are you saying?' he asked in a low voice. 'We're thieves?' It wasn't only the sun making Kevin sweat now. He was livid.

A gust of wind made a loose piece of tin on the shed bang and the galahs that were perched in the trees rose in a squawking cloud of pink and grey. The ghost gum next to the shed battered its leaves against the tin, making a scratching sound. As soon as the gust blew itself out, the land was silent again.

Glenn held up his hands. 'Mate, I'm not saying anything. I'm here making a few enquiries. Kit hasn't identified any cattle losses, but he's seen fences down and vehicle tracks. On both sides of the fence. He reported one when he first came and saw me. Been more since. And there's been a few animals butchered. Looks like a professional job each time.'

'We've got our own cattle as rations, Senior Sergeant King. And as for tracks on both sides of the fence, that's because they've come from my side, from Spinifex Downs onto Deep-Water, not the other way around.' Kevin's heart was beating fast from saying all of that aloud. And to a copper. His dad would be disappointed if he'd heard the conversation. He wanted to glance around to see if he could see Jackie somewhere, but he didn't dare take his eyes from Glenn's in case he saw that as a sign of guilt. 'And your "making enquiries" sounds to me like an accusation.' His voice was low.

Glenn threw up his hands and cleared his throat. 'Look, Kevin, we've got off on the wrong foot. I'm not here to accuse you of anything. I'm trying to work out if we've got a problem around here. Gathering information.'

Kevin regarded the man standing in front of him and wondered how much he could trust him. The comment about cattle heading towards Spinifex Downs had certainly sounded like an allegation but his face was open and honest. Maybe he just had a shit way with words.

'Gather your information without accusing me of something, then,' Kevin finally said.

'Like I said. Wrong foot and all. Just seems that there're a few things that are indicating we might have someone pinching stock. Have you noticed anything that's raised your antenna? Your older stockmen are good trackers. Have they been out and about the station?'

Kevin turned around again and resumed walking towards the shed. 'Come on, let's get out of the sun. It can make a man go mad.' He didn't turn to see if Glenn was following him.

Inside, he dumped the bread and milk on the workbench and pulled up a couple of ten-gallon oil drums. 'Sit down.' He perched on the side of one and adjusted his jeans, before taking off his hat and letting it fall on the cement beside him, raising a puff of dust. His pocketknife, attached to his jeans, pushed into his hip, but he ignored it.

Glenn's boots clipped on the cement and he sat down too, then he spread his hands and said, 'Tell me what's going on, Kev. I'm here to listen. We can't let whatever's happening out here get out of control, you know? There's only one of me.'

Kevin twisted a piece of baling twine around his fingers and heard what Glenn was implying: he couldn't stop a melee between neighbours without reinforcements. He thought about what to say while Jackie's voice echoed around his mind: *Don't go to the police, boy.*

Kevin wrestled with himself. It was fine for his father to say that, but he was a new generation. He was here to make a difference to his people, to bring pride back. He'd seen it as a young man: his people turning away from work and slumping into the deep abyss of alcohol. Without dignity or self-belief. That's why he'd applied for the scholarship—so he could help bring that pride back to those he cared for so deeply. But would telling this copper about his suspicions take away the respect he'd earned since he'd been back here? But, like he'd said to Jackie earlier, if they kept letting people walk all over them, how could they be a proud people?

In the end, Kevin couldn't see any way around it. He needed to talk about what was going on. If his suspicions were right, Spinifex Downs was going to continue to be a target forever.

He told Glenn to stay where he was and went out to his ute. Grabbing the video camera, he brought it back and held it out to the policeman. 'The screen is pretty small so I guess you won't be able to see much, but on here is a video that shows how my bore was sabotaged. The pump rods were undone and—' he hit the play-back button, with the screen facing Glenn '—here's where the cattle have gone over the fence into Deep-Water Station.' The wind blurred the sound, but they could both still hear Kevin's voice on the footage.

'Look at this—the staples have been pulled out of the post and these couple here haven't been nailed back in. Cattle tracks here and here.' The camera raised up and moved as Kevin walked across the boundary fence and into Deep-Water Station. The deep cattle tracks were clear in the orange soil, as were the broken branches of the bushes. The cattle had clearly been hurried through.

The video stopped and Glenn looked up but didn't say anything for a moment. 'Why do you think the bore was deliberately incapacitated?'

'We pin our couplings so they can't work their way loose. I remember there were issues with that when I was a kid. They'd come loose and then the bores wouldn't pump. I made sure that wouldn't happen.' He paused as another gust of wind hit the side of the shed and the sound of banging tin grew louder.

'I found the pin lying on the ground. Whoever did it wanted me to know it had been done deliberately. You'll see when you watch the whole thing.' He paused the video again to show the stainless-steel pin glinting in the sun against the red soil.

'Can you get this footage to me, please?' Glenn asked, fishing in his pocket and handing over a business card. 'Got internet out here yet?'

'Yeah. We do. Pretty slow though. I don't know if the video will email but if it doesn't I'll save the file onto a disk. I'll work it out.'

'And you're sure you've lost cattle?'

'Me and two other fellas have been over that paddock three times. We've checked every hidey-hole there could be and the cattle that should be in that paddock aren't there anymore.'

'How many?'

By now Glenn had his notebook out and had started to jot down the things Kevin was saying. That made Kevin nervous. He'd already said more than he wanted to.

'There were two hundred in there. Cows, pure Brahman. Three years old. They were the first lot of girls I got on the ground after I came back. Bred from some really beautiful sires I sourced from Queensland. Great milkers.'

'Got the tracking tags in them? NLIS tags?'

'Yeah, and they're all branded. The calves won't be of course, but the cows are.'

Kevin watched as Glenn wrote down something else and tapped his pen against his mouth.

'You haven't reported this.' It was a statement not a question.

'Nope.'

'The obvious question here is why.'

Kevin wound the string around his fingers again as he tried to frame his answer. 'There's a lotta history, you know?'

Shifting on the drum, Glenn squinted. 'History?'

'Between your crew and mine.'

Glenn didn't say anything, so Kevin continued. 'Fact is that my dad and the Elders here don't trust the coppers. They don't want me to say anything.'

''Cause they reckon I'm bent. Now who's chucking rocks at people?'

Glenn's tone was hard, and Kevin could hear the resignation in his voice. 'Look, Kev, I've worked pretty hard to get a relationship with everyone, no matter their skin colour, since I turned up here ten-odd years ago. This isn't about race, mate, it's about some lowlife thieving bastard who needs to be caught.'

Kevin didn't want to be swayed by the impassioned speech, but he also needed someone to talk to. He didn't want to lie down and take what was happening anymore. Still, he had to resist a little—or at least get across his point of view.

'The police, they always take the whitefellas' side. Not ours. And in the past we've been accused of things we haven't done.' He leaned forwards, making sure that Glenn was listening to him. 'We've had to take the rap for some of the whitefellas. You can't blame the Elders for not liking that and being distrustful of you. Their memories are very long.'

'Have I caused any of that?' Glenn asked.

Kevin paused and raised his eyebrows. 'Not that I know of.'

'Then don't tar me with the same brush as the coppers before me.' Glenn crossed his arms and stared at Kevin.

'Historical hurt and all that,' Kevin answered quietly.

'So you're going to let some bastard get away with taking everything you're working towards?'

Anger flared again. 'You think I like this?' Kevin almost yelled. 'You think I like my neighbours coming onto my land and taking my cattle? I'm hamstrung by the past, no matter how hard I try to change it! Old hurts still haunt us.'

'Okay, stop right there.' Glenn held up his hand. 'Kit Redman was the person who made the report about the cattle. I can't see him doing that if he was stealing them himself, can you?'

'What?' Kevin looked at him, not understanding.

'That's right, mate. It was Kit who came to me. He's not doing this. It's someone else.'

Kevin was silent as he raced to process what Glenn had just said. 'He came to you?'

'He did,' Glenn confirmed. 'Last week.'

'Okay.' The string twisted harder around his work-worn fingers.

'You want to make that report?'

Glancing over his shoulder, Kevin took a breath. 'You gotta understand, I'm worried about how Dad and the Elders will respond, but yeah, Sergeant, I want to report some of our cattle being stolen.' He looked down, hoping he was doing what was best for everyone.

Glenn leaned over and clapped Kevin on the shoulder. 'You're doing the right thing, mate. I'll make sure you're looked after.'

'What happens now?'

'Well, I need that video, like I said. I don't care if you put it in the post to me, but I need the footage ASAP. I'm going to head off to another few stations and make some more enquiries. When I get back to Boogarin, depending on what I find, I'll probably ring the stockies. See if they can come up and have a look around. All right if I use the access road to get across to Paperbark Valley?' He named another station to the east of Spinifex Downs.

Kevin nodded.

'Right-oh, I'll get on then. Make sure you get in touch if you need anything or notice something unusual.'

'Will do,' Kevin said, sounding more certain than he felt. 'I'll wait to hear from you.'

'I'll be in touch soon.' Glenn held out his hand and Kevin shook it. Just before he got into his vehicle, he turned back to him. 'You fellas coming in to the rodeo on the weekend?'

'Some of us will be,' Kevin nodded. 'It's a bit hard to keep everyone away.'

'See you there then.'

Two minutes later the troopy was out of sight. The dust it stirred up hung in the air for a while, without a breeze to shift it, just like Kevin's thoughts.

'What'd he want?' Jackie appeared with a short leather whip in his hand. He cracked it, then checked the cracker.

'I reported the cattle missing.'

Jackie didn't say anything but cracked the whip again, a little harder.

'I had to.'

'Nah. Nah, you didn't. Now he's going to be saying that we're pointing the finger at the other station owners. I told you, boy, we don't do this. Don't report things.'

Chapter 7

The spotlights lit up the unloading ramp and the rest of the saleyards as Dave and Bob stepped along the walkway.

It was still dark, and the bitter cold made Dave wish he'd put a T-shirt on under his shirt and jacket. Saleyards always seemed to be freezing cold and muddy, no matter the time of year.

The smell of sheep and shit hit Dave and he breathed the odour in. To him, it smelled like home; he stopped and watched the busyness for a few seconds.

Men in green or red shirts were penning the sheep with expertise, guiding them with plastic pipes and checking the numbers against the paperwork. The sheep baa-ed as their hooves clicked on the cement floor and the gates and chains rattled loudly.

The calls of 'Hup, hup! Get up!' were loud and Dave watched as a couple of kelpies ran up and down the race, encouraging the sheep in a particular direction with short, loud barks. He couldn't help but smile. Men stood in the middle of the raceway, closing the gate when one pen was full, then opening another gate and guiding the next mob into another pen. Further out, away from the roof-covered yards, Dave could see the twinkling tail-lights of the trucks as they reversed into loading ramps and ran off more sheep to be sold. This was a world he loved.

'Dave?' Bob called above the racket and waved him over. 'Son, I want you to meet Bundy. He's the auctioneer. Bundy, our newest recruit, Dave Burrows.'

Dave bristled at 'son' but smiled and held out his hand.

'Glad to meet you, Dave. You need anything, just ask.' Bundy grasped Dave's hand in a strong grip and then clapped him on the shoulder. 'Hopefully we won't have too much work for you.'

'I'm ready if you do,' Dave said.

'Big yarding today?' Bob asked.

'About ten thousand. Big enough. The buyers will have to open their pockets a bit if they want to get their purchases. Couple of blokes from the eastern states here chasing lambs. Price is a bit high for them at home.'

'Should keep things interesting.'

A young girl stuck her head out of a demountable hut and yelled to Bundy, 'You're needed here!'

'Ah, bugger. Looks like I've got to go. I'll catch you both a bit later.' He nodded and walked quickly across the railing to the building.

'They're the offices,' Bob said with a jerk of his head towards the direction Bundy was walking. 'All the paperwork that comes with the animals goes in there once the count has been verified. So if you need any documentation, best idea is to make friends with one of the pretty little things in there. They're a good source too. Know most of what goes on in the yards. Who's who and who's where. That sort of thing. These are big yards—set on nearly fourteen hectares. They hold a lot of cattle . . . and a lot of sheep.'

A man wearing a two-way hooked to his belt and a heavy oilskin coat walked past and openly stared at the set of horns on Dave's jacket.

'Tell me again why we're in uniform?' Dave said. The light-blue shirt had a set of large horns, not dissimilar to the R.M. Williams logo, embroidered on the left-hand side, and again on the outside of his jacket. He'd thought it was odd that Bob had told him to come dressed like this. Surely if someone was going to be doing anything underhand at the yards, the stockies would want to be in plain clothes?

'I know what you're thinking, we should be in plain clothes so we can see if anything illegal is happening. Son, it doesn't work like that. These fellas need to know who we are, so they can come and talk to us.

'This uniform, it's not as obvious as the ones the street boys wear. It just subtly lets everyone know who we are and, if they need us, they can come and track us down to have a yarn privately.'

Dave nodded. He figured if he turned up at the sale-yards once every couple of weeks it wouldn't take long for people to know who he was whether he was in a uniform or not. It would be the same crowd of auctioneers, yards men and buyers every week.

'Bob! Good to see you, old mate.' A grey-haired man with deep wrinkles around his blue eyes sauntered over.

'Robbie, how you doing?'

'Not going to complain. No one listens anyway,' Robbie said as his eyes turned curiously to Dave. 'Got a new bloke, so I see.'

'Yep. New one on the team,' Bob said and introduced Dave. 'Robbie is the yard manager. Any issues, go to him first.'

'What made you want to hang out in freezing, wet, shit-smelling saleyards, Dave? Only us stupid old buggers choose to do that,' Robbie said, his eyes bright.

Dave liked Robbie at first glance. His wizened face told of many years of experience. *He would've seen a few things and heard a few stories*, Dave thought. Giving a laugh, he said, 'I don't know what you mean. This is my ideal job!'

Robbie nodded. 'I'd have to agree with you, lad, but thousands wouldn't. Where you from?'

'Originally? From a farm just out of Northam. More recently I've been in Barrabine.'

'Gold country? Obviously you didn't make your fortune 'cause you wouldn't be here if you did.' He turned to Bob. 'Anything going on that I need to know about?'

Bob shook his head. 'Not a thing. Just wanted to bring Dave on his first excursion, you know. Introduce him round.'

'Grant's back today. You make sure you catch up and introduce young Dave here.' He turned to Dave and explained,

'Grant's in charge of unloading the trucks and getting the cattle to the right pens.'

'Holidays finished already? Did he get a tan?' Bob asked.

'More than that. He got himself engaged.' Robbie gave an exaggerated wink.

'Silly bastard,' Bob said with a laugh.

'He doesn't think so,' Robbie said. 'Anyway, make sure you go and find him, all right?'

'We'll do just that, mate. No worries.'

Dave nodded farewell as Bob guided him up onto selling rails above the pens and cast his arm out. 'Tell me what you see here, Dave.'

Dave looked around. There were sheep of every age and size. Some with wool, some shorn. There were a few blokes leaning into the pens, checking the mouths of ewes, and others feeling the ribs of prime lambs. Fat scoring, seeing how much cover the lambs had, to make sure they were neither too skinny nor too fat for the butchers. They had to be just right.

Like the porridge in the Three Bears, Dave's grandfather used to say.

'Okay, those fellas over there,' Dave pointed to two men who were now inside the pen and feeling the lambs all over. 'They'd be buying for the abs, I'd reckon.' He resisted looking over at Bob to see if he was right. 'And that one there,' he pointed to a man and woman, dressed in jeans and thick jumpers, with beanies on their heads. They were leaning against a pen of ewes. Dave had noticed the man inside the pen, about five minutes before, tipping the ewes over, checking their udders were in good condition and making sure they didn't have a broken mouth. 'I think they're farmers looking for replacement ewes.'

Bob nodded.

'I personally wouldn't buy replacement ewes out of sale-yards, because here is where everyone else's culls are, but,' Dave shrugged, 'guess everyone does things differently.'

'That they do.'

Bob crossed his arms and leaned against the rail. 'Now, you've told me a bit, but tell me more about what you see. Look at the sheep.'

Dave looked again. 'Various mobs of sheep. There're ewes, wethers, lambs . . .'

'You're not hearing me, son. What do you *see*?' Bob looked at him intently, his hands indicating the sheep that had already been penned.

A flicker of anger touched Dave's belly. 'This a trick question?'

Bob shook his head. 'Being a stockie is about looking, not for what's there but for what isn't.'

Dave wanted to snap at the man for talking in riddles, but he held his tongue and tried to understand what Bob was saying.

'Take this mob of ewes here, who have got a bit of red in their fleece. What does that tell you?'

'They've come off red dirt country. Station country most likely.'

'Bingo!' Bob pointed at Dave and nodded. 'And these ones here. The grey ones.'

'Off different land—more likely southern where the soils are lighter coloured.'

'Exactly. Now, see here.' He walked along the rails until he came to a pen with about thirty wethers in it. 'What's wrong with this pen?'

Looking at the sheep, Dave couldn't see anything. They were all shorn, looked the same . . .

'You're looking for what's *not* there, son.'

Clenching his jaw, Dave looked again. Then he saw it. 'One is coated in red dust and the others are all grey. If they were all from the same place, they'd be a uniform grey. And it's a bit bigger than the others. Producers in the north like big framed ewes.'

'Spot on! Buy the man a beer! Let's go and check the penning card,' Bob said as he climbed down the ladder to the ground. 'See, that will show you where they've come from, how many should be in the pen, all that sort of stuff. My guess is that there's a pen of ewes next door that look like they've come down from up north, and one has jumped the fence, but it's always good to check. It's all about traceability. Tracking the animal from farm gate to plate.'

'Geez, in all the years I was filling out the paperwork for the truckies when we sent sheep off, I didn't see it in terms of the big picture.'

'So many farmers don't.' He jumped the fence and grabbed the ewe with the red dust coating and held it tightly in between his legs. 'Check the ear tag and mark against the penning card, son,' Bob said.

He read out the tag and the number of animals that should be in the pen, then checked the card on the next yard. 'Yeah, it's jumped the fence.'

Bob nodded. 'Give me a hand and we'll put it back over.'

Climbing into the yards, Dave grabbed the hind legs and together they flicked the wether over the fence and in with its mates.

Bob cast his eye over the rest of the mob, then grabbed another sheep. 'See here?' He pointed to the ear, where the ear tag should've been. 'If you give me a pair of side cutters, I'll show you how easy it is to get a tag out of an ear. A mutilated ear like this one could be a couple of things— a dog attack or some useless fuck on the lamb-marking cradle didn't know how to use the markers properly. One in a penful isn't a problem. But if you get thirty out of fifty, then that's when you take another look. Do you get my meaning?'

'Yeah. Yeah, I do. Someone might have tried to change the earmark so the animal can't be traced.'

Look for what isn't there. In his mind he could hear Bec's favourite *Play School* song—'*One of these is not like the other . . .*'—and that's what he had to look for.

'Of course, all that I've just showed you there is circumstantial. You need proof to back it all up, but circumstantial is a good start.' He clapped Dave on the shoulder and climbed over the railing. 'Come on, let's get back to the office. If we don't get going soon, I'll miss my lunch meeting.'

❧

The office was empty when Dave and Bob arrived back. On the whiteboard Lorri had scrawled: *Gone to check camera on Avon.*

'Wonder where the others are,' Bob muttered as he flicked through the messages on his desk. He held one up and read it a couple of times before handing it over to Dave. 'Here you go. You follow up on this. I gotta head out. Greg and I are meeting for lunch.'

Dave didn't bother asking who Greg was. He guessed that Bob was heading to the pub again for what seemed to be his daily special—parmi and beer.

Taking the message, he read it and a smile started. 'Leave it with me,' he said.

'Good man. Catch you later.' Bob left the office and Dave sat down. Placing his hands on the top of the desk, he pushed down. 'God, it's good to be here,' he said quietly. He looked at the photo of Mel and Bec on his desk, before focusing back on the message.

Ring SS Glenn King from Boogarin Stn.

Dave wished there was a bit more information. Still, all he had to do was pick up the phone and call and he'd know what it was all about. His heart thudded with excitement and, before he could think about it any longer, he snatched up the phone and dialled the number.

Chapter 8

Boogarin Rodeo Day had dawned clear and warm, but by the time the crew from Spinifex Downs had made it into town it was mid-afternoon and the rodeo was in full flight. A land breeze had picked up and the flags flying above the rodeo ground were fluttering around, being tossed by an invisible force.

Kevin watched in the rear-vision mirror as four utes full of young men from Spinifex Downs pulled into the queue. He knew they would all be wearing large grins and he hoped there would be nothing to dampen their enthusiasm tonight. No broken bones would be an advantage too. The last two annual rodeos had gone spectacularly well, from his point of view, and he'd considered not even coming this time.

Kevin would rather be getting around his cattle or tinkering in the shed than be hanging around in town with a heap of strangers. Tourists seemed to flock to these things—an outback experience. But, with his men attending, he'd had no choice but to come.

'You started this, boy,' Jackie had said. 'You get in there and make sure no one points the finger at our people. Accuses us of taking their cattle. What's done's done. Can't change it now, except to look after our own.'

The Spinifex Downs crew were mostly young blokes, ones who wanted to try their luck riding the broncs or roping calves. They were dressed in their new jeans and brightly coloured chequered shirts and boots, their hat brims as large as their smiles.

The rodeo had been talked about around the fire most nights, and the boys had been practising their grips; one had even gone down south to a rodeo school. Once he'd returned home, he'd taught the other boys what he'd learned. As much as he could without a beast to ride. They'd found an old forty-four-gallon drum and wrapped a girth around it so they could practise as best they could.

As all the boys had climbed into the utes, their laughter and excitement had been felt by everyone. Everyone except Jackie and two other Elders who were sitting under a gum tree watching them, their faces solemn. One had leaned forwards and said something to Jackie—Kevin hadn't been able to hear the words, but from the expression on his father's face, he'd known it wasn't in his favour.

The feeling of foreboding he'd felt when he'd seen the copper's troopy hadn't left him, and there hadn't been any contact with Senior Sergeant King, except for an email thanking Kevin for the video.

But for now, at the rodeo, Kevin knew all he could do was what Jackie had told him to. Go with them and make sure all his young men were looked after—and hope that none of the people who had helped King with his enquiries were going to be pissed off with them. After all, he had made the comment about 'neighbours pinching our cattle'. With any luck, neither his name nor Spinifex Downs would've been mentioned and the copper wouldn't have mentioned what Kev had said.

The three-hour trip to town had seemed to pass in a blur. He'd driven through deep, dry creeks with high red cliffs on either side and large flats of native bush where kangaroos and cattle grazed. Even though the feed was getting tight, the cattle he saw were in good nick. The wedgetail eagles feasting on roadkill and the beautiful white-trunked ghost gums and stony waterways should have captured his attention, but he kept hearing his father's words in his mind: *You started this, boy.*

Anger surged through him. *Well, hell yeah. He had started it*, he thought. *And he'd finish it too.*

He jammed his foot on the brake to stop from running into the back of another ute that had come to a stop in front of him at the gate. Shit! He needed to pay attention. Two cars later, he paid his entry fee and was guided over to the car park, where he let the engine idle for a few moments before he turned the key.

The smell of the camp ovens wafted across the car park, mixed in with hot chips and donuts. It all made Kevin's stomach rumble; he hadn't eaten today. Getting out of the ute, he locked it and turned to look at all the utes and vehicles parked on the dirt area near the rodeo ring. Judging by the number of cars, the whole district must be here.

You started this, boy.

'G'day, Kev,' Jamie Crowden said as he walked by on his way to the main area. Kevin fell into step with him.

'What's happening?' he asked.

'Oh, geez, just a bit of maintenance and fencing really. Not a whole lot,' Jamie answered. 'You?'

'Yeah, same really. Mustering finished a couple of weeks ago and we've finished trucking everything out. The live export market picked up a bit this week. Nice to see a bit of joy in prices. Just wish I had a few more to sell.'

Jamie nodded. 'You're right there.'

A didgeridoo sounded across the oval, then piano and guitar joined in. There was a loud clapping and voices started to sing along and rise into the late afternoon air.

'Got Djolpa here,' Jamie said. 'They're a great band. Should be a good night. And I heard they were bringing in Jimmy Barnes too. Reckon that's why so many have turned up.'

'Make for a good night,' Kevin agreed, looking around for his men. 'Hopefully everyone has a good time and no one gets hurt.'

'Wouldn't be a rodeo without someone breaking something,' Jamie said with a laugh. 'I'll catch up with you, Kev, all right?' Jamie gave him a wave as he stopped in front of the stock agent's tent.

'Later,' Kevin said, taking in the action as he walked. Groups of people were standing around, talking and laughing, all dressed in bright shirts and some in even brighter boots. His eyes stopped at the bar. A dark-skinned man leaned against the wall of the tent, watching him.

Boyd Shepard. He had a habit of turning up.

Kevin looked away without acknowledging him and kept walking. He nodded to a few people he knew as he pushed through the crowd and stopped in front of the rodeo ring, where the clown was running around the edge. Over the loudspeaker the announcer's words tumbled out quickly and Kevin couldn't quite understand them. Then the gate burst open and a bull bucked out into the ring, a rider on his back.

'Here we go ladies and gents! One, two . . . Awww, and he's off,' called the announcer as the clown raced in to distract the bull and the rider got up from the dusty ground and ran to the railing, before hightailing it over the top. 'Let's not forget he needs the full ten seconds for the ride to count.'

The rider wasn't one of his boys, but Kevin watched for a bit longer, his hands hanging through the railing. Another rider entered the ring with the same result as the first, and another one. Every time they came off, Kevin winced, wondering why they felt the need to hurt themselves by riding in the first place.

'G'day, Kev.'

Kevin turned and saw Kit Redman standing nearby, a woman at his side.

'Mr Redman,' Kevin said, nodding.

'Oh, come on, it's Kit, please. You're not a boy anymore, mate.' He nodded towards the ring. 'Going to have a go?'

'Not a chance. The broncs aren't my thing. I do enough that could hurt me without trying to.'

'I'm with you,' Kit said. 'Do you know my wife? Tara, this is Kevin. He runs Spinifex Downs.'

'Yeah, I've heard about you, Kev,' Tara said. 'Doing great things.'

Kevin looked down at the ground. 'Thanks,' he mumbled. Glancing up, he saw Kit's hand possessively placed on Tara's waist.

'We'd better get on. Catch you round, Kev. It's good to see you here.'

'Sure.' He watched as Kit moved his hand to the small of Tara's back and guided her towards the bar. They stopped and talked to another three people before they made it inside, Kit's large laugh cutting across the noise and chatter of the night.

A quick glance showed that Boyd was still outside, watching. Kevin wondered if he was waiting for something.

'Check out those Buckle Bunnies, huh, Kev?' Harry said as he and Cyril sidled up next to him. 'Wouldn't mind . . .'

'Shut up, would ya?' Cyril nudged Harry. 'They'll hear.'

Harry laughed, his slight shoulders shaking. He was almost dancing on his toes as he watched the girls walk by, while Cyril had his head down and was kicking the dirt.

Kevin had never seen either of the boys like this before—they were usually more interested in horses, cattle and prices.

He glanced over at the three girls, who were laughing, engrossed in their conversation with each other. They were slim and young, wearing loud coloured shirts and belts with a large buckle at the button of their jeans. Their hats were clean and, from underneath, long black hair hung down to their waists. They could've been triplets. Maybe they were. They didn't look like they were going to have a go at riding in the rodeo.

'I reckon you fellas should stick to the broncs,' Kevin said with a grin. 'Had a go yet?'

'Nah, not yet. Put our names down, though, didn't we, Harry?' Cyril gave Harry's arm a soft punch. 'We're going to.'

'Yeah. Not gonna chicken out, but I still wouldn't mind having a crack at one of them girls.'

'On a beating to nowhere, Harry . . .'

'Well, look who we've got here.' A voice cut over Kevin's advice. 'The district cattle rustlers.'

Kevin stiffened and turned to see Dylan Jeffries from Cassia Plains and Ethan Schultz from Paperbark Valley standing nearby. Their smiles were mean and their hands were linked into the loops of their jeans as though this was a casual chat. Kevin took a quick look around to see who might have heard their words. Boyd was still standing next to the beer tent, but this time he was turned away, talking. He couldn't see the Senior Sergeant nearby, or anyone else who could help if things got out of hand.

'What the fuck do you mean by that?' Harry bristled instantly and took a step towards them. 'It's not us doing anything.'

'Just what we said, man. Cattle rustlers. Big time. Don't worry, we know it's you lot over on Spinifex Downs and we'll watch until we catch you. Don't think you're going to get away with it.'

'Dylan, don't make accusations you can't prove. You'll just get everyone wound up when there's no need.' Kevin took a step in between his men and the two troublemakers, holding his hands up in a gesture of peace.

A group of young kids walked by, watching curiously, until one of them bumped into Harry, who whirled around with his fists up.

'Harry!' Kevin snapped.

'Mate, how about you fucking back off to where you came from,' Ethan said in a low, menacing tone.

Cyril, whose head had snapped up at the first sign of accusations, gave a little smirk. 'I think we already are.'

A small crowd started to gather, and Kevin glanced around nervously. His dad had been right. These two were going to point the finger. Tell the lies they always had.

'You pricks better watch what you're saying about us,' Harry said back. 'You don't know anything about anything.'

'Enough,' Kevin said warningly. He put his hand on the angry young man's arm to calm him.

'Why should we stand here and take that?' Harry turned to Kevin, his voice loud and sounding like he was itching for a fight.

'Hey, hey, hey, what's going on here?' Kit pushed his way through the group. 'What seems to be the matter, fellas?'

'Just having a chat to the cattle rustlers.' Ethan spat on the ground near Harry's feet.

Harry pushed himself forwards, his fists clenched. Kevin reacted, but Kit got there first.

'Hang on, mate,' he said holding on to Harry. 'Just steady up.' He turned to Ethan. 'I really don't think that was called for. And you should all know that it was me who went to the police and it looks like Spinifex Downs has lost cattle too. So how about you hoodlums get all of the facts before you start throwing blame around.' He looked at the two men, frustration showing on his face. 'I thought we'd got past all this bullshit. This racial shit. You two are a disgrace.'

'What do you mean, got past it?' Dylan took a step forwards, but Kit held up his free hand and put it on his chest.

'Stay where you are,' he said, steel in his tone. 'That's enough.'

Dylan spluttered before saying, 'The government keeps throwing money at these two-bit operations. None of these blokes know how to work the land as well as we do. And to add insult to injury we have to pay our own way! The government just keeps on propping these pricks up. The major issue is that one group of people are given money over another group and they still steal cattle!' Dylan had drawn himself up to full height. The redness in his face wasn't from the sun and he was glaring at Kevin as he spoke.

'Dylan, go home. You're not making any sense. Clearly, you've forgotten we're on their land and the more successful the Spinifex Downs crew are, the better off everyone is. We cannot,' Kit paused for effect, '*cannot* let the past crowd the present.'

'Need a hand here, Kit?' Senior Sergeant Glenn King had managed to push through the ring of bystanders and now stood a few metres away from Dylan and Ethan, his hand on his gun belt.

'I reckon we've got it sorted, haven't we, lads?' Kit asked. 'Everyone's going to go their separate ways and forget this ever happened, aren't you?' He eyeballed each man.

Ethan opened his mouth, but Kit stared at him. 'Aren't you?' The words were loud.

'Come on, Dylan. Stupid fucks don't know when they're getting taken advantage of.'

The two angry men walked away, casting furious glances over their shoulders as they went.

Kevin watched them go, knowing that he could have trouble with them later. Their beliefs were too deep-seated to just dissipate overnight. The two men walked to where Boyd was standing. He turned around and looked at Kevin with a sneer of hatred on his face.

'Right-oh, you lot, nothing to see. On your way,' Glenn told the crowd, who started to move away, back towards the bar.

'Mate, I'm sorry you had to hear that,' Kit turned to the three men. 'I didn't think there was anyone who thought like that anymore.'

Kevin glanced at Harry and Cyril. 'Okay?' he asked.

'Fuckwits,' Cyril snapped, while Harry still looked as if he were a bomb about to blow.

'What happened?' Glenn interrupted.

'Nothing, just a misunderstanding of what people actually believe in this area,' Kit said, shaking his head. 'Got a minute, Kev?' He inclined his head away from the others and started to walk away.

Kevin glanced at his men. 'Just stay away from those two tonight, okay?'

'I've got them,' Glenn said. 'You go.'

'Let me buy you a beer,' Kit said, pushing Kevin towards the beer tent.

'Nah, thanks. I won't have one. I think I need to keep an eye on everything here.'

Kit stopped and faced Kevin, ignoring the fact that people had to walk around them. 'I hope you don't believe we all think like they do, Kev. That way of thinking is not the majority.'

Kevin kicked at the ground before answering. 'Thanks for your words, Kit. They mean a lot.'

Kit held out his hand and Kevin shook it.

Chapter 9

Dave had stopped at the traffic lights and he couldn't control his excitement any longer. He fist-pumped the air. 'Awesome,' he said aloud. 'So bloody awesome!'

Thinking back over the conversation he'd had with Senior Sergeant Glenn King from Boogarin, he wondered what he would find when he and Bob got up north. They were going to have to go, there was no two ways about that.

It had taken a couple of days to get hold of Glenn. Much to Dave's frustration, the phone had kept ringing out. When he'd finally picked up, Glenn had explained the local rodeo had been on over the weekend.

'Had a bit of trouble with the locals calling each other cattle thieves,' he said.

'I'm sure that would stir up some animosity between people,' Dave said.

'That's the truth, for sure. Especially when there're certainly two hundred head of cattle gone from Spinifex

Downs,' Glenn had said. 'Trouble is, the bloke who first reported thought they were taken from his place but in fact they've been taken from the neighbouring property and run out through the complainant's station.' He'd paused before saying, 'At this stage, we're really not sure if Deep-Water Station has lost cattle or not; he was getting back to us on that one. Not long since the mustering has been done, of course, so everyone's numbers should be up to date, but this has happened after that so they'll need to go and get their cattle back in through the yards again and have a re-count, which isn't a simple thing to do. The other consideration is that Spinifex Downs is owned by the local Aboriginal people and their place is surrounded by whites.'

'Why is that a consideration?' Dave had asked.

'Because there's still bad blood between some station owners and Spinifex Downs. There're a lot of old blokes still on Spinifex and some of the old station families, they've brainwashed their young blokes. You know, their fathers and grandfathers have instilled long-held beliefs. Only some, mind you, but enough to make trouble. It's a whole different world up here, mate, and you're gonna be learning on your feet. When are you coming? I can't handle this by myself if it gets out of control. The trouble's already started.'

'As soon as we can,' Dave had promised. He'd hung up and walked around the corner to the pub where Bob would be having his daily special and, before he knew it, they'd organised to leave the next day.

The thrill of the chase was coursing through Dave as he pulled into the driveway at home. He couldn't wait to tell Mel what was happening. He jogged to the front door, the excitement fizzing in his stomach.

He put his key in the lock and pushed open the door, calling out, 'Hi, I'm home. And I've got great news! The saleyards this morning were fantastic; bloody cold, but I met a few of the auctioneers. Learned a fair bit from Bob.' He threw his keys on the table in the hallway and kept talking, even though nobody was answering. 'You know how I said I thought he might be a bit of an old ditherer? Well, by hell he knows some stuff. He taught me—'

Mel appeared at the kitchen door, wiping her hands on a tea towel. 'Great news?' she said, interrupting his flow. 'That sounds good, what is it?'

Dave walked over to her and pulled her into a hug. 'I've got my first case. My first proper case on the stock squad and I leave tomorrow. This is what I've—' He stopped as Mel stiffened, then pushed him away.

'What? Sorry, you're leaving to go where tomorrow?' She put her hand protectively over her pregnant belly.

'To Boogarin, about two days' drive north of here. Bob and I are going—'

Mel interrupted his excited talk. 'For how long?'

'Well, it'll take two days up there, two days back and maybe four days of investigation. Just over a week, perhaps. But we won't really know until we get up there and start talking to the locals. Might be a bit longer depending on what we find. This is exactly what I've been wanting to do, Mel.' He put his hands on her shoulders and smiled at her, still feeling the adrenalin coursing through his body.

'Well, there you go,' she said, turning away from him and walking back into the kitchen, her sarcasm plain. 'I get to sit at home all day with your kids, and you waltz in here and tell me how great your day was and you're taking off for a week. Where's the fairness in that?'

Staring at her retreating back, Dave kicked himself for not reading the signs as soon as he got home. He had been on a high and should have handled this news differently. He sighed and ran his hand through his hair. He'd wear it now.

'Sorry, honey,' he said, following her into the kitchen. 'I should have started that all off differently. How was your day?'

'Not that it matters to you, clearly,' Mel said, a wooden spoon in her hand. 'But it was shit. Thanks for asking.' She slammed the spoon down on the bench.

'Where's Bec?'

'With Mum and Dad. She had another meltdown in the shopping centre and I needed a break.'

Dave looked at her. 'What do you mean "another one"?'

'She has tantrums all the time—when you're not around, Dave. If you'd listened to me, you would have heard me tell you. Bec is very hard to deal with.' She rounded on him, eyes wild with anger.

'I've never seen that. Even in all the time I was on leave, I didn't see that.'

'No, because she's good for you. It's only when you're not here or I take her out in public that she gets difficult. And now you're telling me you're going to be away, as *well* as going to Queensland for the court case. This is shit,

Dave. Just shit.' She leaned against the bench and sagged a little. 'This isn't how I imagined our lives would be once we moved back here.'

Dave wanted to go to her, but he knew she'd reject his advances. It would be best if he kept his distance for the time being.

'Come on, Mel,' he said quietly. 'You know I came back from Barrabine to be with you. This isn't all about me. You wanted to be close to your parents and so here we are.'

'You keep telling yourself that, Dave, but I know better.' Mel stood straight up and crossed her arms, staring him in the face. 'You came back here because you got offered the job with the stock squad. If that hadn't happened, I'm almost one hundred per cent sure you would've stayed in that horrible little town, with Spencer and all your mates. It wouldn't have mattered if Bec and I were there or not.'

A jolt of guilt shot through Dave as he wondered if she was right.

No. No, she wasn't. He remembered the conversations they'd had while he was still in hospital after the shooting. They'd both said they wanted to be together. It wouldn't have mattered where that was. Surely home was where the other was: two arms and a heartbeat.

Maybe not, Dave thought.

'That's not true, Mel. Or fair. Don't you remember what we talked about . . .'

'Who are you chasing up north?' she challenged. 'Someone else who is going to shoot you? What if their aim is better this time? You'll forever be the hero, and Bec and the baby will be without their dad and I'll be without a husband.' She sighed and ran her hands through her hair before turning away. 'Can't you see how dangerous this job is? What you love could take you away from people who love you.'

'Mel, honey, this is what I do,' Dave said carefully. 'It's my job.'

'Well, I hate the job!' Her voice rose in frustration. 'I hate the police force. I wish you'd leave it. Do something that was normal and safe, like . . . like,' she threw her hands in the air, 'I don't know—an accountant.'

As inappropriate as it was to laugh, Dave couldn't help but smile at the ridiculousness of Mel's suggestion.

This time he decided it was worth trying to give her a hug. To defuse the situation. He reached out and held out his arms. 'Come here,' he said.

She took a step backwards but he kept coming.

'I know you're frightened, honey, but I'm not going to let anything happen to me again.' He gathered her into his arms and held her tightly until he felt her relax against him. Kissing her head, he whispered, 'It's going to be okay.'

'How can you even know that?' she said in a small voice. 'How can you even know?'

Mel had gone to pick up Bec from her parents' place and Dave was sitting on the porch with a beer, listening to the hum of the traffic. He kept going over and over their fight.

Yes, he knew he could take some of the blame. He should have handled the whole situation differently but, hell, the things Mel had said had shocked him. He could see what she was saying came from a place of fear—well, he hoped that's all it was—but to actually ask him to leave the job? She knew that's all he'd ever wanted to do, known right from the moment they'd met. That first night they'd walked on the beach and talked about their dreams. He'd told her he wanted to be a stockie. Nothing else. And that would mean trips away because, funnily enough, stock didn't get stolen in the city.

Maybe she hadn't realised what his job would entail. Had he told her enough about it? Did he need to take some of the blame here?

He sighed and took another sip of beer, just as the phone started to ring. 'Burrows,' he said, grabbing the phone that was sitting beside him.

'How's it all going? Settled in yet?' Spencer's voice was clear down the line.

'God, I'm glad to hear from you,' Dave said, getting up to grab another beer. 'It's been great. Been to the saleyards, met a heap of people. But I've had some moments—'

'Oh, yeah, what sort of moments?' Spencer interrupted as if he knew.

'Mel. Tonight.'

'Oh.' There was a pause. 'Tell me about the good stuff first.'

'Got my first case! Gotta take a trip north. Been some cattle stolen from a station out of Boogarin. Bob and I leave tomorrow morning.'

'Ah, I see.' Spencer's voice held meaning. He knew without being told where the 'moments' had come from. 'And how did that go down at home?'

'About as you'd expect.' He grabbed another can out of the fridge and cracked it open as he stood in the kitchen. 'Actually, no. It was worse.' He swallowed half the liquid before he could stop himself.

'How so?'

'She asked me to give up the job.'

The humming down the line seemed extra loud to Dave as he walked back onto the porch and sat down, leaning up against the post.

'Well, that's new,' Spencer finally answered. 'Not unexpected, but new.'

'Yeah.'

Spencer groaned and Dave could hear him scratch at his stubble. 'Now, I want you to hear me out, Dave. Just listen before you say anything. It seems to me that you've got some hard decisions to make. I've seen this time and time again, where plenty of coppers have changed their roles to make their wives happy. They've gone to the country. They've gone back to the city. They've changed who they are and who they want to be, because of the wife. Next thing you know, the wife up and leaves anyway. You know why? Because it's not the job they hate. It's the fact their husband isn't who they want him to be.

'And you can fight for this, fight for your marriage, but it doesn't mean you'll win. If she's not prepared to meet you halfway, Dave, well, you can twist and turn and reinvent yourself into all sorts of roles, but you're only going to make yourself miserable.'

Dave picked up a stick and started drawing shapes in the dirt as he listened. Spencer was right, but he didn't want to admit it. Not yet. He did know coppers who'd changed their lives because of their wives and it hadn't made an ounce of difference. Their marriages had failed anyway.

The silence purred between them again, Spencer waiting for Dave now.

'Dave?'

Dave wasn't sure what to say. 'I know,' he said in a low voice. 'I know.'

'Doesn't make it any easier.'

'She's only saying all of this because she's frightened I'll get hurt again.'

'Of course she'd be frightened. You've been shot! That type of incident brings everyone's mortality home. Tell me, has *she* had any counselling?'

Dave let out a bark of laughter. 'No. If you ask her, she's not the one with the problem.'

'You know as well as I do, that's a problem in itself.'

'I don't think today is the day to bring it up with her.'

Spencer gave a mirthless chuckle. 'Perhaps not. So, tell me a bit more about the job.'

Dave stopped doodling in the dirt and gave a brief outline of what he knew. 'We're going up there to talk to everyone and see what we can find out. Sounds like there is a bit of antagonism between the white station owners and the Aboriginal station owners,' he finished.

'Piece of advice about dealing with the Aboriginal community. They are peaceful people. When you go and talk with them, make sure you sit down in the dirt with them. If you stand to talk, especially to the Elders, they'll take that as confrontational. You've got to be on the same level as them.'

'Sounds like this Kevin is a bit of a goer. He's been down here at an ag college—got some type of scholarship, according to Glenn.'

'Then he'll be different to the Elders, but when you're talking with the old men, they'll be sitting around the fire, so you sit too. It'll make all the difference.'

'Right.' He heard the car pull up into the driveway. 'Sounds like everyone's home. Better go.'

There was silence on the other end of the phone line before Spencer's grave voice said, 'Good luck.'

Chapter 10

The road north was long and straight. Bob and Dave had got started at first light—after Dave had said goodbye to Melinda, who had turned her back on him again, and Bec, who'd been sleeping, her eyes shut tightly, little hands curled up into fists.

His heart had hurt when he'd closed the door and walked down the path, but it hadn't lasted long. The thrill of what lay ahead took over.

By the time Bob and Dave had hit the highway, the sun was high and they'd passed through small towns and wide-open paddocks of green crops. Dave knew there had been good rainfall in the wheat belt and, being early September, the crops were still tall and green, and swayed in the wind, giving everyone who drove through the area a feeling that the land was a living, breathing body.

They'd had to navigate their way around the caravan procession—the wildflower season was beginning, and the grey nomads were heading north to take in their fill of pinks, blues and yellows that stretched across the land. The lethargic movement of the big four-wheel drives pulling the rocking caravans gave Dave a headache as he tried to pass not one but three in a row. The caravaners weren't in any hurry.

Just before dark, they pulled off the main road and down a small two-wheeled track and found a spot to set up camp. The red soil was sticking to Dave's boots as he grabbed the tarps from the back of the vehicle and spread them on the ground to minimise the amount of dirt that would get tracked into their bedrolls. He got the swags down from the roof rack and threw them onto the tarps.

The small clearing, on the edge of a narrow, dry creek bed, was the perfect spot for the night. There were dead trees to provide firewood and the ground was flat—a good thing when sleeping in a swag. He'd slept in places where he'd felt like he was going to slide down a hill!

'Nothing better,' Bob sighed as he took a can, the fifth for the day, Dave realised, out of the Engel fridge in the back of the four-wheel drive. He walked to the front of the vehicle, leaned against the bullbar and stood watching the sun slip below the horizon, while Dave started gathering up sticks to light a fire. His grandfather had always taught him that you did the jobs of the camp first, before sitting down and enjoying the night. Easier to collect wood and set up in daylight than in the dark. Bob hadn't got that memo. Or he was just letting Dave the newbie do it all.

He cracked a few smaller twigs off branches of dead trees and gathered some dried grasses from the clumps of golden feed, then placed them on the ground in front of Bob and put a match to them, watching the orange flames flicker up and catch hold. Walking off, he went a little further afield and grabbed some larger logs and dragged them back to fire. Three trips like that and he thought he had enough to last through the night.

'Just going for a look,' he called to Bob, who was happily sitting in front of the fire, sipping on his beer.

'Don't get lost,' Bob yelled back.

Dave ignored the comment and followed what looked like a kangaroo track. The narrow path wound through some shrubby trees and tufts of thick golden grasses. Stones littered the ground and large red boulders were strewn across some of the heavily wooded areas. A carpet of vivid wildflowers stretched out as far as he could see, covering the ground in red, with the hum of bees darting from one flower to the next. Dave didn't know what sort the flowers were, but their vivid green leaves and tall, bright red flower stems nodded at him in the gentle wind.

Brushing his hand over them, he wondered what Melinda was doing. Probably finishing up dinner and putting Bec to bed. He hoped Bec'd get a bedtime story tonight. One about a brave policeman who was out helping little old ladies across the street and fighting bad people to make Australia safe.

Somehow he doubted that. More likely to be one about a unicorn or a horse. Mel favoured those, whereas he made up stories about policemen and acted them out, causing Bec to fall about in fits of laughter. Never that good when he was trying to get her to sleep, according to Mel, but Bec loved them.

'Dave!' Bob's voice cut through the silence and pulled him back to the present.

'Coming.' As he turned around to head back to camp, he saw movement to the side of him. Letting his eyes adjust, he realised there was an emu camped under a tree. It was almost the same colour as the trunk. The large bird saw Dave too and was up in a flash, running away. Dave watched it go, then turned and headed back.

'Emu out there,' he said as he got a beer out from the back of the troopy and went to sit down. He realised the fire needed more wood, so he stopped and threw another log on.

'There'll be heaps of them. And goannas. Maybe a dog or two. Always see something different when you get up here.' Bob had got the two chairs out from the back of the vehicle and set them around the fire, and was relaxing in front of the dancing flames with another can.

'This is the life. Sit down, Dave!' he said, waving his can towards the chair. 'You're making the place look untidy fussing around like that.'

Dave was stoking the fire. Sparks shot up high in the air with a crackle.

'Need to build up some coals so we can cook tea. Then we're all organised.'

'Plenty of time for all of that. Enjoy the sunset, Dave. Enjoy the fact we're outside and haven't got any pressures for the moment.'

Dave wanted to harrumph at that. He had plenty of pressures. How would Mel feel tonight, not having a phone call from him? He guessed he could find out quickly enough—they had a satellite phone in the troopy—but he didn't want to ask to use it and there wasn't any mobile range here.

'Why didn't you have a beer today at lunch?' Bob asked. 'Reckon you might have to loosen up a bit if you're going to be a stockie. That's how you make friends up here.'

Cracking open his first can, Dave looked at him incredulously. 'I'm not going to have one while I'm driving. Especially driving a cop car. I don't want to lose the job I've always wanted!'

Bob shrugged. 'No traffic coppers out here. We're a million miles from anywhere.' He looked around. 'That's one of the reasons I love being back out here. There're very few rules.'

Not answering, Dave poked the fire with his foot and watched as sparks flew again into the ever-dimming night sky. He could see the evening star now and the shades of pinks and purples were becoming deeper as they faded towards black. Bob was right, he thought as he stretched out in his chair, this was the life.

They were silent, listening to the call of the bush and staring into the fire. Dave wondered if Bob had a family and he asked as much.

103

'Got a couple of kids. In their late twenties. Don't see 'em much.'

'What about your wife? She doesn't mind you being away a lot?'

'Haven't got anyone waiting for me at home. Best way to be in this job, always on the road, or at least a lot of the time. Doesn't make for great relationships when you're sleeping in a swag more than in the marital bed.'

Dave found himself nodding. He had thought the same thing more than once since Mel's outburst yesterday. They hadn't really had time to sort through what she'd said and then he'd had to leave.

'The bush TV could keep us entertained for hours when we were young blokes,' Bob said as he watched the flames jumping around.

'Yeah, one of the best things about camping,' Dave agreed. 'Tell me when you're ready for me to cook a feed. Reckon we'll have steak tonight. I'll get the barbecue out in a minute.'

'I'm probably right for a bit.' He turned to Dave. 'Did you hear me when I said you might need to lighten up a bit if you're going to be a stockie?'

Dave opened his mouth to disagree, but Bob talked on. 'Look at this country here. It's not all about work. It's about the beauty of being free. And a few beers aren't going to end the world for you, you know.'

'But it *is* about work! What happens if we've got to go out and track some cattle at night or something and you're half cut? Don't reckon I'd keep my job if the commissioner found that out.'

Bob scratched at his cheeks and sighed. 'I pity you young blokes. In my day we'd have someone locked up before noon and be on the gas by lunchtime. Often we'd never get home until two in the morning and then we'd front up the next day and do it all again.'

'It's different now.' Dave felt like he was stating the obvious. 'It's not yesterday anymore, it's today and things have changed. A lot.' He put down his beer can and stood up to get the shovel, so he could drag some coals out of the fire and start to cook something to eat.

'Ha!' Bob gave a laugh and got up again for another beer. 'Yesterday was great! Today is boring and tomorrow is gonna be crap. All this occupational health and safety and political correctness is bullshit. Can't take a shit without having to follow the guidelines.' Bob walked unsteadily out into the darkness and Dave heard him unzipping his jeans and then the splash of urine on earth.

Dave dropped his head into his hands. *Please don't ever let me end up a soak like him*, he thought. Aloud he said, 'How about I get some tea happening?' Without waiting for an answer, he found the barbecue plate and put it alongside the fire. Digging the shovel into the glow of red, he dragged out coals and settled them near the fire. He placed the plate over the flames and gave it a bit of a scrub with some newspaper he'd packed for that exact purpose.

'I'll be right for tea, thanks,' Bob said as he came back into the firelight. He held up the can he was holding. 'Just going to sit here and have a few quiet beers and enjoy the night.'

'You'd be better off having something to eat,' Dave answered as he seasoned the plate with butter. 'How about I cook it and you eat when you're ready?'

'Son, I'm telling you. I'm right. I don't need tea.'

'Suit yourself.' Dave sat back down in the chair; he'd ask again when there were more coals.

'Let me tell you about this one case I was on,' Bob said, plopping down in the chair and stretching his feet towards the fire. 'I was working over east in the stock squad and there were reports coming through of a company selling fodder to farmers. The last two years had been pretty dry and the hay surplus was just about exhausted. But this company supposedly had supplies on some of their farms, which they were selling. They'd invoice the farmers for a road train worth of hay and then it would never arrive.'

Dave took a sip from his can and listened.

Bob went on. 'Took a while to track him down, because he was moving all over the country. Accessing his emails remotely and so on. The location of the farm was fictional, as was the hay.'

'Pretty rough, taking advantage of farmers who are already having a hard time of it.'

'Son, I could tell you stories that would make your hair curl.' Bob stared into the fire and Dave could tell he was thinking about a case that must have consumed him.

'What made you get into being a stockie?' Dave asked suddenly.

Bob was quiet for a while, lost in his thoughts, but when he answered he looked straight at Dave. 'I wanted to be a copper so I could help people,' he said. 'I didn't ever think I'd end up in the stock squad. I don't come from a farming background or even have any links back to the land. One day my boss just said I was shifting over. They needed a good detective on a case that was causing the stockies some grief and I was the fella to help.' He scratched his chin and let out a sigh. 'I found I really loved the work—took me a while to learn the animal side of things, but I had a good mentor. Old Monty Ferguson. He was a legend in his own teacup. Pushing up daisies now, but . . .' His voice faded to silence.

Dave glanced over and saw sadness in his face. He let a few minutes pass before he formed his next question. 'What did you like about it?'

'The cockies and the lifestyle. Camping out, all that sort of stuff. The lack of rules.'

Dave hid a grin as he interpreted that as: 'I like the drinking.' At least he was consistent. He glanced at his watch: 8 p.m. already. Bec should be fast asleep by now.

'There're always rules.'

'There sure are, but like I said before, less out here.'

Dave threw a steak onto the barbecue plate and was just about to add the second one when Bob said, 'Not for me, son.' He gave a half-grin. 'Yeah, I knew what you were about to do.'

Smiling, Dave turned back to his steak and watched it cook.

'Stars are incredible out here, aren't they?' Bob said, looking up at the night sky.

'Clearest I've seen them for a long time.'

Bob didn't answer; he kept looking at the stars and drinking his beer. He didn't appear to be bothered by the silence between them.

Dave wolfed his steak down when it was cooked, realising he was really hungry. At home they would've eaten by 7 p.m.

'Well, it's been a big day,' he said. 'I reckon I'm going to hit the hay. Another long drive tomorrow. What about you?' He got up and rinsed his plate from the water tank in the back of vehicle and started to unroll his swag on the other side of the fire.

'Nah, son. I'm happy here for a while.'

Dave took his boots off and climbed in, fully dressed. From the side of the swag, he grabbed his boots and put them alongside him and pulled the canvas over his head, before zipping it up from the inside.

From here he could still see the stars and flickering flames. Silence covered the land, except for a fox bark and the crackling of the fire.

He heard Bob get up and throw another log on, then go around to the back of the car. Next minute Dave heard the creak of the camping chair as he sat down again, so Dave rolled over and peered through the netting to see what Bob was doing.

What he saw was an old man with a haggard face, the firelight flitting across his features. He was sipping from the neck of a whiskey bottle, lost in memories Dave could only guess at.

Chapter 11

Dave still couldn't believe the conversation he was having with Bob. They'd been about twenty minutes away from Boogarin when Dave'd said, 'You were up early this morning. Thought you'd take a bit to get going.' He was feeling under the weather himself. The recurring nightmare of Bulldust chasing him had woken Dave at 2.30 a.m. From there he'd tossed and turned as Melinda and Bec had crowded his thoughts, and his shoulder had ached enough for him to get up and find some painkillers.

'Why'd you think that? Only need a dingo's breakfast.'

Dave glanced at him out of the corner of his eye. The white lines slipped by and they'd edged another couple of kilometres closer to Boogarin by the time Dave asked, 'What's a dingo's breakfast?'

'A scratch, a piss and a good look around. You young blokes sleep too much. There's shit to be done, you know.'

The sun had barely cast a glow from below the horizon when Dave had heard Bob up and stoking the fire. When he'd cleared his blurry eyes, he'd seen that Bob was dressed and putting the billy on the fire. How he'd done that after drinking as much as he had last night, Dave didn't know.

Piss fit was the only explanation. Bob was very, very piss fit.

'I thought you might be a bit . . . under the weather,' he said.

Bob looked across the car at him. 'Son, that's just a normal day in the bush. There's nothing wrong with having a beer—gets good conversations happening. Everyone relaxes when they're having a drink. A lot of information comes when you're sitting around the campfire with a beer in your hand.'

Dave wanted to say, 'Yeah, but there wasn't anyone there to get information from,' but he kept his mouth shut.

'When you go to a country pub or to the saleyards or some place of the like, you've got to talk to people, but you have to listen too. You listen more than you talk. God gave you two ears and all that shit.

'But it's important in the line of work we do. I'll say it again: a few beers loosens tongues.' He held up a finger and wagged it at Dave. 'Take what we're about to do here. Often in conversations it's the same as those sheep I showed you in the yards the other day. It's not what you hear, but what you *don't* hear.'

Turning the steering wheel slightly to take a sharp corner, Dave wondered how, from his comments about being hungover this morning, Bob had turned the conversation to something completely different.

'For example, if cattle stealing is such a big problem up here, how come we haven't heard about it?' Bob said.

'We have,' Dave said, glancing down to check the temperature gauge and fuel. 'We had the phone call. That's why we're here.'

'Ah, but it's the first time. Normally, before we get a call there will be whispers. A conversation in a pub, in the yards. I haven't heard anything of the like, son.' He leaned back in his seat and stretched as far as the car would allow. 'Think about this, Dave. If you meet a good chick in the pub one night, you know, one you might think is a keeper, you're not going to try and get her knickers off that same night, are you? You might have to take her out a couple of times before you try to get her into bed. Same with the people we're talking to—you might have to chew the fat for two hours before they open up and tell you anything. That's why the beer is a good thing.'

Finally, Dave saw what Bob was saying. A few beers and people were more likely to tell you something important. Well, he knew that, he'd just never thought about using it in policing. It also didn't explain why Bob had drunk so much when there wasn't anyone he needed to get to open up. The words 'functioning alcoholic' came to mind and he glanced at Bob again. Yeah, the telltale signs of facial bloat and broken capillaries were there. Dave hadn't noticed them before.

The town sign came into view and Dave switched his thoughts to the copper they were about to meet. 'Do you know this Senior Sergeant Glenn King?' he asked.

Bob nodded. 'Met him once or twice when I was here a few years ago. He's been here a while so he'll know the ins and outs of everything. You know, the spiderweb effect.'

'Spiderweb?'

'Who's connected to who. Pretty hard when we go into an area and we don't know how people are linked. We might be interviewing the woman that the landowner used to date and the relationship didn't end well and we wouldn't know.' He turned in his seat and looked across at Dave. 'Now listen to me, son. And listen carefully. For that very reason, you have to play everything close to your chest. Don't give too much away to these country sergeants, because you don't know the relationships between him and everyone else around. Everything you say will probably get repeated back over the bar or around a campfire.' He gave a bit of a chuckle. 'That's handy when you want to plant a piece of information and use it to our benefit, but not at other times. That copper you nabbed in Queensland was a prime example.'

Dave felt a trickle of apprehension run through him. For an old pisshead, Bob was dead on the money. He'd had no idea that Joe had been dirty, and if Dave hadn't been undercover, he may well have asked him for help at some stage. And that would have set him up for a horrible fall.

'Turn right here,' Bob said, indicating a side street. 'The cop shop is on the left at the end.'

Dave flicked on the indicator and drove down the street until he saw the blue and white sign, with POLICE highlighted by fluoro lights behind the writing. Pulling up, Dave put on the park brake.

The station looked like the town of Boogarin: clean and well cared for. In this town the streets were tidy and the road verges were mowed. The houses were old fibro structures, and although everything was neat, the paint had faded from the sun and there was a coating of fine red dust over the buildings as well as on the leaves of the trees.

Three caravans were lined up next to the tourist bureau, one had the door open and a couple were sitting outside with cups in their hands. Other than that, the street was empty.

The door of the station opened and an older man, about Bob's age, dressed in uniform, started down the steps, a welcoming smile on his face.

'Bob, good to see you, you old bugger.'

To Dave, the greeting sounded like he'd met Bob more than a couple of times. Or maybe that was the way of the north.

'Good to see you, Glenn.' Bob held out his hand and they shook. 'Meet Dave. New bloke. He's the one you've been talking to.'

'Glad to have you here, Dave,' Glenn said. 'Come in, come in.'

The station was a converted house, the same as the rest of the buildings on this street. It had been gutted and turned into a station with a front desk and a large open-plan office. Glenn ushered them in and shut the door. 'Only one of me here, so if the phone rings I'll have to go.' He sat heavily in the chair behind the desk and a loud puff of air left the cushion. 'It'll be all around the place that you fellas are in town. Anyway, it's good to have the professionals here.' He indicated for them to sit.

'What can you tell us?' Bob asked and Dave took out his notebook, ready to jot the important information down so they could refer back to it later.

Glenn went through what they already knew: cattle gone from Spinifex Downs, through Deep-Water Station.

'Kit came and saw me a week or so ago. He was the one who reported the cattle movement through his place. He hasn't been able to pinpoint any stock that has gone missing, but Kevin from Spinifex can—he's missing a couple of hundred head.' He leaned back in his chair and Dave could see he was gathering his thoughts.

'Now, Kit has also reported that he's found carcasses on the side of the road. They've been butchered and he said it looked like a professional job.' He paused. 'History has showed that it's usually Aboriginal people getting a feed when it's dry and the roos are too stringy to eat and they can't find any goannas. Because of that, until recently, when Kit Redman became shire president, there'd always been a bit of bad blood between the white-owned stations and the Aboriginal people up here. So in times gone by relations between them both have been pretty tense. But it's better than it has ever been, so to think that someone has started butchering cattle in the way the Aboriginal mob would is very odd. As is the duffing of cattle—we had that stamped out.

'The other part of it is that some of the station owners around here are annoyed that the government props up the Aboriginal stations.' He held his hands up in a 'what can you do' type gesture. 'Of course, there's nothing we can fix there, but if there are still blokes around who hold a grudge about that, we've got an issue that could flare out of control. To be honest, I didn't think it was such a big thing anymore, but at the rodeo on the weekend there were a couple of blokes who got a bit hot under the collar. Had a crack at some of the young jackaroos from Spinifex Downs.'

'What happened there?' Bob asked.

'Just a few hot words. Nothing physical. But certainly there were accusations of cattle stealing and then the government payments got brought into it. The thinking there is tax-payers' money is being used in a bad way.' He spread out a map on the desk and tapped at a spot. 'Here's Spinifex Downs.'

Both men leaned in and Dave found Boogarin on the map before tracing the road to the station they would need to visit. It looked a good three hours' drive from town.

'Across here is Deep-Water.' Glenn tapped another spot. 'And the boundaries run around here.' He traced a couple of lines with his fingers. 'Paperbark Valley and Cassia Plains are on either side. I went there to chat to the owners; Dylan Jeffries owns Cassia and Ethan Schultz, Paperbark. They're the two fellas that had the run in with the crew from Spinifex.

'Good to know about that,' Bob said. 'Can we take this map?'

'Sure.' Glenn started to fold it up. 'Look, young Kev, he's trying to fix all the issues we've talked about today, and more. He's a good lad, got the smarts. Went to agricultural college down south and hasn't got the same prejudices the old men have got.'

'But he didn't report his cattle missing?'

'No, and I understand why. The Elders have a mistrust of coppers. Again, bad history between old coppers and the Aboriginal people.' He leaned back in his chair and linked his fingers behind his head. 'Nope, the guy who made the report is Kit Redman. Used to be our shire president, like I said. In the chair for fifteen years, so he was. And he's very supportive of what Kevin is trying to do out on Spinifex Downs, as he is with all of the Aboriginal people.'

'Did you go and have a look at the tracks? Get any pics?'

Glenn nodded. 'But by the time I got there, the tracks were aged. Wind and time had made them unusable.' He opened a manila folder and took out three photos. Dave leaned forwards and picked one up, studying it closely.

The Senior Sergeant was right. The tracks weren't clear and precise; the wind had blown the tops off and they were really just worked-up dirt that could have been cattle or camel tracks.

'However, it was obvious that someone had used the yards at Deep-Water—Kit said there hadn't been cattle in those yards for well over twelve months. There was oil on the gates to make them open and slide better, and the grass was flattened.'

Bob ran his fingers over his cheek, scratching as he arrived at his chin, and nodded. 'Well, best we get out there and have a yarn.'

'What? To Kit Redman's?' Dave asked in surprise. 'Why not to Spinifex Downs? They're the ones who had the cattle taken.'

'Yep, that's right. But I want to talk to the neighbours first. Get a feel for the land.' He stood up. 'Thanks for your time, Glenn. We'll get on.'

Chapter 12

There were four utes at the yards as Bob and Dave drove into Deep-Water Station. A mob of cows and calves—all varying sizes and ages—were milling around, creating a cloud of dust that hovered above the yards. The air was still and the cloud hung there, covering everyone in the yards. The stockmen were wearing handkerchiefs over their faces, the women only distinguishable from the men by their body shape and the long hair that tumbled from underneath the large-brimmed hats.

The calves had been drafted into a different pen and were standing at the fence bellowing loudly, looking through at their mothers who were eating hay, unconcerned about their babies, until their stomachs were full.

The cattle were a mixture of white, red and black, and Dave could tell they weren't a single breed, but a mash-up of many. *Liquorice Allsorts*, his grandfather would have said.

'What are they up to?' Dave wondered aloud as he rubbed his shoulder. The driving and constantly having his arms outstretched on the steering wheel was aggravating the ache.

'Looks like they're tagging 'em. See, they've got their heads in the crush and the tagging pliers on the drum there.'

'Yeah, but why? They've been marked. No nuts anywhere.'

'Maybe they didn't have the tags when they marked them. Who knows? That's a question for you to ask, son.'

Dave frowned. He was beginning to hate the word 'son' and what it implied.

They pulled up next to the yards and watched the two men and two women working like clockwork. One of the men was in the round yard, herding the calves into the race, one at a time, while the two women pushed them up and trapped their head in the crush and then the other bloke quickly and deftly used the tagging pliers and put a large tag with a number in the calf's ear. All of them wore large hats and brightly coloured shirts, their jeans dusty. The man at the front looked up as they stopped and gave a smile and wave.

'Friendly type,' Bob muttered as he reached for his hat and got out of the car.

Dave slammed the door behind him and glanced around. The others were looking at them curiously, but the man who seemed to be in charge was heading towards them, one hand outstretched, the other pulling off the hankie that was covering his face.

'G'day, I'm Kit Redman,' he said. 'Sorry, probably look like I've been playing in the dust bowl.' He gestured to the outline of dirt around his sunglasses.

Bob introduced them both and asked if he could have a word.

'I'm all yours,' he answered. 'Gemma, you take over.' Kit spoke above the noise of the bellowing cattle and indicated the men should follow him inside the donga, which was off to the side of the yards.

Kit pulled opened the door and took off his hat as he went inside, giving a loud sigh. 'Glad for the break, to be honest with you. I've been on the go since 4 a.m. Had to do a bore run over to the other side of the place before we started this job.' He sat down on a plastic chair. 'Sit down, sit down. I'd offer you a cup of tea but I haven't got any here. All the gear to make it'—he indicated the kettle and cups sitting on the bench—'but I left the teabags at home, along with my lunch!'

'We're fine, thanks,' Bob said, sitting opposite Kit. Dave got out his notebook and balanced it on his knee, waiting to see what Bob would ask first. He glanced around the room. The fridge at one end was old and the door had a few dents in it. The carton of beer sitting next to it was empty, so he assumed all the cans were already getting cold. On the far wall there was a whiteboard with instructions and numbers of cattle written in black texta.

His eyes fell on some different handwriting right in the bottom corner.

1JMF-014. Dave frowned. That looked like a number-plate and for some reason it was familiar. He jotted it down, holding his notebook so no one could see what he'd written.

'Busy time of the year?' Bob asked, leaning back in the chair. 'Cattle look in good nick.'

'Yeah, we're waiting for the Wet to start, but the country is hanging in there. Looks drier than it is, I reckon. I've been saving the northern part of the station to shift these calves and cows onto, so there's fresh feed out there. Well, not fresh as in green, but fresh as in it hasn't had any stock on it for a few months.'

'How are the prices holding up?'

'Not bad, considering. I should be selling the weaners I've got over on the next paddock, but I just want to see if the exporters might have a bit more coin in a few weeks. You know, right towards the end of the season when cattle are getting short.'

'Bit like Russian roulette, isn't it?'

'We're gamblers, that's for sure,' Kit agreed. He spread his hands out and smiled. 'Anyway, what can I do for you fellas? I guess you're here about the cattle. Not every day the stockies are in town. Got to say, we're glad to have you. Bad business all of this, that's for sure.' He frowned as he spoke.

'Yeah, look, we're just here to have a chat about the things you've seen and experienced. Fact gathering,' Bob said.

'Well, we appreciate you coming all the way up here to do that. It's been a long time since we've had any trouble around here. Taking cleanskins and mustering wide isn't the done thing anymore. We trust our neighbours these days. After all, we've got to live in the same community, so it's just better if we have faith no one is going to rip anyone off.' Kit crossed his ankle over his knee as he talked, and Dave watched his body language. He was being very open.

'Noble thoughts,' Bob said, 'but does it really happen like that?'

Kit nodded. 'It absolutely has been. That's why these slaughtered beasts are so strange, as are the cattle tracks on my place.'

'Yeah, tell me about the slaughtered cattle,' Bob invited.

'I've found five now. More since I reported the first one to Glenn. Just off the track. Looks like it's a professional butchering job. Of course, the blokes from Spinifex Downs were known for doing this, years back, but Kev's got all that sorted now. I'm sure it wasn't them. But whoever it is must have some type of local knowledge. Especially to be able to get in and out of my place without being seen. I've got people here all the time, employees and contractors. Especially this time of year.'

Dave made a note that Kit had called the Senior Sergeant by his first name. Perhaps they were mates?

'Did you take any photos of these butchered animals?'

'Nah, didn't have my camera with me. I just told Glenn about them.'

'Were there any tyre tracks near these beasts?'

Cocking his head to one side, Kit tapped his knee. 'I don't rightly remember,' he said slowly. 'The dirt was all scuffed and I remember seeing boot marks around the carcass.'

'And how had it been killed?'

'Shot.'

Dave saw Bob make a note on his pad and wondered what Kit had just said that was noteworthy.

'How many people do you employ?'

'Eight plus the contract musterers.'

'And they're all on the place now?'

'Contractors have gone. We finished mustering about a month ago.'

'Who's your contractor?' Dave asked.

'Simon Grundy. I'll give you his details if you like.'

'That'd be great,' Dave said, thinking how helpful Kit was being.

'So, you get along with your neighbours well, then?' Bob asked.

Kit nodded. 'Best way to have good neighbours is to have good boundary fences. I've got them and I get along with everyone on the adjoining properties. Dylan Jeffries's place borders one side and Kev and his community the other.'

'No bad blood between any of you? Not even from a long time ago?'

Kit leaned forwards and looked Bob directly in the eyes. 'Like I said, the boys from Spinifex Downs were known for poddy-dodging many, many years ago. They also didn't hesitate to take a few killers.' He paused. 'I reckon that was about ten or so years back. Might've been longer. Kev, since he's come home from down south, he's done a great job of getting that place back in line. Got a beautiful mob of cattle—all the same breed and conformation.' He gave a bit of a laugh and inclined his head towards his cattle yards. 'Unlike mine. I've got different lots of different sorts and colours. Nothing uniform like Kev has over on his place. My old man always believed that having different breeds mean you had access to more markets. I'm not sure if that's right these days, or if it ever was, but it worked for him so I haven't changed anything since he died.'

'How long has Kev been back up here?'

'Geez, I'm not sure,' Kit rubbed his chin. 'Got to be at least a couple of years.'

'The relations have only been better since he came back?'

'They were getting better before. I used to be on the shire council. President actually.' He gave a self-deprecating grin. 'Part of what I wanted to achieve while I was there was good relations between pastoralists, both us whites and Aboriginal, the mining companies and the towns-folk. I guess you could say that I started the understanding process and Kev's helped it along.' Kit shrugged, as if this was just part of what he did, but Dave could see he was pleased with himself.

Bob asked a few more questions and then stood up. 'Thanks for your time, Kit. We appreciate it.' He held out his card, and Dave dug in his pocket for his and passed that over too. 'If you think of anything else we should know about, give us a call.'

'Like I said earlier, we pastoralists are grateful you're here. I'd like to get this under control as soon as possible. I don't want all my good work undone.' He stood up and Bob and Dave followed.

'We'll certainly do our best.'

Outside, the station hands had made quick work of tagging the rest of the cattle; there were only a few stragglers left in the back pen. Dave walked over to the yards and leaned against them, looking in.

Bob came and stood next to him.

'Did you see the numberplate written on the whiteboard?' Dave asked him quietly as they watched a girl hunt two calves up the race.

'Yeah.'

'That's our numberplate. Didn't realise until just now.'

Without looking at their car, Bob said, 'I know.'

'But how could . . .' Dave stopped and frowned. 'How could they have known what our plate number was before we even got here? We spent all of an hour, tops, in town and we were only at the police station, and the servo when we refuelled. Our vehicle is unmarked.'

Bob turned to him. 'Bush telegraph,' he answered simply. 'That's why you've got to play your cards close to your chest. Someone put two and two together. Especially if word is out about the missing cattle, which it seems to be. We're not towing a caravan, so we don't look like tourists. There're a few big aerials on the troopy. And Glenn said most people knew we were coming. Someone, somewhere, spoke out of school.' He raised his eyebrows. 'Don't have to be a detective to work it out.'

'Suppose it could've been the copper,' Dave said. 'Kit called him by his first name. They could be mates.'

Clapping him on the shoulder, Bob gave a grin, before starting to walk back to the car. 'Now you're cottoning on. Although I'd like to say, just because you found a dirty copper in Queensland doesn't mean we're all that way, son!'

Dave laughed and followed him, giving a final wave to the crew in the yards.

❧

'Tell me what you thought about Kit,' Bob said as they drove over the grid leading to the main road.

'I thought everything he said sounded reasonable. He's obviously done a lot of work to make sure everyone gets along. I'd reckon he'd be fairly well liked and respected by everyone around here, would you?'

Bob was silent and Dave glanced over at him.

'You don't agree?'

'Not really.'

'It was good to see he thinks the Aboriginal station is doing well.'

'If that's really what he thinks.'

Dave thought back over the discussion, trying to pressure test everything he'd heard Kit say. What was Bob seeing that he wasn't? He couldn't find anything. 'What am I missing?' he finally asked.

'Don't judge a book by its cover, son,' Bob said quietly.

Dave wanted to roll his eyes. Sometimes he thought Bob was a walking cliché.

'He's too nice,' Bob continued.

Dave let out a disbelieving laugh. 'Come on! He's the one who first went to the cops. He's not going to do that if he was the one who took the cattle.'

'I'll keep my thoughts to myself for the moment. But I want you to look at the facts, not personalities.'

'The fact is, he went to the cops first.'

'What better way for a criminal to hide other than in broad daylight? If a crim thinks someone will point the finger at him, diverting suspicion by being the one who goes to the police first is genius, wouldn't you say?' He nodded as if he was putting a full stop on the end of a sentence.

'Suspicious sort, aren't you?' Dave said.

'Guess that's what I'm paid for.'

Chapter 13

Driving onto Cassia Plains was like taking a step back in time, Dave thought as he looked at the decrepit buildings and old machinery lying around.

The homestead was small but had a beautiful green garden around it—the only thing looking as if someone cared. The sheds were made of old corrugated iron that looked like it had been rescued from the tip—some were different sizes and all had some kind of stain or rust on them, which made the sheds look older than they probably were. An old wooden horse-drawn wagon was alongside the shed and further on were the yards, which again looked as though they had been made from recycled tin.

A man stood blocking the front gate, his arms crossed and hat pulled down low over his eyes.

'Real welcoming committee here,' Bob said as he watched the man's unfriendly stance.

'Wonder how he knew we were coming.'

'I reckon the phones are ringing pretty hot. Everyone will be talking to everyone. All the stockmen in Kit's yards would know who we are by now.' He got out. 'G'day, mate.'

'What do you want?' the man asked. His eyes shifted from Dave to Bob and away as he spoke.

Dave got out the other side, notebook in hand, and walked around to stand next to his partner.

'Bob Holden and Dave Burrows from the stock squad,' Bob said, holding out his card.

The man ignored it.

'Looking for Dylan Jeffries. You him?'

'Maybe.' He changed his posture and cocked his head to the side, waiting.

'We're here to ask a few questions about some cattle that have gone missing from Spinifex Downs.'

'Accusing me, are you?'

'Nope. Just here to have a chat.'

'You should be talking to those bastards over at Spinifex Downs. Reckon they'll have more information than good upstanding citizens like me.' He took a step towards them.

'Steady on there, mate,' Bob said, holding out his hands in a peaceful gesture. 'We've got to talk to you all so we can build a picture of what's going on in the district.'

'Not interested in talking to you about anything to do with cattle or thefts or whatever you're here for. What I'm gonna do is give you a free piece of advice. Those fellas over on Spinifex Downs are the ones you should be talking to.'

Dave frowned at the man's aggression. Where the hell was that all coming from?

A movement from the house caught his eye and he looked over as Bob started to speak. A little girl holding a teddy bear was walking down the path.

'The fellas over at Spinifex Downs know something about all of this, you reckon?' Bob asked. 'Why do you think that?'

'I know the history of the area. It's always been—'

'Dad?'

Dylan turned and saw the girl looking up at him.

'Get inside. I'll be back in a minute,' he said.

'Hello, what's your name?' Dave squatted down to look her in the eye, but she put the teddy bear in front of her face and didn't answer.

'Dad?' Her voice was muffled.

'Get inside, Maria! Now!' Dylan yelled and the little girl turned and ran down the path, her bare feet crossing the cement with a soft thwadding sound.

Dave stood up, arranging his face into a neutral expression.

'As I was saying,' Dylan continued, 'my thoughts are that it couldn't have happened to nicer people. If the cattle have actually gone missing. Which I doubt. More likely they've pinched them from a neighbour and trucked them back to their place. I didn't make the complaint, so I don't want to be dragged into this. So how about you get the fuck off my property!'

'Hold your horses there, mate,' Bob said calmly. 'What's the problem here?'

'I don't like anyone on my land. Black, white or brindle. I've told you everything I know about the cattle—I didn't do it. And if they have really been taken, I'm glad it happened to the oversubsidised bastards out there. Now you can leave.'

Dave was stunned into silence this time and he looked at Bob.

'Okay, sure,' Bob said. 'You've made it clear. We'll get off your property, but if you do need any assistance, here's my card.' He waved it towards Dylan, who looked at the card as if it were covered in cattle shit, before snatching it and turning away to stomp down the path.

Bob was just about to open the door to the vehicle when he called out to Dylan's retreating back, 'Dylan, if I hear a snippet from anyone that you've been taking your anger out on that little girl of yours, I'll be back to arrest you.' He hopped in the car and slammed the car door shut, telling Dave to drive.

Dave turned the troopy around and headed down the drive, trying to avoid the potholes. He glanced in the rear-view mirror to see what Dylan was doing. He'd disappeared into the house. 'Jesus, what the hell was that about? That poor little girl.'

Bob didn't answer.

'Anyway, like you said, the welcoming committee,' Dave continued. 'You'd have to think he had something to hide, wouldn't you? The way he wouldn't let us past the front gate.'

'Don't forget what Glenn said to us: there's a lot of history between the people up here. Some of them just can't let it go. Looking around the place, it looked to me like a living museum. His views and thoughts match that,' Bob said quietly. 'I bet he's got a wife in the house who doesn't get out past the garden and that's probably the way his dad and grandfather treated their wives. They will have drummed their opinion of the station communities into Dylan and, if that drumming's been long and hard enough, it's near impossible to change someone's opinions. I mean, look at the place. He's living back in the 1940s, with attitudes to match.

'Surely that can't be the only reason. He really didn't want us there.'

Looking out the window, Bob didn't answer straight away. 'You know what I reckon?'

The question was rhetorical, so Dave didn't bother to say anything.

'I reckon there was more truth in what he told us today than what I heard from Kit Redman.'

Dave just shook his head as if Bob was mad.

❧

Bob had told Dave about a waterhole he'd heard of that was nearby, so they decided to camp there for the night rather than go back to Boogarin. It would make for a short trip over to Spinifex Downs in the morning.

After a lot of driving and a few wrong turns, they found the place and started to set up camp. By the time they'd finished, Dave needed some painkillers for his shoulder and he started the exercises the physio had given him. Bob sat in his usual chair, with his usual beer in hand, staring into the fire.

As the sun set, the birds came in to drink, sending up deafening screeches. Dave walked to the edge and watched the orange rocks reflecting in the pool. There were gum trees with vivid green leaves surrounding the edge, and the gentle breeze was sending little ripples across the surface. He wished Mel was standing alongside him to see the beauty here. The voice of his cousin Kate from South Australia popped into his mind.

You think she'd see it as beautiful? More likely she'd see dirt and no comfort. Never understood why you went for her, Dave.

Shut up, Kate, Dave thought. It wasn't the first time he'd thought about Kate's opinion of his wife. His cousin had never been able to stop her thoughts coming out as words and he remembered the first time she'd met Melinda. Dave hadn't been left with any doubt about what Kate thought of her, but that hadn't stopped him marrying her.

Picking up a stone, Dave tossed it up and down in his hand, thinking about Mel and Bec. He'd wanted to call them tonight, but when he'd checked his phone earlier, there wasn't range.

The anger of the words she'd said to him before he left surfaced again and he hurled the rock into the water. He watched it fall into the deep, ripples spreading out; just like Mel's words, the ripples started small and ended up affecting the whole pool—just like they had affected his whole life. Maybe Kate had been right.

A kangaroo hopped down from the rocks to the water's edge and crouched down to drink. *Bec would love it here*, he thought. *I wish I could show her.* Digging in his pocket, he found his small digital camera and snapped a shot. He could tell her a story about it when he got home.

He heard a twig snap behind him and saw Bob wandering over, beer in his hand.

'What's happening out here, son? Not a bad view, is it?'

'Beautiful,' Dave answered, looking back across the water. 'The galahs are pretty noisy!'

'Just like a gaggle of girls at the hairdressers! You want to call home tonight? You can use the sat phone if you like.' He came to a stop next to Dave and handed him a beer from his pocket. 'Here you go, son. Get that into you.'

Dave wondered if Bob was able to read people's minds. 'That'd be great, thanks.' He popped the top and raised the can towards his partner.

'Go on, then.' Bob jerked his head towards the car and stood at the water while Dave went back to the car and retrieved the satellite phone.

'Hi, sweetie, it's me,' Dave said when he got through. There was a pause as the words beamed up to the depths of space and back down to his lounge room in Perth.

'Hello.'

'How are you? Everything okay?'

'Fine.'

Dave heard the clipped tone and knew that everything wasn't fine. God, how he hated that word. Fine never meant fine. And she was back to those one-word answers. The ones he loathed.

'How's Bec?'

'Good.'

'And bub?'

'Good, too.'

Geez, it was going to be like pulling teeth. He wanted to ask how long he'd have to do penance for, but decided it wasn't worth inflaming the situation. Not while he was away.

'What did you do today?'

'Doctor's appointment. But don't worry. Everything is fine.'

There it was again. Fine.

'Can I talk to Bec?'

She didn't answer, but Dave could hear her walking. 'Honey? It's Daddy.'

'Daddy!'

'How's my little princess?' he asked.

'I had fun at Gran and Gramps today. We went to da playground.'

'Did you? Did you have a swing?'

'Yep!'

'Do you know what I saw today, Bec?' He looked up at the darkening sky. The sun's light hadn't completely gone so he could see the shine of the evening star against the deep mauve sky.

'What?'

He imagined her staring up at his face, her eyes wide as she waited to hear. His heart gave a little pump of sadness. Missing Bec was the hard part about this job.

'A kangaroo! He came right down in front of me and had a drink at the waterhole we're camping next to tonight.'

'A real kangaroo?'

'Yep, a real one! I saw it hopping and everything.' He thought of the little girl at the station today and the fear he'd seen in her eyes as she'd tried to get her dad's attention. Bec's tone was so different, full of awe and wonder.

'Wow!'

A bird call sounded above him and he glanced up again. This time a lone wedgetail eagle soared in the fading light.

How far away from his daughter he was.

Mel's voice was in the background. 'Finish up now, honey. It's time for bed.'

'Bye, Daddy!'

'Nigh-night, sweetie.'

'Go and jump into bed and I'll be there to read you a story in a minute, okay?'

Dave heard Bec answer and then Mel was back on the line.

'I better go,' she said.

'Mel . . .'

'When are you coming home?'

Dave gave a sigh of frustration. 'I don't know yet. Probably another week. We've—'

'A week?' Her tone turned frigid. 'So, you'll just get back and then have to go again? To Queensland? Dad said it would be like this but I didn't believe him.'

'Yeah, maybe.' He would've loved to have grabbed Mark by the throat about now and squeezed, because Dave knew where this conversation was going to end up.

'Bloody hell, Dave, how do you think I'm feeling back here? This job just about kills you and I'm left to patch you up, then not one day back into it and you're on the road again! What about Bec and I? Let alone the birth of *our* baby.'

'Come on, Mel, you know this is how it has to be.' He glanced around, hoping that Bob couldn't hear what he was saying.

'I'm sick of it. Listen to me, Dave. I'm really sick of it. Maybe Dad's right when he says you enjoy being away more than at home.' The line went dead.

'Mel?' He took the phone away from his ear and looked at it. 'Mel? Goddamnit!' He put the phone back in the case and stomped around the back of the troopy to get another beer. Popping the top, he drained it in one mouthful, then got another one. 'Damn it to hell!' he whispered ferociously. Fucking Mark and his fucking opinions. He always managed to get inside Mel's head.

He saw sparks from the fire shoot up into the sky and he realised Bob must be back.

Peering around the edge of the vehicle he saw Bob was standing next to the fire poking at the coals.

Dave fished around in the fridge and drew out another beer and took it to Bob, before he slumped into his chair.

'Trouble at home, son?' Bob asked after a moment or two of quiet.

'I don't want to talk about it,' Dave said, taking another gulp.

'Ah.'

They sat in silence, Dave going over the conversation in his head—the words he'd wanted to say but hadn't.

I love you, Mel, but you've got to stop doing this to us!
I don't know if I can fight it anymore. I love the job and you!

'You right there, son?'

The words filtered through the yelling in his head and
Dave refocused on Bob. 'What?'

'You're about to crush the can in your hand. Come on,
out with it. A problem shared is a problem halved.'

Dave shook his head. He just wanted to hit something.
Yell at Mel. Tell her father that he needed to stay out of
their business.

Bob turned and looked at him. 'Son, if you think you're
going through something none of us have been through
before, then you're kidding yourself. If you want to take on
the life of a stockie, you'll have to get used to communicating on the phone and being away from home.'

Frustration and anger at Mel made Dave stand up so
quickly his chair fell over backwards. He pointed at Bob.
'You don't know or understand me,' he said heatedly. 'My
circumstances are a bit different to everyone else's.'

'Are they? Why do you think that?'

'Look, I just don't want to talk about it.' Dave stomped
around to the back of the car and pulled another beer
out of the fridge. He didn't need it yet, but he had to do
something. The rage inside him was almost at boiling point.

'You're not Robinson Crusoe, son,' Bob called out to
him. 'Every stockie I know has been on that island you're
sitting on at the moment.'

'Fuck, what is it with your stupid clichés? And while we're at it, I'm not your son. Don't call me that. It's just fucking patronising.'

'Now, now, son, don't have a crack at me. I know it's not me you're pissed off with. Come and settle down. All of us have had our troubles over the years. It goes hand in hand with the job. No point in getting all worked up over it.'

'At least I'm not trying to drown my issues at every opportunity,' Dave snapped back.

Bob shot to his feet and took two steps towards Dave, pointing a finger at him. 'Boy, you need to go and wash your mouth out,' he said menacingly. 'You've got no idea what I've lived and seen and you couldn't even imagine, so don't bother trying. You might've got yourself shot through your own stupidity, but don't think that makes you a hero or above anyone else. So sit the fuck down and shut your mouth, before I shut it for you.'

Instantly ashamed of himself, Dave dropped his head. 'Sorry. I don't where that came from.'

'Yeah, you do. You're angry and frustrated at your missus. Don't take that shit out on me. Apology accepted. Now sit down and drink your beer.'

Bob sat down and stared into the fire without saying another word. Dave followed his lead.

Chapter 14

Kevin kicked the coals back into the fire and made sure it was safe before walking back to the shed.

On the way, he stopped to handball the footy with the five little boys who were running along the creek edge, chasing the football David Wirrpanda had signed.

Harry and Charlie had left earlier to go out and check two of the bores on the eastern side of the property and Cyril and Nicky had gone west, while he was at the homestead, waiting.

He knew the stockies were coming; he'd received the phone call from Kit. Annoyed they'd seen the other station owners first, Kevin had decided he was going to be ready for them when they arrived.

'Just a heads-up, mate,' Kit had said. 'Stockies are around. They've been to see me and Dylan Jeffries, and I reckon they're coming your way next.'

Kevin had been pleased they'd arrived until he'd heard they'd visited all the other surrounding stations before coming to Spinifex Downs.

'Why would they have done that?' he said to Jackie.

'Just like all whitefellas,' Jackie answered. 'Always listening to other whites first.'

'They should've come here first.'

'They were never going to.'

'I'll sort it, okay?'

'You keep believing that, boy. They're not goin' to take any notice of you.'

'Maybe not, but by the time I've finished with them, they'll have a different point of view,' he answered. He had a white anger burning in his stomach.

Jackie walked into the bush beside the shed without another word.

With a sound of frustration Kevin kicked at the forty-four-gallon drum lying on its side at the entrance to the shed. Inside on the cement was a trailer with a broken tailgate, so to keep busy, he got out the welder and started to patch the steel together. Better to stay active than get so furious that he didn't behave well when the coppers turned up.

The sparks flew around his hands, some landing on his bare skin, but he didn't notice, concentrating only on joining the two pieces back together again.

In the distance a dog barked, then another, and another, and he realised his visitors were here. He lifted the visor

142

on the helmet and looked out into the bright daylight to see if he could see any dust. Too late. A white troopy had already pulled up, the tall aerials on the back the only things giving it away as a police vehicle.

He took off the helmet and checked his work briefly, wiping his brow, before walking outside to greet them.

'You must be Kevin,' the older of the two men said. 'Bob Holden, Stock Squad. This is Detective Dave Burrows.' He was frowning as he talked and gave Kevin the distinct impression he didn't want to be here.

'G'day,' Kevin answered, nodding his head towards them.

'You've had some trouble out here?' Bob said.

'Yeah. A bit.' He felt the anger whirling in his stomach as he answered.

'Want to tell us about it?'

Squatting down, Kevin began to draw in the dirt, not answering. Bob squatted down too, then Dave. The older man rubbed at his head as if it hurt and Kevin started to believe the words of his Elders. There really wasn't any point in dealing with the coppers. They weren't going to help him. Not this older one anyway.

Finally, Kevin looked up. 'Not sure why you're here,' he said. 'You've already been to all the white man stations getting their story. It was my cattle that was stolen, so why didn't you come here first?' He made sure he kept his voice calm and quiet.

Bob snorted and gave a jerky nod as if he was furious that Kevin had questioned his policing methods. 'Just the way the stations are laid out, son,' Bob said sharply. 'Yeah, we did, we went to Deep-Water first, then on to Cassia Plains. Once we finish here, we're off to Paperbark Valley.' He shrugged. 'We're just following the map.'

'But they've given you their story first. Swayed your thinking.' Kevin stood up now and the other two shot up after him.

'Now hang on there just one minute!' Bob snapped. 'This is a district matter, Kevin. Other people are involved, not just you. You've been targeted, son, and it sounds like Kit has been too. Maybe even set up. Yeah, we've talked to others already, but it doesn't matter which order we've spoken to everyone. We're keeping an open mind and we're here to listen to your side of things now.'

'You and your condescending white talk,' Kevin snarled. He wasn't sure he could hold himself together now. He'd been wrestling with his decision to report the stolen cattle and now all the guilt, fear and worry from going against his Elders was boiling to the surface. 'You will have already formed your opinion, I'm sure. You're not here to help us. Just like everyone else.'

His raised voice brought three young men out of the bush.

'You right, Kev?' one asked as they came to stand behind him.

'Yeah.' He didn't turn to look at them.

Bob took a deep breath and raised his eyes towards the heavens, before speaking with exaggerated patience. 'Mate, I really think we've got off on the wrong foot here. And I'm sorry about that. My fault. Look, we've come to help you all. We don't care whether you're black or white. Dave here and me, we're police for everyone. Don't know what experience you've had with other coppers, but we're straight up and down. All right?'

The young man didn't hear the words. Just the tone: impatient, annoyed and irritated. Pretty much how Kevin was feeling himself. He looked at the men and the younger copper started to talk.

'Look, I reckon we probably need to calm down. Why don't you and I go for a drive, Kev? You can show me what paddock the cattle were taken from and where it all happened. What do you think?'

'Yeah, good idea,' Bob said. 'You lot fuck off and I'll hang around here.'

Kevin bristled but Dave quickly intervened again.

'Where's your ute, mate? Let's go, yeah? Have a look around.' He walked over to his car, grabbed a bag and hoisted it over his shoulder, before waiting expectantly.

Kevin considered what the younger bloke had said. Maybe he'd be okay. Maybe, like him, this younger cop wouldn't have the preconceived ideas that the older generation had. Maybe he should give him a go.

'This way,' Kevin said. 'You boys, you go back. I'm right here.' He turned and walked to his ute and waited until Dave got in, then drove away.

❧

In the passenger's seat, Dave kept checking the side mirror, worried that Bob might leave without him. Bob was suffering this morning. He had a hangover from the night before and Bob was in a seriously bad mood. In the time they'd spent together—which wasn't long, Dave admitted—he'd never seen Bob anything other than professional, no matter what he'd had to drink the night before.

But last night Bob'd brought out a bottle of Wild Turkey Honey Whiskey. Rocket fuel. A drink to give even the most seasoned of drinkers a hangover.

Dave felt bad. Maybe his accusations last night had brought up Bob's buried memories. Or maybe he just loved drinking. But Dave's instinct told him there was something Bob was trying to forget and last night had brought it a bit too close to the surface for comfort.

This morning the sun had risen before Bob even moved in his swag and his normal cheerful persona had been replaced with an angry, dark mood that Dave knew was fuelled by a monstrous headache—he'd seen Bob popping some painkillers just before they packed up camp. The old bloke had hardly said a word in the hour's drive to Spinifex Downs.

Now here he was taking it out on Kevin.

Bob wasn't the only one suffering, Dave thought darkly. The painkillers Dave had taken just before arriving hadn't kicked in yet. Sleeping on the ground and the rough roads weren't his shoulder helping either.

'Sorry about Bob,' Dave said as they went over a cattle grid and turned towards a line of hills in the distance. 'He's not feeling that well today.'

Kevin didn't answer.

'His heart's in the right place, you know. He's genuinely here to help.'

'Why'd you go to all the other stations first then? It would have made more sense to come here.'

'Just like the old fella said—we were following the map. All those stations are on the way here.' Dave shrugged and looked out the window. The country was floodplain leading towards hills, but he still couldn't see very far in front—tall, spindly trees blocked the view.

'Sounded like he was talking down to me. Especially when he called me "son".'

Dave gave a laugh. 'Yep, that's Bob all right. He calls me son all the time. Annoys the hell out of me. In fact I had it out with him last night about that. Didn't do much good though. First thing he said to me this morning was: "How'd you sleep, son?"' He shook his head. 'But he wasn't being condescending towards you. I was there and I heard the conversation, he was just trying to get some facts about what's happening out here.'

Kevin chuckled and Dave thought he saw his shoulders relax a little. Then he slowed the car to a stop and turned to face Dave.

'What you need to know is that I've put my head on the line for you lot,' he said. 'The Elders, they didn't want me to say anything. Reckon there's too much history of white coppers not helping us blackfellas. I'm trying to make them see that all that has finished—that you will help us and our community. I need your help—no, *expect* your help—so I can keep control and build the respect within my community. Without that, I can't do the things I've come back here to do.'

'Mate, I promise you, we are here to help everyone. You've got to know we'll follow the leads and see where they fall. If they point to your fellas or to Kit or to anyone we've talked to, we'll make sure the book is chucked at them. We're straight down the line.'

Kevin nodded. 'That's all I ask.' He put the ute in gear again and started to drive off.

Dave watched as the orange soil passed under the ute. He thought about what he knew of the crime then ordered his thoughts into questions.

'How often do you head out on a bore run?' Dave brought his notebook out of his shirt pocket and opened it to a new page.

'This time of the year? Only about once a week. We've just finished mustering and know that all the mills are in good working order. We've sold the young stock. It's only the water we need to keep an eye on now. But with the size of the place, those bore runs can take up to three days to complete, depending on what we find. I usually send one bloke in each direction so we can cover everything a little more quickly.'

'And you pump the water into a tank then down into a trough?'

'Yeah. If someone shut my bore off, the cattle have to drink all the water in the tank before the trough goes dry and they start looking for water.'

'How long would that take?'

Kevin thought about that. 'Cattle drink about sixty litres of water a day. Can be more if it's hot. Our tanks hold ten thousand gallons of water, which works out at about forty-five thousand litres, so they're going to go dry in about three to four days. Say three, to be conservative. That's four days without water by the time we realise there's a problem, and when it's hot up here, being without water isn't an option. They'll go looking for it. The more they walk, the thirstier they get, the more dehydrated they get. Then the outcome isn't good.'

'Could the cattle have put pressure on the fence and busted through onto Deep-Water while they were looking for something to drink?'

'Of course. They'll walk up and down a fence line until they find a pressure point they can get through. And don't forget cattle can smell water—some say up to eight kilometres away,' Kevin said thoughtfully. 'Dunno if that's true or not, but the old fellas have always told me that. Guessing if they can smell it, they'll go looking for it, and if there's a fence in the way, they'll find a way through.'

Dave wrote a couple of notes and then stuck his pen in his mouth as they continued to drive.

'This bore here,' Kevin said, pointing to his left, 'has got about a hundred head on it.'

Across the flat land the tussocks of grasses were dry and brown, but the leaves of the trees were a vivid green. Red shiny cattle grazed contently across the plain and Dave could see the windmill head turning lazily in the breeze.

'You get enough wind up here to run these things?' Dave asked suddenly. 'What happens if you don't get any for a week. Got any solar or fuel pumps?'

'We've got back-ups if we don't get the wind, but it's rare we have a problem. Most afternoons get windy.' Kevin turned the wheel and started heading over to the bore. 'See here, cattle aren't straying too far from the water. At the moment there's enough feed around that they don't have to go looking.' He pointed to some heifer weaners that were lying down under a cluster of trees, chewing the cud. 'These are my girls for next year's breeding. I bought a couple of real good bulls from Queensland and bred these. Good quality stock is important in any set-up, but up here I reckon it's essential.'

Kevin edged the ute in closer and came to a standstill. Two of the heifers stood up and flicked their tails lazily, while staring at the ute. Their ears twitched back and forth, listening to the unusual noise of the engine, trying to work out if the vehicle was a threat.

'They're beautiful, aren't they?' he said in a reverent tone. 'See how good their structure is—legs are solid, as they need to be for this type of country.'

'They sure are.' Dave looked at the well-bred cattle and then out across the country. Everything he saw here looked like it was well maintained. Impressive really. Especially after what they'd seen at Cassia Plains.

Kevin put the ute back into gear and drove across to the windmill. 'See here?' He pointed to the shaft of the mill and Dave could see what Glenn had showed them photos of back at the station: stainless steel pins, locking the couplings together so they couldn't become unscrewed, no matter how many times they pumped up and down.

It was clear from the well-maintained equipment and the evidence photos that the cattle had not simply pushed through a fence looking for water. They had been stolen.

Chapter 15

Bob wasn't anywhere to be seen when they arrived back at the homestead, but Dave was relieved to see the troopy still parked in the same spot. He wasn't sure why he'd been worried that Bob would take off and leave him behind. As a copper, you needed to be able to trust your partner. But he hadn't ever seen Bob in a mood like he'd been in that morning.

Maybe it was because he'd thought the pull of the booze might be too strong for Bob. He'd wondered whether Bob was able to hold his drinking at a consistent level or whether he'd end up going off on a bender. He wished he'd thought to discreetly ask someone in the office about what it was like being on a job with Bob; that way he might have been more prepared.

'Where's he gone? Hope he's not poking around in my shed,' Kevin said.

Dave put his hand on the bonnet of the troopy. Warmth filtered up through his fingers, caused more by the sun than the engine.

'Bob!' Dave called out and then walked onto the track to see if he could see him. Nothing.

'Would he have gone down to the community?' Dave asked. 'How far is it from here? Maybe he wanted to talk to the Elders.'

'He'd better not have. I don't want him bothering everyone down there. Come on, we'll go and look.' Kevin waved towards the track and started walking.

Dave could hear kids laughing and women singing. It sounded more like chanting and he asked what it was.

'They'll be teaching the young ones,' Kevin said. 'Probably cooking roo or goanna or something and while they're doing that, they're always teaching the kids how to sing, or cook, or paint. The Elders know so much and we have to make sure that knowledge is passed on.'

Dave nodded. Campfire smoke drifted towards them and there were a couple of dogs barking in the distance. The tall gums were standing silently on the bank of the creek and Dave could understand why these people had such a connection to the land. The country was beautiful and it was theirs.

The dirt track curved to the left and as they came around the corner Dave could see Bob sitting with an old man underneath a tree, next to a fire. They each held a pannikin.

'Ah shit,' Dave said aloud, without meaning to.

'What?'

153

'Nah, nothing. Sorry. Just thought of something.' Dave hoped there wasn't Scotch or beer in that pannikin.

Then Kevin stopped. 'What's he bothering the old people for? He shouldn't be talking to them,' he said and started to jog across to where they were sitting.

'He'll be fact finding,' Dave said, quickening his pace too. The change in the man was sudden. Gone was the bloke who was happy to chat and loved his job. The distrust was clear in his voice.

'Hey! Hey you, copper,' Kevin yelled out. 'What are you doing here? Shouldn't be talking to the old men. They deserve your respect, not your shit.'

Dave groaned inwardly, hoping Bob wouldn't retaliate. He knew from his drive with Kevin that his reaction was only because he'd gone against the Elders' wishes, rather than anger towards a white man copper. The Elders had told him not to talk to them and Kevin had wrestled with the decision and gone against them. Now he'd be wanting to protect his people from his decision the best he could.

Bob and the old man looked at them as they approached and the old man raised a hand to wave them over.

'What are you doing?' Kevin repeated.

Bob stood up and held his hand out to the angry young man. 'Son, like I said, we got off on the wrong foot.'

'I'm not shaking your hand.'

'Kevin!' The old man barked. 'You show respect to the sergeant.'

'What?' He rounded on Jackie.

'You know better than to disrespect a man when they've offered their hand.' Jackie got to his feet and glared at his son.

Without looking back at Bob, Kevin spoke to his father. 'You're the one who hasn't got any respect for the coppers! You're the one who told me they were all about the white man.'

'Kevvy, this man, he's different. A good man. I've talked to him. Don't leave him hanging.' He nodded towards Bob's hand, which was still outstretched. Dave could see it was grudgingly, but Kevin held out his own hand and they shook.

'That's the way, son,' Bob said. 'Don't you worry, I'll make sure everything is okay for you. Promise you that.' He paused. 'Sorry about before. I had a bit of shit on the liver and shouldn't have taken it out on you.'

The sound of laughing children came closer, dispersing the tension between the men and Dave turned to see a group of about eight young kids surrounding a white woman, all talking to her at the same time. They disappeared up the steps and into a demountable, which Dave assumed was the schoolroom.

'What about you, young fella?' Jackie turned to Dave and broke into his thoughts. 'Are you a good man too?'

Kevin looked over at Dave and spoke before he could. 'This is my father, Jackie. And, yeah, Dave's a good man.'

Jackie smiled, showing a missing top tooth. 'Then we have two good men. Two good men who'll get to the truth.'

'We'd better be off,' Bob said, turning back to Jackie, who was standing by now, and nodding. 'Thanks for the yarn.'

'You keep being a good man, Sergeant.'

❧

Dave took the driver's seat and waited until they were out of sight of the sheds and homestead before he asked, 'What were you doing back there?'

'Talking to the Elders. Jackie was the only one I could find. He didn't want to talk at first, but then he realised that I was there to help. I've been up this way a few times before and dealt with similar issues. I've learned a bit along the way. He was okay. Respect is a big thing with Aboriginal people. Sitting next to him on the ground was an important thing to do.'

Dave recalled Spencer's advice had been just that.

'Did you find out anything of interest?' he asked.

Bob was quiet for a while and then he said, 'We talked a lot about the old days. I understand why he is very distrustful of the police.'

Dave wanted to ask what the reasons were, but he waited, thinking Bob was going to say more. Kilometre after kilometre slipped away before Bob spoke again.

'What you have to understand is that there are a lot of people out here who are distrustful of the police and they're concerned their own private business is going to be shared with the whole community.

'These Aboriginal stations have had a bad rap. The owners were accused of not looking after their cattle. Not being able to run the station. Jackie, the old man, he doesn't want any of that happening again. But he also doesn't want to cause trouble with his neighbours by making accusations; he doesn't want any conflict. And he certainly doesn't want people to think the cattle are missing because of their management. And when cattle go missing like this, there are three thought processes by those who don't know. One, people can't look after their stock and they've walked through broken fences out into Crown land; two, they've been stolen; and, three, they've died.'

'They haven't died,' Dave stated flatly.

'I agree. Everything I saw on that station was in good nick. Professional. What I'd expect from a good operation. They didn't die from lack of water or feed or poison. They might be dead now, of course; might've been taken to abattoirs. There's no doubt in my mind they've been stolen. What did you find out?'

'Pretty much everything that you've said. Kev is passionate about his job. You should've heard him when he was talking about his cattle. He's put a huge amount of time and effort into getting this place running well.

'He told me that when he arrived back here there were pieces of tin missing from the shed, old cars lying around, and everything was pretty much in disrepair. It took time, but he finally got a few of the lads rounded up to help restore things to the way they should be. He just wants his people have a high regard for themselves and he thinks the way to make that happen is by giving them something to be involved in, something to take pride in. I've got a lot of respect for that man back there.'

'Yeah, everyone has said that Kev's a great bloke and doing good things.' Bob paused. 'But that also makes me suspicious.'

'Why?'

Bob paused. 'I guess I understand the mentality about not reporting the cattle when they were first stolen. Especially after talking to Jackie. But there's something not adding up. I can't tell what it is yet. I almost think they know who did it but they won't say.'

'What, you reckon Kev knows who it is?' Dave turned to Bob in surprise.

'No . . .' His voice trailed off. 'No, I don't think he knows, but I think the Elders do.'

'You think it's inhouse?'

'Nope, not that either.' Bob scratched his chin thoughtfully. 'Wish I could put my finger on it.'

'So what now?'

'Well, no one has accused anyone else. There aren't any leads. Really all we can do is document everything. Go home and write everything up. It's a bastard really, because I know there's more here than we're seeing, but we can't be away any longer. Let's go and talk to this other bloke at Paperbark Valley, then head home, I reckon.

'See, even if I got a warrant and we searched all the properties around here, and we found those cattle, the story is going to be that they walked there. Pushed through the fences. Whomever's place we found them on is going to say they didn't know they were there—big swags of land. Can't be everywhere all of the time. Plausible deniability.

'You know we have to prove it beyond reasonable doubt, and we can't do that unless we catch someone in the act of taking them. No jury is going to convict because we found cattle on a bore on, say, Cassia Plains. They just walked there; cattle walk and cattle stray.'

'Long way to come without any results,' Dave said, but his heart leaped at the thought of seeing Bec.

'Unfortunately, that's the way it is when you're dealing with this type of thing. Like I said to you when we first came up here, I haven't heard anything; not a whisper on the grapevine that there is any type of trouble up here. To have two hundred head of cattle stolen without there being any warning is pretty unusual. I think we'll be back up here before too long. This is a watch and wait and see case—can't be hurried.

'Anyway,' he gave Dave a wink, 'you'll be needed in Queensland soon.'

Chapter 16

The house was in darkness when Dave arrived home. He frowned and glanced at his watch. Close to 6 p.m. His family should be here.

He'd tried to call Mel earlier in the day to let her know he'd be home soon, but she hadn't answered.

Flicking on the light, he hoped there would be a note in the kitchen. Maybe they were at her parents' house having tea.

Fighting back disappointment, Dave thought about the trip back. He and Bob had shared the driving and made good time so he could be back for dinner. It was the first time Dave had seen Bob go without a drink for twenty-four hours. As soon as everything was unloaded, he'd headed for home, hoping to be able to read Bec a story and show her the pictures of the kangaroo.

Only to arrive to an empty house.

'Unbelievable,' he muttered, going to the fridge and grabbing a beer. He wanted to rant and rave but instead he went out to the back verandah and sat under the stars. 'I'm not going looking for you, Mel,' he said to the sky. 'Especially if you're at your dad's place.'

He got out his phone and checked it again, making sure he hadn't missed a call, but there was nothing. Restless, he got up and went back into the house, into Bec's room. Everything looked normal there—the bed was made, the stuffed teddy bear he'd bought her when she was born was propped up against the pillow, and only the little bag Mel always packed with spare clothes had gone.

Then he checked their bedroom. Nothing out of place there. Well, one good thing was it was clear she hadn't left him again. That thought had seeped into his mind when he had first arrived home, but now he knew they'd be home soon.

∾

An hour later, his anger got the better of him and he went back out to his car and drove to Mark and Ellen's place. There was Mel's car. He pulled up and looked at it, trying to work out whether to go and knock on the door or just wait for them to come home.

'Fuck it,' he snarled. 'I tried to tell you I was coming.'

He got out and slammed the door, before stalking up the path and rapping loudly on the door.

It didn't take Mark long to open it.

'Oh, you're back, are you?' he said without saying hello.

'Yeah, I am. Is Mel here?'

There was the sound of little feet running and then Bec came into the light. 'Daddy! Daddy!'

Dave bent down and swept her up into his arms, ignoring Mark's glare. 'Hello, my little princess, how are you?'

'I'm good, Daddy, but I've missed you. Did you see any more kangaroos?'

'Not this time, but I've got a photo to show you of the one I did see.' He saw Ellen come into the hallway and he gave her a wave with his free hand.

Suddenly he realised there was something wrong.

'So, is Mel here?' he asked, looking straight at Ellen.

'Come into the kitchen,' she said. 'There's more room in there.'

Still carrying Bec, he followed his in-laws down the passageway. He wasn't sure what he was about to be told, but he was certain it wasn't good. Had Mel lost the baby? Oh god!

Putting Bec down, he kept a hand on her shoulder for comfort. 'So, where is she?' Dave asked. 'Is the baby okay?'

Mark turned around to face him. 'She's in hospital.'

'Yes, Mummy's in hospital!' Bec parroted. Dave pulled her closer to his legs.

'Why?'

'It's nothing too serious, Dave,' Ellen broke in. She took a step towards him, her hands outstretched. Her perfectly manicured nails and smooth hands reminded him of Mel. 'Everything will be fine, but the doctor thought it was a good idea. Just so she could have a rest.'

'You don't go to hospital to have a rest,' Dave said, staring hard at his mother-in-law. 'What else is there?'

'Mel's got high blood pressure . . .'

'You didn't think to get hold of me and tell me?' Dave turned on Mark and spat the words at him.

'Daddy?' Bec turned her face up towards him and held out her arms.

Dave was too busy staring Mark down.

'We thought you'd be too busy with work,' Mark answered. He smirked. 'We're happy to be here when you're too busy for your family.'

'Daddy!' Bec's voice was urgent.

'Mark!' Ellen snapped. 'Take Bec into the bedroom. Daddy will come in to read you a story in a minute, darling.' She reached out and smoothed a hand over Bec's hair.

'Hang on, you thought I was too busy with work to want to know my wife was in hospital?' He glared at his father-in-law. 'What sort of person do you think I am?'

'Now, boys,' Ellen said. 'Stop it, not in front—'

'You know what you would be doing if you were any sort of a husband? You would be taking parental leave to look after your wife, so she didn't get into this situation in the first place. But don't worry, since you're so busy, the doctors can look after Melinda and we'll look after your daughter, take on your responsibility.'

'Daddy?' Bec's voice held tears in it as she patted Dave's leg to get his attention.

Somehow his daughter's voice filtered through the red mist of rage. Dave took a breath, gathering himself and squatted down. 'It's okay, sweetie. Go with Granddad and he can read you that story. I'll be in once I've finished talking to Gran.' He kissed her forehead. 'I'll be in shortly, I promise.'

Mark reluctantly took Bec's hand. 'Come on, what story should we have tonight?' He threw a glance full of hatred over his shoulder as they left the room together.

'I'm sorry, Dave,' Ellen whispered as the footsteps faded into the bedrooms further towards the back of the house. 'I'm sorry, he's just been so angry. I don't know what's got into him the past few years. I just can't seem to talk sense into him anymore. He worries me.'

Dave flicked his hand. 'Doesn't matter. Tell me about Mel.'

'They were worried about pre-eclampsia.'

'What the hell is that?'

'The most simply put, it's protein in the urine and high blood pressure. She had a lot of swelling around her ankles and because she was running after Bec and was on her feet all day—'

Dave grunted and she held up her hand. 'I know you have to be away, Dave, don't say anything right now, just listen. Because she had to look after Bec, having a decent rest was impossible. See, if she has bed rest, which she's getting in hospital, her blood pressure should come down. But if it doesn't, they might have to bring the baby on early. I understand the only cure is the delivery of both the baby and placenta.'

Dave ran his hand through his hair and looked around as if for an answer. 'I just don't get why you didn't call me.

When did this happen? I'd left the number for the satellite phone on the fridge at home.'

'Oh, did you? Mel didn't tell me you had one. If you hadn't come home by tomorrow, I was going to find the station phone number and call there.' She reached out and put her hand on Dave's arm. 'She'll be okay, you know. This can happen in the later weeks of pregnancy. She's in the right place. If something does go wrong, the doctors will know about it straight away and fix it. They've hooked a monitor up so they can see the baby, hear its heartbeat and make sure it's not distressed in any way.'

Dave took that in. *Distressed in any way.* This high blood pressure thing sounded more serious than Ellen was admitting. 'And Bec?' he finally asked. 'What about . . .'

'Bec can stay here. I know you'd love to have her at home, but it's not practical with your work. I understand that. You can come and see her every night, have tea with us, whatever works for you, but understand that we are here to support you through this.'

Dave gave a laugh, but there was nothing joyful about it. 'That's very nice of you, Ellen, but I'm not sure Mark is on the same page.'

'He'll have to be. When times get rough, families have to pull together.'

Dave had a fleeting thought of his mother and two brothers who hadn't done that for him when his father had kicked him off the farm all those years ago. *Not always,* he thought.

'What hospital is she in?'

Ellen turned back to the bench and picked up a piece of paper. 'Here are the details,' she said. 'Room five on the third floor.'

Staring at his wife's writing on the paper, a wave of emotion overtook him. He'd been hundreds of kilometres away when she'd needed him.

'I'll go to her now,' he said. 'I'll just say goodnight to Bec.' He turned to leave the room then stopped. 'Thank you,' he said quietly.

❧

'Visiting hours are over, Mr Burrows,' said the woman at the front desk of the hospital. 'I'm sorry, I can't let you in. It's very late and the nightshift staff have started.'

'I'm her husband, surely you can let me in,' Dave said. He'd been trying to persuade her patiently for the last five minutes.

'Doesn't matter who you are. You'll disturb the other patients.' She crossed her arms and stared at him.

'Look, could you make an exception just this once. I'm a policeman and I've been away for work. I haven't seen my wife since she was admitted.'

The woman looked at him again and then sighed. 'You men—workaholics, always away—I don't know how your wives put up with you.'

Sensing a weakening, Dave didn't say anything.

'Oh, all right then. Off you go. Take the second lift on the left. But make sure you don't make any noise.'

'Thank you. I could kiss you I'm so grateful.'

'That won't be necessary.' She ducked her head and looked back at the computer, but not before Dave caught the glimpse of a smile.

Not needing to be told twice, he found the lift and pressed the button. When he got to the third floor, he found the signs pointing to room five. He peered inside to see Mel dozing, her dark hair spread across the pillow and the outline of her belly under the blanket.

He went in quietly and pulled a chair up next to the bed. Reaching out he took her hand, hoping she would open her eyes, but she didn't.

Instead she just said, 'You're back.'

With his other hand, he pushed her hair back from her face. 'Yeah, honey, I am. What have you done to yourself? Why didn't you call me?'

'What have *you* done to me might be the better question.' Her tone was cold.

Dave nearly reared back only he wasn't sure he'd heard her correctly. 'Sorry?'

Now she did open her eyes and turned to look at him. He was startled at the iciness in her eyes. 'What you did to me,' she repeated.

'Honey, I think this is something that happens to women sometimes. I asked the nurse when I first got here. I know you're probably frightened—'

'Yeah, it does. You're right. But when you can't rest because your husband isn't at home, that's when the doctors put you into hospital to make sure nothing bad happens to the baby. Do you know I could *die* from this? The baby could die because of this! Yet the job is still more important than me and your daughter. And your unborn child!'

Dave took his hand away. 'Mel, sweetie, I didn't know you'd been admitted until I got home tonight. I wasn't told. If I'd known, I would have caught a flight home. The job is never more important than you all.' He took a breath, hoping Mel would offer some kind of olive branch, but she remained silent. 'Look, don't upset yourself anymore. Go back to sleep and we can talk about this in the morning. Do you know when you can come home?'

She ignored the question. 'Give up the job, Dave. Please. For me and the kids. Just give it up.'

Stifling the anger that roared up inside him, he stood and went to the window to look out. 'Maybe it's just better if I come back tomorrow when you've had a good night's rest,' he said.

'Can't do it, can you?' she said.

He felt like she was taunting him. Asking him to prove how much he loved her and the kids. 'Let's talk about it again when you come home. I'll see you tomorrow.'

Dave left the room without kissing her goodbye.

Chapter 17

'Why is she doing this?' Dave snapped down the phone to Spencer. 'I just don't get what she wants me to do.'

'Pretty clear to me,' his friend answered. 'She wants you to give up the job. Question is, what are you going to do about it?'

'What can I do? She's just about to have our baby! I can't not be here for her.'

'So you'd give it all up because she asked you to?' His tone was incredulous. 'Surely not.'

'No! Yes! Fuck, I don't know. What a shitty, shitty spot to be in.' Dave slumped down on the floor, his back up against the wall. 'I don't know,' he said again, this time very quietly. 'I really don't know what to do.'

'Mate, I don't know what you should do either. What I *do* know is that when you're a stockie you're going to be away a lot. When you're on the beat in uniform, you're going to be on nightshift sometimes, not just daytime hours.

Dave, what we do isn't easy on anyone. Doesn't matter which part of policing you're involved in, there're crappy hours and crappy shifts. That's just how it is.'

'I know, I know.' He let out a frustrated sigh. 'Bob said that too. Have to get used to communicating on the phone and being away. I don't mind talking on the phone, but a phone call doesn't help with the practical things, does it. That's what she's saying now; she needs help at home.'

'What about getting a nanny?'

'I don't think anyone except me is going to cut it somehow. Well, that's the impression I got. She actually said, "What have you done to me?" as if I'm to blame she's got high blood pressure. But in a way I guess I am, because I wasn't there to help and let her rest like the doctor said. I didn't even know the doctor had told her that.'

'Dave, listen to yourself. You're making excuses for her. Do you really think that if you'd been there her blood pressure wouldn't have gone up? I don't know much about these things, but I'm guessing it would've.'

'If you ask her father it wouldn't have.'

'We know he's a tosser.'

Dave didn't feel like laughing but he couldn't help it when he heard Spencer's sour tone.

'I'm hoping it will all blow over when the baby is born. You know that she's just feeling really vulnerable at the moment. I understand having Bec and trying to run the house would have been a lot more work without me around. And to be fair, she's had me at home for a couple of months, so I guess she got used to me being there.' He was quiet while he took another sip of beer. 'Her family have been helping out while I've been away, so it's not like she's been completely on her own.'

'Can I be really blunt?'

Dave harrumphed. 'You usually are.'

'Mel saying you not being there is an excuse she's using to try to make you feel guilty. You've just said yourself the folks have been helping out. I don't think she's been without help as much as she thinks she has. Christ on a bike! You've only been back at work for a week and a half!'

Dave let that sink in. He'd already had those thoughts but hadn't wanted to say them aloud. Instead he said, 'I don't know how she thinks we're going to live if I don't work.'

'I've got a bit of an idea about what she might have in mind,' Spencer said.

'Daddy's money? She knows me better than that. Not a chance in hell I'd take help from that arsehole.'

'Hmm, well, I guess you'll have to have that conversation sooner rather than later if that's what she's thinking.'

They both fell silent and Dave's mind flew through all sorts of scenarios. He could give up work and get a job as a stockman at the saleyards. Maybe he could become a stock agent—he'd have the qualifications. Still, all of those jobs meant being away from home for long hours. Maybe he'd just become an accountant as Mel had suggested.

Like hell.

The only figures he liked were stocking rates and estimated breeding values.

And what about Brisbane?

'This court date, Spencer, like I told you last time, it's right around when the baby is supposed to be due. What can we do about that?'

'Yeah, you need to try to shift it. Ring the DPP and see if you can organise to give your evidence by video. That should keep everyone happy. You'll have to cite family reasons—something really important that you can't leave the state for, because they're not going to be thrilled by the idea. They much prefer people in their courtroom.'

'I guess my wife having some sort of life-threatening illness is important,' Dave said dryly.

'I guess it is,' Spencer agreed. 'Do you think it's worth Kathy going to visit her and having a chat? She talked her around last time.'

'I'd like to say yes, but I think it's gone past that. And why should Mel have to be talked around? If she doesn't want to be with—' He broke off as he felt a bubble of hurt in his chest. He tried to breathe through it. How could their relationship have come to this? 'Anyway, I've got to try, don't I? She's about to have our second child and I know what it's like not to be a part of Bec's life, so I can't let that happen.'

'I'll be here to support you in whatever decision you make, mate.'

Dave opened his mouth to say something more about Mel but decided there really wasn't anything left to say. Instead he said, 'Speaking of *mates*, have you got any idea how much bloody Bob Holden gives me the shits? He keeps calling me "son" and, man, he can put away some piss.' All of Dave's pent-up rage came spilling out as he talked. Somehow, he knew it was all to do with Mel, but Bob was bearing the brunt of his anger now.

'What's wrong with calling you "son"?' Spencer asked.

'It's the connotation, isn't it? Little boy, who doesn't know much. Hang with me and I'll teach you. For fuck's sake. I didn't come down in the last shower.'

'Dave, mate, calm down! It's a nickname. An affectionate nickname in our business is something you earn—you know that. The little bit I do know about Bob is that if he's calling you that it's because he likes you. Maybe he sees something special in you. A protégé.' He paused. 'I reckon you could be blowing all that out of proportion, you know. Probably because of what's going on in your personal life.'

'No, I'm not,' Dave snapped. 'Bob's really bloody annoying. I had words with him about it when we were camped out one night. He just kept coming and coming with that stupid word. The more he drank, the more it came out. And—' Dave paused for effect '—I can't believe how he can function the next morning with all the beer he drinks. One night he was drinking whiskey and he was *still* up before me. Although,' Dave conceded, 'there was also one morning he was in a filthy mood 'cause he had a hangover. He'd been drinking rocket fuel, so I'm not surprised he had the mother of all hangovers. Trouble was, he took it out on the bloke at Spinifex Downs when we went to interview him. He's fucked to be around when he's like that.'

Dave could feel his heart hammering in his chest as he tried to get all his feelings out.

'Let me tell you a little story about Bob,' Spencer finally said. 'You of all people know that we don't always have the full story about people. I bet the stock squad think you've got your shit together. You've single-handedly broken up a cattle-stealing operation. You've been shot and come back, and you've worked your way up to the job you've always wanted. You've got a wife and child, with another baby on the way. From the outside, it looks like you've got it all and everything is rosy, doesn't it?'

Dave went to say something, but Spencer kept talking.

'But you and I know that's not the case. So do you reckon it could be the same with Bob? Yeah, he drinks a little too much, but is there a reason for it?'

'Well, yeah, I—'

Spencer interrupted. 'Have you ever noticed his hands?'

Dave blinked. 'What? What about them?' As he spoke a picture of Bob's left hand holding a beer surfaced: pink, scarred tissue snaked across the top of his hand, devoid of any hair.

'They've got scars on them. Burn scars. It's why he wears long sleeves all the time. You know how he got them?'

The sinking feeling that he had made a huge mistake started in Dave's stomach. 'How?'

'When he was a young copper, we were working out of the same station, like I told you. One night, Bob and his partner tried to pull over some little pain in the arse for running a red light. Now this arsehole decided he didn't want to stop for the law, so he put his foot down and took off. What do you reckon Bob did?'

'Chased after him.' Dave's stomach churned. He thought he might know where this story was headed. To a nightmare.

'That's right. The pursuit was legit, they'd radioed in and done all the right things.' Spencer stopped talking.

'What happened?'

'The arsehole who ran the red light ploughed into a family of four. He was killed, and so was the father and one of the children. Bob pulled the mother and the other child out of the burning car. See, now in our eyes he's a hero because he's saved two lives. In his eyes, he's a murderer because it was his decision to chase the car.'

The word 'murderer' hung in the air between them.

Dave dropped his head into his hands and closed his eyes. What a freaking judgemental prick he was.

'I wonder how *you'd* go, thinking you were a murderer of innocents?' Spencer continued softly. 'The booze is how he manages. There are plenty of functioning alcoholics out there. Bob may or may not be one, and I guess if he is the grog will get him in the long run, but he's a damn good detective. He just has a few ghosts in his past that need chasing away at times.' Another long silence. 'And, mate,' Spencer finally said, 'I'm pretty sure you would want your colleagues to look after you, inside the fold, if you'd turned that way after you'd been shot.'

Dave couldn't imagine his life without all his colleagues; they weren't just workmates, they were family. 'Yeah, well, I fucked that up, didn't I?'

'Don't reckon. Bob is a good bloke and I'm sure you already know that. Just all this other shit has got you mixed up. And rightly so. There's a lot riding on your shoulders.'

'Yeah. Look, Spencer, I've got to go. I'll ring you later, okay?'

'Always here, mate. You know that.'

Dave put down the phone and went to get changed into his running gear. He had to move to get rid of what he was feeling: anger, frustration. Defeat. Like he was on a runaway train and unable to get off.

Walking briskly out to the footpath, he did a couple of stretches then took off, not knowing where he was going, just that he needed to clear his head. There were too many thoughts rushing around.

He heard Bob. *Boy, you need to go and wash your mouth out. You've got no idea what I've lived and you couldn't even imagine.*

He was right. How did you live with yourself when you had two people's deaths on your conscience? Rightly or wrongly, a person couldn't not feel responsible in that situation. Dave knew *he* would. How could he judge Bob?

More images of Bob's hands came to him: on the steering wheel, holding a pen, a phone. Every time Bob looked at his hands and the damage that had been done, he would remember. Bob would never be able to lose sight of the fact that two people had died as a result of a decision he had made.

'Shit,' he muttered as he jogged through the pale light of the streetlamp. 'Shit, shit, shit.' He felt like punching something, but instead he started to run faster.

The shooting and recovery had left him out of shape and it didn't take long for his lungs to burn, but he kept going. If he kept pounding the pavement, surely all this confusion would dissipate.

Baby, Mel, Bec, job. With each footstep he said one of those words in his mind. *Baby, Mel, Bec, job.* His legs kept pumping and he ran on, concentrating only on the words, the streetlamps lighting the way.

Mark's words echoed around too: *We thought you'd be too busy with work.*

Was that really what his family thought about him? That he put everything else before them? A sense of shame rushed through him. Surely not. He loved them all. Well, except for Mark. Mark could go fuck himself. Mel, Bec and the new baby—they were his world.

But so was the job.

Letting out a groan, he slowed to a walk, trying to drag oxygen into his lungs, then stopped and bent over, his hand on his hips.

The feeling of needing to punch someone hadn't gone. He turned to a tree on the footpath and shadow-boxed at it. Right, left, right. Jab! Right, left, right. Jab! He kept going until he couldn't anymore, then he turned his back on the tree and leaned against its rough bark.

The choice was impossible.

Did he even have to make a choice?

And, if he did, what the hell was the right one?

Chapter 18

Carrying her bag out to the car, Dave walked alongside Mel, his gait matching her slow waddle. He'd spent as much time at the hospital as he could. Not that there had been a lot of conversation while he'd been there. Mel had had her head stuck in a book and he'd read the *Farm Weekly,* or handwritten reports for Bob on the time they'd spent in the north. At least he'd been in the same room as her.

At night he'd gritted his teeth and knocked on Mark's door so he could see his daughter. He'd eaten tea with them and then put Bec to bed, before heading back to the hospital to see Mel.

Surely they'd all see now he was committed to his family.

At the office he'd followed up with phone calls to Kevin and Kit. He'd spoken with Glenn, who had told him there was nothing new happening in and around the Boogarin Shire. He'd visited the saleyards again and had not found anyone who knew anything about the cattle missing from Spinifex Downs, or seen anything amiss.

More importantly, he'd apologised to Bob for losing his rag once again. Their conversation had made Dave feel better.

'Gotta say I'm sorry for the stuff I said up north,' Dave had said. 'I understand a little better after talking to Spencer.'

Bob had clapped him on the shoulder. 'It's all good, son,' he'd said. 'And your situation isn't that easy either, I know. It's a bastard of a barrow to push, but you'll get to the top of the hill in time.'

Dave had turned away, still wanting to roll his eyes. Freaking clichés.

However, with that apology the strong sense of family he'd always felt within the police force had returned. He didn't feel on the outer or not part of the team. And the stock squad closed in around him as he left early and came in late. They answered his phone and checked his emails, knowing he had to be at the hospital. Their loyalty brought home to him why they looked away when Bob was having another beer.

That was one of the things he loved about being a copper, the close-knit family they became when they joined. And Dave had been looking for that since his father had kicked him off the farm. The coppers were his family now. And Mel and Bec, and soon the new baby.

'I'll get the door,' Dave said to Mel as he put her bag in the back of the car. He held the door open as she heaved herself inside.

'I'm really over this,' she said, putting her hand to her stomach and rubbing it gently. 'Anytime you want to arrive, little one, I'm more than happy.'

'I know, honey,' he said as he got into the driver's seat and started the car. 'Only another two weeks to go. And like the doc said, bub might come early after everything you've been through. If we're looking for a little ray of sunshine, that's it, don't you think?'

'Maybe.'

Dave drove towards his in-laws' house, trying to pat down the ever-present anger he felt when he was going to see Mark. The man was becoming intolerable and Dave was astounded that Ellen could live with him.

Yesterday, at the hospital, Mark had strode into the ward while Dave was there.

'When are you going to be discharged, Melinda?' Mark had asked. 'Has the doctor told you yet?'

'No, he's not going to make a decision until we know if Dave can get leave. He doesn't want me going home to an empty house.' As she'd said the words, Mel had looked at Dave pointedly.

'I spoke to Bob about holidays yesterday—' Dave started, but Mark interrupted.

'If he can't care for you, we will,' he said. 'You know that. If you want to get discharged, do it now and I'll take you home. If you're out of danger, you need to come home.'

'If you'd let me finish,' Dave said, standing up, 'I'm trying to get some leave. Trouble is I'm in a new job and

I don't have a lot up my sleeve—especially since I had all that other time off.'

Mel turned to Dave. 'Then I'm going to have to go to Mum and Dad's.'

'We don't even know if you're allowed to go yet!'

'I know, but if the doctor knows I'm going to be looked after, I'm sure he'll discharge me. They could use the bed for someone else then.'

Dave knew that he couldn't argue, and he couldn't put into words how much he hated the smug look on Mark's face.

Now, pulling up in the driveway, he turned in his seat and looked at Mel. 'I have to go back to work this afternoon because I have a phone hook-up with the Department of Public Prosecution.'

Mel turned to him, anger on her face, but he held up his hand.

'It's not what you think. I'm trying to get an adjournment of the trial until after the baby is born and you're back on your feet. I don't know how successful I'll be but I'm going to try.'

Dave watched her face soften and her mouth turn up into a smile. 'That's good news,' she said.

'Don't get your hopes up, though, sweetie. But I will try. If that doesn't work, then I'll ask for a video link-up.'

'I'd feel so much better knowing you weren't in Queensland,' Mel said, shifting uncomfortably in her seat. 'If you go there, those people might try and kill you again.'

'You do understand that my identity has been suppressed, don't you?' Dave asked. 'It's not like they know who I am, or where I'm from.'

'But they might have more contacts within the police department who can tell them.'

Dave took her hand. 'They're not going to find me. There were no records of me on the police database when I was undercover. Everything in the computer system was hidden. The only two people who knew who I was while I was in Nundrew were Spencer and Justin. You don't have to be concerned about another dirty cop passing on my information because it's not there.' He was losing patience with the 'someone might murder you' attitude that Mel was adopting. Did she think the police department was incompetent?

'Hiding your identity isn't enough, Dave,' Mel said. 'I'm scared of losing you. I need to know that you're safe, and staying here is the only way.'

They looked up as Mark came out onto the front steps of the house and stood waiting. Dave felt the familiar urge to punch his father-in-law but instead he took Melinda's face in his hands and kissed her, long and hard.

'I will be safe,' he promised her.

❧

'Can you tell me why you need an adjournment?' Hal McCure asked as he leaned towards the computer and looked at Dave.

The video call had been set up in a small room off the main office of the stock squad and Dave could hear Lorri talking to Perry outside.

'The stress of this case, concerns about my safety in particular, has caused my pregnant wife to have some medical issues that are putting her and our unborn child at risk,' Dave answered, his hands clenched into fists on his knees. 'I need to be here with her.'

'Where is she now?'

'At her parents' place.'

'But she's been in hospital?'

'Yes. She was discharged this morning.'

Hal wrote something on a legal pad and moved his head from side to side. He looked like he was thinking hard.

'Pretty difficult to get these cases moved, Dave, to be honest with you. This date's been set for four months and the defence is against adjourning it.'

'Have you asked them already?'

Hal shook his head. 'No, but I've heard rumblings that Reeve Perkins is chafing at the bit to get at you.'

Dave shrugged. 'Let him chafe.'

'Like I said, it's not that easy. And to be perfectly honest, you would have had more chance of getting the date shifted if she hadn't been discharged. To let her leave the hospital, well, the doctors must not believe there is a risk to either your wife or your unborn child. They wouldn't have let her out otherwise. No, Dave,' he shifted in his chair, 'I think this will be hard to get changed. Where did you say she was right now?'

'At her parents' house.'

'Yeah, see, again, there are people who can look after her, which frees you up.'

'I think you can understand that Mel would rather it was me who was doing the caring.'

'Yes, of course. However, you can't forget your duty to the state.'

Dave patted his hands on his thighs nervously. He had to get this changed somehow. 'Okay, if we can't get an adjournment, can you try for a video link?' he asked, desperation beginning to flood through him. He'd been sure that the DPP would understand the situation he was in and try to shift the trial to another time.

'I can try for both. However, I'm telling you it will be difficult. I'll advise the defence of our intention to change but it won't be up to either them or me, as you know. It will end up in front of the judge and he'll make the decision.' The lawyer put his glasses on top of his head and rubbed his eyes while he spoke. 'You'll just have to hope that he's feeling nice and generous on the day I see him. Now, while I have you, let's proof your evidence.' Hal flicked over a few pages on the pad in front of him and picked up his pen again. 'I need you to summarise your undercover job, please.'

'Right.' Dave took a moment to gather his thoughts then started. 'I was asked to infiltrate a contract mustering business called the Highwaymen, as it was alleged they were stealing cattle. The Highwaymen were a professional mustering team, one of the few around the north of Queensland, so they were a legitimate business, but with a side operation running.

'As you know we need to prove things to be able to charge, so we had to catch them in the act. Or hear a confession. I was in charge of getting an admission from them. As it turned out, I not only got a confession but I was involved in an illegal muster. I was there on the ground when they trucked stolen cattle from the station they were mustering to their holding station in the Northern Territory.'

'Can you tell me in your own words what happened the night you were shot?'

Rubbing his face, Dave closed his eyes and saw a flash of light against a dark sky and heard the dogs barking. He felt the damp earth as he crawled through the trees in desperate search of the river so he could escape, then there was nothing but heat in his arm.

'Dave?'

'Ah, sorry. Yeah. I arrived at the depot with a bottle of whiskey. Senior Sergeant Parker had asked me to try and extract more information from the person of interest, Bulldust, who was also known as Ashley Bennett. I had hoped I might be able to get him to talk if we had a few drinks.'

Hal held up his hand and continued to make notes on his pad.

Dave stopped and took a drink of water, waiting for Hal to indicate he could start again.

'Did you see anyone else at the depot when you arrived?' Hal asked.

'I did not. What I did see was a set of linked cable ties on the kitchen table. I knew I had to get out of there fast.'

'Why was that?'

'Cable ties had been used to restrain a murder victim linked to Ashley Bennett and Scott Wilcox. I assumed my cover had been blown and they were looking for me. Their intention wasn't to let me leave alive.'

Hal indicated for him to keep talking.

'By the time I had made the connection, both men were in the kitchen—'

'What men?'

'Sorry,' Dave said. 'Ashley Bennett and Scotty Wilcox. Actually, I need to amend that. By the time I made the connection, both men were in the doorway leading into the kitchen. I saw Ashley first, then when Scotty stepped out from behind him I knew I was in trouble. I had been told earlier that Scotty was Bulldust's enforcer. The one who took care of business.'

'What sort of business?'

'Anything that needed taking care of—whether it was to kill someone to keep them quiet, or to shift cattle on quickly because there was a threat. But when Larry Jones told me this, he was meaning more along the lines of murder.'

'And who is Larry Jones?'

'The truck driver for the Highwaymen mustering operation.'

'I see. One final question for now, Dave. How did you realise that First Class Constable Joe Ross was working for Ashley and Scott?'

'When I was being chased I saw a police car. I flagged him down and got into the car. Joe Ross was the driver and he immediately locked the doors so I couldn't get out.

'I asked him to take me to a police station. He said he would take me "where there is judge and jury" and then he drove back towards the depot. Didn't take Einstein to work out who he was going to take me to.'

Hal wagged his finger. 'Do not say that in court. That's an assumption. Stick to the facts. He talked about judge and jury and what else?'

Dave could hear Joe's mocking tone as he said to him, 'Not talking? Cat got your tongue?' Dave focused on the question and pretended he was in court.

'Ah, he asked who I really was, because he didn't think I was who I said. At that point he drove straight by the police station and kept going.'

'Right. Good. I'll prep you a little closer to the time. Now, you would have heard we're charging First Class Constable Joe Ross with conspiracy, corruption and attempted murder.'

'Attempted murder? Why? He wasn't even there when I was shot.'

'He's party to the offence because he tried to take you back to Ashley and Scott.'

Dave frowned. 'Geez, counsellor, I reckon you're drawing a pretty long bow there.'

'Maybe a charge that carries a minimum of fifteen years imprisonment here in Queensland will help convince him he needs to roll over on Ashley and Scott. We're aiming to offer a plea deal to drop that charge if he helps us. Anyway,' he looked at the gold watch on his wrist, 'I have another appointment. As soon as I know about the adjournment, I will get back to you.'

Dave thanked him and pressed the disconnect button, before letting out a long breath. He took out his phone and sent a text message to Mel: *Think I've got it sorted,* even though he wasn't feeling confident.

Chapter 19

Kevin pushed the answering machine button and heard a deep gravelly voice on the line. *'Kev, Detective Bob Holden here. Letting you know we've put alerts out on your cattle, like I said we would. Haven't had any bites yet. Dave's been to the saleyards a couple of times but there's been no sign. Give me a call when you come back in. Cheers.'*

Picking up the phone, he dialled the number that Bob had left for him and waited for him to answer. He'd been hoping that it would be Dave who called, but he couldn't be picky when it came to which detective he dealt with. His dad thought this detective was a good bloke, so he would have to trust his dad's instincts on this, even though he didn't want to.

'Burrows.'

'G'day, Kevin from Spinifex Downs here,' he said, pleased it was Dave who'd answered the phone. He'd liked Dave when they'd driven around and was sure he was going to be a good support. Plus he'd noticed the gleam in Dave's eye which had said that he wasn't the type to give up.

Kevin sat down at his desk and got out his diary to record the phone call's details.

'G'day, mate. How are things up your way?'

'Not too bad. Nothing else has happened, which is a bonus. Well, not that I know about!'

A screech of laughter reached him, and he turned back to the window and saw four children in bathers diving into the waterhole. Even with the warmth outside, he knew the crystal-clear water would be freezing—it was deep, so deep the sun wouldn't penetrate enough to heat it.

Better them than me, he thought.

'That's always good,' Dave said. 'Glad to hear it. Although I don't have any news for you, I'm afraid. The alerts we put on the cattle, through the abattoirs and trucking companies, nothing has come of them. Fellas at the saleyards don't know anything either. We'll keep our eyes and ears to the ground, obviously, but right now there's not much more we can do. Unfortunately this is a wait-and-see game.'

Kevin blew out a heavy sigh. 'Pain in the arse. They were good breeding stock.'

'Insured?'

'Yeah, which is helpful in getting replacements, but it's going to be hard to replicate the genetics and, of course, it puts me twelve months behind.'

'What about the other cattle you said you were missing over the last few years? Were they breeders as well?'

'Nah. I had about four hundred bullock calves taken last year; that's just less than half a triple road train. I've had bulls that I haven't been able to find too, but I've put that down to just not being able to find them when we've been mustering.' He shrugged. 'You don't always find every beast when you muster. Some of the bulls, they get street-wise and canny. They know how to beat the choppers and bikes. Scrubbers.'

'Four hundred?' Dave was incredulous. 'And you didn't report them?'

'At first, when I realised what was going on, the numbers weren't as big. I didn't understand what was happening. Just thought they'd wandered off and died. You know, bitten by snakes or something. Cattle are curious and seem to love to sniff things and they often get bitten on the nose. That's what I thought when it came to the bulls. But then I talked to the old men and they said someone had probably taken them. Like they were used to hearing about this kind of thing.

'The second lot, yeah, I knew something was amiss then. But even then the Elders said not to report the thefts. They didn't think the law would be applicable to us.'

'Fuck.'

Kevin watched the kids swimming, thinking how ridiculous it was he hadn't reported the cattle thefts. He wondered if it made him look suspicious.

Dave broke the silence between them. 'If I didn't know better, I'd almost say you've been targeted.'

'Yeah.'

'Anyway, Kev, leave it with us. Trust us—we will do the best we can.

'Cheers, mate,' he said and hung up the phone.

The smell of old smoke was drifting in and Kevin went outside and stood on the verandah to see if there were any fires still alight. The day before, some of the Elders had taken the young boys out into the scrub and started to burn some spinifex and bush. Getting rid of the grasses made the goanna holes easier to see, and they would've been hunting them today. Maybe there would be goanna cooking on the fire tonight.

He looked around the community he had started to clean up. The eight transportable houses were perched back from the creek. The junk that had surrounded them when he'd first arrived home was now cleaned up and all the front yards were tidy. There weren't any gardens, but every morning the women raked a brush broom over the soil, leaving it free of footprints and leaves.

The children were clean and tidy and loved learning in the schoolroom the government had provided, and Hayley, the teacher, was loved by everyone.

Kevin nodded contently. Yeah, he'd made a difference, but he still had some more things to fix. He would find out, with the police's help, who was taking his cattle.

Stepping down off the verandah, he walked over to the waterhole and stood beside Hayley. 'All good?'

'Oh, hi, Kev. Yep, everything's fine. Look at little Yarran there.' She pointed to a boy who was swimming underwater.

'There's no way you'd think he'd grown up in the desert. He can swim like a fish!'

'He's the one we'll have to send out when they go fishing then,' Kevin said with a grin.

'Hey, Kev!' A little girl with a mop of wild curls ran by, chasing her sister. Her smile was wide when she saw him.

'Hi, Yindi. What are you up to?'

'Running!'

He laughed. 'Yep, it looks like you are.' He walked further into camp and stopped to talk to a couple of the women before seeing Jackie and two other Elders sitting at the campfire underneath the white bark river gums. It looked like they had been there for a while.

The lyrical words of his native language reached him. He was fluent in his own language, but he hadn't had much use for it while he was down south. It made him feel safe and comfortable when he heard it now, and he loved listening to it. Hearing the old men speak kept his ear in and he found himself repeating what they were saying in his mind. Repeating the inflections and words.

He sat himself down next to Jackie and watched as his father scraped a flat stone over the edge of a boomerang to smooth it out as he talked to the other men. They were sitting cross-legged, the fire reflecting in their eyes, and they turned to nod at him as he joined them.

They radiated peace when they sat like this: still, their hands on their knees.

'How are you, boy?' one of the men asked in English.

'Good,' Kevin answered.

'The cattle good too?'

'Yep. When're the rains coming this year?'

'Long time to go yet.'

Kevin reached out and took a pannikin which was sitting on the ground with two tea bags in it; a billy was boiling on the coals. He poured himself a cup, then shook in some sugar from a tin and stirred it with a stick.

'I had a message from that detective down south,' he said.

The men didn't answer him, but he could tell they were listening. The wind picked up and tossed the leaves of the trees about, and a small amount of raised dust blew across the creek. In that moment of breeze, the flies were finally still.

'Nothing to report, by the sounds of it.'

'Won't be,' said the first old man.

'They're gone,' the second Elder said simply. 'Long gone.' He nodded as he talked.

Jackie was quiet as he continued to work on the boomerang.

Taking a sip of the tea, Kevin placed his fingers in the dirt, before swirling them around. 'What do you mean, long gone?'

'Just that. They're gone and won't get found. Just like the others,' Jackie finally spoke.

'We didn't report the others.'

'Not what I meant,' Jackie said.

'The detectives are looking for them though. They've got alerts out.'

'Don't push too hard, boy,' Jackie said, looking up.

'What?'

'Just what I said. Don't push. Bad things might happen.'

A dog of many different breeds wandered up to the fire and sat down next to Kevin. He reached out to stroke its head, anxiety rising in his stomach.

'I don't know what you're telling me,' he said.

'In early times there was trouble between the white-fellas and the community. Our people used to disappear. Police always said that they've gone walkabout.' He leaned over to Kevin and spoke very clearly. 'But they never came back. Them disappearing? It was never "just walkabout". The cattle would disappear and so would our people. I'm worried that might happen to you.'

'Come on, Dad, you know people walk off all the time.' Kevin glanced at the other two old men, but they weren't looking at him. They had gone quiet and were looking at the ground.

'You haven't seen it.'

Kevin frowned, frustrated now. 'You're not telling me anything I can understand. If you've got something to say, tell me so I can do something about it.'

'You don't know what I've seen. What we've all seen.' Jackie indicated in a wide arc to the other Elders. 'When I was a boy, things used to happen. I don't want to think about that. We don't want to talk about that. But you need to know that the white law isn't going to take our side.'

'They will. They're good men, you said so yourself.'

'You're not listening, boy. I'm telling you. I saw things when I was young that I'm not going to talk about because of bad spirits. I'm *not* talking about it. I don't want that to happen to you. You're good here. Doing good things. The coppers won't help.'

'You know it's not like that now. Those fellas are here for us. If they can find the cattle, they will. I thought you liked the sergeant.'

'Yeah. Yeah, I like the sergeant. I could see in his eyes he spoke the truth. That don't mean the law will take our side.'

Kevin turned to look at his dad. 'Are you saying that whitefellas took our people away and killed them?'

'Boy, I'm not talking about it. You just need to know that bad things happened in the past. Same thing might happen to you.'

'How do you know our people just didn't take off out into the bush or get bitten by a snake?' He was grasping at other possibilities because what he was hearing was too frightening if it was true.

'Don't be stupid. The old people knew the bush. That's not gonna happen to them.'

The two other old men stood up quietly and walked away.

'Where are they going?' Kevin asked, trying to understand his father's riddled talk.

'They don't want to be here while I'm talkin' about this. I'm not telling you what happened back when I was a boy, 'cause we can't talk about it. Bad spirits. But you need to watch yourself.'

Another gentle gust of wind and Kevin looked up at the trees, the leaves dancing with the invisible force, and he wondered what his father could have seen to make him frightened to report cattle theft to the police and to distrust the law so much.

Chapter 20

Reeve Perkins slammed down the phone in annoyance then snatched it straight back up again. He didn't want to make the next phone call, but it would be better to get it done straight away rather than waiting.

'Bulldust. Reeve,' he said when the call was answered.

'Yeah? What do you want?'

'We've got some trouble. I've just had the DPP Hal McCure on the phone. Seems they're looking for an adjournment.'

'What the fuck for?' Bulldust snarled.

'Witness X has a personal emergency and he's not wanting to leave where he is.'

'I don't give a fuck whether he's got an emergency or not. Just get him here.'

'It's not as easy as that,' Reeve explained hurriedly. 'This request goes to the judge. If he agrees, I can't stop it. Sounds like he's interstate somewhere, because if he can't get an adjournment, then he wants to give evidence by video link.'

'That don't mean anything, does it? He could be in the next room but still on video.'

Reeve doodled on the paper in front of him. 'Yes, good point,' he agreed.

'What's this personal emergency?'

'The story is that his wife is sick. Whether it's true or not, who knows. He might be trying to avoid coming back here. I can ask for evidence that she's unwell, which will hold things up a little.'

'Have you found out who he is yet?'

'No. Nothing there. I have an investigator on it. All he's been able to find out is that the bloke is definitely police.'

'How'd you find that out?'

'I'm not privy to how they investigate, but that fact was mentioned in the last conversation I had with the PI. Anyway, we already knew he was; just hadn't had it confirmed.'

'Yeah, I guess you're right there.' Bulldust paused. 'How come you can't find out his name then?'

Reeve swallowed and said, 'Everything to do with this guy has been suppressed. The judge ordered that when Joe Ross was first charged and went before the court. It can't be reversed unless we have good reason to ask for it.'

Bulldust chuckled. 'We do have good reason.'

'Not one that's going to work for the judge, I'm guessing. And whatever your reason is, as your lawyer, I don't want to know.'

'Yeah, probably a good idea. Don't agree to the adjournment. Do everything in your power to make sure it doesn't happen. I want that fucker in Brisbane.'

'Right.' Reeve put down the phone and stared at the blank notepad in front of him. He'd never thought he'd end up taking dirty money and defending a lawless man. But Bulldust owned him, as he assumed all the people around the man were owned. One day when all of this was over, he'd ask some of the others—he knew who they were, because he'd defended them.

Larry Jones had driven the truck for Bulldust and was part of the Highwaymen musters. Now he was in jail at the Brisbane Correctional Centre, as was Chris Mooney who flew the chopper during the illegal musters, and George Dellaney, who had been the general dogsbody.

All of their cases had been simple. They'd pleaded guilty and gone to jail. Bulldust didn't want them anywhere else, because he knew they wouldn't roll over on him.

Defending First Class Constable Joe Ross was a whole different story. He was a dirty copper who knew the system and knew how to make deals with the DPP. Somehow, Reeve had to keep him protected from that and loyal to Bulldust.

How Reeve wished he'd never gone to Nundrew on holidays—what a ridiculous place to decide to ride his motorbike. He hadn't gone there by himself; he'd been with two other blokes who rode bikes as well. And the decision to go to Nundrew had been his mate's.

He also wished he'd never come across Shane, Bulldust's daughter.

Embarrassment flooded through him as he remembered how Shane had danced close that night in the pub. She'd even rubbed her groin against his. The thought of having her in his bed had driven him wild. It hadn't been long before they were tumbling out into the night, towards his hotel room.

His mates had turned a blind eye to the fact he was married with three young kids. They'd all done things they'd never tell anyone about while on these sorts of trips. The old rule. Boys Only. What happened on Boys Only, stayed on Boys Only.

Bulldust, however, hadn't been too happy to find his daughter straying. He'd gone to work and found out who Reeve was. Two days later, as he refuelled his bike at the local servo, Bulldust had pulled up next to him and leaned out the window.

'Reckon you might be the fella I'm looking for,' he'd said.

Reeve remembered looking over to see a large man with a bald head and long beard.

'Don't think so, buddy,' he'd replied. 'Don't know your face at all.'

'You're about to 'cause you slept with my daughter a couple of nights ago.' Bulldust had got out of the car and Reeve, a slight man, had seen how tall he was. And strong.

Trepidation had flooded through him, but he'd tried to act unconcerned. He'd hung up the fuel hose and turned to face the man. 'Free country. Didn't see her complaining.'

'No,' Bulldust had agreed. He'd leaned forwards and leered in Reeve's face. 'But Sal, your wife, might. Oh, yeah,

Reeve Austin Perkins, I know all about you. Graduated from Western Sydney University fifth in your law class. Worked at Bentley and Co for the first three years of your career, then moved out to start your own business, which isn't doing that well, is it? But don't worry. I'll probably be able to help you with that.

'Married Sally Jane Frank in October twelve years ago and have three beautiful girls aged six, eight and ten. The model family. Surely, as a father, you must understand how unhappy I am you thought you needed to have relations with my daughter. A man like you. A failure. I'd want so much more for my daughter.'

Reeve's eyes had widened as Bulldust continued to talk. He knew everything! How?

'Here's my offer to you. One, you stay the fuck away from my daughter. Two, I'm going to become a silent partner in your business. You'll find two hundred k in your business bank account already and you—' he looked hard at Reeve '—are going to work for me when I need you.'

Something in Reeve had made him want to fight back. He wasn't going to take this lying down. He was a lawyer! He knew the penalty for blackmail was fifteen years. 'And what if I don't?' he'd sneered with a confidence he hadn't felt.

'Then I guess poor little Sal is about to have her world turned upside down when these arrive in her mailbox.' He'd handed Reeve an envelope, and Reeve had known straightaway what was inside. 'Imagine what the girls will think of their daddy when they come home from school and Mummy has these strewn all across the kitchen table.'

Reeve had paled as he'd realised he was caught. There was nothing he could do now. Not if he wanted life to continue on the way it always had. He'd made his bed and there he would have to stay.

Bulldust had obviously sensed he'd won and had climbed back into his car. He'd given Reeve a wink. 'Guessing by the look on your face, we've got an understanding. I'll be in touch.'

That had been five years ago. He'd only ever needed to help Bulldust out once and that had been a small piece of legal advice on the sale of a property. Easy stuff. Nothing to do with blackmail or anything illegal.

In fact, until six months ago, Reeve had been able to almost forget that Bulldust even existed. Until the phone call. Four of his employees had been picked up by the cops and one was a dirty copper.

And that was the end of the forgetting.

∿

Four days later, he was in front of the judge with the DPP, Hal McCure, standing alongside him.

'Your Honour, we are opposed to the adjournment. This date has been set for many months and to change it now will impact not only on my client, who has a right, when found innocent, to be back with his family as soon as possible, but also on the lawyers. This isn't the only case I have. My calendar is full for the rest of the year,' Reeve said, clasping his hands together as if begging.

'And you, Mr McCure,' the judge said, his eyes shifting to the next lawyer, 'what is your reasoning behind the request?'

'Your Honour, Witness X's wife is seriously ill and pregnant with her second child. We are asking that he is able to remain until the child is born and his wife is well again.'

Reeve spread out his hands as if to say, 'Really?' 'I object, Your Honour.'

The judge adjusted his glasses and glared at him. 'You've already stated that.' He paused. 'Mr McCure,' the judge turned to the tall man standing in front of the bench, 'I take it that the wife is in hospital.'

'No, she's been discharged, sir.'

'She has no one else to care for her?'

'Witness X is caring for her now,' he said.

'That doesn't answer my question. Is there no one else to care for her? No family? Friends?'

Reeve felt his heart kick up a notch. Maybe the judge liked his argument. Maybe, just maybe. He needed to make sure that the judge didn't let the adjournment happen. He wasn't sure what Bulldust would do to him if he didn't prevent the delay.

'She's with her parents.' Hal looked down at the paperwork in his hands and frowned.

'If she is with her parents, Mr McCure, why are we here?' the judge asked, looking over his glasses.

Reeve saw his opportunity. 'Your Honour, while I understand the concerns of the witness for his wife—and no one should have to leave an ill family member—the fact is his wife is in the care of her *family*. Therefore, he is not the sole carer. Surely she should be able to stay where she is while Witness X is here. I will endeavour to have him in front of the court for as little time as possible. And under the circumstances, Mr McCure would do the same, I am sure.'

'I have to agree with you, Mr Perkins.'

'And what about the protection of the witness?' Mr McCure broke in. 'Let's not forget that Witness X was shot. We need to be aware that there are two other exceptionally dangerous criminals still at large. They may well be plotting to try and disable my client, sir.'

The judge looked down and appeared to be reading something. 'Yes, two of the main suspects haven't been sighted since that night,' he said, half to himself.

'Your Honour, if I may, if that is the main reason that the witness doesn't want to attend the trial in person, then surely the city police are able to supply some kind of protection,' Reeve appealed.

McCure rounded on him. 'I don't think you've been listening, counsellor! My client has a wife with an illness who is about to give birth. Does your wife have children? Would you have wanted to miss the birth?'

'Enough!' The judge looked up and frowned at both the men. 'I appreciate Witness X's circumstances, Mr McCure, but I need to allow the court to have the best evidence and I prefer people here in my courtroom. The city will offer protection to Witness X. Let's not forget that an officer of the law is on trial here. This is an important case. Motion denied.'

'Sir, could I draw your attention to the other option of a video link-up?' Mr McCure hurried to say before the gavel had fallen.

Reeve quickly responded. 'In fairness to my client, I need to speak to this, ah, Witness X face to face. Mr McCure here brought the charges against my client and I believe I have the right to pressure test this evidence at the highest level, which is, as I'm sure you'll agree, face to face.' Reeve hoped his argument would stand up. He had to make sure this man turned up and his face could be seen and his identity discovered.

'Again, denied, Mr McCure. Witness X will be here to give evidence in two days' time.'

Reeve wanted to punch the air with excitement, but he had to keep focused. 'Just one more thing, Your Honour.'

'Yes?'

'In regard to the suppression order. At the moment Witness X is unknown to us. All we have is his deposition. We need to know who this gentleman is so we can prepare our case accordingly.'

'Your Honour,' Mr McCure just about shouted, 'you understand the sensitivity of this case. I ask you do not remove the suppression order. Have I not just mentioned the dangers of this case!'

'You're right, Mr McCure. There is a sensitivity to this case. The suppression order will stand.'

Without another word the gavel fell and the lawyers were dismissed.

Chapter 21

Dave couldn't believe what he was hearing. He looked down at the notepad in front of him and saw he'd written one word. *No.*

'And you can't change it?'

'No, Dave, I can't. The judge has ruled and once that's happened it's set in concrete. You need to be on that plane tomorrow and giving evidence in front of the court the next day. Get it organised.'

'Fuck.' Hanging up the phone, he ran his hands through his hair, then jumped up, agitated, and paced the room. He wanted to ring Spencer, but there would be nothing his friend could do. He would just have to be in Brisbane tomorrow. He grabbed his wallet from the desk and shoved it in his back pocket. He put his hands on the desk and leaned forwards, breathing deeply. How was he going to tell Mel?

Bob looked up from his office. 'What's up?'

'Judge denied the adjournment.'

Bob typed something then got up and came out into the room. 'When do you have to go?'

'Tomorrow.'

'Right. I'll take you to the plane.'

'It's not that part I'm worried about.'

Bob nodded. 'I know. You'd better go and get Melinda sorted. Let me know what time your flight is.'

'That's if I'm still alive then,' Dave muttered, grabbing his jacket from the back of his chair and heading out the door.

Outside, he decided to walk to Mark and Ellen's house. It was only about four kilometres away and he needed to clear his head. And to get his story straight. Not that there was anything kinked about it, but he had to somehow put a positive spin on what was going to happen.

'Damn it!' he said again. He shouldn't have promised. *You didn't promise,* he thought. *You just told her you thought you had it sorted.*

That argument wasn't going to stand up and he knew it.

The door opened before he could knock and Melinda stood in the doorway, her hair up, looking beautiful. Dave had to admit the rest was doing her good—the dark shadows under her eyes were fading and the tension had gone from her shoulders.

Maybe being away from me is helping her, he thought.

'God, you're a sight for sore eyes,' Dave said as he leaned down to kiss her. 'Why aren't you resting?'

'I have been. I got up to go to the loo—this baby just wants to sit on my bladder! Then I saw you walking up the drive. How come you've walked?' She stood back to let him come inside. 'And what are you doing here in the middle of the day?'

'Felt like the exercise. Where's Bec? And your parents?' he asked, ignoring the most important question.

'Mum's hanging some clothes on the line and Bec's helping her. Not sure where Dad is. Probably in his office watching the share prices.'

'Let's go into your room,' Dave said, putting his arm around her.

'Why?' She turned to look at him. 'There's something wrong, isn't there?'

He sighed and took her hand. He couldn't sugarcoat the news. 'I'm sorry, sweetie, the DPP rang a little while ago. The judge denied the adjournment. I have to go to Brisbane.'

Mel let out a gasp and her hands flew to her mouth. 'No,' she whispered.

'Yeah.'

'When?'

Dave waited a second before placing his hands on her cheeks and bending down to kiss her again. 'Tomorrow,' he said against her mouth.

Mel wrenched away from his grasp. 'They'll see you. They'll know who you are! Then they'll know who we are.' The frightened words ripped from her as she backed away from him, holding up her hands as if to ward him off.

'I promise they won't, Mel. The cops are picking me up and the DPP told me today I'd be staying at a safe house. I'll have protection all the time. The judge has ordered it.'

'But what if they get through? People like that could have a sniper rifle or something. They might be able to get at you like that. The police mightn't even see them and you could be dead!'

Mel's face was pale and she was breathing hard. Dave had to get her to calm down; he didn't want her to go into labour or faint.

'Here,' he took her hand again to lead her over to the couch. 'It'll be okay. I promise.' The repeated words were beginning to feel empty, but he had to keep reassuring her.

'You've said that before, but you can't be sure. How can you be?' Mel's voice was high and strained and her hands were over her stomach as if to protect the unborn child. 'Dave, you can't go, you just can't.'

'Sweetheart, I have to. I'm sorry. I don't have a choice in this. This court case is so much bigger than me.'

At those words Mel seemed to gather herself. She breathed deeply through her nose and glared at him. 'And you wonder why I say you love the job more than me.' Standing up, she walked to the window and looked out. 'What should I tell Bec when she's six and she's asking about her father? Well, honey, Daddy had to go to Brisbane to talk about some bad men who tried to kill him once. He had to go, said he didn't have a choice and while he was there the bad men who tried to hurt him before got to him and he came home in a casket.' She swung around. 'But don't worry, he was given a state funeral for his trouble. Or even worse, what if they track you back here and take Bec, or harm all of us?'

'Mel—'

'What's going on here?' Mark stood in the doorway.

'Dave's just telling me how he has to go to Brisbane tomorrow to give evidence. The judge denied the adjournment,' Mel said calmly.

'I see.' Mark shook his head. 'Still, I don't know why I'm surprised.' He stepped into the room and walked to Mel. Putting his arm around her, he said, 'We're here.'

'Can I ask you, please, to look after Mel while I'm away?' Dave asked, swallowing every amount of bitterness and anger he held towards the man. Maybe if he could get Mark onside, Mel would change her attitude.

Mark eyeballed him with dislike. 'Yes, I can look after your family since you're unable to. Or unwilling to. I won't let my family down.'

Biting back a sharp reply, Dave thanked him, although all he wanted to do was yell at the injustice of it all. 'I'll just say goodbye to Bec and be off. I've got to pack and get ready.' He didn't tell them he had a few jobs left to do at the office, or that he couldn't wait to get out of this house. It was better to say goodbye now and make it quick.

He went out to the clothesline where Bec was standing on an upside-down bucket helping Ellen by handing her the pegs.

'Hi, princess,' he said, picking her up and giving her a cuddle.

'Hello, Daddy! I'm helping Gran.'

'And it looks like you're doing a wonderful job.' He kissed her cheek. 'I have to go away for a few days, honey, so I'm not going to be coming around for dinner. But I'll be back really soon.'

'Where are you going?' she asked, looking at him.

'A place called Brisbane. It's a long way from here. I've got to catch a big plane to get there.'

'Like that one?' Bec pointed to a jet above them. 'I like watching them.'

'Yep, just like that one, princess.'

'Okay. Bye, Daddy,' Bec said, putting her chubby arms around his neck and squeezing.

He put her down and Ellen placed her hand on Bec's shoulder. 'Can you run inside and see Mummy for a sec, darling? I need to talk to your dad.'

They watched her go and Dave turned to Ellen. 'Thanks for having them here. Mel's pretty upset and I just want to let you know that I don't have a choice here. If I don't turn up, I'll be held in contempt of court and that can carry a jail term. I haven't told Mel that, but someone needs to know. I just want you to understand that I have to go. I *have* to.' His voice broke before he said, 'I didn't think it was worth adding fuel to the fire in there by saying that.'

'It's okay, Dave. I'm retired, as is Mark. I'm more than happy to have them both here. In fact, it's quite nice, after you all being such a way away over there in Barrabine.' She paused. 'But I do have something I want to say to you.'

Ellen reached down for another piece of washing and started to peg it out. 'Sometimes, when you marry a person, they're not that same person in thirty years' time. And sometimes you don't like who that person has become. Mark isn't the man I married, Dave. He's had a few kicks during life, which I think have made him put up walls and barriers, but when I first met him he was a charming, charismatic man. Now he's sullen and mean.' She picked up another piece of clothing and continued along the washing line.

'When you lived in Barrabine, it was easy for me to be swayed by what Mark was saying. You were working long hours, and Mel had followed you to a godforsaken little town that had no prospects for her. Or your children. You'd taken her away from us.

'Since you've moved back here, I can see that the assumption I made wasn't right. Instead, I see how great a dad you are to Bec and how good you are with Mel. How you look after them both so well. Which of course means you need to go away sometimes.' She stopped and looked over at him. 'Perhaps the problem isn't you, but my husband and my daughter. She's certainly stubborn when she gets set on something, which she has with your job.'

Surely he was being set up here. Ellen had never been so nice.

'That's good of you to say,' he stumbled over the words.

'Dave, I've given up a lot of myself for the wishes of my husband and daughter and it's only now I realise how much. Don't let that happen to you, because you are doing a great job in very difficult circumstances.' She patted his arm and turned back to the clothesline. The conversation was finished.

࿇

Bob pulled into the driveway as the sun rose over the roofs of the houses. A dew had settled on the lawn overnight, but the sky was a clear blue and, with the heat not far away, it wouldn't take long for the dew to dry.

'Not the same watching the sun rise in the city as it is in the bush,' he said when Dave had thrown his duffle bag in the back and settled in the passenger seat.

'Dead right there,' he agreed.

Bob glanced over at him. 'How'd you go last night, son?'

'Pretty rough.' Dave looked out the window, not wanting to talk about the way he'd left the house. Mel had been silent and cold, and Mark had smirked at him as he closed the door. He'd thought, as he walked down the paved driveway, looking at the lawn, manicured to within an inch of its life, that he was playing right into Mark's hands. He wanted his daughter to himself and Dave was handing her to him. Only because Mel was letting it happen!

He thought back to Spencer's words about changes that so many coppers had made and how they never quite satisfied the wives. Dave wondered if Mel was one of those women who couldn't be satisfied. If so, there really was only one choice. Not wanting to think about that anymore, he changed the subject. 'Anything interesting happen yesterday after I left?'

214

'Lorri charged two twenty-three year olds with growing the green stuff down on the Avon River.'

'Ah, she got them! Good on her, she'll be happy with that.'

'She had a bit of a grin on her face when she came in last night, for sure.'

'All through the video evidence?'

'Yep. Pretty hard to deny it was them when their sorry faces are looking straight down the lens of the surveillance camera. And she also got the numberplate of the motor vehicle they were in. The DPP have charged them already and their hearing is next week. Hope the magistrate doesn't give them bail.'

'You'll have to shout her a beer for me.'

Bob turned to look at him. 'You can do that yourself when you get back, son. You're not going anywhere for too long.'

Tapping his fingers on his knees, Dave nodded. 'I'm not worried. Bulldust and Scotty might be dangerous, but they're gutless when it comes to showing their faces to the law. They won't want to risk being caught. I just want the whole saga to be over and done with.'

'I get that. The stockies over there are good fellas. You know some of them. They'll have you covered.'

He swung the car into the airport drop-off and came to a stop. Dave got out and picked up his bag and looked at Bob over the roof of the vehicle.

'Good luck,' said Bob, holding out his hand. 'Stay safe and have a good flight.' He checked his watch. 'I'm off for a meeting with Dicko.'

Dave grinned, knowing that was code for a parmi and a beer. 'Cheers. Let me know if there're any developments with Kev and everything up north.'

'That'll still be here when you get back, son.'

'Gives me something else to think about, instead of worrying if Bulldust is out for my scalp.'

'You just said you weren't worried.'

Dave threw his bag over his shoulder, feeling his shoulder protest. 'Maybe a bit,' he said quietly.

Bob nodded. 'Sure, then, I'll call you if anything develops. Don't reckon too much will happen there for a while though. Wouldn't be clever to strike again when we've just been there.'

'Thanks, Bob.'

'No worries, son.'

Dave walked towards the terminal without caring that Bob had called him son, knowing he had a mate who had his back.

Chapter 22

Disembarking from the plane felt like déjà vu to Dave. He hoisted his duffle bag over his shoulder and started to disembark with the rest of the passengers. Someone bumped into his back and Dave turned to eyeball them.

A pretty blonde girl smiled at him. 'Sorry,' she said. 'Everyone is always in such a hurry to get off the plane, aren't they? So much pushing and shoving.'

'Yep, you're right there,' Dave said, looking around.

He'd been watching for familiar faces since he'd arrived at the Perth airport. Or people who might be following him. So far, so good.

While he'd been waiting to board, he hadn't stopped walking the terminal—he had been like a shark, moving all the time. Watching, waiting for prey, except this time he would be the prey. He knew if he kept moving, he'd pick up on a tail soon enough.

The ticket he'd been issued was in cattle class, but he had two empty seats next to him. He watched people, not bothering with the movies or music, settling back in his seat and scrutinising every face that walked up and down the aisle.

By the time they landed, he knew every face from economy class.

As he was herded off the plane by the tide of people around him, he spotted Senior Sergeant Justin Parker, his handler at Nundrew, standing in the arrivals lounge. Next to him were two blokes built like rugby players, both wearing stock squad uniforms.

A grin broke out on Justin's face when he saw Dave. 'It's good to see you, man,' he said, grabbing Dave's hand in a strong grip. 'Really good to see you. Especially looking as well as you do.' He gave Dave's chest a slap. 'Shoulda seen him when I last did,' he said to the two men standing next to him. 'He was broken, for sure! Dave, meet Detective Sergeants Josh Becker and Dane Hill. They're your protection for the next few days.'

'Good to meet you, fellas,' Dave said, shaking hands with them before pulling Justin into a manly bear hug. 'Good to see you too, mate.'

'Come this way,' Dane said, pointing to a door marked for airport staff only. 'We've got a car waiting down there.'

'What's the back entrance about?' Dave asked, following the three men and nodding at the airport cleaner who opened the door and let them through.

218

'Just a precaution,' Justin said as they clattered down echoey stairs. 'Because Bulldust and Scotty are still outstanding.'

Dave frowned as he saw the unmarked car with dark windows. 'You heard something I haven't?' he asked. 'They got a contract out on me?'

'Haven't heard that on the street and we've got eyes and ears out there. Nah, the judge ordered this, so don't get too alarmed by our friendliness! Just doing what we're paid to do.'

Josh took up the commentary. 'We've got you in a hotel on the outskirts of the city and we've put security measures in place there too.'

'Has there been any sighting of them at all since they shot through?'

'Not a whisker. It's like they've disappeared from the face of the Earth.'

'Where do you think they are?'

'My gut feeling,' Justin broke in, 'is that they've headed out deep into the bush. Holed up on a station where there's no one else around. Pretty easy to hide out there if you want to. We've been watching their bank accounts and there's no movement on them. My guess is they've had cash stashed somewhere, or money in accounts we haven't managed to trace yet.'

Dave looked out the window and saw they were going to take the Story Bridge over the Brisbane River.

'What about Bulldust's daughter?' Dave asked.

'We kept an eye on her for a while, thinking Bulldust might get in contact, but there was nothing there either.' Justin looked over his shoulder at Dave. 'She's starting to make a new life in Sydney. Got a unit and made some friends. Took her a while to get on her feet.'

Dave nodded, remembering how close Bulldust and Shane had been. He was sure the news that her father was a crook and a killer had come as a dreadful surprise to her. That type of information would take a bit of getting your head around. Especially when some of the last words she'd heard from Bulldust were: 'I did it all for you.'

The car turned into an underground carpark and came to a halt next to a lift.

'We'll be waiting for you when you come back down,' Josh said.

'Where're we going?' Dave asked. 'Thought we were headed to the hotel?' He was in need of a shower and a quick kip.

Justin got out and indicated for Dave to do the same. 'Surprise.'

'Don't like surprises.'

'You'll like this one. Come on.'

They rode up in the lift in silence. When the door slid open, Dave realised they were on the top floor of the police department building. Standing in front of the commissioner's office.

Commissioner Bryce was on his feet, his hand extended. 'Welcome, Detective Senior Constable Burrows, welcome,' he said. 'Come this way.'

'Thank you, sir,' Dave said, glancing around. What the hell was he doing here? He followed the man into his office where a framed certificate was on the commissioner's desk.

'We want to express our thanks. We here in Queensland are very grateful for the work you did while putting yourself on the line. Unearthing the bad apple we had among us.

'I would've loved to have been able to present you with your award in public, but it was better to keep it inhouse to protect your identity, considering the other parties are still outstanding.

'Detective Senior Constable David Burrows, I'm presenting you with the Commissioner's Commendation Award for Bravery.'

Dave felt a rush of embarrassment and pride. 'Thank you, sir,' he said as they shook hands again. 'Thank you.'

'You identified people responsible for the murder of three innocent men, occasioning an attempt on your own life, and we are proud to have you in the force.'

Justin, Commissioner Bryce and the young female constable, who were the only people in the room, clapped and Dave couldn't help but reflect on how great it felt to be appreciated, and how horrible it was when you weren't.

∾

'Right-oh, we're off to the coppers pub just across the road. You'll be safe with all of us there,' Justin said, nodding to a stone building. 'Got close protection and surveillance outside, like we will at the court. Not taking any chances with you; you're not getting murdered on our watch!'

'Fucking hell, cheers for that,' Dave said incredulously. Living in Western Australia, away from the reality of the court case, he hadn't thought much about Bulldust and Scotty and the threat they posed. Now that threat was in his face and he couldn't ignore it any longer.

'And while we're talking about the court, just so you know, you'll be taken in and out through the sallyport.'

Dave frowned; that's where the prisoners entered and exited. Not usually witnesses. They were certainly being cautious.

'Look, fellas, can we catch up for drinks after the trial? It's nice that you're being so friendly and all, but I'm feeling like the bloody prime minister with this personal security team!' Dave said, looking first at Josh and then at Dane, walking either side of him.

'Don't worry. We've got this pub being watched within half a k radius. And I reckon you'll be on a plane straight back home again as soon as the judge dismisses you, so we gotta make the most of having you here now.' Justin pushed the door open and let Dave walk through. 'Need four XXXXs, love,' he said to the bartender.

Dave put his hand in his pocket to get out his wallet.

'Don't bother,' Dane said. 'Your money isn't any good here. You're with us now.'

'Cheers,' Dave said.

The bartender lined up four XXXXs and Justin picked up his. 'Here's to you, Burrows. Good job.'

Dave nodded and held his beer up in a 'cheers' gesture, then took a long sip.

'What's going on over in your neck of the woods? I hear you're with the stockies now? That should suit you,' said Justin.

'Haven't been there long, but I caught a case up north.' He explained that it sounded like Spinifex Downs was being targeted and that some station owners resented the Aboriginal stations for receiving government funding for bores and purchases of cattle when they didn't.

'Same issue over here,' Josh said as he put his beer down and nodded for the woman to line them up again. 'It's a shame that some people think like that, but I can understand why they do. Some stations run like clockwork—you know, the people have a lot of pride in what they do and everyone in the community helps out. Others are just an excuse to funnel money into the local communities.

'Two different sets of rules for two different people. I can understand why the white owners might get upset.'

Justin turned to Dave. 'How's your wife going? She was pregnant last time I heard.'

Dave took a long sip of his beer then put it on the mat. He realised that since he'd got on the plane, he hadn't given Mel any thought. He'd been consumed with watching people and thinking about the evidence he was going to give.

'Yeah, due any day.' He took another sip. 'Gotta admit, things are a bit rocky with everything that's gone on.' Looking down at the counter, he wiped the condensation from his glass. 'And coming over here didn't help matters.'

'You won't be the first or the last, mate,' Justin said, clapping him on the shoulder. 'Have another beer. And let's order some steak so this bloke can get an early night and be on the money for tomorrow.'

∿

'Stand back, please,' the guard called as Dave got out of the police car flanked by Justin, Dane and Josh.

There wasn't really anyone to stand back—all the media crush and interested people were out the front of the court and now here he was, where all the prisoners stood, waiting to be taken into the courtroom.

'Mate, we'll be here when you've finished,' Justin said. 'Good luck.'

They hustled him inside to a windowless room, where Hal McCure waited.

'Dave, we've had one day of court proceedings so far. Both the DPP and the defence have given their opening statements,' Hal told him. 'First Class Constable Joe Ross will be in the dock, on your right, when you walk in; however, there is a partition between him and where you will be seated. He won't be able to see you. The court is closed for your evidence, so there will be no one in the public gallery. The defence lawyer is Reeve Perkins. A good enough criminal lawyer, but not the best. You will be known as Detective X.'

'Okay.' Dave's knee jiggled up and down and he realised that he was nervous.

'Let's go.'

Having been sworn in, Dave took his seat and looked at Hal McCure. Hal would question him first, then the defence.

'Detective X, can you tell me in your own words how you came to be working in Nundrew for the Highwaymen mustering team?' Mr McCure asked.

'Yes, sir. I was approached by a Senior Sergeant in my unit asking if I would be willing to go undercover and infiltrate the Highwaymen mustering operation to gather evidence they were committing the crime of stock stealing.'

Mr McCure walked down to the dock and stood in front of Dave. 'That's very brave of you. How did you become employed by Ashley Bennett, also known as Bulldust?'

Dave explained about the meeting in the bar where he had fought two of the Highwaymen's employees and the unexpected breakfast meeting with Bulldust the next morning.

He outlined in detail the legitimate musters he was employed on and the illegitimate ones. He talked about the other employees and how Bulldust came to own people, to make sure they were indebted to him, so he could control them.

'And how did you meet the accused?' Mr McCure asked, waving his hand towards Joe.

'The first day I arrived in Nundrew, I knew I had to create a scene to get the attention of the police. I flogged the bike I was riding down the main street above the speed limit and then parked it on the verandah of the pub—in a place you normally wouldn't park. Joe Ross was one of the police officers who came to ask me to move it. We had words and I ended up being taken into custody.'

'So, to be clear, Joe Ross did not know you were an undercover policeman?'

'He did not.'

'Who in Nundrew did know?'

'Senior Sergeant Justin Parker was my handler.'

'I see. And what was Officer Ross's role within the police station?'

'Objection, Your Honour,' Reeve Perkins broke in. 'How would an undercover policeman know that? He wasn't involved in the day-to-day running of the police station.'

'Sustained.'

'I'll rephrase. Can you tell us what Officer Ross's role with the Highwaymen Mustering team was?'

'I believe it was to vet potential employees and pass on information which may help the Highwaymen decide what stations to hit. Any type of information that would make it less likely they would get caught.' He paused. 'Basically using police privilege to help criminals.'

'No further questions, Your Honour.'

Reeve Perkins rose slowly and walked to stand in front of Dave. 'You and my client didn't have the best relationship, did you?'

'I was in town to do a job. That involved me having a few run-ins with the law. It was always Joe Ross who arrested me.'

'Mmm. And I wonder how we can believe testimony from a policeman who lies. After all, that's what you did, didn't you? Came into town under a false name, gave a false story as to who you were and what you did? Pretended to be a drifter, from all accounts.'

A flutter of anger filtered into Dave's stomach. 'I did what the police department asked me to do.'

'Which is just what my client did. And now, well, here he is on the stand.' He raised his hands in a 'go figure' gesture. 'Detective X, where are you stationed?'

'Objection!' Mr McCure jumped to his feet before Dave could answer. 'We're not here to identify the witness.'

'You're skating on thin ice, counsellor,' the judge glared at Mr Perkins.

'I apologise, Your Honour.' Mr Perkins paced the floor before looking at Dave. 'Detective X, I put it to you that when my client picked you up, after you were shot, you assaulted him.'

'That is incorrect.'

'You assaulted my client and twisted his words to suggest he said he was taking you to Bulldust.' Mr Perkins voice became louder.

Dave matched his tone. 'No, I did not.'

'Objection, leading the witness!'

'Sustained.'

'Again, Detective X,' his tone was sarcastic now, 'I put it to you that my client was actually taking you to hospital and you were delirious from blood loss.'

'No. He stated he was going to take me back to see Bulldust as we were driving in the opposite direction to the hospital.'

'The fact is you were badly wounded. Blood loss causes confusion. How could you possibly know or remember what was going on?'

Dave's voice was loud and tight. 'I remember exactly what happened that night. I'd been shot and had to flee for my life. The moment I thought I'd found a sanctuary, with the police . . . and then it was clear I'd got into a dirty copper's car—'

'Move to strike from the record, Your Honour! Hearsay,' Mr Perkins shouted above Dave's testimony.

'Denied. We might have an adjournment to let the detective gather his thoughts.'

Fifteen minutes later, Dave was back on the stand, giving cool and calm evidence. He answered the questions without emotion.

Finally, it was over. Mr McCure said, 'Your Honour, we'd ask that the detective be excused and allowed to return home, due to his current set of personal circumstances.'

The judge nodded. 'Yes, Detective, we appreciate the sacrifices you've made in leaving your family at this time and travelling here to revisit the events before the court. You're excused and may return to Perth.'

Dave froze. The judge had just revealed his hometown.

Chapter 23

'Oi! Kevin? Kev? I can hear a plane,' Charlie came running into the shed where Kevin was changing a tyre on his motorbike.

'Where?' Jumping up, he ran outside and looked up. The sky was empty of anything except the sun.

'Can't see it, boss, but it sounds like the eastern side. And it's low.'

Standing still, he closed his eyes and listened. The distant growl of an engine reached him, and he turned around slowly until it seemed louder. It was coming from the east, Charlie was right. Where his two-year-old heifers were.

'Maybe nothing,' Charlie said.

'Maybe,' Kevin replied. 'But I don't trust a plane flying over Spinifex Downs these days. Come on, let's go for a look. You take Nicky and head towards the boundary and I'll go to the mill. It's not that far off midday. All the cattle should be camped around water and sleeping in the shade. If they're not, then I guess we've got something to work with.'

Following the two-wheel track, Kevin drove over the cattle grid and into the three thousand acres where his heifers were paddocked. He was proud of these girls that he'd bred and couldn't wait to see what sort of progeny they produced. They would be quality, he knew that.

Bumping around the termite mounds and slowly winding his way along the edge of the creek, he couldn't see any cattle. A feeling of disbelief started through him. Surely whoever was taking the cattle wouldn't be so brazen as to take them in the middle of the day?

No cattle.

He drove along the fence line searching for tracks—any kind, cattle, vehicles, dogs. There weren't any, and there weren't any cattle either.

Driving the creek line, he came out near a patch of trees where he knew the cattle always slept. Relief flooded through him as he spotted about thirty heifers standing under the branches. But they weren't the relaxed cattle he was used to seeing, chewing the cud and flicking flies away with their ears.

As soon as they saw his ute, the leader's ear twitched forwards and she took a few steps back and shook her head at him. The other cattle, jittery, stepped sideways, and then one turned and ran in the opposite direction, tail in the air, taking the rest of the mob with her.

'Some bastard has buzzed them,' Kevin muttered. 'That's

why they're skittish. Whoever was up in that plane has been spotting.'

Kevin stopped the ute and got out, listening to see if he could still hear the drone of the engine. Nothing. He always got there too late! Fury burned through his stomach as he thought back to what Jackie had told him. *Cattle went missing, then their people did too.*

Surely whoever was doing this now wasn't the same person who had been doing it when his father was a young jackaroo? And people wouldn't go missing now. But what was the connection between the two and why was Spinifex Downs being targeted like this? It didn't seem to Kevin that anyone else was having cattle stolen. Not that he'd heard about anyway.

Grabbing the two-way mic, he called Charlie and Nicky. 'Where you boys at?'

It was Charlie who answered. 'Just off the boundary, boss.'

'See anything?'

'I reckon you might want to come and have a look at this.'

'Shit,' he muttered. He got directions and drove to where Charlie and Nicky were against the boundary.

'Don't look good, Kev. I reckon someone has taken some of our cattle. Not many, but look at this,' Nicky said, pointing to disturbed ground. The dirt was kicked over from many hooves running over the top, and there were a few branches broken on the bushes as if the cattle had rushed through, not taking the time to find the clearest path.

Kevin went back to the ute, grabbed the camera he'd started to carry with him all the time and took some photos.

'And here too,' Nicky pointed out. Truck tracks.

'What? Why the hell didn't we see them before?'

'Maybe the plane was leaving when we heard it?'

'They're getting game. In the middle of the day! Look here,' Kevin pointed. 'Reckon this is a small truck—a rigid body. See how the tyre tracks are thinner than a road train's would be? Yeah, that's what they've done. Come in here to grab a few and then got out quickly. Wouldn't take long at all. Find a small mob camped up, run them along the fence and then into the back of a truck. Bob's your uncle.' He took more photos, then walked the fence to see if there were any wires broken. The only damage he came across was a couple of wooden posts that had been pushed hard and were now leaning on an angle.

'Maybe it wasn't today,' Charlie said slowly as he squatted down and traced the tracks with his finger. 'Maybe they were here yesterday and the plane has nothing to do with what we're seeing here.'

Kevin turned to look at the young man. 'Any reason you say that?' he asked.

Charlie pointed to the tops of the imprints. 'They're not as clear as they'd be if they were made today. Just a little bit of wear from the wind.' He stood up. 'These tracks, they could've been made today, but they might be a bit older than what you think.'

Considering that piece of information, Kevin made a decision. 'You fellas stay here,' he said. 'Maybe do a run around the paddock and see if you can see anything else— if they've hit another part of the paddock we haven't seen yet. I'm going to follow these tracks. They're not getting away with it this time. Whether they were here today or yesterday, I'm going to find the bastards.'

Yanking open the door, Kevin got into his ute and followed the truck tracks that arced back to the road leading from Spinifex Downs. He drove slowly, his elbow hanging out the window and his neck craning to see the tracks. It was only a small truck, he was certain. One that might carry only ten or twelve beasts. *Who around here had a truck like that?* he wondered. Most of the stations called in transport companies who used road trains or triples. Some stations had their own trucks to cart cattle from one side of the property to another—the distances were so vast, it made it easier to truck them—but, again, the trucks were big. Not some small farm truck.

He trailed the twisting and turning the truck imprints until he looked up and realised where he was: right on his driveway that led straight to the main road. That highway was sealed. He wouldn't be able to follow them any further from there.

'Damn it!' Instead of stopping straight away, he kept following, until he saw the tracks turn onto the road. There was a thin trail of dust from each wheel on the bitumen. The further down the road it went, the less dust there was, until it disappeared altogether.

Snapping pictures so he had evidence of which way the truck had turned, he then wheeled the vehicle around and drove back to the community.

'What's wrong, boy?' Jackie called as he flew past him and into the office.

'I told you they'd do it again,' he spat, snatching up the phone. 'Yeah, it's Kevin from Spinifex Downs here,' he said when his call was answered.

'G'day, Kev. How can I help?' Glenn King asked.

'I've had a plane over my place today. I know it was spotting because the cattle are all stirred up. Not on the waters the way they should be. Look like they've been chased.' He was breathing hard, watching Jackie, who was standing in the doorway, watching him.

Glenn sighed deeply. 'Right-oh.'

'And there's truck tracks. Looks like they've run cattle down a fence and onto the back of a truck. Not many, but I can still see what's happened. I tracked them to the main road, but that's as far as I got.'

'Can you confirm the truck was on your place today?'

Kevin opened his mouth to answer when Charlie's words came back to him. *Maybe it happened yesterday and the plane had nothing to do with it.*

'I guess I can't be certain,' he answered slowly. 'But the cattle were still real stirred up when I was out there, so whoever has been there, they hadn't been gone long.'

'So they could've been there within twenty-four hours of you finding the tracks and the cattle missing?'

'Yeah,' Kevin admitted grudgingly.

'Did you get some photos of the scene?'

'Yep. Took a heap.'

Kevin heard Glenn sigh again. 'You're not going to come out?' Kevin asked.

'There's not a lot I can do really, Kevin. If you've seen that they're on the main drag, I can't track them anymore than you can.'

'What about putting an alert out on the truck?'

'I'd love to, but what sort of truck are we looking for? Do you see what I mean? So many trucks this time of the year shifting stock.'

'My cattle will be in the crate.' His voice rose. Surely that was obvious!

'I understand, and I can let people know to be on the lookout for them, but that's about all I can do, mate. Get me those photos and I'll put them on file.'

Kevin slammed the phone down, his heart thumping in his chest.

'Told you white man's law wouldn't help us,' Jackie said from the doorway.

'I'm not finished yet,' he snapped and picked the phone up again. 'Is Dave Burrows there, please?'

'Not at the moment, sorry. Take a message?'

'Or Bob . . . Bob, can't remember his last name.'

'That you, Kevin? It's Bob here, Bob Holden.'

'They've been here again, Sergeant. Taken some more of my cattle. I've seen the tracks.'

'Whoa, slow down there,' Bob said in a calming tone. 'Start from the beginning.'

'My boys, they heard a plane and we went to look,' he said and told Bob everything he knew so far. 'And the copper in at Boogarin, he said he can't help me.'

'Did he?' Bob asked. 'Well, don't worry, I'll put an alert out on your cattle. Give me the details. Heifers?'

'Yeah, the new breeding stock I showed Dave when you fellas were here. Brand is 9SP for Spinifex Downs.'

'What type of cattle?'

'Red Brahmans.'

'Got some pics of them? Or any that are like them?'

'Yeah, I got some.'

'Okay, can you get them to me so I've got something to show the boys at the export and saleyards when I put an alert out? And anything else you've got that might help identify them. But, mate, I've got bad news for you. Being heifers, I doubt they'll be going anywhere bar another property.'

'The truck turned south, Bob,' Kevin said. 'I could see the dust on the bitumen.'

'Okay, that's good to know too. Look, stay vigilant. Dave and I will be up ASAP.

'Now, while we're getting organised to drive up there, I want you boys to run around and muster that paddock. Get what's left into the yards and do a count. We need to know exactly how many are missing.' He paused. 'Have you got somewhere closer to the community that you can run these cattle?'

Kevin thought for a moment. 'Yeah, I can bring them in around the community here. It'll make a bit of a mess, but it won't be for long.'

'Good man, you do that. And can you get out all your figures, from calf marking to sales? Weigh bills and sale transactions so we know what has legally gone off the place. We'll do a full muster when we get up there and find out what the hell we're dealing with.'

'Sure thing.'

'Right, we'll see you soon.'

Hanging up the phone he looked at his father who was still standing in the doorway. 'They're going to help us.'

Chapter 24

Bulldust checked his phone and saw the call was from Reeve Perkins.

'What have you got?'

'You won't believe it. The judge dropped a bomb today! The DPP will be fuming.'

'Why, what'd he say?'

'He let out of the bag that the detective is from Perth. He actually said, "You can return home to Perth."' Reeve sounded like he was still in shock. He was sure there'd be ramifications for the judge. Apparently the DPP lawyer had frozen when he'd heard it, but he was never going to call it out in court and embarrass the judge.

'What's he look like?'

'About six foot two, dark brown hair and blue eyes. He's wearing a pretty nice suit. Black, but my guess is that he'll change before he gets to the airport. Who'd want to sit in a suit on a six-hour flight to Perth?'

'Heading there now, are they?'

'I'd say so. Security bundled him up and out quickly. You won't be able to identify him; they've taken him out through the back entrance. Reckon they'll keep him close until he's about to board that plane.'

'Thought as much. We're in a car outside and can't see him. Fucking people everywhere.'

'Maybe try to catch him at the airport.'

'That'll be a waste of time if he's surrounded by coppers. I'll get someone to the Perth airport tonight. Should be able to pick him up that way.'

Bulldust hung up without saying goodbye, then rang his brother.

'Detective from Perth. All we know. I'm on it.'

'Good,' Scotty replied.

Bulldust hung up again and started flicking through his contacts. He found the name he was looking for and dialled.

'Bulldust, what a long time,' drawled the whiskey-rich voice of Missy Harper.

'It's been too long since I've seen you, sweetheart. What are you doing?'

'Not waiting around for you if that's what you're wondering.'

'You've broken my heart.'

'Sorry, sweetie.'

'Got time to do me a favour?' Bulldust looked up as the throng of people near the courthouse began to move. They'd obviously been told the celebrity detective had given his evidence and was now out of the building. He'd have to move; he couldn't take the risk that a cop might see him. Even clean-shaven and with his hair cut short he was worried about being recognised.

'Anything for you, honey.'

'There's a bloke getting off a flight from Brisbane tonight. Not sure what airline he's flying, but I need you to follow him. Tracking people without being caught, that's what you're good at.'

Missy laughed, deep and throaty. 'I know that's what I'm good at, but I hope you've got some more information for me. I could follow anyone home with what you've told me so far.'

'He's a cop. Just given evidence against one of my employees, who's looking at a long stint inside.' He went on to give the description Reeve had given him. 'I want you to follow him home. Find out where he lives. And if you can get his name that would be even better.'

'Good thing I like a challenge,' she said. 'Leave it with me. I'll ring you when I've found him.'

'Cheers.' He put the phone down and started the car, pulling away from the kerb slowly so as not to draw attention to himself. He badly wanted to drive to the airport and see if he could pick this bloke out of the crowd, but he knew it was too chancy.

In this line of work, patience was a virtue.

❧

'Fuck, I can't believe the judge said where I was from in the courtroom.' Dave ran his hands through his hair.

Justin held out a cap. 'Come on, put this on. What I wish is that you weren't so bloody tall. You stand out.'

Dave took the cap and pulled it down firmly over his ears and put his sunglasses on.

'Better let someone at home know,' Justin said, glancing over his shoulder as they hurried through security and towards the boarding gate. 'Get them to meet you. I'll call Spencer when you're on the plane and update him.'

Pulling out his mobile phone, Dave called Bob. 'Got a problem. The judge told the court I was from Perth.'

'What the—'

'You're telling me.'

'Hold your horses, it was a closed court wasn't it, son?'

'Not the point.'

'Surely there won't be anyone in there who would pass it on?'

'Joe Ross would if he got the chance.'

'He wouldn't be in contact with Bulldust, though. He's in custody, isn't he?'

'Nah. He's not. He was bailed, so he's still going home every night. If I know Bulldust, I reckon he'll be keeping a close eye on him and making sure he doesn't spill his guts for some immunity deal. I would almost bet they're in contact somehow.'

'You're fucking kidding me? What was the judge thinking?'

'He wasn't, obviously. Anyway, can I get you to get me out of the airport on the QT?'

'Leave it with me.'

'Please make sure my family are safe, Bob.'

'I'll get the guys on duty to do a couple of drive-bys over the next few days. I'll get everything else organised. What time do you land?'

Dave told him, his eyes roaming around the airport.

'Right. Now while I've got you, a heads-up. Kev rang and they've got trouble up there again. We'll need to drive up tomorrow or the next day at the latest.'

'Beautiful, that's going to go down a treat.'

'Yeah, sorry about that.'

'It's the job, all good. Can't let that bloke down. Sounds like too many people done that in the past. See you in a few hours.' He hung up just as they called his flight.

'Thanks for everything, mate,' he said to Justin.

'Safe flight home. Hope everything picks up for you over there. We'll make sure we keep our ears to the ground and let you know if there're any problems. You do the same, yeah?'

They shook hands and Dave joined the line of people boarding the plane to Perth.

❧

Bulldust checked the screen on his phone as it rang in the console of his car. Missy.

'How'd you go?'

'Hello to you too,' she said.

'Sorry. I'm a bit fucking antsy. Hello.'

'This bloke must mean a fair bit to you.'

Bulldust stared out the window of his car. He was parked on the edge of the Brisbane River, watching the Wheel of

Brisbane turn lazily around. Before Missy's call he'd been seething at everything that Dave had taken away from him. He hadn't seen his daughter, Shane, since he and Scotty had run that night. Just for that he would willingly kill Dave with his bare hands, let alone the loss of income and loss of lifestyle he'd caused.

Briefly he wondered if Dave was this bloke's real name—it was how he'd introduced himself at the pub. Dave Barrows.

'Yeah, I need to have a conversation with him, for sure.' Bulldust cracked his knuckles as he spoke.

'Okay, here's what I know so far. There's only one flight in from Brisbane tonight, so he should be pretty easy to track. While I was at the airport, I noticed a bloke who turned up in an unmarked cop car. Thinking that might be related to your man, I followed him in.'

'What sort of car?'

'Four-wheel drive, troopy. Unmarked and covered in mud.'

Bulldust nodded to himself. Ah, well, there you have it. Sounded like the stock squad to him. And that would make sense; a detective coming from WA to go undercover in a mustering contract business would have needed the bona fides to do it and Dave had just that. He'd fooled Bulldust and all the other blokes in his contracting team. No one had ever questioned that Dave could do the job. He'd seemed like he'd lived and breathed cattle all his life.

'Right. And who was driving?'

'That's where things get a bit interesting. An older bloke who was wearing a blue shirt with what looked like long cattle horns on the pocket. I shadowed him for a bit and heard him talking to the airport staff about needing to get a passenger off the plane quietly, so I knew I had the right bloke.'

'Did you manage to get a name?'

'Nope, no name, but I accidentally bumped into the old bloke on the way out and saw that his shirt read *Stock Squad*, so maybe that will help you.'

'I'm sure it will, thanks, Missy. Still follow him when he gets off tonight. Just because he's being picked up by the stock squad doesn't mean he's one of them.'

'Right-oh, I'll ring you back in about an hour. That's when the flight's landing. Now I know what car I'm looking for, I'll sit back at one of the roundabouts and get on their tail when they come out.'

'Don't lose them,' Bulldust growled.

'This bloke isn't leaving, he went out and parked his car, then went through security. I'm guessing he's sitting up at the gate where your boy is going to get off so he can grab him straight away.'

'Right, well you know how to do your job. I'll leave you with it.'

'I'll ring you when I'm on their tail.'

'Cheers.'

Bulldust hung up and narrowed his eyes. The coppers must be worried that he and Scotty were going to try to nail this guy. That would explain the tight security around him. Obviously he had a weakness though—Reeve had said he'd sought an adjournment because he had a sick wife. Maybe he could get at this so-called Dave through her.

Anyway, once they had a name and knew where he lived, it would be easy to cap him. But it wouldn't be done without a bit of torture and Dave knowing exactly who had him.

He didn't usually let himself think about Shane, but as he sat there overlooking the river, his thoughts drifted towards his daughter again. Bulldust couldn't get her look of disgust from his mind. There were nights he dreamed about her yelling at him, asking him, 'What have you done?' The horror in her eyes. She'd never said she didn't want to see him again—the words hadn't needed to be said. He knew. Shane had been his life since she'd been born and now she wasn't. Clenching his hands around the steering wheel, he squeezed hard, wishing it was Dave's throat and he was crushing the life out of him.

That night, after everything had turned to shit and they had known the cops would be coming after them, he and Scotty had split up. He'd headed towards Lightning Ridge in his ute, knowing he'd be able to hide out in an old mine until the heat had died down. He'd swapped number-plates with some spares he had in case something like this happened. He and Scotty had always had escape plans in place in case they were exposed.

Scotty had made it very clear that Bulldust was to blame for the whole mess.

'You were the one who employed the fucker,' he'd said. 'I told you he smelled off when I first met him.'

'If Joe couldn't find anything on him, then how the hell did you expect me to be able to?'

By the light of the moon, they had glared at each other, before Scotty had jammed his finger into Bulldust's chest and backed him against the ute. 'You were too keen to replace the fella you killed, that was the problem. You needed more manpower and you let him in too quickly. It's your fault. Not mine or anyone else's. Yours. You've fucked up a good thing and you're gonna have to wear it. Now we're probably facing charges of attempted murder of a police officer. Jesus, Bulldust.'

'He mightn't make it. We saw all the blood on the ground, so we know he was hit.'

Scotty had shaken his head and got back into his ute. 'Stay the fuck away from me.' Then he'd driven off, leaving Bulldust to work out where he was going to go and what he was going to do.

In Lightning Ridge, he'd found a derelict shanty and had lain low there. He'd thanked whatever god there was that Scotty had insisted they always had a large amount of cash stashed in secret spots and Bulldust was able to live on the smell of an oily rag.

Two weeks passed before Scotty had calmed down enough to call Bulldust.

'We're gonna get that fucker,' he'd said.

'I've already thought about that,' Bulldust said. 'I read in the paper they're charging Joe. He'll have to come back for the trial. We'll get him there.'

'Good idea. Get in contact with that lawyer of yours. You'll need to make sure Joe doesn't turn on us too.'

'Already in hand.'

'Good. Well, I'm going bush for a while. Not sure what'll happen to my place, but I'm sure the coppers will search it at some stage. If I'm not there, they won't find me.'

'Pricks will take all of my vehicles and everything at the depot, I guess. Fuck, I wish I'd never set eyes on that bastard.'

'Heard from Shane?'

'No.'

'Stay out of trouble then. I'll talk to you later.'

Bulldust remembered sitting outside drinking beer, looking up at the stars, thinking about Shane and wanting to ring her. So many times, he'd stood in the phone box on the main street of Lightning Ridge, late at night. His fingers had hovered over the keypad; sometimes he'd even started dialling her number, when he'd had to stop. He couldn't risk getting caught. Once Dave—if that was his name—had been dealt with, then he'd think about how he was going to handle Shane. Somehow, he had to get her to understand he'd done everything for her.

The anger made his chest tight and he took a few deep breaths through his nose, trying to stop the feeling of wanting to smash something. The rage wouldn't help.

His phone rang, providing a welcome distraction.

'Missy.'

'Honey, you're going to want to pay me extra for what I've just found out,' she cooed down the line.

'Sounds like you've had a win.'

'I picked up the troopy like I said I would. There were two heads in there, and the one in the passenger seat matched the description best as I could see.'

Bulldust listened, wishing she'd get to the point.

'Didn't take long for me to get in behind them. They drove to an empty house—well, it looked that way. Lights were out and there was mail in the mailbox. The passenger went inside and not ten minutes later the garage door came up and he drove off.

'Got a bit curious about where he was off to so soon after getting home, so I followed him to another house and guess what was inside?'

'A woman?'

'A pregnant one. And a child.'

'The address?'

She told him and he wrote it down.

'Did you get his name?'

'As a matter of fact, I did. I watched through the window of the second house for a while and realised he wasn't leaving any time soon, so I went back to the first house and checked the mailbox and went around the house to see if there was an easy way in. There wasn't but there was some mail.' She paused for effect.

Bulldust wanted to jump down the line and squeeze the words out of her. 'And?' he snapped.

'His name is David Burrows.'

'Barrows? As in wheelbarrows?' Bulldust was incredulous. He was that freaking brazen to use his own name?

'Burrows as in a wombat burrow.'

Bulldust was silent, too busy seething to be able to say anything.

'You still there?'

'Yeah. What's with the two houses?'

'I got a theory on that. There're also two older people in the second house. I think they're either her or his parents and the wife and kid are staying there while he's away. Helping out maybe. Or maybe she doesn't like being by herself.'

Or maybe he was worried I'd come for her, Bulldust thought.

'How much do I owe you?'

'This is on the house, honey, just so long as you look me up when you get back over this way. I'm guessing it won't be long.'

'Who knows,' he answered, not giving anything away. 'But I will do. Thanks, Missy. Thanks a fucking lot.'

Chapter 25

'How did it go?' Mel asked after Dave had read Bec a story and put her to bed. They'd made an agreement when he'd rung her earlier that they wouldn't talk about anything volatile in front of Bec.

'It's all done and dusted,' Dave said, leaning back against the couch, reaching to take her hand. 'All behind us.'

There wasn't any point mentioning the judge's indiscretion; that would only inflame the situation yet again. Tonight, Mel had been happy to see him when he walked in through the door, giving him a hug and telling him to put his hand on her stomach because the baby was kicking. He didn't want that feeling to fade just yet.

'How's everything here?'

'The doctor is happy with my blood pressure—it's still high, but it's dropped a little since I left hospital. I'm spending most of the day on the bed, which helps apparently.' She looked a little embarrassed. 'This blood pressure thing is a bit stupid really—I mean, how many women have babies and they don't have this problem? Here I am, perfectly healthy, having to lie down all day.'

'I don't think that's the case, sweetie. I'm sure there are loads of women who have high blood pressure and you've got to do what's good for the baby and for you. How's Bec been?'

'Very well behaved. Seems she loves being with Mum, who has endless patience. You need that when you've got a kid asking "Why?" all the time.' She changed her tone to a child-like one. '"Mummy, why do you put the milk in the fridge? Why do you have to cook the veggies? Why . . ."'

Dave laughed. 'They've got to learn somehow,' he said.

'I guess, but it's really annoying!' Mel smiled then turned her body towards him. 'So, the court case is really all over?'

'It is for me. Joe wasn't sentenced while I was there; there was still more evidence to be heard. Justin was next on the stand after me. I guess I'll hear what happens when the verdict is handed down.'

'And there wasn't anything that went wrong? You didn't see anyone who looked like the guys who used you as target practice?' she smiled, trying to make her words light, but there was an underlying brittleness there.

'Not a sign of anyone,' he answered reassuringly. 'No, all was quiet on that front. I reckon they've forgotten all about me. Probably more worried about trying to stay hidden from the police.' He paused. 'The nice part was that I got a Commissioner's Commendation Award.'

Mel narrowed her eyes. 'What's that for?'

'Bravery.'

Watching her chew the inside of her lip, it seemed to Dave she was trying to work out what to say. Surely congratulations wouldn't be too hard.

'How nice they acknowledged that you almost died for them,' she finally said. 'And that your children were almost without a dad.'

Now it was Dave's turn to work out what he was going to say. He was beginning to get sick of the snide remarks. He didn't die and neither Mel nor Bec was without him. 'Well, I was appreciative anyway.'

'And now you're going to be able to stay home.' There was some excitement in her voice.

Dave's heart sank. He'd been hoping to have a little more conversation with her before he had to tell her the bad news.

'Well, I have some news about that. While I was in Brisbane we found out there had been more cattle stolen from the station we were at last week,' he said quietly.

Mel cocked her head to the side as if she didn't understand what he was saying. 'What does that have to do with you?'

'As the investigating detective, I have to go back up and make more enquiries. Kevin, the manager up there, hasn't had anyone to support him through all of this and I promised I would. I can't let him down.' As he said the words, he expected Mel to fire back something like how about supporting *her*.

Instead Mel pulled back from him and moved down to the other end of the couch, not meeting his eyes. 'You're going again?' Her voice was flat.

'Yes.'

'When?'

'Tomorrow morning.' Dave stood up, put his hands in his pockets and rocked on his heels while he waited for her to say something else.

Mel wouldn't meet his eyes, but looked at the floor, shaking her head in disbelief. 'Tomorrow?'

Dave didn't answer. There was nothing to say.

Mel stood up and walked out of the room.

'Shit.' It was Dave's turn to shake his head and he dropped back down onto the couch. He put his head in his hands, not knowing what to think. This trip away could be the last straw, and the lack of emotion in Mel's response was unnerving. Normally she'd yell and get angry.

'Congratulations. You really know how to upset someone, don't you?'

Not turning at the sound of Mark's voice, Dave said wearily, 'I don't have a choice.'

'You sound like a broken record.'

I feel like one, he thought.

'Let me get this right. You're going back up north. No point in Melinda moving back home if you're not going to be there.'

'No.' Dave stood up again and looked at his father-in-law. 'No, you're right. There's not.'

'You bemuse me, Dave,' Mark said, walking over to look him in the eye. 'Ellen and I are more than happy to help you financially and yet you still run out the door to go to work every opportunity you get. Don't you love my daughter? Because from where I stand, it doesn't look like it. You seem very selfish.'

Dave realised this attitude was what he was going to be fighting his entire life if he and Mel stayed together. She wasn't strong enough or didn't want to stand up for Dave in front of her father, and Dave wasn't sure he had enough fight left in him to keep battling everyone.

'I do love Mel, Mark,' he said quietly. 'You can't imagine how much I love her and Bec. Your offer to help with money is appreciated, but you know as well as I do that I'm never going to accept it. I love my job—not more than my family, as you think. What you need to understand is that police have responsibilities to the people they help. To the victims of crime. They rely on us. We can't let them down, because they don't have anyone else. They put all their hope in us and trust that we'll find who has hurt them or their family. I can't walk away from that.' He sighed and held his hands out. 'I'm sorry if you feel that attitude lets down Mel and Bec, but this is who I am.'

For once Mark was quiet.

'If Mel and Bec could stay here while I'm gone this time, I'd certainly appreciate your care of them. The other thing I need to tell you is that the judge let slip that I live in Perth. You'll need to keep an eye out for anything unusual. I'm not worried—there's no talk on the street that they're going to try to come after me—but you just need to be aware if you see anything strange.'

Mark's face turned red.

Taking a step closer towards Dave, he looked at him through narrowed eyes. 'If you've put my daughter and granddaughter in danger, you'll never hear the end of it from me,' he spat.

'You think I like this any more than you do?' Dave's temper finally found its way to the surface. 'I don't. It couldn't be avoided, and we are doing everything to make sure that nothing happens to anyone. There will be coppers doing a few drive-bys to be on the safe side. I *did* just say I'm not expecting any trouble. All I'm asking is for you to keep an eye out for anything unusual.'

'If anything happens to them . . .' Mark broke off and stormed out of the room.

'Well, that went just about the way I expected it to,' Dave muttered as he dropped back onto the couch.

'I'm sorry, Dave.'

He looked up and saw Ellen, then shrugged. 'It is what it is,' he said. 'Guess I'd better get going. Got to pack and everything.'

'I know this is tough for you. I heard what you said to Mark about victims relying on police. I hadn't ever thought about your work like that and I'd bet my bottom dollar that neither have Mark or Mel. You do what you need to do. Like I said last time, you're doing really well in difficult circumstances.'

Dave stood up. 'Thanks, Ellen. I can't tell you what it means to me to hear you say that. Can you . . .' He swallowed. 'Can you tell Bec that I think about her every day?'

'Of course I can.'

'I'll be hard to get hold of up there. The mobile range is pretty haphazard. With any luck I'll only be gone about a week anyway. If the baby arrives, call me and I'll come straight back.'

'I'm sure nothing will happen between now and then. When the doctor examined Mel last, he said the birth was still a way off.'

Dave nodded. 'Thanks again.' He let himself out of the house without saying goodbye to Mel and drove away.

❧

In bed that night, Dave lay staring into the darkness, thinking about Mel. He could smell her shampoo on her pillow and it made him miss her.

Rolling over, he tried to get comfortable, but the bed seemed lumpy tonight. The nightmares still plagued him and there were nights he didn't want to go to sleep. Tonight was different. Even so, he couldn't drift off; there were too many thoughts rushing around in his mind.

He thought about Spinifex Downs, and if there had been any more cattle stolen. He thought about Bob and what they'd do when they got back to Boogarin. They'd need to do a muster. Maybe muster some of the neighbouring properties to find out what cattle were where. If they found Spinifex Downs cattle on another property, that would make for an interesting investigation.

He thought of Bec and her smile. The way she called out, 'Daddy!' when he walked through the door. How her chubby little fingers held his hand and hugged him tightly.

What would he do if she wasn't in his life?

A tear leaked out of the corner of his eye and he felt it roll past his ear and drop onto the pillow. 'Shit!' He thumped the pillow now and sat up just as a noise exploded over his roof. It sounded like hail raining down.

Leaping out of bed, he dropped to the floor, crawling to the window to see if he could see anything from there.

The noise sounded again. *What the hell?* His heart was racing as he peered over the ledge of the window, then he heard loud whispers.

'I know that's a copper's place. I seen him turn up in that copper car. Reckons we can't work it out 'cause it's unmarked. Fuckwit. See what he thinks about someone scaring the shit out of him.'

'Fuck the coppers.' The sound of laughing, then another round of rocks on the roof and running feet.

Dave relaxed. Kids.

He turned and leaned his back up against the wall, not having the energy to chase them. Didn't matter. They hadn't been Bulldust or Scotty and they weren't chasing him, only wanting to cause a bit of mischief.

His heart began to slow. Would the brothers actually come after him, he wondered, or did he just have the wind up him because of all the security measures there'd been in Brisbane? He wasn't sure, but he knew that Bulldust and Scotty were bad enough to want to come after him. But were they brave enough to risk getting caught trying?

Chapter 26

'Glenn, what we really don't understand is why you were so unhelpful to Kevin when he rang you about these cattle,' Bob said from across the desk in the Boogarin Police Station.

Dave and Bob had driven through the night and made it to the town in good time. It was early morning and they'd been waiting for Glenn to arrive so they could ask a few questions before heading out to see Kevin.

Glenn spread his hands. 'Mate, I'd had a brawl in the pub the night before and was taking statements from the five fellas I had to lock up—by myself. He couldn't tell me when the truck had been on his property. Maybe the theft happened a week ago! I know he thought there had been people on his place that day, but he didn't see them. They could've been five hours away by the time I got out there to have a look.'

He shrugged. 'What do you want me to do? He's asking me to look for a truck. But what sort? He's crazy if he thinks I can pull over every truck and look at the paper-work. Too big a job for me—you blokes got any idea how many trucks are on the road at this time of year?'

'Anything negative towards the blokes at Spinifex Downs is going to be counterproductive. It would've been great if you'd done something. You're looking for red cattle, with the earmark and brand of their station. Pretty easy when you think about it.' He stepped up to the map which was hanging on the wall and looked at it. 'I do get your point about timing, though.'

'Sure, if you've got the resources, which I don't. Anyway, it's your job to do that sort of thing, not mine. I can't keep running around looking after these boys out there. I've got other jobs on too, you know.'

Bob crossed his legs and regarded Glenn for a while. 'Again, what I don't understand,' he said slowly, 'is why you're being so down on Kev and the situation. What's your reasoning?'

Glenn regarded both men then leaned forwards and put his elbows on the desk. 'It's like this,' he said. 'Boogarin has been a nice quiet town for a while now. Seems to me the community out at Spinifex Downs are stirring up trouble. They're pointing the finger at some of the other station owners. That type of thing doesn't make for good relations. I don't want any trouble up here. You boys have got no idea what kind of problems this might cause.'

'So, what, you want to sweep it under the carpet?' Dave asked, just as Bob said, 'Yeah, I understand. No one wants to think cattle stealing is going on in their backyard. But

I don't think you can say "the community", do you? You know as well as I do, it was Kevin who made the report. And, hell, you were the one who got him to do it, or have you forgotten that?'

'Nope, I have not. But I didn't think it was going to keep on going. Thought you blokes would come up here and get everyone settled down and life would go back to normal. Doesn't sound like that's going to happen now. And, no.' Glenn looked at Dave. 'No, I don't want it swept under the carpet, but I don't want any unrest either.'

Dave frowned. 'Sorry, going back to your point about accusations. I think I've missed something here. I wasn't aware anyone had pointed the finger at anyone. Who's Kev claiming has done it?'

'His neighbour.'

'I think you've taken that conversation out of context. He hasn't named anyone, but his cattle have been stolen, and it's clear cattle have gone from his place through Deep-Water Station. To me that isn't accusing Kit Redman.'

'Yeah, well, it's yet to be shown the stock have even gone. By the time I got the photos and went out there, all the evidence was unusable. You said so yourselves; we can't be one hundred per cent certain that's what happened, can we? Sure, we got a report, but that doesn't mean it's actually happening.' Glenn shuffled a few sheets of paper around on his desk and then looked up at both men.

'You're kidding me, right?' Dave got up and paced the floor, disbelief in his voice. 'Surely you remember how hard it was for Kevin to make the decision to talk to the coppers?

And the trouble it's putting him in with community—they aren't happy he's done that, are they?'

'Maybe the Elders know better than he does. They've been around longer. I wonder if Kev's not making trouble for trouble's sake. Maybe he's trying to cover up bad management.'

'Bad management?' Dave spat in disgust. 'You've been out there! You've seen how well that place is run. Kev's caught flak from his own community by reporting this and your inaction only reinforces their views about the police. I think you're scared of what the outcome might be!'

'Okay, okay, fellas, let's just calm down a bit here,' Bob said, frowning at Dave. 'Look, Glenn, I understand your concern and your thought process. You need to know, that's not what we're seeing here. Don't forget we're stockies and we've been on heaps of different stations and farms and seen differently managed places. There's something else at play here—we just need to find out what that is.'

'Well, I'll leave it to the experts,' Glenn said. 'Keep in mind that uneasy relations between station owners make for hard policing up here. And that there's been bad blood with these two stations before.'

'We'll be sure to remember that, Glenn,' Bob said, getting up. 'Thanks for seeing us today.'

'Where are you headed now?'

'Spinifex Downs to begin with, then we'll work out where after that.' Bob turned towards the door.

'How long do you reckon this will take?' Glenn asked, standing too.

'Who knows. Long as a piece of string, this type of investigation. Just got to see where it takes us.'

'Boys,' Glenn said, 'I want my patch to go back to the way it was before this all started. You know, I got blokes coming in from the communities and stations, having a few beers at the pub and then getting hot under the collar. I haven't had to break up a fight here for years and suddenly there've been two in the last few weeks.

'It's pretty hard for me to run a tight ship when I'm on my own. And let me tell you, it's not going to be long until we have a full-blown brawl.'

Bob nodded understandingly. 'We'll do our best to get it sorted as soon as we can, Glenn.' He opened the door and bright sunlight streamed inside. 'Oh, and one more thing, can you tell us who has a fixed-wing aircraft around here?'

'As in personally owned?'

'Well, anyone really. Company, if there is one. Yeah, and private.'

'The company up here is called Ocean Air. I think they've got two—they do tourist flights and so forth.' Glenn hitched up his pants and went over to a filing cabinet. Picking out a manila folder, he read through. 'Kit Redman has one, flies it himself. Dylan is a pilot too and owns a chopper, but not a plane.' He ran his finger down the list. 'All of the other ones are well outside the area that you're looking at. Like hundreds of kilometres outside.'

'Can I get a copy of that list?' Bob asked.

'Sure.' He took it out, put it on the photocopier and pressed a button.

'How did you get this information?' Bob asked.

'When you've been up here as long as I have, you learn to keep notes. I've got information on things no one else would have, because they wouldn't have ever thought it was important. In fact, I can tell you what year Greg and Dorothy Janson got married and when they had their first child. The fact that Stella Grace had her fiftieth birthday at the pub and her ex-husband Murray turned up, got drunk and started a fight with the new husband, Jeff Grace. That was the first year I arrived.'

'That's fantastic to know, Glenn. Nothing like a bit of local knowledge. That sort of thing helps us outsiders a lot.'

'That's why I'm telling you that they might be causing trouble just for trouble's sake.'

Bob nodded and held his hand out to Glenn. 'We'll certainly keep all of that in mind. Thanks again.'

❧

In the troopy, Dave pulled on his seatbelt and snapped it into place, a sneer on his lips. 'What the hell was that about?'

'I think that's one frightened copper,' Bob answered, putting the vehicle into gear and reversing out.

'What, 'cause he's got someone leaning on him to get us to go away?'

Bob gave a laugh. 'Dave, Dave, Dave, just because you discovered a dirty copper in outback Queensland doesn't mean you're going to find one in outback Western Australia. Don't judge everybody by Joe, son.'

'Well, seriously, what the hell was all that "covering up bad management" shit?'

'That is plain ignorance. He's frightened about things getting out of control in his town and someone getting hurt. Think about it, one bloke and five or six big strong men from out on the stations? He's not going to have a huge amount of control if a fight gets out of hand, is he?'

Dave fiddled with the air-conditioner. 'I guess not.'

'How would you feel if you had to break up something like that without back-up?'

'Yeah, not too good, I guess.'

'So cut him a little slack.' Bob swung the car onto the highway and headed towards Spinifex Downs. 'But I will give you a little piece of advice. You're going to have to be careful with old Glenn now.'

'Why?'

'He's going to think you're against him, since you gave him a bit of a tune-up in there. I was trying to get your attention to shut up, but you didn't seem to be getting the message.'

'I was pissed off.'

'That was obvious. Next time take the hint and pipe down. If he thinks we're suspicious of him, we won't be able to get him to talk to us, and we're going to need his inside knowledge without giving him all the info we're learning in the investigation.'

Dave knew that Bob was right, but he was still pissed off. 'Yeah,' he said and turned to look out the window.

'Tell you what, can you get on the laptop before we lose mobile range? Let's do a little poking around on who owns Deep-Water, Cassia Plains and Paperbark Valley. Just because we think we've met the owners, doesn't mean we have. Family set-ups and all.'

Turning around, Dave got the laptop off the back seat. 'What do you think we're looking for?' he asked as he turned it on.

'Who knows until we find it but, when we do, we'll know.' Bob smiled, staring straight ahead. 'Don't worry, we'll know.'

❧

Pulling in at Spinifex Downs, Dave could see the effect that the last lot of stealing had taken on Kevin.

His shoulders were a little more stooped than they'd been before, and his eyes were bloodshot, no doubt from lack of sleep.

'Glad you're here,' Kevin said to them both, shaking their hands.

'How did you go with the muster?' Dave asked as they walked up into the office.

'Boys and I went around that paddock five times. There were supposed to be one-fifty in there, but there's only ninety.' He pushed the weigh bills and a pile of other notes in Bob's direction. 'I got everything you asked for, Sergeant. And we shifted the heifers in around the community here. Then I decided to post the boys on lookout, so they've all been out in the bush, watching and waiting, but we haven't seen or heard anything since.'

'Let's go back to the beginning—the noise that you heard was definitely a fixed-wing plane?'

'Yeah. Choppers make a different noise. Like a whoop, whoop sorta thing, but planes, they drone on, only time they really change tone is when they're altering speed.'

'Okay, and when you mustered last you put one hundred and fifty Brahman heifers into the paddock that sixty are missing out of now?'

'That's right.' Kevin put his hands in his pockets. 'Sergeant, I bought some security cameras. Put them up on the windmills and gates. There're only three and I can't cover all of the boundaries, but I had to do something.'

'Great idea, mate,' Dave said before Bob could answer. 'We would've done that if you hadn't. Have you had any hits yet?'

'Nah, only the occasional roo.'

Dave wrote the information down, then while Bob was still quiet, formed his own question.

'Have you ridden the paddock boundary? No sign of a fence being pushed over where they could've wandered away into a different paddock?'

Kevin went to the wall and poked his finger at the map pinned up there. 'This is the paddock the cattle were in,' he said. 'You can see it's two paddocks inside the boundary that backs onto Deep-Water. If they were real thirsty or being mischievous, they'd still have to get through another three fences before they were off our place.'

'And you're going to tell me you've been around those paddocks, aren't you?' Dave said.

'Yep. Three times. On bikes and in utes. The sixty cattle we're missing from this paddock, plus the other two hundred, aren't on Spinifex Downs. They've disappeared.'

Chapter 27

'We've got about an hour before it gets too dark to set up camp,' Bob said. 'I think we should swing past Deep-Water. We've got time.'

'This late?'

'Yep, this late. They won't be expecting us at this time of night. Let's just head over there and see what we see.' He put the troopy into gear and pulled back out onto the road from where they had been parked under a tree, writing up their notes after talking to Kevin.

'You still think it's him?' Dave said. 'The local celeb?'

'No, I'm not saying that at all. You've always got to keep an open mind, which you're not doing about this bloke 'cause you decided you liked him and he was helpful. I'm being the balancing voice here.'

Dave held up his hands in defeat. 'Okay, I'm hearing you. I'll be on guard this time.'

'Tell me again who owns this place?' Bob asked, concentrating on the road.

'It's in the name of C.G. and T.J. Redman. Christopher Geoff and Tara Jane. They trade as Deep-Water Pty Ltd.'

'Wonder where Kit comes into it then.'

'That'd be his nickname, wouldn't it? Christopher can be shortened to Kit.'

'Really? Sounds bloody stupid to me. Why don't they just call him Chris?'

'Who knows. I'm not Glenn King who keeps notes on everyone,' Dave said.

'Okay.' Bob turned back to the issue at hand. 'Kit and Tara are both partners together and there's no one else involved. That's good to know. Sometimes when there's families, there're brothers in partnership with brothers and it all gets a bit messy tracking everyone down. No extras in this lot. And the trading name is Deep-Water. It's not unusual to keep the same trading name as the generation before. Buyers know the quality of cattle they're going to get from each trading name. Does that make sense, son?'

'Yeah.'

'And has either Kit or Tara got any priors?'

'Not that I could find. Not even a drink-driving charge.'

'And what about the others?'

'As in Dylan and Ethan?'

'Uh-huh.'

'Interesting. Dylan has an assault charge against him— pounded some poor bugger in Perth three years ago. Didn't hurt him too much, but he went to court, pleaded guilty and got off with some community service hours.'

'Where'd he do them?'

'In Boogarin—helped the local council weed and tidy the streets, that sort of thing.'

'That must've dented his pride. All the people he knew driving past and seeing him.'

'Then Ethan Schultz, he's got a spent conviction for failing to secure a firearm correctly. Nothing came of that.' Dave tapped his fingers on his knees as he watched the sun start to sink on the horizon. The deep pinks and reds of the north were intense, and he wound down his window a little to breathe in the cool night air. 'You sure we're not heading there too late? Won't it be dark by the time we get there?'

'No, it won't, I've got it calculated we'll arrive just as everyone will be sitting around having a beer and yarning about the day. Sometimes, son, that's the best time to turn up, because you're not expected and everyone is a little less on guard.'

Half an hour later, they were driving across the cattle grid into Deep-Water Station.

'Look how clean these posts are next to the grid,' Dave said. 'You'd reckon they should be covered in red like everything else is. Wonder why they're so white. Someone must've washed them.'

'Or they're freshly painted,' Bob said. 'Got to say, this is a great road—not many station roads are so smooth, they're usually full of potholes and corrugations. These have been graded recently—see how the gravel hasn't actually set yet? It's still all fluffy? Care and maintenance. Kit's on the job.'

Dave looked at him slyly. 'Or he's just covered up the tracks of a small, rigid body truck.'

Bob looked over at him, a half-grin on his face. 'Now who's the suspicious one?' he asked.

'That's what they pay me for,' Dave answered, in Bob's own words and turned to look out the window with a wide grin on his face. This was the sort of banter he had with Spencer. Maybe they'd make a good team yet.

They followed the wide, freshly graded road towards the homestead, past the cattle yards and through a creek, until they saw a tennis court and two old huts on the side of the road. Four dogs—an Alsatian, two staffies and one kelpie—came to greet them, the Alsatian growling as they pulled up next to the shed, in which there were two utes. Kit and another bloke, both dressed in blue shirts and denim jeans, were leaning over the back of one ute, having a beer.

'And there you go,' Bob said with satisfaction as he looked at the two men. 'Don't know that fella. Be good to meet him.'

Dave frowned. 'What do you mean?'

'Well, Kit has someone working here, or just called in. That bloke might know something we don't. The more people we talk to the better.' Bob pushed open his door and got out, putting his hat on his head. 'G'day there, Kit. How're you going?'

'It's Bob, isn't it?' Kit said, holding out his hand. 'And Dave. The stockies who turned up here the other day.'

'You've got a good memory. Good to see you.' Bob turned to look at the stranger, who hadn't moved since they'd arrived. The tall, tan-skinned man leaned against the ute. 'G'day,' Bob said to him, walking around to shake his hand.

'G'day.' The man and Kit looked at each other and Dave caught an expression flicker across Kit's face, too quickly to identify.

'Bob Holden, and this is Dave Burrows.' Bob introduced them. The dogs barked loudly and jumped around Dave as he tried to reach out and shake the man's hand.

Kit seemed to gather himself. 'This is Boyd Shepard,' he introduced them.

'Good to meet you, Boyd. You from around here?' Dave leaned against the ute and pushed his hat back on his head.

'I'm from—'

'You boys want a beer?' Kit interrupted.

'Wouldn't say no,' Bob said. 'Always keen to have a sip, hey, Boyd?'

'Especially after a long day.' Boyd drained his can and put it on the tray of the ute. 'I'll have another too, mate,' he called.

Kit walked towards the shed, talking over his shoulder. 'Yeah, we've had a busy day, shifting cattle into fresh paddocks.'

Dave glanced around and saw two motorbikes parked outside the shed and a grader sitting in the middle of the road. It looked like the driver had decided he'd had enough for the day, and just turned the grader off right then and there and got out.

'So where are you from, Boyd?' Bob asked.

'Oh, round and about really. Just here catching up with Kit for a couple of days. I don't see him much.'

'Sounds like the life,' Dave said.

'What brings you blokes back up here so soon?' Kit said, walking back with two cans in each hand.

Dave watched Kit as he returned. There it was again. Another tiny glance that was a signal of some sort.

'Boys over at Spinifex Downs need a bit of a hand. Had a few more cattle stolen,' Bob said.

Handing out the beers, Kit stopped and looked over at him? 'Geez, really? I hadn't heard anything about that. Bloody awful. How many?'

'We're still sorting through all of that.' Bob cracked his can and drank deeply. 'You hadn't heard anything, huh?'

Kit shook his head. 'No, mate, if I had've I would've been on the phone to Glenn straight away. I don't like how this is headed. Like I said last time you were up, I worked hard to make sure this sort of thing had stopped happening. Specially when those boys like Dylan Jeffries and Ethan Schultz are as hot-headed as they are. I had to stop what could've been a fight at the rodeo a while back. They were about to have a go at the blokes from Spinifex Downs over this very matter. Worries me, I can tell you.'

'No doubt. Must be tricky when there've been so many years when nothing like this has happened and then—bang!—up it all starts again. Is there anyone new in the district?'

Kit frowned as he thought. 'No, mate, I don't think so. There's always the transient work force at mustering, but they're kept so busy, they wouldn't have time to get around the district causing havoc like this.'

'You think it must be someone local?' Bob asked.

'Well, I'm not saying that either, Bob.' Kit shook his head. 'Don't put words into my mouth!' He gave a smile. 'Cattle stealing is from another generation, is what I'm saying. It's from back in my father's day rather than now.'

'What about you, Boyd?' Dave asked, turning to look at him. Boyd's mouth was set in a hard, grim line as he wiped condensation from the can. 'You think the same?'

'I reckon. And I know nothing about any cattle being taken. Kit here mentioned it a few weeks ago when you were up here last time, but I never hear much about anything.'

'How's the investigation going? You can't have any idea about who's done it if you're asking these sorts of questions. What about knowing where the cattle could be?' Kit asked.

'Not yet,' Bob said. 'Early days. Always hard to investigate these types of activities without catching someone red-handed. But we'll keep at it. Neither Dave nor I are ones to give up, are we, mate?' He turned to Dave.

'Not me,' Dave said, taking a sip of his beer.

'Yeah, the interesting thing about this one is that it seems there's been a small truck used. Like the rigid farm trucks you use down south, not the big road trains you blokes have up here. Know anyone who has a similar truck?'

Dave watched as Boyd glanced around the yard before shaking his head.

'A lighter truck?' Kit said. 'Well that's an interesting thought. I haven't seen one. Don't even know why you'd bother with a tiny truck up here. I only ever use semis when I'm shifting cattle and that's what we all use. Too expensive to do it any other way when you've got to cart the distances we do.' He drained his can. 'Now listen, you blokes want to stay for tea? I've got to get back to the house to make a few calls, but you're more than welcome. Tara's used to whipping up extra food.' He turned towards the house and yelled, 'Tara!'

'Oh, yeah, that'd—' Dave started to say but Bob spoke over the top of him.

'Thanks, but no thanks.' Bob put the empty can of beer in the back of the ute and reached down to pat one of the staffies that had plopped at his feet. 'Dave here has been away from his young family too long, so we're trying to wrap everything up as quickly as we can. The only way to do that is to keep pushing on and I think we'd better get back to town tonight.'

'Long drive,' Boyd said.

'Yep. That's the life of a stockie. Thanks very much for the chat, boys. And the information.' Bob turned to Dave. 'You can drive, mate,' he said, just as a woman appeared on the verandah.

Kit waved her away. 'No need for you,' he called. 'They're not staying.'

With a small nod of her head, Tara acknowledged him and went back inside.

Dave started the car, setting up a round of barking from the dogs who had been lying panting at everyone's feet. He waved as he put the troopy in gear and turned towards Boogarin.

Bob took his pen out of his pocket and wrote something on his hand. 'Did you see those looks between Boyd and Kit when we first got there?' he asked.

'I saw something. I wasn't sure what it meant.' Dave flicked the lights to high beam and concentrated on the road in front of him. He didn't want to hit a beast.

'I think it was a "don't tell him any more than you have to" type look.'

'What did you just write down?'

'The regos for both utes there. Let's find out who this Boyd Shepard is and what type of relationship he has with Kit Redman.'

Chapter 28

The smell of bacon and eggs reached Dave as he opened one eye then the other.

He looked around the little room he'd spent the night in and groaned. The mattress was so lumpy, he should've got his swag out and slept on the floor.

A thump sounded on the door and then he heard Bob's voice. 'I've told you before, you young fellas sleep too much. You getting up or what? Or you too busy giving yourself a hand shandy?'

'Piss off, you old fuck,' Dave muttered. 'I reckon I've had about three hours' sleep,' he called back. He didn't mention the nightmares that had woken him twice.

'And I've had even less because I've cooked breakfast. Come on, we've got shit to do.'

'Is there coffee?'

'You and your fucking coffee.' Bob gave the door another bang and Dave sat up.

They'd booked in at the caravan park because it had been too late to set up camp anywhere and it offered a twenty-four-hour reception. *God knows why,* Dave had thought. *Can't be too many people turning up here at midnight.*

Dave got dressed and was tucking his shirt into his jeans as he pushed the door open and was greeted by the glare of the sun. 'Shit, sunnies,' he muttered. 'God, I feel like I've got a hangover.'

'You're acting like you've got one too,' Bob called out.

'Just a late night and a horrible bed,' Dave said as he walked towards the communal kitchen where Bob was serving up bacon, eggs and toast.

'You'll have to harden up, son. Here, get that into you.'

Dave took the loaded plate. 'Cheers.'

'Right, plan for today,' Bob said, cutting a large piece of bacon and shoving it into his mouth, 'is we're going to borrow an office at the station and do some research.' He pushed a piece of paper over to Dave. 'That's what you're checking out for me.'

'Right-oh.' He read it and folded it up before putting the paper in his pocket.

'Have you phoned home, son?'

Dave's fork stopped halfway to his mouth as a feeling of dread seeped through him. 'No.'

Bob looked at him hard. 'Maybe you should do that first while we're in town and there's phone range.'

'Yeah, yeah,' Dave said and got up to make himself a coffee. 'Instant coffee, horrible shit. I'd be better off drinking tea.'

Bob chuckled. 'City ponce.'

❧

They walked across the road to the station, Dave's phone burning in his shirt pocket. He'd tried to ring Mel at Mark and Ellen's house but there hadn't been an answer. Maybe Mel was at a doctor's appointment. He hoped that's all it was, but it was unusual for at least Ellen not to be there.

'G'day again, Glenn,' Bob said as he pushed open the door.

'Thought it might be you fellas,' he said, getting up. 'How'd you go with everyone yesterday?'

'Yeah, not too bad. Had a chat with Kev. I can see the toll this is taking on him.'

'Oh, yeah? Get to talk to Kit or anyone else?'

'Did a bit of a drive around before we ran out of light. We did get to Deep-Water, but not for too long, just enough time to tell Kit we were back up here and to let us know if he heard anything. Got back here about midnight and checked in over at the caravan park.'

'Yeah, I saw your vehicle over there when I came in this morning. So, how can I help you today?'

'Well, Glenn,' Bob leaned on the front counter and put his chin in his hands. 'We really need to borrow an office with a phone and a computer. Got somewhere you can put us?'

Pointing to a closed door at the back of the room, Glenn said, 'You can borrow Tictack's office. He's not needing it where he is.' He opened the door to let them behind the counter, then walked them to an office door.

'Where's Tictack?' Dave asked. 'I thought you were a one-man band here.'

'I am. Tictack was my dog. He used to sleep in there. He died a month ago.' His hand on the knob, Glenn turned and looked at them. 'Do you think you'll be here for a while?'

'Who knows, mate,' Bob said cheerfully. 'Guess we'll be here for as long as it takes us.'

Dave nodded to Glenn and gave him a ghost of a smile as he walked past him into the office. The furniture was minimal but comfortable and the most important items were sitting on the desk: the computer and the phone. 'Sorry about your dog.'

'I'll grab you another office chair,' Glenn said.

'Cheers,' Dave answered and pressed the computer's on button, before wiping his hands clean. A fine layer of dust lay across the equipment.

Bob met Glenn at the door and took the chair from him. 'Thanks for everything, Glenn.' He closed the door behind him and took his notebook from his pocket. 'Right, you make the call to the office down south and run those regos for me. Hopefully we'll get Boyd's surname. Then you do your magic on the computer, because I'm sure you'll be quicker than me,' he told Dave. 'I've gotta couple of phone calls to make.'

Snatching up the phone, Dave dialled the number and waited. 'Lara, I need a rego run please,' he stated his name and number and then the plate—2IHP-054.

He could hear her typing and there was silence once she'd put all the information in.

'Boyd Paul Shepard of . . .' she reeled off the address and date of birth and driver's licence number, while Dave wrote it all down. He thanked her and hung up the phone.

The computer took a while to fire up, but when it did, he pulled up the police database. Typing in *Boyd Paul Shepard* he waited, hoping for a hit while the wheel spun around and around.

Bob was on the phone and Dave worked and listened at the same time.

'Listen, matey, we're out bush and I need a name run to see if he's linked to any businesses. Got time to do that for me?'

Pause.

'Yeah, sure, sure.' Bob laughed. 'Anytime, mate, a beer and parmi, all yours.'

Pause.

'Right-oh.' He reached out to Dave and waved his hand for the information Dave had just written down. 'Yeah, one Boyd Paul Shepard. Just whatever businesses he's involved in and if there're any flags on him. Cheers, buddy. Appreciate it.'

Pause.

'Yeah, yeah, on this number. I'm in Boogarin.'

Pause.

'Yeah, mate, I know, way out in the sticks, but it's good fun. Catch ya later.'

Dave put in the web address for the Department of Agriculture's brand register and in the search engine typed % *Shepard*. The percentage was the wildcard and he knew from something Bob had said on his first day, the wider the search the easier it was to find the brand you were looking for.

Five pages of brands and information came up and Dave looked carefully through each one, trying to match the name and address he had from the rego number.

They worked silently between them, until the phone rang, startling them both.

Bob snatched it up. 'Holden,' he answered. 'G'day, mate. What'd you find?'

Pause.

Bob reached out to grab the pen from Dave and wrote down a couple of notes. 'Yeah, good. Ah-ha. Really?'

The surprise in Bob's voice made Dave look over at him, and glance at his notes. There was something underlined. *BPS Enterprises.*

Dave nodded and went back to the computer screen, scrolling down and reading. The words were blurring in front of him and his head felt fuzzy from the lack of sleep last night. He needed another cup of coffee. Getting up, he paced the floor and did a couple of squats to get the blood flowing, and then went out to Glenn.

'Mate, is there anywhere I can get a coffee?'

'Instant in the kitchen, or if you want something else, head over to the pub. Mae will do you a good brew there.' Glenn didn't look up from the computer.

'Thanks.' Dave went outside and jogged across the road. He ordered three coffees and then took them back, putting a cup down on Glenn's desk before handing one to Bob and sitting down at his desk.

Reading through the grid that had come up on the computer screen, he checked the name and address for a BP Shepard. Not Boyd. The address was wrong. Next one, next one, next one.

'Bingo,' Dave muttered as he reached for his coffee. 'That's you, isn't it?' He read the information and scrolled down again. Not one but two properties. 'Check this out,' he said to Bob. 'Here's the brand 90P0 and the earmark.' He tapped the numbers which correlated to the earmark then went on: 'Owner name: Mr BP Shepard, address, trading as BPS Enterprises. Property ID number, and property name: Shepard's Run. But check this out. There's another property right underneath here, same brand and all, except different address. One is out of Gascoyne Junction and the other is further south near Mullewa.'

'South of Gassy Junction, huh?' Bob said, leaning back in his chair. 'You know, I'd reckon that not mentioning he was a station owner is pretty interesting, don't you?'

'He certainly wasn't forthcoming with information.'

Bob pointed his finger at Dave. 'That's my point. And . . .' He pulled out the map that Glenn had given them. 'Look here.' He traced a road with his finger. 'If whoever stole these cattle from Spinifex Downs turned south when they left, as Kev said, that's heading down that way.'

'Circumstantial,' Dave said.

'But interesting, son.'

'Hang on, let me see if I can find him and come up with any other information.' Dave plugged in Boyd's name and in a second the search was complete. He read through the headlines but there was nothing—no names or photos that correlated with the Boyd he had met. 'Pretty unusual not to even be mentioned in the *Farm Weekly* or *Countryman*, isn't it?' he asked around the pen he was chewing.

'Depends. Maybe he never goes to the stock yards. Maybe he keeps out of them because he doesn't want anyone to know his face. Obviously people up here know him, but there's no need for anyone down south to, especially in and around the saleyards, if he keeps out of their way.' Bob picked up the phone and put it on speaker. 'Let's ask Kev if he knows anyone by the name of Boyd.'

'Spinifex Downs?' Kevin's voice came down the line.

'G'day there, Kev. Bob Holden here. Dave Burrows is with me and you're on speaker.'

'G'day, officers. Have you got some news?'

'No, mate, but I'm wondering if the name Boyd Shepard means anything to you?'

The line hissed with silence and Bob glanced at Dave with his eyebrows raised.

'Yeah, it's a name we know up here in the community.'

Bob was looking down at the desk now, concentrating. 'What do you mean, a name you know?'

'We all know him here, but we never see him, see? He doesn't come here. Better that way.'

'Are you saying he was part of your community?' Dave asked, thinking back to Boyd's tanned skin.

There was banging at Kevin's end and then his voice came through the speaker a little clearer. 'I had to go into the office,' he explained. 'It goes back to Deep-Water Station. Kit's father. He had a relationship with an aunty of mine. Boyd's her son.

'See, Kit's mother died and his dad used to come over here, to the community. Visiting. There were lots of girls here. Not so many in town.

'He managed to charm my aunty away. Took her back to Deep-Water. One day she turned up back here, pregnant, you know?'

Bob's face was grim, and he was shaking his head. Dave figured he'd heard this type of story before.

'When Old Man Redman found out she was having his kid, he kicked her out. Said something about it not being right that a black woman's child should be raised with his white son.

'And the other son was Kit?' Bob clarified.

Dave mouthed, 'Half brothers,' with a look of surprise on his face.

'Yeah. Aunty, she came back to us to have the baby, and one day they both disappeared. The Elders and men, they searched. They called in people from the neighbouring stations to help, and she was found. By Old Man Redman. My aunty, she'd perished. Too much hot sun. But the baby was still alive. That's when Redman decided he was going to look after Boyd. Take him back to Deep-Water.'

'But he said he didn't want to raise Boyd with his own child?' Dave said.

'I know,' Kevin said. 'No one really understood his change in heart. I guess he was sad when he found Aunty dead and he knew that he'd done something wrong.'

'Does Boyd ever come to Spinifex Downs to see you?'

'He has done, but not for a long time. I don't think he likes it here.'

Chapter 29

Kevin hung up the phone and put his head in his hands.

He didn't want to admit his dad had been right, but he was beginning to think that finding out who was responsible for the cattle thefts might cause more trouble than it was worth.

'Who were you telling that story to?'

Kevin looked up and saw Jackie standing in the doorway. He got up and walked over to his father. 'Let's sit outside. There are days I hate being inside.'

Together they walked over to the campfire that was smouldering closest to the office and sat down cross-legged in the sand.

'Who were you telling that story to, boy?' Jackie repeated.

'That was the police on the phone. They rang to ask if we knew the name Boyd. I told them we did.' He dug into the sand and let it drift through his fingers, liking the feel of the earth on his skin.

'Why are you telling them?'

'I was putting the story into context for them. The history. Why we know him.' Kevin frowned. 'There was nothing wrong with telling about his past was there?'

Jackie picked up two sticks that were lying close to the fire and started scraping them together. 'That Boyd's no good,' he said, not looking at his son. 'I tell you, boy, he's not nice. He was raised by a wicked man. One who hated our people.' Jackie's voice got low. 'He told a lot of lies and now you, boy, you've told those lies to the police. Told you not to talk to the police.'

'What lies?' Kevin asked flatly.

'Once you hear the truth you can't unhear it, boy. But I'll tell you the real facts: she was one of them that they made disappear. The ones we don't talk about.

'He wanted that boy, but your aunty, she didn't want to go with him. He treated her badly. Hit her. Just like his son hits his own wife now. That's why she didn't want to go with him. She came back here to have the baby. When he was born, she disappeared.' Now Jackie wagged his bony finger. 'But she didn't disappear! She was taken. During the dark time. Taken, boy, you hear? He wanted his son back and she wouldn't go, so he took her. Next thing, she was dead. They blamed us, the whitefella coppers.

'But you know, boy, you know we don't treat our people badly.' Jackie closed his mouth and looked into the fire. 'Told you not to talk to the coppers.'

'Why didn't you tell me this before now?'

Jackie shook his head. 'We don't speak about people who have gone. You know that. No point, no one believes us. That boy believes those stories his whitefella father fed him. He hates us—you be careful around him.'

'Did Old Man Redman kill Aunty?'

'She was found dead and the baby alive. A baby is weaker than a woman. You think about that, boy.'

❧

Dave's mobile phone rang as he was trying to find out which agent Boyd Shepard sold his cattle through. Glancing at the screen, Mark and Ellen's home number flashed up.

A flicker of guilt ran through him. He hadn't given much thought to Melinda or the situation at home since he'd been back up here. There had been too many other things going on.

Not knowing who he was going to be speaking to when he answered, he just decided on, 'Burrows.'

'Dave, it's Ellen.' She sounded breathless and the guilt hit Dave's stomach with full force.

'Ellen? Everything all right?'

'It's Mel. We had her at the doctor today and her blood pressure was high again. They decided to induce her. He didn't want to wait.'

Dave stood up, but realised he didn't have anywhere to go, so he sat down again. 'What? When?'

'Early this morning. I tried to call you a couple of times, but I just got your message bank. It wasn't the sort of thing

I wanted to leave a message about, so I've kept ringing until you answered.'

'I'll be back as soon as I can. I'll catch a flight. Has she had the baby yet?' Dave didn't know which question to ask first.

'You're a dad again, Dave. Another little girl. A very quick birth and both she and Alice are okay.'

'Alice?' As far as Dave could remember, he and Mel hadn't talked about names.

'That's what she's named her. Dave, I'm sorry . . .'

'Doesn't matter, Ellen,' Dave said. 'As long as they're both okay. I'll catch the first flight I can, okay? What hospital?'

Ellen gave him the details and said goodbye.

'Shit!' Dave got up and paced the edge of the room. 'Shit, shit, shit.'

'Don't worry,' Bob said. 'We'll get you on the first flight we can. I'll drive you to the airport now and get something organised ASAP.'

They were both solemn-faced as they looked at each other, realising the ramifications of Dave not being there for his daughter's birth.

'Congratulations,' he added.

'God almighty, can you imagine—' Dave broke off.

'Son, you don't need to come back here until you've sorted things out at home, okay? Take your time.'

'She's gonna kill me.'

'Well, look on the bright side, better than Bulldust getting hold of you. At least Mel killing you might be quicker and less painful.'

'Ever the little ray of sunshine, aren't you?' Dave ran his hand through his hair. 'How did it all get to this?'

'Come on, go and grab your things and I'll run you out to the plane.'

Dave knew that Bob didn't have an answer. Opening the door, he jogged back to the caravan park and threw his things into the duffle bag. As he checked he had his driver's licence and ID in his wallet, his eyes fell on the family picture they'd had taken on the day he'd come back from Brisbane after getting out of hospital.

Mel was smiling widely, her arms around Dave's waist, with Bec on her hip. The gentle swell of her stomach was touching his and he was leaning down pressing his lips to her hair.

'Shit, Mel, I'm sorry,' he muttered. 'Sorry I wasn't there. Sorry that all this stuff has happened to us.' He looked at it a moment longer and then snapped his wallet shut and grabbed his bag.

❧

The flight was the longest Dave had ever endured. When they touched down, the relief that coursed through him was almost overwhelming.

He ran through the terminal and hailed the first taxi he saw. 'I need to go to Princess Margaret Hospital, as quickly as you can,' he said, throwing a fifty-dollar note onto the front seat. 'I'm a copper.' He flashed his ID.

The driver didn't say anything but put his foot down and screeched away from the kerb.

Please let her be happy to see me, Dave thought as he watched the cars race by. *Please.*

'Cheers, mate,' Dave said with relief as they pulled up in the drop-off bay at the hospital. Keep the change.' He handed him another fifty and yanked the door open, almost tumbling out in his haste.

Five floors up and he stood nervously in the doorway of Mel's ward. The butterflies in his stomach were almost as bad as when he'd stood at the altar waiting for Mel to walk down the aisle. Taking a couple of deep breaths, he tiptoed in and saw Mel in bed, on her side, her back to him.

There was a crib next to the bed and her hand was inside. He thought she might be stroking the little girl's cheek.

'Hi,' he said softly.

Even though Mel wasn't moving, it seemed to Dave as if she froze as he spoke. Putting his hand out, he touched her shoulder.

Mel turned over and sat up. 'Hi,' she answered.

Still cautious, Dave sat on the edge of the bed. 'How are you?'

'Okay. The birth was all fairly fast, but I'm okay.' She nodded towards the crib. 'Meet your daughter. I called her Alice.'

'Pretty name,' he said, not moving but looking into her eyes. 'I'm sorry.'

Mel shrugged. 'Can't change it now.'

'You're upset?'

Mel's mirthless laugh made Dave realise how much trouble he was in.

'Wouldn't you be? We knew there wasn't any point in trying to get to you—that you would've been out on a station somewhere. The doctor said we could wait until we got a hold of you, if it was today, but I didn't want to. Thought it was better to have Alice and get hold of you when we could.'

Choosing his words carefully, he continued to stroke her hand. 'I guess I'm the other half of this and I'm very upset I wasn't here.'

Mel swallowed and didn't meet his eye. She stayed silent.

This unnerved Dave. He really wanted to get up and go and look at his beautiful new daughter, but something kept him sitting on the bed looking at Mel. In the end she said in a singsong voice, 'You know, Dave, I feel our whole life is about you. About the job. I don't feel valued or loved or that you're invested in Bec, Alice and I.' Her lilting tone sent shivers up Dave's spine.

'Mel—'

'No, I think you should hear me out. Think about the last three weeks. You've been up north twice and to Brisbane. I've been living with Mum and Dad. Bec has been out of her routine and her home. Neither of us should have to do that.

'You've barely been here and, when you have, we've been fighting. You can't say it's the best for us all.'

'No, I agree.' His heart ached at everything she said. How could he fix this and still stay married? Spencer's voice came to him: *I've seen this time and time again, where plenty of coppers have changed their roles to make their wives happy. They've gone to the country. They've gone back to the city. They've changed who they are and who they want to be, because of the wife. Next thing you know, the wife up and leaves anyway. You know why? Because it's not the job they hate. It's the fact their husband isn't who they want him to be.*

He took a breath. 'What do you want to do about it?'

'You haven't been listening, have you? I've asked you to leave the job.' She folded the sheets between her fingers just as Alice started to stir. Looking at the watch Dave had given her for their wedding anniversary two years ago, she said, 'Alice is due for a feed.'

Dave got up and went to the crib, staring in. Squinty eyes stared back at him, a downy black cover on her head. Alice's fists flayed through the air and she made sucking noises.

'Hello, little one,' Dave murmured, his voice catching in his throat. 'Welcome to the world.' Gently picking her up and kissing her head, he handed her to Mel, who unclipped her bra and latched Alice onto her breast.

She drank greedily and Dave smiled, reaching out to stroke her arm that was thrown up over her face.

Dave paused, wondering if he should say what he really wanted to. Surely this wasn't a conversation to have with his wife when she had just given birth. Too late! The words tumbled out. 'And now I've got a question for you.'

Mel looked up and met his eyes for the first time.

'What happens if I leave the job and I take up something boring, like you suggested. An accountant. What if you weren't happy with the hours I had to keep at tax time?

Then what? I've given up a job I've worked towards for years and things still aren't working between us.' He held out his hands, appealing to her.

Alice let out a little cry and they both looked down at her.

'I don't know,' she said quietly.

'What I'm asking, Mel, is it really the job, or is it me?'

Mel's head snapped up. 'The job, of course!'

'Are you sure? Because if it's me, we're never going to fix the problem. If I change jobs, I'm going to lose a part of me that's really important and you still mightn't be happy.'

Mel's eyes widened and Dave could tell he'd shocked her with his words.

'I'm going to get a coffee and come back, okay?' he said. 'Can I bring you anything?'

She shook her head and just before she dropped her gaze towards Alice, Dave saw the glistening of tears in her eyes.

Chapter 30

Kit waved as two tourist vehicles drove down the main street of Boogarin. He continued along the pavement until he came to the farm merchandise store and pushed the door open.

'G'day there, Sally,' he said to the girl on the front desk. 'Digby around?'

'Hello, Kit. How are you? I'll see if he's free.' She picked up the phone and dialled a number. 'Kit's here to see you.' She listened and then waved Kit to go through. 'You know where you're going,' she said and turned back to her computer.

Kit walked down the passageway toward Digby's office, stopping to say hi to the people behind the merchandise counter.

'Got a pallet of lick blocks I can take home with me?' he asked one of them.

'Sure, Kit. Your ute out front? I'll get them loaded up for you.'

'Good on you, fella. Cheers.'

Kit greeted a short, ruddy-faced man standing at his office doorway. 'How you going, Digby?' He walked towards the stock agent, his hand outstretched.

'Good, Kit. You? Come on in.'

They took their seats and Kit leaned back, crossing his legs. 'How'd that shipment of cattle from Darwin port a couple of weeks ago end up?'

'Arrived and docked without any problems,' Digby answered. 'We had a couple of vets on board to make sure the cattle were well looked after. No problems at all, even with the temps a bit higher than were forecast.'

'Good, that's real good. Now, listen, I wanted to talk to you about getting some forward contracts for next year. Got any idea what sort of money we're talking yet?'

'Nothing's come through, but I can make some enquiries. How many are you talking?'

'Maybe three hundred micky bulls.'

Digby whistled. 'Nice. That a few more than usual?'

Kit shook his head, his face hard. 'Nah, Boyd's got a few agisted on my place at the moment. Be easier to leave them there than truck them south.'

'Agisted up here? Ha! Usually it's the other way round. Well, I'll see what I can get organised.' He wrote down a few notes and looked up with a smile. 'I'm sure—'

Kit was standing, leaning on the desk and towering over Digby, his voice soft and menacing. 'Not "I'll see what I can get organised", Digby. You *will* find someone to take those cattle. No ifs or buts. Otherwise,' he drew a finger across his neck, 'you know what happens when I don't get what I want.' He watched as Digby drew back. Giving a brittle smile, Kit nodded. 'Don't forget to work with me—' He broke off as loud voices sounded outside the office.

'You fuckers, you been out stealing any cattle lately?'

Digby, still clearly unsettled by Kit's threat, looked at him. 'That sounds like Dylan Jeffries,' he said. 'I bet the boys from Spinifex Downs are out there. Better go and break that up before they wreck my office.'

Kit held up his hand. 'Just let them have a go at each other, bloody dickheads! I'm sick and tired of nursing these idiots.' He eyeballed Digby again. 'Have I made myself clear about shifting those cattle? Don't fuck me around. And don't be passing judgement on where Boyd agists cattle.'

Muffled voices filtered through the door. 'You're nothing but a wanker, Jeffries!'

'We've gotta intervene.' Digby danced on the spot, his eyes between Kit and the door and whatever was happening beyond it.

Kit took a step towards Digby. 'You haven't answered me.'

'I'll shift your fucking cattle, Kit,' Digby snapped as the sound of a fight starting up reached the office. 'I always do, you two-faced son of a bitch.'

Kit glared at him and stood back. 'Knew you'd see it my way.' He rearranged his face into a concerned smile. 'Now, let's just hold on a minute before we go out there. Have a listen first, never know what you might find out.

Hotheads all of them, and at some point whoever is stealing cattle won't be able to keep their mouth shut.' He got up and opened the door a crack, looking out.

'This is my shop and I want them shut down,' Digby said.

'And this is my town and I run things the way I want to.'

Digby kept jiggling. The words were clearer now the door was open. 'Not anymore it's not,' he said quietly.

'Don't you go pointing the finger at us, you white prick!' Sounded like Harry from Spinifex.

'Now, boys,' said one of the merch guys.

'We know it's you. The money the government gives you all to prop you up, it doesn't keep you in cigarettes and booze, does it?' said Dylan Jeffries. 'You've gotta take other people's cattle to make everything work out there.'

'Not on our watch, arsehole. We know it's you lot who are coming onto Spinifex Downs. You've been doing it for years, you whitefellas. Always trying to throw the blame on us. Well, not anymore. We've got Kev now. And he's going to find out who's doing this.'

'Guys,' came the muffled voice of another merch bloke, 'you really need to stop this. Break it up. Dylan, how about you get outside and calm down?'

'What, so you're going to send *me* outside to calm down, not this cattle-thieving prick?'

'I—'

Kit opened the door further and stepped out to intervene.

'You fuckers are gonna go for a row,' Harry said. 'We've got cameras on our place now and we're gonna know if you go there. If your face turns up on our camera, mate, we'll be straight to the police to get you locked up.'

'You watch what you say, you black prick. No copper is ever gonna believe you. And you wouldn't know how to breed cattle to save yourself. That's why you lot have to steal.' Dylan threw a punch that Harry dodged.

'Right-oh, boys. That's more than enough. Harry, Dylan, back away, put down your fists,' Kit said, striding towards them. 'What are you lot thinking?'

'You know as well as I do that they're the ones stealing the cattle, Kit,' Dylan said, breathing hard.

'Actually, I don't.' Kit stood in front of Dylan and stared at him. 'All I know is Spinifex Downs have had cattle stolen. How you think they've stolen their own cattle, well, I don't know. Have you had a think about that?'

'Maybe they're just dead from bad management,' Dylan snarled. 'Or trying to get an insurance payout.'

'I think you know that's not the answer,' Kit answered calmly.

'No, we don't!'

'What's going on?' Kevin came running through the door. 'Harry, get here now. Next to me.' He grabbed hold of Harry's arm and pulled him away from the crowd of people.

'It's all right, mate, think we've got these two hotheads sorted,' Kit said, pushing his hand into Dylan's chest. 'Jesus Christ, Dylan. If that was the case, don't you reckon the government and animal welfare would be all over them like a rash? And we'd know about it, because we'd smell the carcasses and see them when we flew over. Grow a brain. Sometimes you make me wonder what goes on in that head of yours.'

Kevin grabbed hold of the back of Harry's shirt and pulled him back to the merchandise desk. 'You sit down there and shut up,' he said.

'Sorry, Kev. He got me so worked up.' Harry hung his head.

'I can see that. Just shut up. We don't need any more trouble.' He turned to Digby, who was standing behind Kit. 'Sorry, mate, is there any damage? I'll pay for it,' he said.

'Nah, she's right,' Digby answered, looking around. 'Just get him out of here. Dylan, you too, go on! Get out of here and only come back when you can treat each other with respect. I don't give a shit what colour your skin is. Respect! Hear me?'

Kevin gave Harry a little push. 'You heard the man. Get out of here. I'll be out in a minute.'

Kit watched as Harry went out the front door and Dylan out the side, then turned back to Digby.

'Geez, I didn't see that happening today when I left home,' Kit said, for the benefit of the other people in the room. 'We've got to put a stop to this somehow, don't you think, Digby?'

'Yeah, sorry about that, Kit, Digby,' Kevin said. 'Harry's not usually one to cause trouble.'

'Guess if you get accused of being a thief, there's only so much a bloke can take,' Digby said, running his hand over his head, glaring hard at Kit. 'You right over there, Sally?'

Kit looked over and saw Sally coming out of the ladies' room.

'Yeah, all fine. I was ready to call the cops if I needed to,' she said, waving the cordless phone.

'You're all over it,' laughed Kit, breaking the tension in the room. 'Well, I'd better get out of here. Got other things to do today. Kev, you got a moment?'

Kevin nodded.

'Let's walk,' he said. Over his shoulder, he said, 'Catch you all later.' His eyes fell on Digby and he winked, before walking out the door.

Outside Kit leaned against the wall in the sun, flicking his sunglasses down over his eyes. 'Hope those detectives from down south are going to get this sorted soon. We really don't want a fight up here.'

'I know and I've told them all that. Like I said, Harry's pretty quiet. That's why I brought him instead of Charlie. There would've been a worse issue in there if he'd come.'

'Mate, have you got any idea who might be doing this to you? Like I said, I just want the shire to go back to the quiet, peaceful place it can be. Not with all this tension and shit.'

Kevin shook his head. 'If I did, I'd be knocking on their door.' He crossed his arms.

'Such a bugger. Such a bugger.' Kit sighed as if the weight of everyone's problems were on his shoulders. Then his head snapped up. 'Harry said you blokes have got cameras rigged up out there now? Great idea.'

Staying quiet, Kev kicked the ground.

'Where'd you put them?'

'Around about.'

'Well, mate, you don't have to tell me, I just think it's a great idea. Taking the initiative, you know? Hopefully that'll help the cops.'

Kevin nodded. 'That's the plan,' he said.

❧

Dave walked back into the ward, not knowing how Mel was going to greet him. Truth be told, he rarely knew how she would react to him when he came home.

Alice was back in her crib and Mel was up, dressed in her dressing gown, sitting in a chair and looking out the window.

'I'm back,' he said. 'Brought you a coffee.'

'Thanks.' She didn't turn away from the window, so he put the coffee on the table and went to look in the cot.

Alice was wrapped up in a pink baby rug, sound asleep, with her eyes tightly shut. Reaching forwards he stroked her cheek, thinking his heart might burst.

'She looks like Bec did when she was a baby,' he said softly. 'Like you.'

'I think she looks like Mum.'

Dave looked again. 'Maybe a little bit. She's got the cutest chin and that comes from you.'

Finally Mel got up and came to stand beside him and they looked at Alice together. He wanted to put his arm around her shoulders, but he wasn't sure how he would be received, so he didn't move.

'What are we going to do?' Mel whispered.

Dave didn't answer.

'I'm sure it's the job,' she said.

'You don't sound certain.' He glanced sideways at her and saw she was staring at Alice.

Mel turned to him. 'I am.'

Dave nodded. A tiny bit of hate started, like a small balloon in his stomach, and he tried to push it away. He couldn't hate her. She was his wife.

Should a wife ask you to give up something you love? he wondered. *Should anyone?* Spencer's words came to him again: *No one should ask anyone to give up something they love.*

He took a breath. 'I don't think I can give up the job.'

The air felt thick and heavy and Mel let out a small sound—a cry or groan, Dave couldn't be sure.

She went and sat back down in the chair and rubbed her eyes. 'Stalemate,' she said.

Alice started to stir, and Dave reached down to pick her up. He cradled her in his arms and rocked her back and forth, bending to kiss her, his head touching hers and his eyes shut.

What did the future hold for her? For him? For them all?

'I think you should go,' Mel said, sounding like she'd given up.

'What?' Dave didn't move, although his voice rose in surprise.

'Go back up north and do what you've got to do. Maybe we can sort this out when you get back. Just leave, Dave. You won't be happy until the case is finished, so you might as well finish it, then we'll work something out when you're back and you can concentrate on us.'

'Mel, come on, sweetie. Don't be like that. I don't want to leave you within twenty-four hours of you having a baby. Our baby.'

'Hmm, well, you weren't here for the birth, so I don't think you not being here will make a difference to me. I'll be in hospital for a few days and I'll just go back to Mum and Dad's until you get back.'

'And you'll come back home then?'

'Yes, I will.' She gave a brittle laugh. 'I didn't think I'd ever say this, but maybe we should go to counselling, Dave. We don't seem to be able to break any new ground when we talk. We go over the same thing every time. It's tiring and boring and we're not getting anywhere.'

'Look, Mel,' he put Alice back in her cot and turned to his wife. Squatting down in front of her, he took her hands. 'I'll do whatever it takes to make us work. If you want to go to counselling, let's give it a go. But I won't give up policing.'

'You sound like Meatloaf,' she answered without a smile.

'I won't do that,' he said, hoping he'd make her smile. He'd always been able to.

Withdrawing her hands, Mel looked away. 'Go, Dave. Go and do what you have to, then come home. We'll work everything out from there.'

Chapter 31

Dave disembarked the plane and glanced up at the sky as the humidity hit him in the face and the small bush flies buzzed around his head. He'd tried to sleep through the flight, but images of Alice and Mel kept going through his head. Mel and her lack of interest in him and their relationship—acting as if she'd already given up on him. Alice with her long eyelashes touching her cheeks as she slept, and her little rosebud mouth moving as if she was sucking at her mother's breast. Walking out the door of the hospital had been one of the hardest things he'd ever done, leaving his family behind, not knowing what the future held for them.

In the terminal there were only a handful of people picking up bags and looking around for loved ones. Dave could see the troopy through the sliding doors and he grabbed his duffle bag from the conveyor belt and strode outside, trying to put his wife and two daughters out of his mind until this case was finished.

'Good to have you back,' Bob said, and Dave was grateful that he didn't ask how the visit went. The fact he was back within twenty-four hours of leaving probably told the story anyway.

'What's happened since I've been gone?' he asked, clipping on his belt. 'Any updates?'

'Well, young Harry from Spinifex Downs and Dylan Jeffries from Cassia Plains had a bit of a to-do in the merchandise shop yesterday. Only heard about it when Glenn came in and told me. They were both throwing accusations around.

'Apparently Kit Redman was in town and broke it up. Once it was all over, Kev hightailed it out of town, his young lad in tow.'

'Ah bugger,' Dave said, scratching his head. 'I don't know why those two had to go around casting aspersions.'

Bob turned the corner onto the main road and headed south. 'Come on, I'll bring you up to speed with what I've found out. Do you need a coffee before we get on the road? Too early for a beer.'

'Didn't think I'd ever hear you say that! Where're we going?'

'To a little station called Avaglong. Out of Gassy Junction, son.'

Dave's head whipped around. 'Boyd Shepard?'

'I thought we'd pay him a little visit. How about that coffee? It's a bit of a drive.'

'Yeah, that'd be good.'

Dave went into the pub and ordered two takeaways. Mae looked him up and down. 'You run away for the day yesterday?' she asked as she set out two cups.

'Had a couple of little jobs to do at home, yeah,' Dave said, wondering how she'd noticed when he'd only ever set foot in the pub once to get a coffee.

'Yeah, Glenn and Kit were here for lunch yesterday and I heard them talking. Said you had to go home 'cause your missus had a baby.'

Dave grinned. 'Yeah, that's right. A little girl.'

'Congratulations! What's her name?'

'Alice. She's a little ripper!'

Mae looked up from the milk she was pouring and gave him a hard look. 'Why are you back up again so soon then? Shouldn't you be at home at your wife's beck and call, changing shitty nappies?'

'No, we've got an understanding,' he said, wishing she'd hurry up. He didn't need to be reminded.

'Hmm, maybe *you* do. I'm sure she doesn't.' Mae poured the hot water in and pushed the cups over the counter. 'I don't think I'd be that happy with a husband who flew home to see me for twenty-four hours then went back to work. I'd watch yourself if I was you. Might go home and find there's no one there.'

'I'll keep that in mind,' Dave said, wondering what gave her the right to pass judgement on his life. He dropped the correct money on the counter.

'Yeah, bit of advice for free!' She winked. 'Us women need to stick together.'

Dave raised one of the coffees at her and went outside, his heart beating just a little faster.

'Damn,' he muttered. Getting back into the car, he leaned his head back against the seat and closed his eyes. Bob didn't say anything, only put the vehicle in gear and drove off slowly.

'Kit and Glenn were in the pub yesterday having lunch,' Dave finally said.

'Oh yeah?'

'Mae was offering some maternal advice.' He looked over at Bob. 'Glenn and Kit were in yesterday for lunch and they were talking about Alice's birth. Mae overheard them.'

'Hmm, Kit and Glenn?'

'Yeah. Got me thinking about something.'

The white lines flew beside the troopy as they drove towards Gascoyne Junction. Termite mounds, large as a six-foot human and vivid red, stood out against the flat landscape, while scrappy grasslands coloured the ground. The sky stretched out in an endless blue.

'We know they're mates, those two.'

'Mmm.'

'Remember how Glenn had changed his attitude towards Kev and the community when we got back up here?'

'Like I said, son, I think that's ignorance rather than anything else. He's allowed to have mates, you know.'

'Yeah, yeah, but it's worth noting.'

'Sure is. Now listen. Going to the airport yesterday gave me an idea. I decided to charter a plane and go for a fly.

Told Kevin what I was doing in case he had someone shoot me out of the sky but didn't tell anyone else.

'Gives you a whole different perspective up there, I tell you. And this really is God's own country—the ranges and gorges. Do you know, we flew over a couple of waterholes where we could see the reflection of the plane? Beautiful.' Bob took a sip of his coffee and went on.

'We flew the boundary of all properties that border Spinifex Downs—Deep-Water, Cassia and Paperbark.'

Dave couldn't help himself. 'What did you see?'

'To be honest, not much. But there were a couple of things that caught my interest. On Cassia Plains, I remember Dylan saying that they hadn't sold any cattle for twelve months. If that were the case, there shouldn't be any truck tracks in there, should there?'

'Unless it was the fuel truck,' Dave suggested.

'Good point. There were tracks in. We flew low enough to be able to see them. I got the binoculars out and had a real good look. And you're right, maybe they were bringing in fuel, but the fact of the matter is that they're there. So that's number one.

'Two, I rang my mates at the saleyards and asked if there had been any Brahman cattle sold through there in the last three months. They faxed through thirty-two weigh bills for me to look at.'

'Yeah?' Dave turned to look at him. 'Do tell.'

'Three of those weighbills were for BP Shepard Enterprises. He's sold ninety Brahman steers and fifty cows.'

Dave's heartbeat kicked up another notch. 'Seriously?'

'True story.'

'What are we doing now then? Why aren't we arresting him?'

'Come on, Dave, you know we have to prove this without doubt! We need photos of him pinching the stock from Spinifex Downs, or the stock in the saleyards with the wrong brand being sold under his trading name—even then, a good judge will call that circumstantial. Nope, we've still got a bit of work to do yet.'

❧

Dave followed the map with his finger, then looked up. 'Turn right here, reckon it should be Courtabilly Road. Then Boyd's front gate is about three k down here.'

Bob checked the speedo and worked out the kilometres. 'It should be about . . . Yeah, look. There it is.' He pointed to an open gate to a dirt track leading into the farm.

Two minutes later they were pulling up at a homestead that looked like it hadn't had a woman's touch in many years.

'Hello?' Dave called out.

Bob walked up the steps of the house and banged on the door. 'That's bloody disappointing, he's not here. We'd better check the shed and see if he's down there.' He gave a wink and Dave knew that they didn't need a warrant to enter the property if they were looking for Boyd.

Around the back of the homestead, towards the shed, there were sheep yards. Large weeds were growing up through the rails and Dave could see where wooden boards had fallen off and split. He would've bet his last pay cheque that wild dogs had made it too difficult to keep sheep here.

Further on there were cattle yards that were just the opposite: shiny, new steel ones. Dave walked over to them and pushed the gate into the crush open and shut. It slid like a dream.

'Reckon these are used a fair bit,' he called to Bob, who was over in the shed. 'Nice tidy set. Bit like the ones we saw Kit and his crew working in at Deep-Water that day.'

'Fresh shit there?'

Dave glanced down. 'It's not steaming but I'd say a week or so old.'

'Come and look at this.'

Dave went to the shed and waited for his eyes to adjust to the gloom. In the corner was a small white truck.

'Doesn't have a cattle crate on it,' Dave said, going closer.

'No, but there's cattle shit on the tray. The crate's been taken off.' He rubbed his finger along the edge of the tray. It came away with red dust on the tip. 'It'll be here somewhere.'

'Shit, Bob, look at this,' Dave bent down and put his fingers on a wheel. 'Red dust.'

'Yep. Take down that rego number, will you? Think we should see if it's registered to anyone we know.'

Dave jotted it down in his notebook. 'Should we take some photos?'

'Can't really. Haven't got a warrant.'

'Shit!' Dave said. 'Reckon we've got enough to get one?'

'Not yet. Everything is still circumstantial. Run that plate and we'll have a bit more of an idea. I think Boyd is involved somehow. Who might know if Kit has anything to do with his extracurricular activities? We'll have to work that out.'

'I'm still not convinced about Kit's involvement,' Dave said. 'I reckon he's worked too hard for too long to keep people united in this shire. It doesn't make sense for him to want to see Kev and his community hurt.'

'Told you before. Best place for a criminal to hide is in plain sight. No one would ever suspect Kit of stealing cattle.' Bob looked around. 'There's more to this. It's bigger than just the stock. My gut tells me it's to do with the history between the Spinifex Downs community and Boyd, but I . . .' His voice trailed off. Taking a breath, he started to walk outside. 'We're just going to have to keep digging.'

'Wish I could see some cattle,' Dave said.

'You and me both. Bugger to come all this way and not sight Boyd, too. Anyway, that was the risk we took. Come on, let's get into mobile range and you can ring about the rego.'

Fifteen minutes later, Dave hung up the phone. 'It's registered to Boyd.'

'Mmm. Let's call Kev. I've got a couple of questions for him.'

Dave dialled the number and Kevin answered.

'Real pleased you called, Dave. I've got something for you.'

'What's that?'

'The alarm on the cameras went off last night. There was someone here—not an animal. A person.'

Dave glanced across at Bob, who held one hand up as if to say, *What's going on?*

'Did the camera capture an image?'

'Yeah, Sergeant, it sure did.'

Dave chose his words carefully. 'Do you recognise the person?'

'I know who I think it is, but I'm not saying. I don't want to be the one who gets accused like we did in town. You'll have to come and get the camera.'

'What you tell us, mate, it's not going anywhere. You can give us the information.'

'Nope.' Kevin was firm. 'When can you get here?'

'We're coming now. But we won't be there before dark. We're quite a way away.'

'Come tomorrow, then. Don't want you to drive in late at night; kids will be asleep and you might frighten the old people. First thing in the morning, dawn. The camera's not going anywhere.' Kevin hung up before Dave could say anything else.

'Let's get back up there,' Dave said to Bob. 'He's got an image on the camera, but he won't tell me who it is. Doesn't want to be seen to be making accusations.'

Bob swore. 'Ridiculous!' He pushed the accelerator down and headed north again.

Chapter 32

With an east wind blowing and a half-moon, the ute approached the community without its lights on. Boyd knew the wind in the trees-tops along the creek would make sure no one from the community heard their approach.

'Pull up here,' he whispered. 'Need to be a long way away from them otherwise they might hear.'

Kit pulled into a bushy scrubland area so the ute wouldn't been seen, and reached over into the back, bringing out a bag. He upended it onto the front seat to check the contents. Gaffer tape, cloth bag and a steel bar.

'Here.' He handed Boyd a balaclava and a set of gloves. 'I would've been a lot fucking happier if you'd managed to find those cameras before we did this. We're going to have to be really careful.'

'I looked,' Boyd said. 'Nothing on the front gate, or the mills near our boundary. I took the night-vision goggles, but there wasn't anything. I reckon the bastards are bluffing.'

Kit's hand shot out and grabbed Boyd by the shirt front. 'You'd better be right, otherwise we're both going down.'

Boyd brought his clenched fist down on Kit's arm. 'Don't pull your arsehole crap on me. You forget, I know you better than anyone and your bullying won't work with me.'

Kit let him go and they glared at each other through the dark night, their chests heaving. Finally, Kit nodded. 'You're right. Sorry. Bit uptight about this. We're good.' He held up his fist and bumped it against Boyd's.

'Glad to hear it. You should know better than to take your temper out on me. Got me stuffed how you actually held it together while you were in public office.' Boyd stalked off into the bush, leaving Kit behind.

'Could've done with those night-vision goggles tonight,' Kit whispered loudly.

'You don't need goggles,' he threw over his shoulder. 'You've got me. I was only wearing them before because I was looking for something.'

Boyd didn't hear Kit's answer. Everyone thought his brother was the golden boy. The local celebrity, never put a foot wrong. People wouldn't believe he hit his wife or yelled obscenities until his jugular stood out and his face was fire-red.

Not like him; ever the drifter, the half-caste who didn't have a mother. People would believe anything about him. He'd heard the blokes at the bar call him a sly dog. He hated that he'd never fitted into either the black or white worlds, while his brother slipped effortlessly between the two.

The brothers were intertwined by blood and history. And some sort of half-arsed love that meant they could battle each other to within an inch of their lives, but if anyone else turned on the other, they were a united force. Their father had always impressed upon them that there was no one more loyal than a brother and so that's how they were.

Brothers. In arms. Devoted until the end.

'Get back here,' Kit hissed through the night and Boyd stopped until Kit caught up.

'Dickhead,' Boyd muttered as he heard his brother stumble over a bush. 'Right?' he asked as Kit found his feet.

'Let's get this over with. Have you worked out a plan yet?'

'We'll snatch him as a warning. Keep him alive. Let everyone think he's dead, but we'll let him walk home. Then there'll never be any trouble with this mob again, while he's alive.'

They moved stealthily along the creek bank towards the community. The shadows of trees danced in the moonlight as they walked and the night sky smelled like rain was coming.

Boyd held up his hand as a dog started to bark. The two men froze, and another dog started, then another. Holding up his hand, Boyd indicated to wait until the noise had died down.

It didn't take long before everything was silent again. Boyd walked on again, taking a track through some shrubby bushes towards the manager's house.

They could see a glint of moonlight on the tin shed, and in the distance a cow bellowed.

At the bottom of the stairs into the house, Kit and Boyd stopped and listened. Gentle snoring came from within.

'Surely it's only him in there?' Kit asked.

Boyd nodded, just as a dog barked, this time much closer. Both men hit the ground and lay there.

A voice from the community yelled out. 'Shut up, you mongrel dog!'

The dog, shocked into silence, whined and lay down, the chain rattling against the tin kennel.

Pointing upwards, Boyd indicated they should climb the stairs. The snoring was getting louder.

With light feet, they pulled open the front door, which gave a squeak. They both stopped and listened. All still quiet except for the snoring.

They entered the house and, with a few more hand signals, tiptoed towards the bedroom.

The curtains were open and they could see the body of the man they were after lying on his back, his arm thrown up over his eyes. His head was just off the pillow. Perfect.

With slow, gentle movements, Boyd picked up the pillow and placed it over Kevin's face, then fell on the sleeping man to hold him down. Shocked into wakefulness, Kevin started to struggle. The pillow muffled his cries and his arms lashed out, trying to hit the unseen perpetrator.

Putting all his weight onto the struggling man, Boyd rolled until Kevin was pinned under him face down. Kit pulled Kevin's arms behind his back, tearing at the tape at the same time.

Kevin gave more muted cries while Boyd lifted his weight slightly to let Kit get to Kevin's hands.

Feeling freedom, Kevin instantly twisted away and got his head out from underneath the pillow, followed by one of his arms.

'Hel—' he started to yell. Boyd smashed his free fist into his face and Kevin went quiet and limp. The sting of the punch followed by the smell of blood made Boyd panic.

'Quick! Come on,' Boyd snapped at Kit, who was still tearing off pieces of tape. He managed to get one arm behind Kevin's back and then the other one. Kit bound them tightly, put the cloth bag over Kevin's head, then rolled him onto his back.

'He can't walk,' Kit whispered. 'He's out cold. We'll have to carry him.'

'Not sure we can do that, the ute's about half a k away.'

'Well, how else are we going to get him there? Why the hell did you hit him anyway?'

Kevin groaned and started to move. This time it was Kit who snatched up the steel bar and struck Kevin's head beneath the bag. There was a horrible crack of steel on bone and Kevin stopped moving.

Boyd and Kit looked at each other, then Kit leaned forwards and listened for breathing.

Nothing.

'Fuck, I think I've killed him.'

Boyd put his hand roughly on Kevin's chest and felt it move. 'Nah, these blackfellas got hard heads. Trust me, I know, I've got one. He'll be right for now. Come on.'

Pulling the cloth bag off his victim's head, Boyd tore off another piece of tape and put it over Kevin's mouth, before binding his legs as well.

'Put the bag back on his head,' he instructed as he wound the tape around Kevin's waist, pinning his arms to his side. 'That'll teach the fucker,' he said as he broke the tape off.

'Look at this,' Kit said, indicating blood seeping through the bag over Kevin's head. 'We're going to leave a trail.'

'Won't matter, just so long as we get the hell out of here now. They won't find us once we're in the ute. Come on, grab an arm.'

They seized an arm each and started to drag Kevin's limp form from the house. His legs made a thudding noise as they walked down the steps and a dog barked again.

'This is no good,' Kit hissed. 'We're going to have to get the ute, otherwise they'll hear us.'

'Keep going,' Boyd muttered. 'Just keep going.'

They stumbled their way across rocky ground for a few hundred metres until they reached the bushy scrublands they'd come in through.

'We're out of sight now,' Boyd said, relaxing a little. 'And with the wind in the trees the dogs won't hear us. You right to keep going?'

Kit stopped and wiped his forehead. 'Would have been better to make him walk. Didn't mean to hit him so hard.'

Boyd gave a nasty laugh. 'Nah, anyway he'd just yell and give us up. Not how I planned it, but better like this,' he said. 'Don't worry. He'll get everything he deserves.'

Kit and Boyd linked arms under Kevin's shoulders and they trudged on in silence, pushing branches and sticks out of their way.

A few minutes later Kit stumbled and fell heavily, the unconscious man landing on top of him.

'Fuck.'

'What?'

Boyd heaved Kevin off Kit and tried to help him up. 'You right?'

'Don't know,' Kit answered, breathless. He placed his foot on the ground and pressed. 'Fuck!' He breathed heavily through his nose, trying to get rid of the pain. 'No. No, I'm fucking not.'

He tried again, with the same result.

'Mate, I'm not going to be able to walk much. Can you get the ute?'

'How the hell are we going to get the ute in here? We're in the middle of the bush!' Boyd snapped.

'You're going to have to drag him to a clearing and load him up from there. I'll try to hop to you.' He used the branches of the shrubs around him to pull himself up, swearing under his breath.

Boyd wanted to hit something. Could this go any more wrong? He grabbed Kevin and started to drag him again, hoping Kit would be able to follow the noise and use the trees to help him along.

Before he knew it, he also stumbled under the weight he was dragging.

'Boyd? You right?'

Puffing. 'Yeah. Just came a cropper too, but I haven't hurt anything. I think we're far enough away that I can get the ute in now. Where are you?'

'Not far behind. You go, I'll watch Kev.'

Boyd listened as Kit hopped along a few metres, and then he saw him emerge from the bush. They both looked at Kevin's body lying on the ground.

'He's not going anywhere.'

Kit slumped to the ground next to Boyd, his hands massaging his ankle. 'Shit,' he whispered quietly.

'How bad is it?'

'Better not take my boot off. Don't think I'll get it back on.'

'Damn it to hell,' Boyd muttered.

'Come on,' Kit snapped at him. 'Get going. We've gotta get out of here before daylight.'

'I fucking know, all right?' Boyd got up and started towards the ute, stopping only to listen to the noises of the bush. A dog, a light breeze and the leaves rustling against the branches and bush. He knew when the engine started it was going to be loud.

'Shit,' Boyd said.

❧

Jackie awoke to the sound of barking. Not just barking, howling. Instantly alert, he rose from the ground and walked outside.

He thought he heard the rumble of a vehicle, but then the wind gusted and the leaves rustled together and the sound was gone.

322

Standing still, he listened longer. Harder. And a feeling of dread overcame him.

With light feet and sure steps, Jackie walked quickly to the homestead. 'Kevvy?' he called out. 'Kevin?'

Silence.

Climbing the stairs, he reached out to flick on the torch he carried. His eyes adjusted to the light and he stared at the floor.

Blood. Drag marks.

'Boy?'

Padding towards the bedroom, Jackie looked in, already knowing what he was going to see.

The bed was empty and there was blood on the sheets.

'They've taken him,' Jackie said to himself, uneasiness slipping into his body. 'Stupid boy, I knew this would happen.' He stared at the empty bed before going outside and sitting next to the fire, where the last embers were still glowing.

'The past always comes back to haunt us,' he whispered.

He remembered bygone times. The noise of cattle hooves thundering through thick bush; the sound of stock whips and horses. The shouts of men as they rounded up cattle that didn't belong to them. Staring hard into the embers, he hardly heard one of the other Elders come and sit down next to him.

'He's gone?'

Jackie turned at the sound of his friend's voice, then dropped his eyes. 'Yeah.'

The old man put his hand on Jackie's shoulder. 'Is it happening again?'

'Nah. It will just be Kevin. That will be their warning. They won't take anymore.'

'Until next time.'

Jackie's head snapped up. 'There won't be a next time.'

'The boys will want to talk to that police bloke.'

'I said it before and I'll say it again. No cops. This time they'll listen to me. Kevin is being made the example.'

The sun was beginning to peep over the horizon when two of the younger men, Harry and Charlie, came out of their houses, stretching. Seeing the Elders next to the fire, they came over.

'What's going on?'

The two men looked up, their eyes red. 'Kevin has gone.'

'What do you mean, gone?'

'Out bush, you mean?'

'Nah.' One of the Elder's shook their head.

'He won't be coming back,' Jackie said.

'Who's taken him? What are you talking about? Someone has taken him? The same as been taking the cattle?' Charlie sank down into the sand and stared hard at the men. 'If he's gone, we gotta call the cops. Someone's taken Kev!' His voice rose as he looked around, as if he were hoping to see his friend appear out of the bush.

The Elder leaned forwards. 'No cops,' he said. 'No cops. There's been enough damage done.'

Jackie looked out over the creek and nodded, before looking at Harry and Charlie. 'No police,' he reiterated. 'I seen this before. He's not comin' back. Kev's not coming back.'

Chapter 33

'What the hell is going on here?' Dave asked as they pulled up at Spinifex Downs. The whole community seemed to be gathered around the fire, some sitting, some standing, but all looked bewildered and frightened. The silence as they stood there gazing at the police vehicle was unnerving.

Jackie came and stood looking at them without speaking. A sad stare. A stare that could see through most things. Then he turned and walked away.

'Shit,' Bob said, throwing open his door. 'Something's happened to Kevin.'

They followed Jackie down to a smouldering campfire, pushing their way through the quiet crowd.

'What's happened, Jackie?' Bob said, squatting down in the dirt. 'Where's Kevin?'

'I told him no police. He wouldn't listen.' Jackie turned his head away from them.

'Tell us what happened. Do you know what time? When it was?'

'It's the same as before, white man takes what he wants. I got nothing to say,' Jackie said stubbornly.

'We're here to help,' Dave said. 'We don't want any harm to come to Kevin either. Can you tell us what you know?'

Charlie came and sat down next to them. 'I've been up to the house. There're blood and drag marks coming out the front door and down the steps. I tracked 'em to the bush but they disappeared after that,' he said.

'You keep your mouth shut, boy.' Jackie's head came up and his voice rose. He looked at every person surrounding him, jiggling his knee up and down in agitation. 'No more! Kev's gone. Nothing can be done. No cops, no nothing.' He held his fingers to his lips.

Bob caught Dave's gaze and inclined his head towards the house.

'Can you show me, Charlie?' Dave asked in a low voice.

He nodded and pointed in the direction of the house.

'No, boy. No!' Jackie's voice broke, but Charlie and Dave kept walking, ignoring the old man's pleas, while Bob sat there and listened.

'Do you know what happened?' Dave asked Charlie as they walked away.

'Nope. I woke up early and felt there was something different. The dogs had barked a lot during the night and that's not normal. When I got up, the old men were sitting around the fire. That's unusual too, so I went to sit with them, waiting to hear what was wrong.' He bent down and pointed at a spot on the ground. 'That's blood, I think.' He paused as Dave looked down and took a photo. 'Someone came into the community but we didn't hear them in time to stop them.'

'Do you know if anyone woke up before you did?'

Charlie shrugged.

Cyril fell into step with them. 'I reckon I saw something,' he said.

Dave turned to look at him. 'Can you tell me?'

'Got up to take a piss. The dogs woke me. Went out and was doing my business, and I heard a thump at the main house. The dogs let off another round of barking and I told 'em to shut up. Someone else had yelled out earlier when they'd been barking, so they must've been sneaking up on foot, I reckon.'

Dave stopped walking and turned to look at him. 'You didn't go to investigate?'

Cyril shook his head. 'Nah. Coulda been a roo hopping through. Sometimes those big fellas, they make thumping noises like that. Still could've been roos.' He shrugged. 'We mind our own business here.'

Dave nodded. 'What was the moon doing last night? Would these people have been able to see without torches?'

'Yeah, not well, but enough. Specially if you know the country. It was a half moon, but that's plenty bright enough to get by.'

Jotting down that information in his notebook, Dave said, 'Let's go and check out the house then.'

'Here,' Charlie called. He had walked on ahead and was now standing in front of the house, pointing at the ground. 'Drag marks.'

Dave took the camera from the bag and looked at the tracks. 'Looks more like toe marks, doesn't it?' he said, more to himself than anyone else. 'And there doesn't look to be any other sign of struggle, so maybe they knocked him out.' He snapped another couple of photos. 'Let's go inside.'

'Here, Dave,' Charlie pointed again. 'More blood.'

Bending down, Dave looked at the small spots. Drips, almost. Not a lot of flow, so not a large wound, but enough to leave a trail. And to suggest he was only unconscious, not dead. Well, not from blood loss anyway.

Dave followed the trail up the steps and looked around the front entrance to the house. It was sparsely furnished—a table, chairs and off to the side an office with a computer sitting on the desk and a phone alongside it. On the wall, Dave could see a large map of Spinifex Downs and marks to show what paddocks the cattle were in. A whiteboard with lists of jobs and phone numbers was hanging next to it.

On the other side was the bedroom. A double bed with tangled sheets and blood. Again, it didn't look like there had been much of a struggle. Nothing upturned or tipped over.

Dave took more photos in silence, while Charlie and Cyril stood at the doorway, their backs turned. They didn't want to see.

Dave followed the drops of blood back outside and down the steps. 'Can you boys follow this trail?' he asked. 'I can see it when it's easy like now, but I might need you fellas a bit up there where the ground gets hard.'

'Jimbo is already on it, boss,' Charlie said. 'He's tracked 'em to the bush over there. Come on. Harry went and got him earlier. He's the best tracker of all of us.'

'Hang on, I need to take photos of what we're seeing and draw a map of where they've dragged him to.'

'No time for that. Let's go.' Charlie was already striding off, leaving Dave no choice but to follow.

Five minutes later they were deep in the bush and Jimbo was standing still, looking at something on the ground.

'What have you got?' Dave asked as he got closer.

'See here. Drag marks of Kev's feet and two footprints on either side, but here'—he pointed to broken branches and a scuff mark—'he's fallen over and then there's only one set of prints dragging him.'

'So we've got two perps. One who's hurt himself and one who's still draggin' our boy?'

'Think so. See, 'cause the way one of 'em walks has changed too. One footprint, rather than two. It's deeper in the soil, which means he's putting more weight on it. He's hopping. And, here, more broken sticks as he's held on for balance.' He pointed to a snapped branch.

Dave took more photos of the tracks. 'Still blood?' he asked.

'Yeah, here and here.' Jimbo indicated some spots Dave would never have noticed. The soil had sucked the blood into the earth, leaving only a dark spot on the ground.

'Come on,' Jimbo indicated for them to follow. 'Here are some ute tracks. They head off in the direction of Cassia Plains.'

Dave, now out on the road, looked around. Strange that they should head towards Cassia Plains when he was sure it had been Boyd and Kit. They hadn't found anything to link Dylan to the investigation. Trying to put them off? Slowly, he turned in a full circle, listening and looking. 'How far is the community from here?' he asked.

'About five hundred metres that way,' Jimbo said, pointing north.

'That's the same direction as Cassia Downs, so how did they get by you without you hearing?'

'Dogs were barking and the wind hides sounds.'

'You would have seen the lights of the ute.'

'Not if they didn't have them on.'

'It was light enough to drive without them? Driving's different to walking.'

'This road is wide until you get past the creek. After that they could have put the lights on and we wouldn't have seen anything.'

Dave nodded and wrote some notes. 'Guess we need to follow the tracks as far as we can,' he said, squatting down and taking more pictures.

'Jimbo's your man,' Cyril said. 'He'll help.'

'Good. Come on, let's head back to Bob.'

'What have you got?' Bob asked Dave as they walked into the camp area.

Dave noted that Bob was still sitting with Jackie, and by the frustrated look on Bob's face, he hadn't had any luck in getting the Elders to talk to him.

'Certainly drag marks and blood. Jimbo's happy to track for us.' He glanced across at Jackie, who held his hands up.

'I told him and now I'll tell you—I'm not talking to the coppers.'

Dave kept talking. 'He's been taken from the bedroom without a struggle. Somehow they've overpowered him and I reckon he's been rendered unconscious because there hasn't been a struggle while they've carried him to the ute. Just some drops of blood.'

'Murder?'

Dave shook his head. 'I don't think there's enough blood to indicate that, unless death was caused by something else, like strangling.' He glanced at Jackie as he spoke, hoping he'd see a softening in his stance.

Nothing.

'Have you found the camera?' Bob asked.

Dave looked at him aghast. 'I'd forgotten all about it. I wonder if the other blokes know where it was situated.'

One of the Elders spoke. 'Kev didn't tell anyone where he'd put them.'

'Bugger it. Right, let's go and ring Glenn,' Bob said and got up from the ground. He looked at Jackie, who refused to meet his eye. 'Not going to get any help here.'

A feeling of frustration swelled in Dave's chest. All the inroads they'd made with the community had been thwarted by this kidnapping. Surely they'd want to find Kevin and get him back alive?

'I'll find him, Jackie,' Bob told the man and turned away to follow Dave.

❧

'Glenn, mate, we've got an incident out here at Spinifex Downs. Young Kev has been taken by two suspects. I need you to organise eyes in the air for me.'

'What? Who's taken him?' Glenn's disbelief was obvious even from three hundred kilometres away.

'We believe Boyd Shepard is one suspect.'

There was silence on the end of the phone. 'Surely not. He's part Aboriginal. He's *from* that community.'

'Raised by his white father, from what I understand.'

'Yeah, but the Aborigines don't turn on their own.'

'Well, there's an exception to every rule. We found a rigid body truck at his station out of Gassy Junction, covered in red dirt. I've got proof he's sold red Brahman cattle through the saleyards recently. And he's Kit's half-brother, as you know, which makes me a little suspicious since the first lot of cattle went out through Deep-Water's yards.'

He paused. 'You know, Glenn, you said you had a lot of information on most of the people around here. And you've been saying all along that there's a lot of history between the white and Aboriginal stations. What else has happened between the Redman-Shepard camp and the community at Spinifex Downs?'

Glenn was silent for a moment. 'All I can tell you is the folklore. It was well before my time, a different generation.'

'Give me the rundown so I know what I'm dealing with.'

'Kit's father got a woman from that community pregnant. He didn't treat her well so she came back to her family, had the baby and then went walkabout. She was found dead and the baby alive. As the father, he had the right to take his son and raise him in the white man's world, which he did.'

Silence hummed down the line.

'See, I have a problem with that story because a baby is so small and tiny and would dehydrate so much quicker than an adult woman. Has anyone ever thought that perhaps he murdered her and took the child?' Bob finally asked.

'No one has ever said that. Not even a whisper.'

'Hmm,' Bob said as he remembered some of the comments from the Elders.

White man's law doesn't look out for us.

Because no one bothered to follow it through.

Dave ran inside Kevin's homestead holding a security camera in one hand with a smile on his face. Bob looked at him quizzically but continued to talk to Glenn.

'Okay, if you could get eyes in the sky. We're looking for a ute headed towards Cassia Plains. Stay in contact, okay?'

'Sure thing.'

Bob hung up the phone and stood up. 'What have you got?'

'Check this out,' Dave said. 'Harry brought the camera back here. Here's the image.' He held out the camera. On the screen was a grainy photo of a white ute.

'Can you enlarge that in any way?'

'I'll connect it to Kevin's computer.' Dave fossicked through the top drawer of the desk until he found a likely looking cable, connected the camera to the computer and flicked the mouse. A shot came up. 'See here. Here's the numberplate. Same as the one that Boyd was driving when we pulled up at Kit's place a couple of nights ago.'

'Is there anything that shows us who was driving? Tell me that camera has got night vision?'

Dave smiled. 'Sure has.' He flicked across and there, outlined against green grainy background, were two faces. Boyd Shepard and Kit Redman were staring through the windscreen, their eyes on the road as they drove.

'Got 'em,' Bob said. He turned to Dave in a hurry. 'You get on the road. You said one of the boys could follow the tracks? Take him with you and see where they go, but for fuck's sake, make sure you stay in touch. I'll cordon this area off and make it a crime scene.' He looked at his watch. 'I reckon they've got maybe three hours' head start on you, and you've got about eight hours of daylight left. They'll be travelling quicker now the sun's up and you'll be able to go quickly too. We'll get that plane up ASAP. The pilot'll be able to radio you info.'

Dave nodded and started to jog down the steps.

'Channel 40,' Bob yelled out. 'Keep the two-way on channel 40 and make sure you've got the sat phone out.'

Chapter 34

'Dumb fuck,' Boyd said as he drove the ute away from the community, the moonlight helping him see the way.

His headlights weren't picking up the road as well as they should—one was out after he'd hit a roo early on.

'We wouldn't have had to do this if that idiot had kept his mouth shut and listened to the old people.' He turned the wheel sharply to avoid a pothole. The wheel clipped the edge and they bumped heavily along the road. He swore as the steering wheel was reefed out of his hand.

'Jesus, slow it down a bit, mate,' Kit said, hanging onto the handrail. 'Last thing we need is to have an accident with Kev on board.'

Boyd glanced over at his brother and shook his head. 'We should be getting out of here as fast as we can. Anyway, I've been on this road enough to know where the tricky bits are.'

'Have you been coming over here?'

'Yeah. At night, when everyone is sleeping. I come and I watch the old people. Make sure they don't tell anyone anything. Last time I was here, I went and stood at the end of Jackie's bed. I did that to remind him. Remind him that the people from Spinifex Downs need to keep their mouth shut about what happens out here.'

'What did he do?'

'Stared at me. But I scared him. I know I did.'

'Didn't work,' Kit said in a defeated tone. 'They still talked.'

The ute bumped on and Boyd put his foot down even harder. 'I reckon those coppers will turn up real quick.'

Kit nodded. 'Yeah, they're not going to stick to any of the unwritten laws we have up here. That's the bloody problem when you bring outsiders in.'

'You got Glenn tucked in?'

'No need. He already knows the rules. Shouldn't be any trouble with him.'

Boyd glanced over. 'What, you haven't paid him off?'

'Nope. Was never going to. He's my mate.'

'He's a copper! Fuck, you've left him to chance?'

'Sure have. He'll be fine,' Kit said confidently. 'Where are we going to leave *him*?' Kit nodded towards the back seat.

'Gonna stash him out in one of the old bunkers on Crown land. Leave a bit of water and shoot through. When he comes to, he'll be able to get himself back home again.' Boyd pushed his foot down harder and the ute sped up. 'That'll teach them to get involved with coppers. They were never my people. Remember how Dad used to tell us stories about how they didn't go looking for Mum? If it wasn't for him, I'd be dead, and they have to pay for that. Pay for not loving a white man's kid.

'They don't know how to run stations anyway. Like Dad used to say, they wouldn't know how to look after the stock. Best we have them. But you've added something personal now. The fact that they abandoned me in the bush.' He looked over at his brother.

'Did the cattle even mean anything to you, or was it all about getting back at them?' Kit asked.

'I don't give a fuck about the cattle *or* the money. It was never about that. It was about seeing them turn against each other. The Elders are upset Kev's gone to the cops, and, now he's gone, well, they're not going to cause us any trouble. He'll be frightened when he turns back up again. We'll be able to walk all over the place and take cattle whenever we want and they'll let us.'

Kit watched as Boyd tightened his hands on the wheel and smiled. 'No more problems from *them*. When Kev goes back to the community, Jackie will be angry, start to shut him out. The others won't want him around because he's caused trouble. This'll be a massive warning to them all. They'll toe the line for a lot of years to come.'

The road become rougher—the little-used track was full of corrugations. Overhanging branches were whipping along the side of the ute. A couple of times Kit threw his hand up to protect his face from the branches, even though he was inside the cab.

From the back seat came a muffled moan. Boyd drove faster again, the steering wheel shaking under his grip.

'Mate, slow down,' Kit said again. 'I'm sure there's a—'

He hit the roof of the cab as they nose-dived into a ditch and came to an abrupt halt. The noise of crumpling steel rose into the now-light sky along with the screech of galahs. And then there was silence.

'You okay, brother?'

Boyd's voice broke into Kit's haze of pain. When he opened his eyes he saw a wall of red dirt rising in front of him.

'For fuck's sake, you idiot,' Kit snapped, rubbing his head where it'd connected with the roof. I told you to slow down. No point in killing us in the process!'

Boyd looked back and saw that Kevin had been thrown forwards and he was now awake and struggling against his restraints. 'Need to knock him out again, can you do that?' he asked, jamming the ute into four-wheel drive reverse and gunning the engine.

Kit watched his brother's leg, waiting for him to let the clutch out, and braced for the jerk when he got out of the ditch, only to find that the wheels were spinning.

'Fuck,' Boyd muttered and stopped.

'Rock it out,' Kit snapped. 'Change gears from reverse to first and keep rocking the ute back and forth.'

Finally the wheels finally gripped and they reversed out.

Kit looked over at his brother and grinned. 'Bit of excitement.'

'That we could have done without.'

In the back, Kevin made another whimpering noise. 'I'll give him another whack,' Kit said. 'He's so far gone it won't take much to knock him out again. Stop when you get out on the road.'

Boyd pointed the ute back out onto the road and started to drive. The ute limped forwards, shuddering, and Boyd had to grip the steering wheel hard to hold on.

'Flat tyre,' Kit said, glancing around nervously.

'And steering, I reckon.'

'Fuck.'

Boyd stopped the vehicle and they both got out, Kit gasping as he tried to put his foot on the ground. 'You'll have to get under and have a look,' he said. He held onto the open door as Boyd got down on his back and shimmied under the vehicle.

'Steering rod's bent.'

'Back tyre this side,' Kit said.

'Can you grab the spare?'

Kevin kicked at the door, his foot connecting with steel. He continued to bang against it.

'Mate, I can't walk, if you hadn't noticed! Oh, for fuck's sake. Stop doing that!' Kit hopped to the back door, reefed it open and hit his passenger again. Kevin went still and Kit slammed the door shut. 'Just change the fucking tyre and let's get going.'

'Going to be hard with the steering the way it is,' Boyd said, getting out the jack. He grunted as he put it under the axle and started to lever it up.

Ten minutes later, with the tyre changed, they limped off again.

∽

Following Jimbo's directions, Dave drove carefully along the overgrown two-wheel tracks, hoping with every corner they rounded to see Boyd's vehicle broken down.

'Which way are we headed now, Jimbo?' he asked, leaning forwards to look out the window at the sun.

'North, boss. Bit of Crown land up here. Might be heading there 'cause there's a track that heads back to Deep-Water.'

'You don't think Cassia Plains?'

Jimbo shook his head. 'Nah. If it's Boyd they'll be heading back to Deep-Water. He knows this country as well as I do. And Dylan and Boyd don't get along. They won't be working together.'

'How do you know that?'

'They had a punch-up at the rodeo four years ago and Dylan said never to come near him again.'

'Do you know what it was over?'

'A woman.'

'That'll do it every time. Who got the girl?'

'Dylan.'

Dave nodded and swung the wheel of the troopy to avoid a deep ditch.

'Stop!' Jimbo yelled.

Dave slammed his foot on the brakes. 'What the fuck?' His heart was pounding. 'What've you seen?'

Jimbo was out of the ute and on his knees before Dave could yank the handle of the door open.

'Look here, they've been stuck. He's nose-dived into the ditch.'

It was easy to see what Jimbo was talking about now that Dave was on the ground. There were deep grooves in the dirt where they'd reversed, and soil had been sprayed out from the wheels as they'd tried to get the tyres to grip.

Jimbo was further down the road now. 'They've had a flat tyre. See here.' He pointed to the indentation in the ground and Dave snapped more photos. 'And look how the tread is heavier on one side of the ute. I reckon they've damaged the steering.'

'You're a legend, Jimbo,' Dave said, impressed. 'I would have missed that without you. Right-oh, let's get going again. We'll keep at them.'

Dave increased his speed as he drove, hoping Kit and Boyd were only just in front. He'd calculated that changing the tyre would have cost them fifteen minutes and with the damaged steering their speed would be much slower. Maybe they could gain on them.

He jerked the wheel to take a sandy corner and the back of the ute swung outwards. As he came out of the slide, he pressed the accelerator harder for more power.

Glancing across, he realised Jimbo was hanging on hard. 'Okay?' he asked.

Jimbo didn't say anything, only stared ahead. Dave gripped the wheel harder and watched the road, making sure he avoided any potholes or trees, anything that could damage the vehicle.

'Cattle around here, boss,' Jimbo finally said.

'What do you mean?'

'They walk on the roads sometimes.'

Dave lifted his foot a little and the troopy slowed a fraction, just as the CB burst into life, causing both men to jump.

'Stock Squad, Stock Squad on channel 40, you got a copy, Dave?'

Dave recognised Glenn's voice over the scratchy radio. Slowing down, he picked up the handset: 'Stock Squad receiving. Yep, got a copy there. Where are you, Glenn?'

'Mate, we're about twenty k east of Spinifex Downs heading in a north-east direction. In the air.'

Dave looked up; nothing but blue sky. A quick glance at his GPS to read his position showed they weren't that far away from each other.

'Roger, Glenn, we are about twenty-five ks ahead of you, heading in a similar direction on an overgrown track. Moving towards Crown land.'

'Copy that, will call when we have you in sight.'

Returning the handset, he looked over at Jimbo. 'Reinforcements have arrived, Jimbo. Just what we were looking for. Make things a bit easier if they can pick up Kit and Boyd and direct us to them. Sort of feel like I might be chasing a phantom because I don't know where they are!'

'Tracks are still there, boss.'

Dave nodded, focusing on the twin tracks they were following, snaking through the scrubby bush.

Suddenly the track seemed to come to an end, thick branches covering where the track should have led. He slammed the brakes on, then threw the vehicle in reverse, trying to see where he'd missed a turn.

'See anything, Jimbo?'

'Let me get out.'

Dave stopped the vehicle and both men got out and ran back the way they'd been driving.

'Here!' Jimbo pointed to a spot about twenty metres back. 'They've gone east, straight through the scrub. Broken branches.' He walked in and disappeared from view. 'There's more of a road here and I've got the wheel tracks,' he called.

Running back to the car, Dave kept reversing carefully until he came to where Jimbo had disappeared, and there he swung the nose of the ute around before carefully driving in. The bush opened up and he could see the road easily again.

'Quick! Jump in, mate,' Dave called. He stopped the car long enough for Jimbo to climb in through the passenger door and then headed off in pursuit of the unseen vehicle.

'Stock Squad, Stock Squad, channel 40. Got a copy, Dave?'

Dave grabbed at the mic. 'Yeah, Glenn, loud and clear. Where are you?'

'We were tracking slightly south of your current location and nearly missed you but picked up a reflection from your windscreen. Just about overhead of your location now. You should have eyes on us in about one minute.'

'Copy that. Can you see where this track is heading, over?'

'Yeah, Dave, it's going to get pretty rough in about five hundred metres, but you should make it through okay. Deep creek with a rocky bank you'll have to get up. After that, you'll swing east again in about a k. There appears to be another river coming up in a few ks.'

Dave visualised the rivers criss-crossing the land, tall gum trees lining the banks and rough outcrops of rocks dotted everywhere. He'd have to be careful he didn't get a flat tyre.

'Up there, boss.' Jimbo pointed out the plane in the air just above them.

'Got eyes on you, now,' Dave said into the mic. He thought for a minute then depressed the button. 'Glenn, can you see any other vehicles in the vicinity?'

'That's a negative. We haven't sighted anyone else. But we're on the lookout.'

'Maybe best if you can swing ahead of us and see if you can pick up anything. We saw a while back that they'd gone nose-first into a ditch, and Jimbo tells me they've damaged their steering so they may be having issues or have broken down. They've also had a flat. They're going to be slower than us and I want to catch them.'

'Copy that, will sweep ahead and keep you informed. I have relayed our position back to Bob on my sat phone. He is liaising with the district office and getting further resources out here . . .' The static on the radio broke up the last few words, but Dave got the gist of what Glenn was saying.

'Good job. We're looking for a Land Cruiser ute or similar based on the tyre tracks. Definitely a four-wheel drive. But check out anything you see as they may have another vehicle out here.'

There was a silence before Glenn answered again. 'Copy that. Are the suspects known to us?'

'Affirmative.' Dave wasn't going to say anything more. Channel 40 was the public channel of every truckie in Australia, not to mention the tourists. Trouble was, Glenn didn't have a police radio in the plane he'd hired and Bob didn't have one back at Spinifex Downs, so they didn't have a secure channel.

A thought crossed Dave's mind.

He picked up the sat phone and dialled Glenn's number. 'Boyd Shephard and Kit Redman,' he said when Glenn answered.

'You're kidding me?' Glenn sounded astonished at the news.

'I wish I was.'

Chapter 35

Hanging on to the steering wheel for dear life, Boyd felt like his arms were going to shake loose from their sockets. The steering rod had been damaged so severely he was lucky to be able to hold it on the road at all—the left wheel kept fighting to tear itself away from the front suspension. He gritted his teeth and kept on driving.

'Lad,' his father had once told him, 'there're millions of acres up here and plenty of spots to hide bodies without being discovered. But, just in case they are found, it's best not to let them turn up on your station.'

'Where should we put them then?' he'd asked.

'Have a look at this,' Old Man Redman had said, pulling back a large bush to reveal a deep cave under the ground. 'Army built these bunkers back in the war. They're all over the place if you know where to look and most people don't because they don't even know they're here. Government likes to keep these things quiet. Best thing about them? They're on Crown land. Anyone could've put these bodies here.'

'There're some in there?' Eighteen-year-old Boyd's eyes had been wide as he'd peered into the gloom.

His father had laughed. 'I'll tell you all about it one day, lad, but needless to say, yep, there are a few bodies in there that no one will ever know about.'

They hit another deep crevice and Boyd was pulled back to the present as Kit let out a cry.

'God almighty! How much further until we hit the main track?' he groaned, clutching at his ankle.

'Not far until we stop,' Boyd said. 'Just over the next ridge.'

'Thank fuck for that. We need to get to the bunker and get rid of him and the ute. I'd reckon everyone would know what's happened now, with Kevin missing and all. But whether they've tied it to us or not, or if they've talked to the coppers, we can't be sure. Those cameras could've fucked us over.'

'Nah, I said before, I reckon they're bluffing. Didn't find any trace of them.'

Kit looked out the window. 'If the coppers are involved, they'll have the planes up spotting and there'll be people looking for us on the ground. That Bob, he knows enough about the Aboriginal people to have trackers on us.'

'We've got time on our side. They couldn't have discovered Kev was gone until daylight and then it will take the police a few hours to get out there and track us. I think we're fine for time.'

Then Kit turned on Boyd and snapped, 'We should have been there hours ago and we would've been if you'd listened to me and slowed down!'

'Yeah, yeah,' Boyd answered lazily, grabbing the wheel back as it bounced out of his hands. 'So you've told me every five minutes since it happened. Stop repeating yourself.'

Boyd directed the ute up the winding track and crested the low ridge. 'There we go,' said Boyd with satisfaction as he looked out over Crown land, which was covered with trees, grasses, termite mounds and deep valleys. The ridges sent out long shadows across the land. 'Not long now.'

One hundred metres ahead was a graded track.

Kit heaved a sigh of relief as the bumpy road became smooth. They turned south and headed towards the low range of red hills that stretched away from them to the east.

'Be there in about twenty minutes.'

'Good,' said Kit. 'We drop Kev and this ute and head back to Deep-Water like nothing happened. Need to get back there before anyone comes looking for us.' He paused. 'You're certain this ute can't be traced to us?'

'I told you, it came from a mate who stole it years ago. Nothing to tie it to us. We push it into the bunker and anyone looks they will just think someone dumped an old wreck. The bunker slopes down and goes in about eighty feet and is black as night, so why would anyone bother? Plus, like Dad said, hardly anyone knows about them.'

'Have you been in there?' Kit asked. 'Really?'

'Yeah, mate. I've walked down to the bottom.'

Kit looked ill at the thought of walking down into a musty, airless cavern.

'Want to know what's in there?'

'I already know.'

'Yeah, but you don't know how many.'

'No, I don't. Let's keep it that way.'

Without speaking, they continued along the track at a sedate pace, the shuddering front end threatening to give out at any time.

❧

Jimbo pointed as the pilot completed another swoop along the bottom of the red ridge. The fact that the plane banked to pass over the hill again meant they'd seen something.

Dave wanted to stop and watch, give his shoulder a break. It was aching from the effort of holding the steering wheel in rough conditions, but he had to keep his foot down.

'Reckon they've spotted something, boss,' Jimbo said. 'They're banking.'

'Stock Squad, Stock Squad, channel 40, do you have a copy, Dave?'

Dave grinned and gave Jimbo the thumbs-up. 'Affirmative!'

'We have a vehicle travelling east on the old bunker access road south of your location. A white Toyota ute.'

'Roger that,' Dave answered, the urgency in his voice clear. 'Any idea how far we are from that track?'

'Hold five.'

Dave flicked on his flashing lights so the plane could locate their vehicle more easily. The plane swung back to the north.

'Roger, Dave, we have you in sight. You're about one k from the track and I would guess you are about fifteen kilometres behind the ute. I'm tracking the suspects.'

The slowness in Glenn's voice indicated to Dave he was looking through binoculars, watching the other vehicle as he spoke into the radio.

'Suspect's vehicle is travelling very slowly.'

'Copy that, we'll see if we can pick up the pace a bit. Any way you can slow that ute down even more?'

'We'll see what we can do, Dave. Push on as quick as you can. I'll update Bob with our location and see how far off the cavalry are.'

'Cheers, Glenn. Good luck.'

Dave looked across at Jimbo. 'Sounds like we're a goer,' he said.

Jimbo looked over at him but didn't say a word, and Dave realised he'd made a mistake. Jimbo was a talented tracker, but he didn't want to be in the midst of the take-down. The fact remained that whether Boyd identified with his heritage or not, he was part of their family.

Still, nothing could be done about that now. Dave resumed his focus and pushed the troopy even harder along the rough track, risking everything to find Kevin.

Chapter 36

The screaming of a wheel bearing and smell of overheated metal permeated the cabin of the utility.

Boyd and Kit's progress had slowed again but they still pushed on doggedly, not speaking, each lost in his own thoughts.

The ranges were close to their left, covered in ochre rocks and stone, and dotted with white-trunked gums, but they didn't notice. They were fixated on the bush beside the road, looking for the unmarked track which would lead them to the bunker and a replacement vehicle.

'What's that noise?' Kit suddenly asked as a roar sounded above them.

'Jesus, what the fuck?' Boyd cried out, not knowing what was happening.

The aircraft, when it appeared, was about twenty feet above the ground, coming directly at them.

Boyd swung the steering wheel away from the oncoming plane while Kit ducked. 'Fuck!' he screamed. 'Where did he come from?' He put his head out the window and watched as the plane banked to come at them again.

Pulling back inside, he put his hands over his head and crouched in the footwell of the ute as the plane came in low over them, then swept up and away from the road surface, banking to the left away from the hills.

'Who the fuck was that?' Boyd swore. 'And what the fuck are they doing?'

'Those bastards went to the coppers!' Kit screamed. 'It'll be the younger guys, not the Elders. Shit, I should have made sure they wouldn't talk before we did this! I thought the Elders would keep the young blokes under control!' Kit reached over into the back of the ute and took out a rifle, before turning on the CB radio and punching at the scan mode.

It burst into life and Boyd and Kit looked at each other in horror as they heard: 'Stock Squad, Stock Squad, got a copy, Dave?'

'Glenn,' Kit whispered. 'That's Glenn's voice.'

Boyd turned on him. 'You said we wouldn't have any trouble with him! Stupid prick!'

'Copy, mate, what's the update?'

'Just scared the shit out of them. We've buzzed them but there's not much else we can do. There are two occupants in the ute but I can't ID them. Couldn't see a third occupant but it's dual cab, so might be on the back seat. They have made it to the hills and are still tracking east.'

'Shit, shit, shit,' said Boyd, pushing his foot down hard, without any result.

'Listen, Dave,' Glenn continued, 'we're about out of fuel. We're gonna have to leave you. We will head to the closest station and refuel and get back up as quick as we can. I will update Bob as to the current situation.

'Also, they appear to be having car trouble. Not sure how much further they will get. We're turning to head back now and we'll be as quick as we can.'

Kit peered up into the sky and saw the plane turning towards Cassia Plains and disappearing into the distance.

'Copy that, we are on the track now.'

'Get this thing off the road as soon as you can!' Kit yelled above the screeching. 'We've got to hide somewhere.'

'Don't panic,' Boyd said in a calm tone. 'We'll outrun them. And we have the advantage of knowing where we're going.'

After another kilometre Boyd swung the disabled vehicle off into the bush. 'Here we go. The bunker track,' he said. 'Only a k up to the entrance and we can get rid of the body and ute, then we're free, brother.'

'Dunno how you make that out,' Kit said. 'How the hell are we going to explain what we're doing out here?'

'Get thinking. That's your problem, not mine. You're the one who's got everyone thinking you're a fucking saint. I'm going to have to get rid of everything. I won't have time to think.' He glanced at Kit and grinned at the scowl his brother had been giving him all his life.

The trail weaved under a dense canopy of eucalyptus trees, and the smooth surface of the road quickly changed to rocky outcrops as they started to drive up the ridge.

It only took the first jarring impact and that was it for the front suspension. The ute slewed to the left and came to a grinding halt, tipping to one side.

With a quick look out the window, Kit could see that the wheel had buckled under the engine and the ute was leaning precariously close to the ground.

'Fuck!' screamed Boyd, forgoing any pretence of calmness now. 'Fuck it!'

'Get out,' yelled Kit, trying to scramble out of the window without hurting himself. 'Ugh, fuck.' His teeth were clenched in pain as he managed to crawl away, while Boyd shouldered the driver's side door open and clambered out.

'You good?' Boyd puffed, running around to Kit. 'You good, brother?'

'Yeah.' They both looked at the inert form in the back of the ute tray.

'How far up to the bunker from here?' Kit asked.

'Too far to carry him. About half a k or more.'

'Well, what the hell are we gonna do about him?' Kit asked the question more to himself than Boyd.

Boyd hopped from one foot to the other then went to the back of the ute to look at Kevin again. Kit knew that Boyd was close to losing it.

'You certain we can't be linked to this ute?' he asked.

'No, Kit, I've already told you. There's no worries there. I got it sorted.' He spoke quickly, then realisation overcame him. 'Fingerprints. We haven't used gloves.'

Kit's face went red with rage. 'Guess we haven't got a choice but to leave it,' he said. 'Okay, go get the stashed ute and bring it back here. I'll see if I can hop down to where we turned off and sweep our tracks away and wipe out the cab. With any luck, Burrows will drive right on past. But for god's sake be quick. We haven't got a lot of time.'

Boyd headed off at a trot and Kit turned and limped down the track. He didn't make it far before the pain was unbearable, so he dropped to his knees and crawled, keeping the injured ankle up in the air.

He was sweating hard by the time he reached the junction of the two roads and he had to lie on the ground to catch his breath.

The roar of an engine reached his ears and he catapulted up and quickly broke a low branch off a nearby bush.

Crawling again, he started sweeping the dust across the surface to cover the telltale tracks of their passing, then swept his way back to the narrow opening. As he checked to make sure he'd covered his own crawling impressions as well, he looked up to see if the entrance to the side road was visible. He decided he could probably fix that a bit more and broke off some more bushes and placed them in among the trees already there to cover the track opening. Satisfied that the camouflage was sufficient, he started to crawl back towards the ute.

Bugger this, he thought as he pulled his body along through the dirt. He was covered in red dust and had prickles in the palms of his hands, but he could move quicker this way than trying to walk.

By the time he made it back, Boyd still hadn't returned, so he pulled himself up by the tyre and looked into the back seat, checking their victim.

Kevin's chest still rose and fell in shallow breaths, and the bag over his head was now stained with the dark dried blood from the head wound.

Boyd was right about one thing, he thought, *they do have hard skulls. A whitefella would be dead by now.*

Turning at the sound of tyres, he watched as his brother arrived in Kit's dual cab ute.

'Let's head back up into the bunker while they pass,' he said to Boyd when he'd stopped. 'Then, if they do see our tracks, they'll be preoccupied with Kev for a while and hopefully we'll be able to get out on the other track that goes straight up over the top of the ridge.'

'That'll be hard going,' Boyd said, putting the ute into gear and doing a three-point turn.

'Not as hard going as jail,' Kit stated.

Boyd drove the ute into the mouth of the bunker and turned the key. The ticking of the engine was loud in the black silence and Kit turned to look over his shoulder out into the daylight.

'You right?' he asked Boyd.

'Yeah, mate.'

'Okay, as soon as they've driven past, we'll deal with Kev and double back from where we came. There's another telegraph track we can go down about five k along the road. You know what this joint is like, roads criss-crossing everywhere. That'll get us back to Deep-Water. We'll have to hightail it though. Once we're there, play it cool and stick to the story.'

'What story's that?'

'We've had water trouble and we've been camping out the last few nights working on the mills. Haven't been home for three nights. Bit dirty 'cause of that. Then we burn the clothes, gloves and boots, everything. Make sure we haven't left anything to chance.'

'What about Tara? She'll know we haven't been out on the station.'

'Tara will say whatever I tell her to say. She still remembers the last time she questioned me on something,' Kit said flatly. 'And even if they find Kev and he lives, we won't have any more trouble with the community, and if he dies, well, even better. Win-win situation really. Just so long as he doesn't give us up.'

'I'm confident he won't do that. Not after this.'

They sat there quietly, waiting to hear Dave's cop car passing. Boyd got up and walked to the entrance.

'I see dust,' he said, looking into the sky.

'And there's the engine,' Kit said quietly.

They waited, holding their breath. So much depended on the next few minutes.

'Look there,' Boyd said. 'Good thing we're up high, we can see him.' They watched the approaching dust cloud through the bush canopy from their elevated position above the track.

'Fuck, he's hooking,' Boyd said, watching the vehicle flying along at a reckless pace. It was upon and past their hiding place in a flash and continued on at high speed around the next sweeping bend.

The brothers turned to each other, their smiles wide.

'Told you, didn't I?' said Kit.

'Stupid prick was travelling too fast to see we'd turned off. He'll be miles away before he realises he's fucked up.'

'Dodged a bullet. Okay.' Kit's tone changed from triumphant to business-like. 'Let's check we have everything out of the ute. We can't leave anything in there that ties us to this. Then we get out of here.'

Chapter 37

'Where are they, where are they?' Dave muttered to himself as they closed in on the range. He'd hoped to see the dust of the fleeing vehicle by now. In fact, he was sure he should have seen it.

His troopy lurched heavily and he turned into the slide as they rounded another tight bend. Jimbo grabbed at the handrails and let out a little moan but didn't say anything.

'Sorry, mate.' Dave risked looking over at him for a brief second then focused back on the road.

On the next straight section Dave picked up the mic of the CB again. 'Fixed airwing patrol, Glenn, you on channel?'

The airwaves were silent and Dave swore. 'Either they're not in the air, or the bloody hills are blocking the reception. And I can't see anything. I really need that plane up there!'

Gripping the wheel, he accelerated harder and watched the speedo climb to one hundred and thirty kilometres an hour, hoping like hell he didn't hit a crevice, pothole or a roo.

Bec and Alice filtered into his mind and he realised he was risking his life again, as he had in Queensland. A high-speed chase through the station country of Western Australia wasn't what he'd promised Mel, that no more harm would come to him.

Jimbo's voice startled Dave from his fixation with the road ahead. 'Sorry, boss, but those tracks have stopped.'

'What's that?'

'No more tracks, boss, they must've turned off back there.'

'Shit,' said Dave as he braked heavily. 'How far back did the tracks stop?' He ran up over the side of the road as he tried to turn around in a three-point turn, and trees and bushes scratched the side of the car.

'Not far, boss, not far.'

Dave accelerated back the way he'd come, rounding the corner at high speed again. As he drove over a small rise, he was greeted with the telltale sight of a vehicle dust cloud some way ahead on the track.

'Well, well, look at that. Well done, Jimbo. That was great spotting. Especially since I was going so fast. They must've pulled off to let us go past. We've got them now.'

'Maybe they changed cars, boss. Not the same tracks.' Jimbo was hanging out the window looking at the ground.

Dave pondered this for a moment. It would have been smart to have another car hidden as an emergency back-up. That would put the cops off. That type of cunning made him want to catch them even more.

'Not far ahead now.'

Another corner and a straight stretch and there it was.

'There we go.' Dave finally got his first glimpse of the vehicle ahead of them, a white dual cab ute travelling normally. But as he closed to within four hundred metres the ute's speed picked up and its dust cloud intensified. The gap between their vehicles began to grow again as the more agile dual cab pulled away from his heavier troopy.

❧

Boyd glanced in the rear-vision mirror and stared. 'Fuck,' he said.

Kit looked at Boyd and then looked out the rear window. 'Where the fuck did they come from? Go, go, go! Put your foot down!'

Boyd jammed down on the accelerator and their vehicle leaped forwards. Kit turned and hunted for glimpses of the stock squad troopy through breaks in their dust cloud on the track behind them.

He switched the CB on again and waited to see if there was conversation between the air and the coppers, but the airwaves remained silent.

'Floor it!' he yelled. 'Get us the fuck out of here, for Christ sake!'

'We shouldn't be running,' Boyd yelled over the noise of the engine and the rattling of the ute as they bumped over the corrugations.

'No choice now, mate. If we weren't done for before, we are now. Only thing to do is outrun them.'

No matter how hard he pushed the troopy, the dual cab kept pulling away from him. Dave realised he was fighting a losing battle. The police vehicle was no match for the lighter, more agile ute. He had to make a decision: keep pushing on, or stop and use the sat phone to alert someone further up the track.

Coming over the next rise he saw the gap between their vehicles had grown even further. Now the other vehicle was only a dust cloud heading for freedom.

'Damn it to hell!' Dave slammed on the brakes and hit the steering wheel in frustration as he slowed to a stop.

Without thinking, he pulled the sat phone from its holder and dialled the number for Spinifex Downs, hoping that Bob would be there.

'Hello?' came a voice. Not Bob.

'Is the policeman still there?' Dave asked.

'Yeah. I'll find him. Hang on,' came the reply, and then nothing as footsteps could be heard walking away from the phone.

Dave turned to Jimbo. 'That road there got a name?'

'Nah, but there's a bunker down there.'

After what seemed like minutes, Bob's voice came on the phone.

'Holden.'

'Bob, it's Dave. Listen quick. I am following a white dual cab eastbound along a road that has a bunker at the end of it; the same road the plane followed the suspects

363

on when they were headed in a different direction. They appear to have swapped cars and doubled back, heading your way. I can't keep up to them. Can you get someone to intercept?' He reeled off the GPS coordinates.

'Mate, just calm down. The plane will be up again in about fifteen. If we can get them overhead, we can follow them. Don't risk your neck trying to keep up. There are too many things that can go wrong in this scenario. We know who they are, we can pick them up later on.'

Dave shook his head—he had no intention of listening to Bob. 'I've got to go. I can still see their dust ahead so I'll follow them as long as I can. Not sure how much longer that will be as I am getting low on fuel. Gotta go.'

'Dave!' Bob barked.

Dave terminated the call and accelerated off in pursuit again.

❧

'Lost him,' Boyd said as they got to the top of a hill and he looked in the rear-vision mirror. 'Can't even see any dust. Maybe they've stopped.'

Kit turned in his seat and looked out across the valley that stretched for several kilometres back.

'Good job, bro,' said Kit. 'Let's slow it down, no point in killing ourselves now.'

Boyd pushed the car faster again.

'All good, mate, we've been driving these roads all our lives. A few more kilometres of distance between us and the coppers won't hurt. I'll move it to the junction, then slow it down from there. We can take the short cut through to your place. I'll hide this out at the old shelter, and we can take the bikes back to the homestead. Those stupid coppers will be running around looking for a white dual cab but it will have just disappeared.' He laughed. 'You know what? I reckon we've pulled this off!' He looked over at Kit, joy and relief in his face.

Kit caught his eye and laughed too.

As they looked back to the road, travelling at a steady one hundred kilometres per hour, both men yelled simultaneously.

A huge bull camel stood in the middle of the road, staring at them.

Boyd reefed the wheel to the left, but it was too late and the vehicle struck the camel a glancing blow to its flank. The impact deflected the ute across the loose road surface and out into the open air of the rocky drop-off at the side of the road.

Kit yelled out as the ute started to tip.

Boyd couldn't make a sound. His eyes were wide with terror as the view from the window went sideways.

The first impact flipped the ute end over end, and then it rolled several times before coming to rest thirty metres below the road surface.

Kit's head bounced off the window and he smelled blood.

When the vehicle finally came to a stop, he couldn't work out where it had landed. He tried to turn to look outside but found his vision was blurry and his shoulder was screaming in pain.

'Holy fuck,' Kit gasped. 'Holy fuck!' Then he remembered Boyd. 'Boyd? Mate?'

His question was met by silence. He tried to turn his head and then realised he was suspended by his seatbelt looking down at the ground. The lower half of his brother's body was beneath him, but his head and shoulders were outside the cab, trapped between the vehicle and the ground.

Not wanting to see the grotesque scene, Kit shut his eyes and lapsed into unconsciousness.

Chapter 38

Dave slowed in order to conserve what little fuel remained. They could no longer see the cloud of dust ahead of them, so their reckless pursuit was over.

'Lost them, Jimbo. What a bastard.'

'Don't reckon, boss,' Jimbo said as they came to the top of a hill.

Looking over at him, Dave said. 'What do you mean?'

'Reckon they've been . . . Yeah. Look there.'

Dave was confronted by the bulk of a camel down on its haunches in the road ahead of him. Braking heavily, he was able to stop before they hit the beast.

'What the hell's happened here?' he asked over the camel's agonised bellows.

The camel's distress was evident as it pawed the ground with its front legs, but it couldn't get up.

'Been hit, boss.' Jimbo looked around for the vehicle.

'Can't leave him like that,' Dave said as he climbed out of the troopy and drew his Glock pistol. The single shot broke the silence as the camel slumped to the ground.

'Hey, boss, look here.' Jimbo had stepped out of the vehicle and was walking to the edge of the road. 'Just like I thought. They crashed into that camel there and went over the side. But, for sure, we wouldn't have known the ute was there if the animal hadn't been in the middle of the road.'

Dave ran to the top of the rocky outcrop that formed the western edge of the road and there below was the crumpled wreck of a white dual cab.

'Shit,' he said and ran back to the troopy. He grabbed the sat phone and hit the redial button.

Bob's voice come over the phone. 'Dave? That you? Where—?'

Interrupting, Dave snapped out his words. 'Bob, get a pen. Suspects have crashed down an embankment and rolled. GPS coordinates are . . .' He reeled them off. 'Wanted to get them to you before I head down to check on them. It looks real bad, mate.'

Bob read back the coordinates and Dave confirmed they were correct. 'Get an ambulance out here as soon as you can and get the Royal Flying Doctor Service on standby. I don't think they'll be able to put down out here but find the closest place.

'Reckon you might need the district boss notified because of the circumstances. I'll head down and check on them now and ring you back.'

He didn't give Bob a chance to respond.

'Jimbo?'

'Yeah?'

'You all right?'

'Yeah. But I'm staying here.' Jimbo sat on the ground next the troopy and looked down at the ground.

'Good man.'

Grabbing the first-aid kit out of the back, Dave picked his way down the steep, rocky embankment, holding on to the trunks of trees to get down without slipping, until he got to the car.

At first glance, he saw Kit slumped unconscious in the passenger seat.

He reached in to check for a pulse. There was one, but it wasn't steady. Dave knew he needed to get Kit out of there are soon as he could.

Looking past Kit, he saw the lower half of another male. Boyd. He hadn't been as lucky. The upper half of his body was trapped under the vehicle.

Swallowing down his horror, he got up and looked around to see if Kevin had been thrown further away from the vehicle.

'Kev's not here!' he yelled back up to Jimbo. There was no answer and Dave didn't want to push it, because he wasn't sure what Jimbo would do. Their cultures were so different, and Kevin was the leader of their community.

Dave started searching, looking under trees and in the treetops, but there was nothing. He went back to the car and looked in the back seat, trying to see if there was any blood.

From where he stood it looked clean. None of the side windows were broken and all that could have happened was that Kevin was thrown out the front. It didn't look like that had happened either.

His heart rate kicked up a notch. 'I don't reckon he was with them,' he yelled. Going to the front of the vehicle he yanked open the door, which thankfully hadn't been stuck shut, and patted Kit's cheek. 'Come on, mate,' he said. He leaned over to try and unclip the seatbelt. 'Need to get you out of here.'

Standing on the upturned vehicle, Dave pulled out his pocket knife and cut the seatbelt, releasing Kit from the car. Breaking his fall, he dragged Kit away from the car, knowing he could be doing more damage but also realising that there wasn't any choice. Out here there weren't any Jaws of Life; they just had to make do with what they had.

Manoeuvring Kit's unconscious body, he got him in the recovery position and, having checked his vital signs, made his way back up to the road and the sat phone.

'One fatality, one touch and go,' he said. 'Can't find Kev. I don't think he was with them. He's not been thrown from the car anywhere that I can find. They must have left him behind somewhere.'

'Right-oh. The plane is on the way to you with a nurse and some coppers. There's another lot heading out by road and I'll go with them from here. Jackie and some of his boys are coming along to see if we can find him. We should be there in an hour or two.'

'Thanks, mate. See you when you get here,' said Dave as he slumped in the seat. Where was Kevin?

❧

It was the low thrum of an engine that made Dave lift his head up and check Kit again, before climbing up and running out into the middle of the road. He turned on his flashing lights in case it wasn't Bob and his crew, not wanting another accident.

The late afternoon heat and flies had taken their toll on him, and the adrenalin he'd felt chasing the two suspects had left his body, leaving him drained, exhausted and with an aching shoulder.

Earlier, Dave had set up a tarp to provide shade from the afternoon sun as the temperature climbed into the mid-thirties and the humidity grew, and he'd sat next to Kit, waving flies away and checking his vital signs every fifteen minutes. Kit hadn't showed any signs of waking up, and his pulse was still unsteady.

Dave had talked to Jimbo about his taking the troopy to look for Kevin, but they'd decided it was better to stay together, so Jimbo had catnapped near the vehicle while Dave kept watch.

Dave had found himself dozing, but his sleep was filled with images of Mel lying in a car, her face pale, with blood at the corner of her mouth. Bulldust was grinning and Bec and Alice were in the back crying. There was nothing he could do to stop him.

'Mate,' Bob said as he pulled up next to him. Glenn was in the passenger seat. 'Plane landed about twenty ks back, on a flat stretch. Too many bloody ridges and gullies through here. Got Leah, the nurse, with us. And Glenn's here to help. Need all the hands we can get.'

'Where's the patient?' Leah grabbed her bag and ran from the car.

'Down there,' Dave indicated, brushing more flies away from his face.

When she got to Kit, she set to work, administering a saline drip and assessing Kit's injuries.

'We're going to need to get him out of here ASAP!' she yelled. 'How far away is the ambulance?'

'Probably an hour,' Bob answered after calling in on the CB.

'Might be too late,' Leah told them. She climbed up to the top of the hill. 'Can we shift him out of here in one of the troopys?'

'Probably not,' Glenn said. 'Don't think we'd get him in there.' He looked ill as he glanced down at his friend.

'Shit,' she said, running her hands through her hair. 'Yeah, you're probably right—too rough to risk getting him back and doing more damage, without him being strapped in properly. This is when I hate isolated nursing. Fuck!'

Bob pulled Dave aside from refuelling the troopy from jerry cans of diesel Bob had brought.

'What do we think happened to Kev?' Bob asked.

'I'm not sure. I'm thinking they've stashed him somewhere.'

'Can anyone confirm there was a body in the ute with Kit and Boyd? Glenn?'

Glenn walked over and rubbed his cheek. 'I'm sure I could see something large on the back seat of the other vehicle, when we buzzed them, but I couldn't swear to it in court. Certainly looked like a body with a bag over its head. I had the binoculars on them.'

'Do you know where the other ute was parked?' Bob asked. Dave shook his head.

Jimbo came to stand alongside them. 'I reckon I know, boss.'

They all turned to him.

'Where, mate?' Bob asked gently.

'Back where I said the tracks had stopped. They must've turned off just before that. I was watchin' them tracks real close and I pulled you up pretty much straight away.'

Dave leaned over and clapped Jimbo on the shoulder. 'Good job. Come on, let's go.'

'Hey, I need some assistance here,' Leah called.

Glenn blanched, then said, 'I'll stay and give a hand.'

Jimbo directed the two-car procession back the way they had come. Forty-five minutes later they approached the hills where Jimbo had lost sight of the tracks. They had stopped several times for Jimbo to ensure the distinct wiggling track made by the damaged front wheel on the Land Cruiser ute was still visible.

'It should be real close,' Jimbo said and Dave slowed the vehicle to a crawl.

'Stop here,' Jimbo said.

Dave stopped the troopy and Jimbo got out, followed by Bob. Scanning the surface of the road, he pointed out the brush marks made by the leaves and followed them until they stopped. He dropped to his haunches and touched a couple of branches on a bush.

'Yeah, look here, tracks been swept with a bush, look here and here, and they go off the road into here.'

Dave and Bob squatted and looked to where he was pointing.

'Shit, I can actually see that,' Dave said, amazed.

'Yeah, but not at one hundred kilometres an hour, boss,' Jimbo said with a grin.

'Geez, I'm glad I had you with me!'

'And here too.' Jimbo pulled out some branches that had been broken off and used to cover the opening. Their leaves were now wilting in the late afternoon heat.

Dave could make out a rough track that headed up the hill away from the road.

'I'll go bring the car up,' said Bob as Dave started up the track at a jog. He needed to find Kevin. Surely they were running out of time.

It was uphill and stony, and Dave slipped several times as he ran, grazing his knee, but he didn't care. Rounding a slight bend, Dave saw the tray of a vehicle ahead. He tried to run faster, but he slipped again.

'Fuck! Kev?' He got up and powered on, reaching the ute. 'Mate?'

Yanking open the back door, he saw Kevin's body, a bag over his head.

No! He was too late. 'Don't come any closer, Jimbo,' he called out.

Jimbo stopped.

Dave got out his pocketknife and cut the tape securing the linen sack. The material was caked with dried blood. Kevin was face down with his arms trussed with tape at his sides. His legs were also bound with tape over his tracksuit pants.

With trepidation Dave reached out and rested his fingers on the unconscious man's carotid artery. The faint pulse sent a wave of relief through Dave's body.

'He's alive!' Dave called out to Jimbo. 'He needs the nurse though. Go tell Bob to get up here quick!'

Chapter 39

Bob and Dave were driving to Spinifex Downs for one last visit. In the back was Kevin and he was heading home.

'Can't thank you blokes enough,' he said through the partition of the vehicle. 'I thought I was a goner there.'

'We thought you were too,' Dave said with a grin that hid the anxious worry he'd felt over the past few days.

When they'd found him, Kevin had been severely dehydrated, with a head injury. Leah had left Kit's side to attend to Kevin and, once again, the situation had been touch and go. She'd been worried they wouldn't get him airlifted to a hospital in time to stabilise him. So Dave and Bob had loaded him onto the back seat of the troopy and driven him to Boogarin at high speed, leaving Glenn to finish cleaning up the scene once the ambulance had picked up Kit, and Boyd's body.

'I still can't work out why Boyd hated us so much,' Kevin said.

'Tara gave me some of Old Man Redman's diaries yesterday,' Bob said. 'Kit and Boyd's father, Nick Redman, was a vicious man, which he in turn learned from his dad, George Redman. Seems George stole cattle from your community for many years. You blokes didn't have your own stations back when George's generation was about, but your community was living on Deep-Water. The Elders used to be his stockmen and they were treated like second-class citizens.

'By the time the government handed Spinifex Downs over to your community, George was dead and Nick didn't like that he'd lost his entire workforce. He plotted a way of getting back at you by taking your cattle.

'It was nothing but pure spite that made George and Nick continue it on: stealing your cattle, then hurting a member of your community to make sure you all kept your mouths shut. A mob of cattle and one person. Every time. They reckoned you'd never go to the police. Old Man Redman probably had a deal with the copper back then to look the other way. Kit and Boyd didn't know any different so they kept going.' Bob scratched his head and looked out the window as Dave drove.

'There was never enough cattle to make Kit's place viable. I looked at the books and they couldn't make ends meet. Free cattle meant more profit without the cost.

'Jackie and the other Elders, they knew it was the Redman family, but just couldn't bring themselves to trust in white man's law to report it. And rightly so,' Bob continued. 'Back then the coppers probably wouldn't have listened. I hope we've changed your mind about our white man's law.'

'I think you've changed Dad's.'

Dave turned to Bob. 'What happens about all the skeletons in the bunker?'

'They stay there, don't they, mate? Unless the bigwigs in Perth say otherwise.'

'Yeah,' Kevin said. 'They're resting now. Don't need to disturb them without reason.'

They arrived at the community, with little kids running around the car, yelling and laughing, the women crowded around the vehicle, big smiles on their faces.

'Looks like you're a celebrity now, Kev,' Bob said with a chuckle.

'Nah, just need to get on and do what I need to do to help my people,' Kevin said.

They slowed to a stop and all got out. Jackie was waiting on the steps of the house. He walked forwards and offered his hand to Bob. White man's gesture of thanks.

'Thank you.' Jackie bowed his head and nodded.

'I'm real glad we could help,' Bob said.

Jackie nodded, walked over to Dave and did the same. For once, Dave was tongue-tied.

'What happens now?' Jackie asked.

'Once Kit is recovered enough, we'll charge him with a heap of offences. Don't you worry, Kev, Kit will go to prison for a bloody long time,' Bob said.

He didn't mention how cut up Glenn had been to find out the truth about his friend. Everyone in the shire was reeling from it. People found it hard to believe Kit had been involved, but with her husband safely locked inside a hospital, Tara had come forward and told of the long-standing abuse she'd suffered at his hands, and Digby had spoken of Kit's threats to ensure the stock sales went through easily and quickly.

Still, some people couldn't accept the truth. Dave and Bob had heard that Mae from the pub had started a petition to stop Kit from going to prison.

'Won't do them any good,' Bob had said. 'I'm going to make sure he stays behind bars for a long time.'

A shadow passed over the sun. Thunderclouds were rolling in.

Jackie came and stood in front of Bob and Dave. 'You are welcome to visit us any time,' he said.

'Yeah, we'll drop past when we're up here next,' Bob said with a grin. 'Hopefully it won't be for a while. Not that we don't want to catch up, but we don't want any more cattle going missing. Now, look, we've gotta head off and take this boy home to his family.' He clapped Dave on the shoulder. 'He's a new dad!'

The women cackled and made rocking movements with their arms and Dave smiled.

'Hold on,' he said. 'We've got something for all the kids.' Dave went around to the back of the troopy and pulled out a large string bag with ten footballs and five netballs inside. 'Have fun with these,' he said as he handed them to the children who were milling around.

A loud crack of thunder brought more cries of delight, and a few fat drops hit the dry ground.

'Might be the Wet arriving,' Bob said.

Kevin looked skyward. 'We can hope.'

Shaking hands with Kevin one last time, Dave and Bob got back into the car and turned south when they hit the main road.

'What do you think you're going to find when you get home?' Bob asked after they'd driven an hour in silence.

'Who knows,' Dave answered, looking out the window.

'Hey, whatever happens, son, I've got your back.'

Dave felt a rush of emotion run through him, but he wouldn't show it. 'Cheers.'

Chapter 40

Dave stood at the front door of Mark and Ellen's house and breathed deeply before knocking.

Mel answered the door and smiled. Alice was asleep in her arms and from deep in the house he heard Bec.

'Daddy's home! Daddy's home!'

'Come in,' Mel said, stepping back from the door.

He leaned down to kiss her and she offered her cheek.

'Here, do you want to hold her?'

'Of course, I do!'

She handed him his daughter and he looked down at her wonderingly. How had two people at loggerheads created such a perfect little being?

He felt an arm slip around his waist and he looked down at Mel. 'Are we good?' he asked.

She shrugged. 'I'm not sure. All I know is that I'm very happy to see you.'

Dave bent to kiss her again, still cradling Alice, and pulled her close for a hug. Kissing the top of her head he said, 'We'll work through this, sweetie. I promise we'll be able to work through it because we love each other.'

'Hopefully that's enough,' she said, her voice muffled against his chest.

❧

Two days later, Mel got Alice out of the baby capsule in the car and put her into the wraparound sling she wore on her chest.

She grabbed a trolley and went into the supermarket. Winding her way through the meat section, she picked up a tray of lamb chops and then bumped into a man with vivid blue eyes.

'I'm so sorry!' she said. 'What a clutz! Must be because I'm sleep deprived!' She indicated Alice sleeping on her chest.

'All my fault,' he said, grinning down at her. 'I'll get out of your way.'

Mel went to move on, but he put a hand on her arm. 'I'm sure I've seen your face before. Are you Dave Burrows's wife?'

A smile spread across her face. 'Yes, I am! Have we met? I'm sorry, I'm terrible with names.'

'It was only briefly, so I'm not offended you don't remember me.'

'Phew, that's lucky.'

'How is Dave? I haven't seen him for a year or so now.'

'He's great. We moved to Perth so he could join the stock squad. Something he always wanted to do. We've got a little girl and now this one.'

'Ah, I'm glad he landed on his feet. Looks like he should be real happy, having such a nice little family and all.'

'Can I tell him you said hello? What's your name?'

The man smiled. 'Yeah, I'd love it if you could pass on my regards. You tell him Ashley said g'day and I'll catch up with him very soon.'

Author's note

Fool's Gold, *Without a Doubt* and *Red Dirt Country* are my three novels that feature Detective Dave Burrows in the lead role. Eagle-eyed readers will know Dave from previous novels and it was in response to readers' enthusiasm for Dave that I wanted to write more about him.

In *Fool's Gold*, *Without a Doubt* and *Red Dirt Country*, set in the late 1990s and early 2000s, Dave is at the beginning of his career. He's married to his first wife, Melinda, a paediatric nurse and they're having troubles balancing their careers and family life. No spoilers here because if you've read my contemporary rural novels you'll know that Dave and Melinda separate and Dave is currently very happily married to his second wife, Kim.

Dave is one of my favourite characters and I hope he will become one of yours, too.

Acknowledgements

The A&U Team: Tom, Annette, Christa and everyone else behind the scenes, from marketing to publicity. You're all incredible and I love how much you care about each and every book you publish. Thank you.

Gaby Naher from Left Bank Literary, agent and friend. A calming influence in the occasionally stormy waters of writing.

The Writing Team: DB, you're brilliant and such an important part of this process. Thank you from the bottom of my heart.

The WA Crew: Carolyn, Heather, Robyn, Lauren and Graham, Ewin, Jan and Pete, Chrissy, Lee and Paul, Al. The best cheer squad and support crew a girl could ask for.

The Family: Rochelle, Hayden, Mum, Dad, Nicholas and Susan, plus the nieces and nephews, Aunty Jan and all the cousins. Love you all so much. And thanks to Ben and

Laurs for introducing me to Wild Turkey Honey Whiskey, so I knew how bad Bob's hangover would be!

The Canines: Jack-the-Kelpie and Rocket-the-Jack-Russell. I really wish you two would get along and I could have both of you asleep at my feet while I write. As it is, I can only have you in my office one at time, but it's nice to have you there at all.

The Readers: 'I can't write without a reader . . .' John Cheever said that. Well, isn't that the truth? There are never enough words to thank you all for spending time with my imaginary friends! I hope you've enjoyed Detective Dave's adventure through the top of Western Australia—let me know over on Facebook or Instagram. I can't wait to get back to the keyboard and start writing his next escapade. Who knows what Bulldust will do . . .

With love,

Fleur x

OUT IN APRIL 2021

Something to Hide

FLEUR McDONALD

Returning to Perth after a near-fatal undercover case in outback Queensland, Dave Burrows, now a Detective Senior Constable in the stock squad, receives an ultimatum from his deeply unhappy wife, Melinda.

Before Dave and Mel's problems can be resolved, Dave is sent to the far north of Australia on a stock theft investigation. He finds two cattle stations deep in a complex underbelly of racial divide, family secrets, long-repeated lies, kidnapping and murder.

Facing one of the biggest challenges of his policing life and the heartbreaking prospect of losing his family, Dave can't imagine things getting worse. But there's a hidden danger, intent on revenge, coming right for him.

ISBN 978 1 76087 682 1

Chapter 1

'I met a friend of yours today,' Mel said as she heaved the heavy shopping bag onto the kitchen bench.

Dave bustled in behind her with Bec in his arms.

'Really? Who was that?' he asked as he set their daughter down and watched her toddle off into the lounge room and turn on the TV. He waited by the door for Mel's answer, listening for Alice's cry from outside.

'I've been trying to remember what he told me his name was ever since I got back into the car.' Her brow creased with annoyance. 'I don't think I took it in. Just after I met him, Alice started to grizzle, and I was keen to leave. There's nothing fun about being in a supermarket with a crying baby.'

'Hold on, I can hear Alice. I'll be back,' Dave said, jogging from the house to lift the newly woken Alice from the car capsule.

The sun was shining, and even the chilly wind that swept down the quiet street couldn't dampen the glow in his chest. Last night Mel had come into their bed for the first time in many weeks. They'd shared whispered talks, cuddles and occasionally a laugh as memories from better times surfaced. When Alice woke and demanded her mother's breast, Dave had fetched her for Mel, then taken the baby back to the cot. Tonight, the spare room would be empty again, he was sure.

Last week's counselling session hadn't brought out anything he didn't already know—Mel wanted him to leave policing. She was adamant. But so was Dave. He wasn't going to do that. He had insisted they could make compromises that would benefit them both and their family.

The counsellor had convinced them to work together. To each make a little more effort at home: for Dave not to walk out the door and go to work when he was angry; for Mel to listen rather than shut Dave out while he told her something she didn't want to hear. For them both to be a little more open-minded and thoughtful of each other.

'Hey, look at you, Miss Alice,' Dave cooed as he unbuckled the straps and picked her up.

Alice gave a couple of hiccupping cries and closed her eyes.

With his daughter in his arms, he nudged the car door shut and glanced around the street—an old habit—before going inside, where Mel was unpacking the perishables into the fridge.

'How did you get talking about me to this fellow?' he asked as he went through to Alice's room and placed her gently in the cot. He drew up the covers and pulled the door to before checking on Bec. She was curled up on her child-sized unicorn couch watching *George the Farmer*, her hair falling over her eyes. Dave smiled and ducked back into the kitchen.

'So?' he asked again.

Mel straightened. 'Well, it was strange. I didn't notice him, then suddenly he was right there in front of me. Almost like he waited and stepped across my path. Alice was in the sling on my front, and I was busy looking down at what I was buying.'

'Uh-huh,' Dave said. He reached into the shopping bag for two tins of tomatoes and put them in the pantry, just as a trickle of concern ran through him.

'I apologised,' Mel continued, 'and then he just said, "Aren't you Dave Burrows' wife?" Or something like that.' She shrugged.

Dave stilled and turned to look across at Mel. 'And what did you say?'

'Yes, of course, you duffer! Are you still looking for proof we're trying?' She flashed him a half smile.

'What?' Dave was confused, his mind full of criminals who might want to take revenge on him by approaching Mel, rather than their marriage status. 'No. But you told him who you were?' He knew he sounded incredulous.

'Well, yeah . . .' She gave a sunny smile. 'He wanted me to pass his regards on to you.'

'Mummy?' Bec stood in the doorway. 'I'm hungry.'

Mel gently pushed past Dave and took out a box of Jatz crackers and cut up some cheese. Dave watched as she put it all on a plate and handed it to Bec, who promptly disappeared back into the lounge room.

'And you can't remember his name?' he persisted, stepping closer to her.

'No. It's baby brain, I tell you. I can't remember what I did yesterday!' She looked at him. 'I'm sorry. I *am* trying, you know.'

Dave put his hands on Mel's arms and looked directly at her. 'Mel, this is important. What did he look like?'

'Ah,' Mel frowned again. 'I don't know . . .' Her voice trailed off.

Dave didn't let her finish before he cut in again. 'Tell me exactly what he said.'

Looking up at Dave, her eyes now shone with fear. 'Oh, Dave.' She swallowed hard as realisation hit her. 'He said he was a friend of yours. From—' She paused and thought hard. 'From out bush, I think.'

Dave wanted to shout the word *Bulldust*. Or *Ashley*. But he knew he couldn't put words in her mouth. One of the first interview techniques taught during detective training was never to do that. 'What did he sound like?' The words snapped out of him.

'Sound?'

Dave's heart was beating hard and a knot of fear was sitting like a stone in his stomach. It was one thing to be an investigator on a case that involved dangerous criminals; it was another to have strangers approach his family. 'Hard voice? Nasal? Deep?' he offered, keeping his tone quiet and comforting. 'Did he speak slowly?'

Mel leaned back against the kitchen bench, her arms folded. 'Um, quiet.' She frowned, the way she did when trying to dredge up a memory. 'Yeah, quiet. He spoke slowly, like he was drawing the words out.'

Dave knew he couldn't prompt her. Couldn't ask about a beard. About vivid blue eyes. About the tattoos on Bulldust's knuckles. The features he knew of Bulldust, by heart.

'Height?'

'Dave,' Mel glanced over her shoulder to the lounge room, then down the passage to Alice's room, 'you're scaring me.'

He wanted to shake her for being so stupid—for admitting who she was, to a stranger who approached her out of the blue when she had their baby with her. It frightened him, which in turn made him angry. It wasn't as if Mel didn't know who Bulldust was, that he was out there somewhere holding a grudge against Dave. In fact, it was Bulldust's threat to kill Dave, and Mel's reaction to it, that had started their recent spate of marital problems. Actually, if he was honest with himself, all of their problems since he'd returned home from being undercover.

'How tall, Mel? Measure him against me.'

She put her hand over his head.

'Hair?'

'I don't think he had any. No, I remember glancing at the overhead light reflecting off his head.'

'Other facial features?'

'I don't think so.'

'No beard?'

'No.' She sounded more certain. 'I remember thinking he needed a shave.'

'Just stubble, then?'

She nodded, running her hands up and down her upper arms. Dave knew the gesture. She was trying to comfort herself. He should go to her. Put his arms around her and tell her everything was going to be okay.

He knew he couldn't. It was more important that he remain the professional detective so he could protect them all.

'Any tatts that you saw? An accent?'

'He was wearing long sleeves. Yeah, long sleeves. A blue cotton shirt. Like a work shirt.'

'For a suit?'

She shook her head. 'No, more like what you wear for the stock squad. Like farmer's wear.' She paused. 'Dave?' She looked at him questioningly. 'He wouldn't be . . .'

Dave spoke calmly. 'He could be. Now, listen to what I say very carefully. I need you to pack a bag for you and the girls. I have to get you all somewhere safe.'

Mel took a step towards him, then backed away as if Dave were the problem. 'I'm scared.'

He grabbed her in a bear hug, not letting her pull away from him. 'I understand that, and I don't like this much either. But we have to take precautions in case this man *is* Bulldust.' He took a breath. 'You need to take the girls and go somewhere safe.'

'But I've got you.' Mel's voice was muffled against his chest.

He sighed. 'That won't be enough. It's me he's after. And he won't stop.'

❧

Fighting the anger rising inside him, Dave drove carefully, his eyes skipping between the road ahead and the rear-view mirror. He'd had enough dealings with Bulldust over the past two years to know that if he was the one who had approached Mel, he wouldn't have stopped at the super-market—he would have followed her home. The man was intent on revenge. Dave had gone undercover to gain Bulldust's trust. He'd befriended him, then betrayed the trust that was between friends. Which in turn had taken everything from Bulldust: his daughter, his business, his freedom, and Dave had seen firsthand what Bulldust did to people who double-crossed him.

Usually they ended up dead.

Mel's description of the man could have been Bulldust. The last time Dave had seen him, he'd had a long beard, but that could have easily been shaved off. It was the voice that interested Dave. Quiet. Slowly spoken.

A drawl. A Queenslander.

A little voice popped up in his mind; Spencer, his mate and old partner from his days stationed at Barrabine, had always told him never to assume. Could be someone from the north of Western Australia. Or the Northern Territory.

Dave glanced over at Mel's pale face, then back to the mirror. He didn't believe in coincidences.

Giving evidence against hardened criminals who had no respect for human life was part of the job, one of the perils of working undercover. What wasn't routine was the error made in court when the judge divulged Dave's home city. He wouldn't put it past Bulldust to do everything in his power to track Dave down as soon as he'd heard that he lived in Perth.

'Daddy, where are we going?' Bec piped up from the back seat.

'To visit your grandparents,' Dave said. 'Maybe have a sleepover. Won't that be fun?' He glanced in the rear-view mirror, but so far there was no sign of a tail.

'But it's daytime.'

'I know, but you might stay for a few hours, princess.'

Mel shot him a look of fury. Since they'd piled into the car she'd been silent, and the familiar distance and white anger she'd been carrying around for months had resurfaced.

The very same emotions they had started to overcome last night.

Fuck it, Dave thought angrily. *I'm going to get you, Bulldust, and make you pay for the grief you've caused my family.* If Mel and the kids weren't in the car he would have hit the steering wheel, but instead he looked around him, always watching his surroundings, and willed himself to stay calm.

'This isn't the way to Granny's house,' Bec said looking out the window. 'We usually go past the playground.'

'I'm taking the long way,' Dave improvised. 'Just for something different.' He wasn't about to admit he was looking for a tail, although he thought Mel probably had already realised this.

Mel shook her head and stared out the window.

A few more turns and back streets and Dave was sure they weren't being followed. Breathing easier, he started towards his father-in-law's house, already thinking about the frosty reception he would receive from Mark.

'Mel?' Dave spoke in a low voice. 'When we get there, I want you to go straight inside, okay? I'll bring the girls. Don't stop and talk in the doorway, just get inside, okay?'

Glancing over at her, he saw anger had replaced fear.

'What have you done to us?' she hissed.

Not having an answer, Dave was relieved to turn into the driveway. 'Okay,' he said as the car came to a halt. 'Off you go. Be quick.'

He watched as Mel ran up the steps and banged on her parents' front door. Mark opened it, staring at her as she caught his arm and dragged him inside.

'Bec, can you undo your seatbelt and climb over the front seat to me, sweetie?'

'You don't like it when I do that. You get mad.' Bec crossed her arms and frowned at him.

Biting down agitation, Dave said, 'I know, princess, but I need you to do it for me today, okay? Come on.'

As if sensing the urgency, Bec unclipped her belt and clambered into the front.

'Good girl.' He gave her a kiss. 'Now, wait here for me. No moving.' He slid out of the driver's door and felt for the gun at his waist as he looked around. The curtain moved in the house and he saw Mark's face staring out.

Dave quickly unbuckled Alice and lifted her out of her capsule, then opened the front passenger door to help Bec from the car. He grabbed the car keys and Bec's hand, and ran with her up the steps.

Inside, he shut the door, locked it and breathed a sigh of relief. Bec let go of his hand as Mark's loud voice shattered the uneasy silence.

'What the hell is going on?'

'Hello, Granddad,' Bec said running towards him, with her arms outstretched. 'We're coming for a sleepover!'

Mark smiled and held out his arms towards Bec for a hug, just as Ellen appeared and offered to take Alice. 'Hello, Dave,' she said quietly. 'I'll take the littlies and leave you to talk to Mark.'

Dave smiled gratefully and handed Alice to her. Waiting until the passage was clear, he said, 'Can we go into your office to talk?'

'A different room isn't going to make any difference to what I have to say to you.'

'But it might to your safety,' Dave snapped back. He felt momentarily appeased when he saw Mark stop for a moment and glance at the front door, before storming off to the back of the house.

'Now, what's all this about?' Mark said as he sat behind the large wooden desk, putting distance between them. He poured himself a brandy but didn't offer one to Dave.

Giving the shortened version of the story, Dave finished with: 'But on questioning Mel, I believe him to be the suspect we know as Bulldust.'

'*On questioning Mel?* Do you realise you're talking about your wife?'

Dave stopped. Falling into police-speak wasn't the best idea when he was talking about his family. 'Of course I do. I'm relaying what's happened. Now I'm going to see Bob Holden at the stock squad and make sure you're all safe tonight. I have to get an investigation underway.'

Mark glared at his son-in-law. 'So, you've finally done it,' he spat, rising from his chair. 'Brought this filth . . . this, this precious work that you ignore your wife for, into *my* house, undermining the safety of *my* family.'

Drawing himself up and barely holding back his temper, Dave said, 'There's no time to argue about this now. The important thing is that I'm going to make sure you're all safe. If you hear, see or even smell anything suspicious, you have to ring triple zero. I'll make sure they have your address listed as priority.'

'Well, there you have it,' Mark scoffed. 'Going to do what you do best. You run off and play policeman while you leave your family in the lurch once again.' Mark put down his drink and walked to the office door, holding it open for Dave to leave.

Bristling, Dave fought his anger and fear. 'This is neither the time nor the place,' he answered, his tone clipped. 'I'll be back as soon as I can. You just need to remember that it's me they want, not Mel, or the children, or you and Ellen.'

'But if they need us to get to you, I don't suppose that'll stop them, will it?'

Dave had no answer as he walked out the door.